# AN EASY THING TO LOSE

E.M. STORM-SMITH

A Pride & Prejudice Variation

Published by
Storm Haus Publishing, LLC
www.StormHausPublishing.com


Publisher's Note: This work of fiction is a product of the writer's personal imaginings. It is not intended to be a factual representation of events, people, locales, businesses, government agencies, or any other entity. While all works of fiction are based on the perceptions, insights, and experiences of the author, any resemblance of the names, characters, places and incidents to actual persons, places or events is completely coincidental.

**Reputation, An Easy Thing to Lose / E.M. Storm-Smith** – 2nd ed.
ISBN-13: 978-1-7374039-0-6 *electronic format*
ISBN-13: 978-1-7374039-1-3 *paperback format*

# DEDICATION

*For Charlie.*
*You can be whatever your heart can dream.*

# Prologue

## Mr. Bennet's Discovery

***Bedford Court, Covent Garden, London***
***6 August 1812; 11:00pm***

***BAM! BAM! BAM!***

Lydia Bennet jolted awake in her temporary lodgings. The clock on the mantel showed it was very late indeed, but the candle by the bed was still burning. Looking around, she was dismayed to find that George Wickham had not yet returned from his evening entertainment.

***BAM! BAM! BAM!***

Whoever was at her door seemed like a mad man and Lydia had no desire to open the door by herself. There were several other boarders at the house, plus the elderly couple who owned the establishment. One of them would surely take care of the ruffian in the hallway without her interference.

***BAM! BAM! BAM!***

"Wickham, I know you are in there! Open this door at once or I shall break it!"

"Papa?" At the sound of her father's voice, Lydia jumped out of bed and opened the door without pausing to don her dressing gown. "What are you doing here?"

Mr. Thomas Bennet shoved open the door with so much force Lydia lost her footing and ended up on the floor.

"What am I doing here? Surely you cannot be serious! I have come to retrieve you and put an end to this shameful behaviour. Where is Wickham? I demand that you bring him to me this instant!"

Lydia picked herself up off the floor and shut the door, while Mr. Bennet opened the water closet and looked behind the privy screen. "What do you mean, '*this shameful behaviour?*' What have I done that is so bad? I am sure Lizzy and Jane would scold me for an elopement, but they are so dreary and dull. They do not know how to have fun. Besides, they are both old spinsters now and clearly do not know how to catch a handsome husband." Lydia clapped her hands and laughed. "Is it not the best of jokes? I shall be married first, of all my sisters! When I come home with my dear Wickham, I shall make Jane sit down one place, as I shall be a married woman and must take precedence now! La, will not Kitty be positively green with envy?" Lydia grasped her father's arm. "But, you shall have to send her to me when we re-join the regiment in Brighton. I am sure I can get her a husband in no time."

Mr. Bennet struggled not to violently shake his youngest daughter. He would save all his strength for her faithless lover. "Where are your marriage lines then? Have you and Wickham been to church?"

"Well, no. Not yet." Lydia recoiled, but regained her composure quickly. "He has some business here in London that requires his time and attention, but it does not signify when we will marry. I am sure my dear Wickham and I shall be married from his parish here in London. I did hope to surprise you all, returning as a married woman, but perhaps it is good you are here now, for I have no money for the wedding clothes, and I certainly need at least ten new gowns and a spencer before we can return to the regiment." She spun around and inspected several items on the dresser. "Oh! And new gloves! Long satin ones for all the parties we shall attend! Oh, la, Father! How lovely I shall be in my new things. And I shall also need a finely fitted mobcap for when I receive the officers. Like Harriet Forster wears. Not one of those old-fashioned draped things. It must be light muslin with some small lace trim. And the small clothes…"

"ENOUGH!" Mr. Bennet had reached his limit. "There shall be no wedding clothes, there shall be no finery. And there shall be no opportunity to insult your sisters further by making them all sit one place down at dinner, for you shall not be allowed to ever again step foot into Longbourn. As soon as you are officially Mrs. Wickham, I shall wash my hands of you. All of your problems and the silly turn of your mind shall be Lt. Wickham's problem the second the register is signed."

"But, Father!"

"No more. You shall be silent now, except to tell me where your worthless young man has gone."

Before Lydia could work herself up to the tears and hysterics that usually produced the result she desired from her father, the door to the room opened once more. Wickham stumbled across the threshold holding a nearly empty bottle of some spirit.

"Lydia, my dear, come here and help me out of this restrictive neck cloth. I have had a poor night at the tables, but… *hic*… maybe tomor-*hic*-row."

Wickham looked up from the floor, where his attention had been singularly focused since coming up the stairs in an effort not to fall onto it. He blinked twice then looked between Lydia and Mr. Bennet.

"Ah, I see we have company. Mr. Ben-i-dict. Ben-ten," Wickham cleared his throat. "Mr. Bennet. How lovely to see you."

Wickham attempted a gentlemanly bow but required the assistance of the dresser by the door to keep upright. As soon as he straightened, Wickham turned on his heels, dropped his bottle and attempted to get back out of the door with great haste. It was the work of a moment for Mr. Bennet to grab the back of Wickham's coat and throw him onto the bed.

Lydia screamed and Wickham made a high-pitched noise that was not at all expected from a grown man.

"Wickham," Mr. Bennet snarled, "so good of you to finally join us. I trust you have concluded your… business… for the night and are now at leisure to discuss the arrangements for tomorrow's wedding."

"I cannot take your meaning, sir. Whose wedding shall we be attending on the morrow?"

"Yours, of course. To my daughter. I am sure that the bishop of St. Paul's will grant me a common license as soon as it is made clear you have been living as a married couple these last six days. We will go there directly at nine a.m., and you shall be married before the first services. I shall sit here, in your chair, all night, to ensure you do not flee the fate which I am sure will bring you no pleasure."

"Papa! How dare you!" Lydia stomped her foot, trying to gain the attention of the two men, both of whom ignored her completely.

Wickham cleared his throat again and shook his head. He tried to put on that charm which had always served him well in tight spots. "Of course, sir. I am perfectly ready to proceed directly to the church, but perhaps we should move back the time of the wedding until ten a.m. so that we might visit your solicitor at nine a.m."

"And why would we need to visit my solicitor before the wedding?"

Wickham smiled and spread his hands in a placating manner. "To draw up Lydia's settlement and dowry, of course. You would not want her to live below her status as a gentleman's daughter. I believe that ten thousand pounds immediately, an annual annuity of one hundred pounds, plus her share of your wife's settlement upon Mrs. Bennet's death shall be exactly what she should have."

Lydia squealed in delight. "Oh, Papa! Am I really to have ten thousand for my dowry? That is marvellous!"

"I TOLD YOU TO BE SILENT, LYDIA! Wickham, you have been amongst our friends and relations for many months, you must know that I do not have ten thousand to dower on Lydia. I cannot even begin to think where such a sum is to be had. You will take her as she is. I shall send her fifty pounds per year, which is already part of the Longbourn entail, and perhaps my wife will see fit to send her enough quality muslin for one or two new dresses a year. But that shall be all! One fifth share of her mother's settlement shall be yours upon my wife's death, and I shall write you a note here, in my own hand, promising such a clause shall be added to my will at my earliest convenience, AFTER you are safely married in the church."

Wickham sighed. "I am afraid that will not signify. I mean to make my fortune from marriage, and if you cannot provide Lydia with a valuable dowry, I will not have her."

"WHAT?" Lydia screeched. Beside her sat an open valise holding certain items, including Wickham's riding boots. Lydia seized upon the heel of his right boot and hurled it directly at Wickham's head. Wickham was normally a man of good reflexes, having had much practice at dodging objects thrown by enraged ladies, but in his inebriated state, he was not able to move in time. The toe of the boot hit him squarely in his eye socket.

"You, crazy, vulgar chit! I shall give you a matching black eye!" Wickham moved to hit Lydia with her own weapon but was once again seized upon by Mr. Bennet.

Using Wickham's momentum against him, Mr. Bennet threw the wastrel into the wall, headfirst, then delivered a strong blow to his nose. "You are as worthless a fighter as you are a gentleman. I shall either see you married before ten a.m., or dead at first light. Which shall it be?"

Wickham spat out the blood from his broken nose onto the floor, splashing Mr. Bennet's breeches. "I believe, *sir*, that I have a better chance of making her an orphan than a husband. I have my pistol here, the finest available to officers in his majesty's army."

"So be it. I shall see you at Chalk Farm Tavern at dawn."

# Chapter 1

## The Dawning of a New Day

***Gracechurch Street, Cheapside, London***
***22 September 1812***

FROM HER PERCH IN THE WINDOW SEAT OF THE SECOND-FLOOR BEDROOM, Elizabeth Bennet watched the sun rise over St. Paul's Cathedral as the great bells announced a new day. Sighing, she put down the letters she had been perusing and looked over to the serene form of her older sister, Jane, asleep in their bed. Soon, the household would waken, there would be four small children to tend and much work to be accomplished before attempting to find oblivion in sleep once again. But for now, the house was peaceful.

It had been nearly a month since she and Jane had come to live with Aunt Madeline and Uncle Edward Gardiner in London.

On the same day Elizabeth and her aunt had been entertained by Fitzwilliam Darcy and his sister Georgiana in the music room of their Derbyshire estate, Pemberley, Elizabeth's father had found Wickham and Lydia holed up in a disgusting one room apartment north of Covent Garden. The next morning, before Jane's letter detailing the elopement had been delivered to Elizabeth, Mr. Bennet and Wickham had met on the duelling field.

At dawn, Mr. Bennet had shot Wickham through the heart, killing him instantly.

Though Wickham may have chosen poorly when he decided upon pistols, as the quiet and bookish Mr. Bennet had been the head of the Oxford shooting club in his university days, the rake did not entirely miss his mark. Wickham's shot went south as he was felled, and struck Mr. Bennet's upper leg, lodging a bullet in the thick bone. Lydia was able to support her father back to the Gardiners' Cheapside home in a hackney coach but was unable to care for his wounds. Before the Gardiners made it back to London, an infection had taken over Mr. Bennet's body.

Mr. Bennet died of his infection on 13 August 1812.

The Bennets' cousin and heir, Mr. William Collins, came to claim their estate, Longbourn, less than one whole month after Mr. Bennet's death. As an ordained minister, most expected he would have given the Bennet ladies more time to adjust to their new situation. However, he gave up the valuable living in Kent at the estate of Lady Catherine de Bourgh in all due haste. Jane and Elizabeth had come to live with their aunt and uncle in London while their mother and three younger sisters moved into the house of their other aunt and uncle in Meryton. Mrs. Bennet had put up a serious objection to Elizabeth's relocation to London, as she blamed their expulsion from Longbourn on Elizabeth's prior refusal to marry her cousin, Collins. London was, in Mrs. Bennet's mind, the best place for her daughters to find husbands, and she believed that Elizabeth was not worthy of any such advantage. However, her brothers, Gardiner and Phillips, were firm in their arrangements, and so Elizabeth and Jane went off to London.

Elizabeth now found it difficult to sleep more than a few hours each night. Every morning, at about four a.m. according to the mantle clock, Elizabeth woke from dreams of a life she would now never have, with a man far too good, whom she loved most ardently. Then, she rose from her bed.

Looking down at her hands, filled with letters between herself and her middle sister Mary, the only member of her immediate family besides Jane who would communicate with Elizabeth, she fought to control her tears. Yesterday afternoon had brought an express rider to the Gardiners' door carrying two missives. One from Elizabeth's Uncle Phillips to her Uncle

Gardiner, and one from Mary to Elizabeth and Jane. Both said the same thing.

Lydia Bennet, the youngest of the Bennet sisters, just sixteen years of age, was with child.

It was the end to all their family's hopes and respectability. Unable to hold in her sobs, and not wishing to wake her sister, Elizabeth donned one of her three full mourning gowns and descended the stairs to the breakfast parlour. Usually this early, only she, Cook, and Mrs. Mathers, the Gardiners' elderly housekeeper, were awake. This morning, however, Elizabeth found her uncle taking his tea.

"Good morning, Uncle. You are up earlier than expected."

Edward stood and filled a plate with morning meats for Elizabeth. "Yes, dear, I have a very early meeting with some of the inspectors from the Royal Imports Office and must be at my warehouse by eight a.m. Whenever I have these early meetings, I fear sleeping too late, so I am up with more than two hours to spare." Edward looked closely at Elizabeth's eyes, normally full of colour and sparkle, but which looked dull this morning. "I see you are still distressed over yesterday's news from Meryton. Did you sleep at all last night?"

"A little, yes, though I confess Jane and I were up late into the night, discussing what must be done. Then I rose at my normal time just before sunrise. So, I am more fatigued than usual."

Edward set down his teacup with some force and rubbed the sides of his temples. "What do you mean '*what must be done*'? Lydia is my problem to solve with your Uncle Phillips. I do not see what you or Jane can do for her until the babe is born. And even after that event, there may be extraordinarily little for her, except some position as a companion to an old tradesman's widow who is beyond caring about her own reputation."

Taking a careful sip of her tea, Elizabeth looked out of the window, avoiding Edward's gaze. "I am going to find a position as a governess or maybe a companion."

"You will do no such thing! I will not have you go into service while I have money in my pocket and breath in my body."

She turned back to him. "Uncle, be reasonable. You cannot keep us forever, and with Lydia's shame now complete, we are fully unmarriageable. As you know, marriage is the only respectable occupation for a gentlewoman, but I cannot expect there to be any man who would want to take me, with Lydia so badly settled." Elizabeth straightened her unused silverware and smoothed out the wrinkles in her serviette. "There is still hope for Jane, for there shall always be hope where there is so much beauty in the face and soul. But I am determined I cannot wait."

"This is wholly unnecessary," Edward blustered and stood up from his chair. "We are not in stress from having you here, and as you are not yet one and twenty, how can you give up all hope of making your own match after the babe is adopted out? Give us the year. Only one year, and you shall see, all may be well again." He returned to the table and stilled Elizabeth's hands from wringing holes in the table linens. "You have the annuity money from the Collinses, and your aunt and I may be able to do something for you and Jane as well, so that there might be something of a small dowry within the year. Then we shall see who would have you."

Elizabeth scoffed. "It was indeed a generous thing for my cousin to provide us each with fifty pounds per year from the savings on the household costs. But if I am smart, I will take only the interest and keep the principle intact for the future. That is hardly enough money to buy fabric for one dress of medium quality muslin! It will not go any distance in enticing a husband. No, I wish to contract a hiring agency as soon as may be."

Elizabeth rose from her seat and came to the side of Edward's chair. She knelt on the floor and took her uncle's hand in her own. "I am more than grateful for the care and expense you have gone to for myself and Jane. We have been welcomed into your home and treated with such kindness. But, now we must be practical. If I take a position, I will be the means of buying my family time. Time for Jane to marry someone well suited. Time for Mary to come take my place here in your house and maybe increase her charm under my aunt's guidance. Time for Kitty to learn from Lydia's folly. Perhaps in this time, we shall be made whole again, all of us."

Elizabeth rose and took her seat once more. She made a considerable attempt to lighten her mood and her smile. "Besides, Uncle, I plan to never marry. I shall instead play governess to Jane's ten beautiful children after some handsome and well-to-do merchant falls instantly in love with her beauty and sweetness."

Edward regarded his niece with a shrewd eye. "And what of Mr. Darcy?"

The clatter from Elizabeth's teacup hitting the table brought the Gardiners' maid running into the dining parlour from the pantry. But Elizabeth waved the girl off. "I am well Gertrude, thank you. There is no mess." She waited until the servant had retreated into the pantry again before addressing her uncle. "I cannot see what Mr. Darcy has to do with our situation. However pleasant a day we had visiting his estate last month, I am certain that we shall never see him again."

Edward harumphed and cleared his throat. "I would not be so sure we have seen the last of Mr. Darcy. Despite your rather complicated history with that young man, he seems the sort to be a loyal friend."

"Complicated is hardly fair. We knew each other last fall in Meryton where he was distant and insulting to everyone." Elizabeth began picking at some lint on her skirt. "I hardly knew him at all, and he insulted me in front of our neighbours the first evening of our acquaintance. No one would expect that someone so far above us Bennets in wealth, connection and consequence to be loyal."

"I believe you have seen much more of him since he quit your old neighbourhood. Did you not meet again in Kent? And of course, we were invited to visit his estate and his sister not two months ago, which, I do not deceive myself, was all on your account. That speaks to knowing him much more than 'hardly at all.' Also, his manner while at Pemberley was decidedly *not* distant and insulting."

Flushed, Elizabeth folded and re-folded her serviette. "This is not a productive conversation. Our situation is unchanged." Finally, she put down the cloth with too much force. "Mr. Darcy is the grandson of an Earl, with one of the largest and most prosperous estates in all of England. He will not associate with disinherited women from a minor gentry estate. Even if he has not heard of Lydia's situation, to believe he might call on me is absurd." Elizabeth looked directly into her uncle's eyes. "I must consider the most likely future, and I must not elevate my expectations."

"No more talk of you taking a position. It is unimaginable that you would do so while in mourning for your father." In a rather uncommon pique, Edward struck the table with his fist. "I forbid it!"

After re-adjusting her teacup, which was unsettled from the table being jostled, Elizabeth sighed. "My twenty-first birthday will be in twelve days, which means I shall be able to contract for myself. And five days after that, we shall be out of the first period of mourning, which allows for some liberty to take calls, go into public, and change from blacks to greys." Elizabeth shook her head and looked up from the table with a determined glint in her eyes. "I am sure that with the time it should take to contract a position, it will be perfectly respectable for me to be seen once I start my service."

Edward looked utterly defeated. He knew it was fruitless to argue any further, but he was also unequal to the disquiet in the breakfast room. Without a word, Edward stood from the table, kissed Elizabeth on the top of her head and took his tea into his study.

Elizabeth, having lost her appetite, poured herself a fresh cup of tea and sipped it in silence, with only her thoughts. After a few minutes in this repose, she began to believe that her uncle's fantastical dreams about Darcy had infected her own mind, not that the gentleman from Derbyshire was ever far from her thoughts. For there, outside the window, in the mews used by the few houses which shared the lane behind her uncle's house, was a massive black horse Elizabeth was sure she recognized.

It had to be Incitatus, for only one animal could be so like its owner in beauty and power. Elizabeth had first encountered this horse, named for the favourite mount of Rome's Emperor Caligula and the only animal to serve as a senator in the Roman Senate, during her stay at Netherfield, the estate nearest her home. Netherfield had been leased the previous fall by Darcy's particular friend, Charles Bingley, and Darcy and come to visit. Jane had fallen ill with a bad cold while visiting with Bingley's sisters, Caroline Bingley and Louisa Hurst, and Elizabeth had come to nurse her favourite sister through her sickness.

On one of her morning walks about Netherfield, Elizabeth had passed the stables and observed owner and mount in a sweet moment. Darcy, back from his morning ride, was trying to brush Incitatus's beautiful black coat while the horse nosed his jacket pocket incessantly. Finally, Darcy reached into his pocket and pulled out a handful of sugar cubes pilfered from the sideboard in the breakfast room. Incitatus happily lapped up the treat while Darcy quietly chuckled, declaring the horse no better than a spoiled child. The encounter had stayed with Elizabeth as the first time she had ever seen a smile grace Darcy's face. He was so handsome when he smiled.

Later that morning, in the drawing room, Elizabeth had asked Darcy the name of his horse, and they were both pleasantly surprised by the discussion of Roman history that continued for more than a quarter of an hour. This discussion was a window to his true nature which, after seeing him again at Pemberley, helped to awaken her love. Darcy would say that the day they discussed Roman history was the day he surrendered his heart to the lively and intelligent Elizabeth. Unbeknownst to either participant, that conversation was also the launching point of another great passion, one born more of jealousy than heart.

Coming back to the present, Elizabeth quickly abandoned her tea, grabbed a handful of sugar cubes from her aunt's sideboard, and dashed out of the door in the kitchens leading directly to the mews. Darcy had called at least once before, several weeks ago. She had seen him as she crossed the vestibule into the south parlour. But since that day, she had not seen him again, nor had she heard her uncle mention him before their conversation not five minutes ago. She could not imagine what business Darcy had with her uncle, but, by now he must have heard of her father's death and Collins's possession of Longbourn.

Rounding the corner of the house, Elizabeth stopped dead in her tracks. There, in the mews, between her uncle's house and the courtyard of St. Michael's, in all his enormous animal glory, was indeed Incitatus. And holding the reins was Mr. Fitzwilliam Darcy.

⁂

Unable to sleep for more than a few fitful hours, Darcy rose from his bed at four a.m. and dressed for the day. Deciding to let his poor valet, Connor, sleep a little longer, he donned work clothes then went down to the stables attached to his large Mayfair house, and saddled Incitatus. Taking Rotten Row south through Hyde Park at a swift canter, Darcy passed Buckingham Palace then traversed the Mall before slowing. Continuing down the Strand, the bells of St. Paul's Cathedral called to him as the sun crested the horizon and bathed London in golden light. Before he knew where his heart had taken him, Darcy stood at the end of a neat street of comfortable but modest homes. The fourth door from the corner, on the west side of the street, held the Gardiner family and Elizabeth Bennet. Without thinking, Darcy led Incitatus to the mews behind the Gardiners' home and dismounted.

Since learning of Wickham's desertion of his post and Lydia's supposed elopement with the rake, Darcy had been desperate to help the Bennet family. He had left Pemberley at first light the day after Elizabeth and the Gardiners returned to Longbourn, and headed straight for London. His aim had been to find Wickham and Lydia himself, but they had already been found, and the reprobate shot, by Mr. Bennet. Darcy had kept up some correspondence with Edward Gardiner in the weeks following Mr. Bennet's death. Yesterday, Darcy had called just as an express rider was leaving. It had been the worst of news.

With the despair of the situation now complete, Darcy had returned home and drunk himself into a stupor after dinner. His young sister, Georgiana, discovered him in a terrible state. She was able to, as only a loving sibling could, gently coax out of him the entire story, including his behaviour in Meryton last fall, the dreadfully rude comment about Elizabeth being *tolerable, but not handsome enough to tempt me* at the assembly where they first met, and even the details about Darcy's insults to her family made during the disastrous marriage proposal. Finally, Darcy admitted how abysmally he had treated his best friend, Charles Bingley, who was still pining after Elizabeth's older sister.

Georgiana had listened patiently, patted his hand indulgently, ordered tea and toast, and then told him to shape up!

*"William,"* she had scolded, in a tone chillingly similar to that of their fearsome aunt, Lady Catharine de Bourgh, *"crying and self-pity are guaranteed not to solve any of the current problems, so what use are they?"*

Then, Georgiana laid out a much better plan in five minutes than he had been able to discern in six weeks. First, she said he must go straight over to the Gardiners' house before the calling hour and ask Edward to speak to Elizabeth. *"I believe she was not indifferent to you while at Pemberley. How are you to know she does not care for you when you have never asked her?"* Second, Darcy was to offer all their collective resources to the disposal of the Bennet family, regardless of Elizabeth's answer to his proposals. *"Be selfless and allow generosity and kindness to rule you."* Finally, Darcy was to engage Elizabeth in the plans and discussions about how to salvage the Bennet family's reputation. *"Do you not love her in part because she has her own mind? Perhaps you should use it!"*

And so, here he was. At barely seven in the morning, behind Elizabeth's uncle's house, hoping to find the answer to his heart's desire.

Finally waking from his internal reverie, Darcy was appalled at his impulsive behaviour. How had he ended up here so early, without a proper shave and smelling of horse? He was supposed to be coming to win Elizabeth's heart, not muck the stalls. There was no way he could speak to her looking so disreputable! There was nothing for it, he would have to go back home, bathe and change, then return in the phaeton.

As Darcy gathered the reins in his hands and turned to mount his horse, the object of his thoughts rounded the corner in significant haste. The moment she saw him, Elizabeth halted, dropping a handful of sugar cubes onto the ground at her feet. Though Darcy remained oblivious to Elizabeth's entrance, Incitatus did not. Seeing the free sugar lying about, the massive animal crossed the short distance to Elizabeth, dragging Darcy along by the reins. Darcy stumbled and crashed directly into the waiting arms of Elizabeth. It was enough to vanquish every rational thought from either's mind. With no thought of her lost father, ruined sister, or any peering eyes, Darcy brought his lips to Elizabeth's waiting mouth for an urgent and passionate kiss.

# Chapter 2

## Surprises

***Gracechurch Street, Cheapside, London***
***22 September 1812***

EDWARD GARDINER WAS FULLY DISCOMFITED BY THE INTERVIEW HE had just concluded with his headstrong niece. Elizabeth was intelligent but young. She must not throw away her life before she was allowed to really live. Edward believed that Darcy held some tender for Elizabeth based on their frequent and intimate correspondence over the past six weeks, but he dared not speak of his suspicions to Elizabeth, as he did not wish to raise her hopes. It was entirely true that with Lydia carrying a babe out of wedlock, most in society would shun their whole family. Edward thought better of Darcy, but he did not want to be the instrument which would break Elizabeth's heart any further.

Rising from his desk, Edward moved with his tea to the back window of his study and looked down on the mews. Elizabeth and Darcy were locked in a passionate embrace. It was both distressing and most welcome.

Edward was not one of England's most successful businessmen due only to his sparkling personality. He was proficient at reading people. The moment Darcy had been introduced to him in the south rose garden of Pemberley, Edward knew he loved Elizabeth completely. Elizabeth's feelings were harder to determine. She was too practiced at hiding herself from her overly excitable mother. Over the three days they spent in Derbyshire, Edward began to suspect that Elizabeth was receptive to Darcy's attentions, but it was the drive to Longbourn that convinced him. Elizabeth was distraught over Lydia's elopement and completely shut down while watching Darcy ride away from the inn at Lambton. Her demeanour during their trip home was forlorn. Both Edward and Madeline had tried to engage her in some conversation regarding Darcy and Georgiana, but Elizabeth evaded their questions. With less than one hour until reaching Longbourn, Elizabeth declared that they were unlikely to see the Darcys ever again, so further discussion of the acquaintance would be a waste of time. Her eyes told Edward all he needed to know. She was heartbroken.

Edward ceased considering the matter until the day Darcy appeared at their door in Cheapside. He was initially shocked to see anyone at the door to his study, since the black drape had been placed on the door less than twenty-four hours earlier. Propriety demanded that only the closest relations could come to a house newly in mourning. But there stood Darcy, one of the wealthiest men in the whole of England, with a reputation for following the rules of society without exception. And he looked dreadful.

He stayed for more than two hours in Edward's study, listening to the whole of the tale and asking invasive questions about the welfare of the remaining family. At first, Edward was cautious. Though it was not his own daughter, if word got out to society in general that one of Edward's wards was so wholly ruined, it could interfere with his business. The elite in society were uncompromising in their connections. But, when Darcy returned the next day, Edward decided to trust the young man.

Edward sent Darcy regular correspondence during the entire affair, and was pleased to invite the man back to his home, twice. Edward hoped that Darcy might still harbour feelings for Elizabeth, but was unsure if he would ever act on those feelings. Yesterday's news about Lydia's condition had certainly been a blow, and Edward had slept little last night, worrying over the matter.

Now, at least he had proof that both young people had their hearts in the same place.

As much as Edward wished to allow Darcy and Elizabeth a little bit of peace after so many weeks of heartache, they were engaged in a compromising position in his back garden, in full view of the mews. Ruination of another niece would be the end of all their livelihoods. So, Edward stepped into the kitchens, asked Cook to send a tray with tea, coffee, and toast for three to his study, and walked out into the morning sun.

*Bliss!*

This was the only thought running through Darcy's mind. Falling into her arms had been a shock, but the moment their eyes met it was clear that all his heart's desires were within reach. Instinct told him to kiss her, and so far, it was progressing wonderfully.

At first, she had been stiff in his arms, but she slowly began to respond. After a few moments, she snaked her arms up to the lapels on his riding jacket and was now clinging to him. Her whole body melted into his embrace, and he took a moment to savour the flavour of her lips. Tea with a bit of honey and milk. Somewhere in his conscious mind he knew he needed to end this and take her back into the house, but he could not give up the feel of her in his arms yet.

*Torture!*

Elizabeth clutched Darcy's lapels and held on tight, but her body was acting on its own accord. How could she let him kiss her like this? It was torture of the sweetest kind. Darcy could not possibly know what he was doing. Lydia's shame was complete, and all the Bennet sisters were now untouchable. Everyone was informed about her father's death and had likely heard about Collins taking possession of Longbourn, but surely, he was unaware of Lydia's condition. They had only learned themselves yesterday. Even if the gossip had spread to the Collinses, an express would have arrived at Rosings yesterday at the earliest, more likely today. Lady Catherine could not have informed Darcy yet. Once he knew, he would regret this kiss. He would ride away on that beautiful horse and never return. She could never blame him. Any connection with the Bennet family would ruin Georgiana, and he could not risk his sweet little sister for Elizabeth's selfish desires.

But she could not bring herself to pull away.

His long arms felt like a shield around her small body. In all Elizabeth's life, she had never felt more cherished than right now in Darcy's embrace. For a fleeting moment, she dreamed about riding away from all her troubles on Incitatus, with the wind in her hair as they left the scorn of society far behind. They could be happy, just the two of them, for the rest of their lives.

But there was not just two of them. Georgiana was Darcy's responsibility, and she was blameless in all of this; a victim herself of the vilest man Elizabeth had ever known. They could not take away her chances of a happy and prosperous life for so selfish a reason.

Elizabeth had sisters to think of too. Lydia was going to need someone to take her baby after it was born. If all the Bennets kept their heads down for the remaining months until her confinement, they may be able to find a respectable merchant acquaintance of Edward's to adopt the child. And while Elizabeth was too old to reasonably consider ever marrying, Mary and Kitty were young enough to avoid spinsterhood. The year after Lydia's confinement, if the girls moved to London, Edward should be able to find them husbands within the merchant classes.

And Jane was so beautiful. Surely, someone would want Jane if for no other reason than to sit peacefully in their parlour after dinner and look upon her serene face.

Yes, Elizabeth's family may have fallen so low as to be totally out of reach of the Darcys, but they still had a lot left to lose. It was time to end this charade and face Darcy's indignation. She must find a position before she brought more shame upon them all.

Darcy finally pulled away from Elizabeth's warm lips but only moved far enough to place his cheek upon her forehead. His arms tightened around her small waist, and he inhaled the sweet scent of her hair soap, lavender and roses.

"Elizabeth, my love, tell me this is not a dream from which I will shortly wake! Tell me that you are really here in my arms and can forgive all my transgressions against your family. Please dearest, tell me you will ease my suffering and agree to become my wife!"

Tears filled Elizabeth's eyes at his heartfelt declaration. This would be the moment she lost him forever. Another rejected proposal, but so different from his last. This time his words were beautiful, and she wished to accept with her whole being. But it could never be.

"Mr. Darcy, I…"

"Ahem! Darcy, Lizzy. I believe we should take this conversation inside my study. Come along, please."

Edward stood at the corner of the house, by the door to the kitchens. "Give that horse to the mews boy and stop gaping at me. It is still early and unlikely that any of the neighbours are yet at their breakfast, but the day is coming fast. It will not do to have yet another scandal on our hands."

Elizabeth scurried into the house while Darcy walked Incitatus back to an open stall in the mews. Edward waited until Darcy walked past him into the house before taking one last look around the back garden and returning inside himself.

Once all three were inside the study and seated at the low table, laden with a tea tray, Darcy spoke. "Edward, I know that it must be disconcerting to have seen myself and Elizabeth in such a tender moment, but I assure you, I am prepared to protect her reputation, immediately."

Elizabeth began to panic. "Mr. Darcy, I cannot imagine how you have come to address my uncle so informally, but I promise I have never given you leave to address me thus! Uncle, I swear to you I have not had any contact with Mr. Darcy since we left Lambton, and I have never before been in such a disgraceful position. I know that it is impossible for Mr. Darcy and I to be wed, and will accept any consequences you choose to inflict on me, but I am sure that no one observed us, so further damage to our family is improbable."

Darcy's heart sank at her rushed words. He turned to her and reached for her hand, but Elizabeth pulled out of his reach. "My love, what are you saying? I was sincere in my proposal. I want to marry you, today, if you will have me. Why would our marriage be impossible?"

"You don't know what you are saying!" Elizabeth exclaimed, with tears in her eyes. "My family's situation is even worse than you can possibly understand."

"Good God! What more could there be?"

Edward cleared this throat. "Lizzy, please modulate your voice. We do not want to be overheard by the staff. Now, I believe that there are some misunderstandings present that need clarification. First, Lizzy, you should know that Darcy and I have been corresponding for many weeks now. I gave him leave to call me Edward more than a month ago. Second, he is fully up to date on the Bennet family situation, including Lydia's condition, of which

I informed him yesterday. Finally, while I can plainly see that you two are in love with each other, I agree with Lizzy that a marriage between you is, at this time, impossible."

"Edward, you can't be serious..."

"Corresponding for weeks! Already knows about Lydia? Why...?"

"Calm yourselves," Edward interrupted. "I am perfectly serious, Darcy. Lizzy, frankly, I told him because I trust him, and the man needed to know. Now," he stood up and brushed a crumb from his jacket. "I must leave in order to meet with the Royal Inspector at my warehouse in forty minutes. You two have much to discuss if you are ever going to come to an understanding. I believe it would be best if we kept this liaison between us for now, so you cannot possibly stay in the house while I go. If you both come with me to the warehouse straight away, we will arrive before anyone else, and you can continue your conversation in the unoccupied office at the end of the front hall near the side entrance." Edward checked his watch and drained the last of his tea, placing the cup back on the tray. "I will join you as soon as the inspection is complete. It may be irregular to allow such a meeting to take place behind closed doors, but I believe you both responsible enough to avoid any real consequences, and this discussion must take precedence if we are to help my nieces."

With that, Edward ushered Elizabeth and Darcy back into the kitchens from the servants' entrance and out the door into the mews. The warehouse for Gardiner Imports was on the next street east from the Gardiners' house. As the hour was still quite early, the three made their way across the street, down the alley, and into the side entrance, without meeting anyone.

Darcy and Elizabeth were silent as they walked, each lost to their private thoughts.

So happy not a quarter of an hour ago, Darcy was now wallowing. He wrung his hands and let his head hang low, not wishing to meet anyone's eyes. *Will Elizabeth ever accept my hand?!*

Elizabeth was not faring much better. *How can he believe that I am marriageable? This is worse than believing him indifferent.*

Before either were really ready, Edward unlocked the door to the unused office once belonging to his father, and ushered them inside. Darcy was handed the key and instructed to open the door for no one but Edward. The door was closed and locked. The silence was deafening.

# Chapter 3

## For the Sake of Our Sisters

***Gardiner Imports, Cheapside, London***
***22 September 1812***

Elizabeth looked around the room. There was a large oak desk with a massive black leather chair against the wall. Two smaller leather chairs sat in front of the desk, and they looked stiff. The desk loomed large in the room and the smaller chairs were in a definite position of inferiority. Perhaps the elder Mr. Gardiner had used the difference in furniture size to gain the upper hand in business negotiations. Whatever the reason, the effect was profound.

In the corner of the room sat a much less menacing couch covered in a dusty white sheet. Darcy was already carefully folding the sheet to avoid kicking up any dust. She followed his silent lead and sat on the edge as far from him as possible with her hands folded in her lap. How does one start such a conversation?

*I love you desperately, but you know you cannot marry me.*

*Think of Miss Darcy! We cannot ruin your baby sister.*

*I could not bear it if you came to resent me for ruining your life.*

That last thought started her tears again. For, if Elizabeth was honest with herself, this was the real reason she would not succumb to any pressure he may lay upon her. If Elizabeth relented and secured her own happiness at the expense of the Darcys' family reputation, he would surely come to resent her. It would be better to live her life as a lonely spinster and have memories of their one kiss than to wake up one day knowing that her husband no longer loved her.

Darcy went from distressed to despondent when he saw her tears. He pulled his handkerchief from his breast pocket and wiped her eyes. With one finger under her delicate chin, he lifted her face to his and placed a chaste kiss on her forehead. "Miss Elizabeth, I beg of you, please tell me what distresses you so."

Honesty was her only choice. "I will not allow my selfishness to ruin your sweet sister. Despite your wishes and mine, we cannot marry."

Darcy looked at her with sad acceptance. She feared his next words as much as she knew they must come.

"My sister is the reason I am here today. She urged me to come and declare myself to you. She does not fear the scorn of society, so why should we fear for her?"

This was not what Elizabeth expected him to say. Something inside her snapped, and all her sadness flashed into ire. "Why? 'Why,' you ask? You cannot be serious! She is but a child and you are her guardian! She has not even come out into society yet. She has never had the privilege of dancing at an assembly or attending a glittering dinner party. She cannot have many friends, and now you wish to relegate her to the untouchables! What can you be thinking? You may not be willing to set aside your selfishness for another, but I am. I will not take her life away before she can live it!"

Darcy dropped both of his hands from her face, rose from the sofa and strode to the one window in the room, behind the massive desk. It was covered with a dirty blind, but seeing the outside world was not his goal. Much like her words at Hunsford after his disastrous and insulting marriage proposal, these accusations cut him deeply. Her reproofs then were not totally unfounded, but if he could not control his temper, this interview would dissolve quickly, and no solution would ever be reached. After several regulated breaths, Darcy turned back to Elizabeth who had collapsed into herself. With her face in her hands, she sobbed silently, tears streaming onto her gown.

What had his sister said last night? *Do you not love her in part because she has her own mind? Perhaps you should use it!* Yes, that was it. He must not give up.

Darcy made his way back to Elizabeth's side. He took her in his arms like he used to hold Georgiana when she had bad dreams as a child. He shushed her softly then relayed his sister's wisdom. "Georgiana told me many things last night, but the most intelligent thing she said was to remind me of your beautiful mind. I believe that we are stronger together than apart, and by working as partners, we will find the solutions that elude us individually." Darcy leaned back and cupped Elizabeth's cheek. He waited until she looked up at him before continuing. "I am totally besotted and wish to never be parted from you. I believe you have confessed this morning to loving me as well. We will find a way to secure our own happiness and protect our families, but we must consider all of the options together and not let the heartbreak of these last weeks overcome us."

Reaching again for the handkerchief he had given her, Elizabeth looked back down. It was hard to argue with him when looking into his sincere eyes. "It would be more than eighteen months before the shame of Lydia's situation could ever be dismissed enough to make me marriageable. And, regardless of Miss Darcy's contention otherwise, I will consider her future. We could not marry until her situation is definite. That could be years yet. I cannot be a burden on my family for so long and my taking a position would do even more damage to my reputation." Trying to make him understand, Elizabeth looked back to his face, allowing the tears to continue to fall. "London society would never allow you to marry a woman who had taken a position, even if I were a companion or governess to a landed family."

Darcy stood and began to pace. "What if I were to supply your uncle with the money to support you and Miss Bennet? Then there would be more to send to your mother and younger sisters." Elizabeth started to shake her head, but Darcy continued. "Not directly, of course, as that would garner suspicion. But I have been considering diversifying my holdings and Charles recently mentioned how well some of his import stocks were faring. This appears to be a large, well-run organization and the state of Edward's furnishings speak of good profits. I could buy in as an investor and free up some of Gardiner Imports' capital."

"If anyone found out, we would all be ruined. Do not forget that my uncle shares our shame as one of Lydia's guardians and the *ton* will assign it to anyone connected to us. A capital investor from such high society will be ridiculed for investing with such a disreputable family."

Stepping up to the window again, Darcy stared out and paused, twirling his signet ring behind his back. "Then, perhaps you could come and be Georgiana's companion, at least outwardly. In reality, we would marry quietly by special license and not announce the union until after Georgiana has a suitor. This way, any money I send to Edward could be masked as your 'salary,' and we could be together."

The hope in Elizabeth's chest was too tight. There was still much to consider. "Miss Darcy already has a companion, does she not?"

Darcy smiled. This was not a true argument, at least not from Elizabeth. He returned to the sofa and sat close by her side. "Yes, but Mrs. Annesley is more of her governess than a debut companion. A young lady newly out who has no mother or older sister to guide her often takes a slightly older companion for social functions. This woman is usually unmarried and serves as her friend as well as her chaperon. Mrs. Annesley does not fit that position, and I was going to hire someone soon for just that purpose. And, Elizabeth, I believe we are beyond formalities." Taking both of her hands, Darcy placed sweet kisses to the back of her knuckles. "Please, my sister is Georgiana, and I would be honoured if you would call me William."

"I cannot think of a greater pleasure, William." Tears once again rose to Elizabeth's eyes, but they were happy tears. After another moment, the crease returned to her brow. "Lady Catherine will never allow me to serve as Georgiana's companion. My ridiculous cousin continues to write her. The letter telling of Lydia's condition is likely already in the post. If you defy her, she will tell all who will listen about my sister, and I will be forced to resign."

Blast his aunt! "Perhaps we need to consider Miss Lydia. How many people were privy to their living situation before the duel? Would it be credible to purchase a forged marriage license for her and Wickham?"

"But my father killed him in a duel. Why would that have taken place if they had married?"

"An enraged father might still challenge the son-in-law to a duel for the heartache caused." An image of himself facing against Wickham for all the worry and heartache caused to Georgiana and now Elizabeth rose to Darcy's mind. Before he could become too upset by thoughts of a man who was now beyond harming his family, Darcy cleared his throat. "Besides, the marriage could not be truly legal, since she was sixteen without a guardian present. But if we confabulated the fact that a ceremony took place, it would lessen her shame. Also, now that she is pregnant, a defective marriage license will be ratified by effect of the common law. She could be considered a widow and the child legitimate."

"Would it be enough for Lady Catherine and my cousin?"

"Perhaps we need to combine all three." Darcy sat back on the sofa and placed his arm on it, behind Elizabeth, inching ever so closer. "If we also bandy about the notion that I had come to an understanding with Edward about a business deal prior to learning of Miss Lydia's elopement, then it gives me a reason to be involved with her restoration. I would not want my substantial investment to be tarnished. I would show my support by taking on one of the elder sisters as Georgie's companion and use the license story in public against any rumours anyone wants to spread. Additionally, I believe we can convince Collins to reverse his course and comply with the marriage license story based on his ongoing connection to the Bennets."

All of a sudden, Elizabeth felt like they could actually do this. Was it truly possible to secure their own happiness and protect their sisters? But the story was getting rather elaborate. A forged marriage license; a secret wedding; a hurried business investment. Plus, playing the part of Darcy's employee during the London season.

Elizabeth turned to Darcy. "William, I can see how the pieces fit together, but we must carefully consider who needs to know which part of the story. If too many people know of our marriage, it will surely slip one day in a most disadvantageous fashion. Also, if too many people know we faked Lydia's marriage license, that will also become common knowledge." Elizabeth looked away from his face, scooted slightly away from his body and fidgeted with the handkerchief in her lap. "Perhaps we should wait to actually marry until after Georgiana is settled."

Alarmed at her withdrawal, Darcy moved again and reduced the space between them. "I do not know if our living under the same roof unmarried is a good idea. I am not a saint, Elizabeth." He adjusted his cravat and gave Elizabeth a serious look when she finally lifted her eyes back to him. Catching his meaning, Elizabeth blushed, then laughed at the tension between them.

Darcy relaxed and reclaimed her hands in his own. "But I agree with keeping the plan as quiet as possible. Georgiana would need to know about our marriage of course, and the Darcy family house servants. That may seem like a large number of people, but my servants are extremely discreet. All of them. Most are from the Grayson-Reynolds family which has been serving us for five generations. If we explain the entire situation to Mrs. Reynolds, she will decide what to tell the staff, and there will be no questions and no breaches of our trust. I believe we should also tell Edward. He can help find any issues we may have missed, and his discretion is assured. Who else in your family we tell is up to you, but I would not tell anyone else in mine. I know what Lady Catherine will say, but the Fitzwilliams' reaction I am unsure of. My uncle, Lord Matlock, is a wonderful man and has always been understanding, but he has a position in the House of Lords to consider. Even Richard I cannot be sure of."

"We should tell no one in my family," Elizabeth laughed, ruefully. "Mother is the opposite of discreet. Mary would abhor the deception. Kitty would giggle and inevitably tell Maria Lucas, and Jane would be burdened by our secret. She has never been able to keep anything from Mamma. No, our marriage will be known only by you, Georgiana, Uncle Edward, and myself. Everyone else shall be told the investment story to explain your involvement."

The smile that shone from Darcy's face was brilliant. Truly, no one was his equal when he smiled. "Does that mean you will marry me, Elizabeth?"

Her eyes sparkled with wit and her left eyebrow rose. Darcy thrilled in the expression, so familiar from their prior sparring matches, yet unseen since she had opened Jane's letter in Lambton. "Do you consider that a proper proposal, Mr. Darcy?"

He laughed out loud. "Yes, woman, I do consider that a proposal, though perhaps not as proper as you prefer. Here, let me prepare for attempt four, so I can appease your high standards."

"How do you come to the number four?"

"First was my abysmal attempt at Hunsford. Second was in your uncle's back garden this morning after a most satisfying kiss. Third was just now. And fourth shall be in a moment." Darcy slid off the sofa. He took off the signet ring from his left middle finger and tested which of her delicate fingers would hold the large ring. Finding that her right thumb was large enough to ensure the ring would not slip off immediately, Darcy placed his signet on her hand and kissed her knuckle just above the thick metal. "Elizabeth Bennet, I have never loved anyone as I love you. I cannot live my life without you by my side. You make me better and I want nothing more than to have you as my partner, body, mind, and soul. Please, will you consent to be my wife?"

"Yes."

# Chapter 4

## Correspondence with a Gossip

***Wilton Row, Belgravia, London***
***22 September 1812***

"Louisa! Hand me those opera glasses."

Caroline Bingley was sitting upon her favourite chaise longue in the north parlour of her brother's London townhouse with her sister. While most would prefer to sit in a south-facing room during the morning hours to take advantage of the light from the rising sun, Caroline had always preferred this spot for its perfect view of S. Carriage Drive, the road surrounding Hyde Park from the south and leading to the fashionable park drives. Though the Bingley townhouse was a few streets south of Knightsbridge, there was the perfect combination of courtyards and one-story buildings directly between the room's middle window and the intersection of Rotten Row and S. Carriage Drive. Here was where Caroline spent hours watching the residents of London on their comings and goings.

"That awful Mrs. Goulding is out and about at this ridiculous hour, pushing her own child around in one of those new-fangled baby carriages. I would be absolutely mortified to be seen walking on Rotten Row without a nurse maid and governess." Caroline scanned Rotten Row again, looking for anyone else she recognized.

"Well dear, I am certainly glad you turned down Mr. Goulding two seasons ago," her sister, Louisa Hurst, said. "Think of the horror, had you been inclined to accept him! Though he is set to inherit a nice estate of more than four thousand pounds per year, having to cart around your own children in London would be unbearable."

Caroline sniffed and turned back to the window. Though Goulding was set to inherit property, Caroline had not been interested in marrying someone not in possession of their inheritance. Playing second fiddle to her husband's mother, or living off some allowance until her father-in-law died, was intolerable. Mrs. Henrietta Goulding, neé Heyer, had been one year behind Caroline at their elite London finishing school. The relatively poor daughter of a gentleman farmer from Kent, Henrietta had not been considered a true competitor in the marriage mart. The death of a wealthy and unmarried uncle had bestowed upon Henrietta a modest fortune last season. Now, seeing her married and pushing around the newest master Goulding, Caroline felt some twinge of jealousy over her security.

Louisa pulled the bell for more tea to be brought up to the drawing room. "At least you know you shall not have to suffer any such insult as the wife of Mr. Darcy."

"I certainly shall not!" Caroline set down her glasses and stood up abruptly. "The wife of one of the most important men in England will have nurses and governesses enough to ensure that I barely have to see my children, let alone take them to the park before breaking my fast."

"Do you think he will propose soon?" Louisa followed her sister's random meander about the well apportioned room. "I understand that Miss Darcy is set to debut in May. You have always said he was waiting to have his sister well situated before making his overtures to you. It would be easier if you were already installed as Mrs. Darcy, though, so you could chaperone the young debutant. Otherwise, he will have to hire a social companion."

"While I cannot bring up the subject directly, for that would be a horrid breach of propriety and Mr. Darcy does not tolerate *any* breach of good manners, I do believe I felt some softening of his resolve to continue to wait. Perhaps if we could see him here for a quiet family dinner before he quits town for the harvest, I might be able to speak with him more intimately. A winter wedding at the Pemberley village church would be lovely."

Louisa looked uninterested in the details of entertaining. The only object she seemed to be contemplating was the new bangle bracelet that her husband, Reginald Hurst, had given her for her birthday. "Do let me know the date and I shall make sure Mr. Hurst and I are available."

Caroline set her mouth in a little tight line. "Unfortunately, the knocker is not yet on the door to Darcy House. I was certain that Charles said he was coming to London after leaving Pemberley early, but according to your housekeeper, Darcy House has been closed to visitors this whole time. I plan on taking a walk in that direction later this week, just to ensure Mr. Darcy is not at home, but I cannot be sure of anything. Do not refuse any invitations for now on my account."

If only Caroline had risen earlier and started spying out of her advantageously positioned north-facing parlour window, she would have seen Darcy flying through the park on his massive horse towards Cheapside at dawn.

"I must say, I am quite annoyed by his silence and Charles's incalcitrant refusal to go and leave his card with the butler. This should have been my moment to ascent to the top rung of the London social ladder." Caroline sat heavy on her chaise and fiddled with the teacup on the side table. "Our sojourn at Netherfield was supposed to be for the benefit of Mr. Darcy seeing my skills as a hostess and running an estate manor, but Charles bungled that as well, by choosing such an ill-suited location and drably furnished house."

Louisa had moved on from examining her bangle bracelet to fiddling with her wedding rings. "Oh really? I thought you were the one to suggest the Netherfield estate, given its short distance from London. If the roads are good, it is not more than four hours in a carriage. Very convenient to maintaining contact with our friends in London."

"I admit that taking an estate lease was my original idea. You know how much grandfather Bingley wanted for Charles to ascend to land ownership. I also admit that I had originally thought very highly of the notion of Netherfield for its location and size. But that was before I had seen the state of the house. It was simply dreadful. I shall be forever glad that I waited to see the condition of the neighbourhood and the furnishings before organizing any entertainment for our friends from London. I would have been absolutely mortified had we offered such outdated accommodations to our elite friends here."

"Well, we are home now, and sooner or later Mr. Darcy will seek out Charles, I am sure of it. Then, we can resume our constant interactions and invitations. Do not fret dear, we shall have you well settled soon."

Caroline tapped her fingers on the arm of her chaise. "It is such an injustice in this world that women must marry men of wealth to have any status! It is not as if I am unworthy to reach the highest echelons of the *ton* on my own merit. I have the finest education, am poised, beautiful, and have an inheritance to rival any daughter of a peer. But, instead of enjoying the position that should have come with my money and accomplishments, I am not even considered a gentlewoman."

Louisa laughed at the thought of becoming a gentlewoman simply with money and accomplishments. "Our father's will did not leave you your money independent of Charles until you marry! Also, unjust as it may be, the rules of society dictate that it takes three generations to make a gentleman," here she dropped her voice to a whisper in case any of the servants were within earshot, "and I do not need to remind you that our grandfather was merely the son of a tenant sheep farmer outside of Halifax."

"Do not think I have forgotten! I was closest to Grandfather Bingley out of any of us." Caroline abruptly stood from her chaise again and began to pace around the room. "Though he might have been born low, Grandfather Bingley was a great man. I am proud to carry on his legacy, gentleman or not."

During his life, Andrew Bingley had worked on the sheep farm with his father and older brothers until his parents could no longer keep him. After being sent on his way, Andrew secured work at a large wool mill in Bradford. He was a shrewd, opportunistic young man, who quickly courted the favour of the mill's owner and rose through the ranks. The other low-born mill workers resented the favouritism showed Andrew, but what did he care? He was going to make something of himself, no matter who he had to step on to advance. After not too many years, Andrew convinced the owner to sign a marriage contract for his oldest daughter. Upon her sixteenth birthday, Andrew took her as his wife and proceeded to produce an heir with haste. Caroline's father, Richard Bingley, was brought into this world as her young grandmother left it. A widower at only twenty-nine, Andrew never truly mourned the loss of his young wife; after all, wives and children cost money. He had what he wanted, the first-born grandson to the mill's owner, and would only have to incur the expense of feeding one additional person on a mill foreman's salary.

As Caroline's father grew, Andrew encouraged a close relationship with his grandfather, the mill's owner. The interaction between grandfather and grandson allowed for natural affection, and years of gentle nudging to fuel an eventual change in inheritance. The aging mill owner decided to overlook his other children and leave his mill, in whole, to his beloved grandson. Andrew was named trustee until Richard was able to take control.

Richard, however, was a disappointment to his father. In manner and temperament, he too greatly resembled his soft-hearted grandfather, but at least he was easily led. Another advantageous arranged marriage between Richard and the only child of a large operation cloth maker in Leeds allowed Andrew to expand his business. Integrating the wool milling and cloth making businesses doubled profits in the first five years of Richard's marriage. Additional automation machinery developed in Scotland allowed even greater savings by reducing the number of workers while maintaining output. The Bingleys quickly amassed a fortune of nearly one hundred thousand pounds.

Richard and his wife, who cared greatly for each other despite their contracted marriage, produced Louisa and Caroline quickly. Though the doctors advised that another pregnancy was not likely to end favourably, Andrew was adamant that there must be an heir. Charles was born a short fifteen months after Caroline and, as predicted, another young woman gave her life in the pursuit of Andrew Bingley's ambition.

Having spent nearly all his adult life kowtowing to the gentry who owned the land of Yorkshire, to buy the best wool at the lowest prices, Andrew knew that neither he nor his son would ever be accepted into their society. Both had worked for the massive Bingley fortune and were well known manufacturers, especially to the Earls of Bradford and Scarborough. Any attempt to make an appearance as a gentleman would be quickly rebuked.

But, if Andrew ensured that they never lifted a finger in his mills, his grandchildren could make the Bingley debut into the *ton*. So, the Bingley patriarch found a beautiful townhouse in Belgravia owned by a spendthrift

Marques who required immediate funds and therefore did not care that the buyers were from trade. The house was close enough to Mayfair to stretch the truth in conversation and, most importantly, it was far from any of the Yorkshire gentry who may make the connection between the young, personable Charles Bingley and his shrewd grandfather. So, Andrew packed up his three motherless grandchildren, hired a buxom governess, and moved to London. Richard was left to manage the mills and was devastated at the loss first of his wife, and then his children, but found himself unable to oppose his father after a lifetime of obeying without comment. He continued to live and work in the Yorkshire mills until he died in a wool fire when Charles was but seven years old. Once again, everything passed to the young Bingley heir with Andrew acting as trustee until Charles came of age.

After moving the siblings to London, Andrew recognized that Caroline was the only one of his grandchildren with the personality to ensure the continued rise of the Bingley name. He began instructing her on how to keep Charles and Louisa in line the same way Andrew had managed Richard. She was educated on the full plan her grandfather had devised all those years ago when he married the mill owner's daughter. Some of Caroline's earliest and fondest memories were of sitting on her grandfather's lap as he told her how to climb the English socioeconomic ladder. Upon his deathbed, Andrew handed his personal journal to Caroline, which included the details of every advantageous opportunity he had ever created for his family. The continuation of the Bingley family social rise passed to Caroline at the tender age of fourteen.

Until last year, Caroline had been extremely successful. Louisa's marriage to Hurst had been easy to arrange. The Hurst estate was a long-standing property on the edge of Kent near Tonbridge and included a seaside house in Brighton as well as a comfortable house in town. The Hursts were one of the oldest families of the *ton*, and Reginald's maternal great-aunt was Lady Sefton, the most prominent and oldest patroness of the ultra-important dancing salon, Almack's Assembly Rooms. Where the Bingley money needed ratification through a longstanding connection to land, the Hurst's land needed money. Louisa's dowry of twenty-thousand paid off the family's debts and allowed improvements to the tenant farms, which brought the estate's income back to a respectable four-thousand per annum. As the second son, and already in possession of more than one nephew, Hurst would likely not inherit, but as part of the consideration for Louisa's marriage, the Hursts gave him title to the house in London and enough of an annual allowance to keep up with the *ton*.

Louisa and Hurst's marriage provided the Bingley siblings a firm footing into London society. Married at eighteen, Louisa was granted access to the events of the *ton* before Caroline was even officially out. Hurst gave Caroline and Charles legitimacy. With Hurst's sponsorship, Charles was allowed to attend Eton, then Cambridge, as the brother of a gentlemen. He was allowed to reside in the gentlemen's dorms instead of being relegated to the smaller accommodations reserved for tradesmen. Caroline made her introduction in Louisa's drawing room and in the company of the elder Mrs. Hurst.

However, despite her careful planning, Caroline was no closer to catching a husband of wealth and title by the end of her third season than she had been at her debut, nearly five years ago now. It had become clear that catching a man with more than a modest estate who needed her dowry to pay his debts, like Mr. Goulding, would be difficult. Caroline would have joyously welcomed an impoverished lord in need of her dowry if there wasn't already an heir for the title. But, for all the influence of the Hurst name, Bingley was still a newcomer to London, and Caroline was having trouble orchestrating an entrance into the highest echelons.

Then, Caroline had been introduced to Mr. Fitzwilliam Darcy at the beginning of her fourth season by none other than her dim-witted puppy dog of a brother. Charles catching Darcy was an unimaginable boon to Caroline. The friendship had grown naturally, and totally without Caroline's manipulation. But, no matter, even a broken clock is right twice a day. Darcy first sailed into the Bingley townhouse the summer after Charles started at Cambridge. Caroline had, of course, heard of the wealth of Pemberley, but since the elder Mr. Darcy was still alive and in no need of an heir, Caroline had initially disregarded both Darcy men as marital prospects. That first summer, Caroline was content to allow the 'boys' to hide in the game room, and saved her best dresses for calling on the wealthy widows with sons to marry off.

But Caroline was not blind. She never failed to notice the superior quality of his clothing, or the pleasing picture he presented wearing them. She also admired his cool and aloof demeanour, which spoke of breeding at the highest level. Upon her first invitation to dinner at the Darcy townhouse, which is decidedly fully ensconced in the Mayfair neighbourhood without any need for embellishment, she also noted the apparent wealth of the Darcy family. Most of the gossips of London's high society mumbled behind their fans that the Darcy estate garnered ten-thousand per annum, but Caroline was sure it was closer to twice that amount. Perhaps the current Mr. Darcy's great-grandfather had earned ten-thousand per annum and society never bothered to update their gossip. Few of even the titled peers surpassed the Darcys in wealth or land holdings.

When the elder Mr. Darcy fell ill and died suddenly the next winter, it was as if Caroline had been given a sign. She felt as though her grandfather was once again holding her on his knee and guiding her down the path to social supremacy. For the last five years since Darcy had taken possession of all the Pemberley property and accounts, Caroline had bided her time. She knew that coming into his inheritance at only twenty-two would be a struggle, but suddenly having to raise his eleven-year-old sister made the job nearly impossible. Caroline guided Charles into making sure the Bingleys were issued regular invitations to Pemberley, and always provided support for the grieving Darcy siblings.

As a young, handsome, and massively rich bachelor, Darcy was pursued incessantly by the match-making mommas of the *ton*. He was so often imposed upon by mercenary ladies, that Darcy never appeared in society without either his cousin, Colonel Richard Fitzwilliam, or Charles, for protection. And where Charles went, so went Caroline. Frequently arriving at a high society event on the arm of the most eligible bachelor in London catapulted Caroline to the top. She was not naive enough to believe that any of her recently acquired lady friends had any interest in her as a person. Each such lady looked on, strictly in jealousy, and with the hope that Caroline would falter at some point. They would be waiting until the end of time. Caroline Bingley does not make mistakes. At the end of this last season, there had been tittering about Caroline deluding herself with visions of becoming Mrs. Darcy. Why would he need five years to make his offer if one was forthcoming? Many of the younger ladies believed that they could supplant the twenty-five-year-old. She would show them exactly how deluded she had become.

Waiting for so long had started to take a toll on Caroline, but she was always comforted in knowing that Darcy had never showed the least bit of interest in any female acquaintance, either in London or around his home in Derbyshire. Additionally, she was not keen to provide Darcy with the required heir too soon, having lost both her mother and grandmother to childbirth. Waiting a few extra years before taking on her marital duty was of no significance. Caroline was confident in her position as Darcy's best friend's sister, and felt as if her influence over Georgiana was coming along quite nicely. When the day came, Caroline was sure that becoming mistress of Pemberley and Darcy House London would be worth the wait.

If only she had not insisted her brother take on that dreadful estate in Hertfordshire. Netherfield was a plague. Jane and Elizabeth Bennet had nearly destroyed all of Caroline's hard work. Her brother was meant for the daughter of a peer, and Caroline was going to be mistress of Pemberley. That chit, with her fine eyes and unkempt curls, would never take Caroline's prize.

The only saving grace from their stay at Netherfield was the discovery of a chatty housekeeper. Grandfather Bingley had always emphasized the use of servants in getting information and doing the dirty work. Oftentimes, those below stairs knew more about the lives of the gentry than they knew of themselves. In each of the London houses, as well as the house in Brighton, Caroline had gained a valuable informant through the high-level staff.

The chatty housekeeper at Netherfield, Mrs. Smythe, had proven to be very valuable with the information she procured regarding the Bennets. It was through Mrs. Smythe that Caroline first learned Lydia Bennet had travelled to Brighton alone, in the care of only Colonel Forster and his young, irresponsible wife. It was too easy. Then, Caroline had received news of Lydia's inappropriate flirtations and attention to none other than Lt. George Wickham. This letter had been received back in July. No other information had yet caught up with Caroline, but her intuition was high. She would bet all her future fortune that whatever family crisis had pulled Elizabeth suddenly from Pemberley in August was the result of Lydia's misbehaviour in Brighton.

Caroline had planned to bring up the topic at dinner on the night Elizabeth and her Cheapside relatives were invited to dine at Pemberley. Fortunately, they had all scurried back to Longbourn and sent Georgiana their regrets before the travesty of a meal could take place. Then, as if sharing Darcy's attention with Elizabeth during her triumphant visit to Pemberley had not been bad enough, Darcy received an urgent missive recalling him immediately to London and cutting their visit to a mere three days. And Caroline still had no idea what was so urgent that Darcy had abandoned his dearest friends.

Finally, the door to the servant's hall opened and Caroline's maid came in with a full tea tray.

Caroline roughly set her opera glasses on the side table. "It is about time, Anna! We were nearly starved up here without any fresh tea. Please take away the old tray when you leave, but first I must know if the post has yet arrived. I am most anxious for any missives that followed us from our summer travels. I do not believe we have had anything since we left Pemberley."

"Not yet, miss. But the carrier usually comes about this time, so Mrs. Kelly is likely to have it soon and always sorts it right away. I will come back with anything as soon as it is ready."

"See that you do. You are dismissed."

Louisa handed Caroline a cup of tea. "I do wonder what has taken the post so long to find us. Mrs. Reynolds must have sent on post from our unexpected early departure to Yorkshire, and then the staff there must have held it for some time before sending it here to London. I believe I have not had a letter from our aunt in nearly six weeks."

"Yes, we've had nothing at all since we left Pemberley." Caroline took a sip of her fresh tea. "I must say, I am not very impressed with Mrs. Reynolds."

"Really! How can you say that, Caroline? She has been Mr. Darcy's housekeeper since he was a child. I am sure he regards her with the utmost respect and affection."

"That all may be true, but what do men really know about the servants? I have made every effort to ingratiate myself with the woman, but she continues to give me the cold shoulder. At first, I tried to be kind and agreeable. I have lately tried to be more authoritative, like what would be expected between servant and mistress, but nothing has worked. This past visit, I spoke outright to Mrs. Reynolds about my… tentative… understanding with Mr. Darcy. Though of course, I did not let her know that there was anything in the formalities still wanting."

"Oh, Caroline, you did not! I would not like to have any report of inappropriateness given to Mr. Darcy."

"It was not so scandalous, Louisa." Caroline looked away from her sister and picked up the opera glasses to spy out the window once more. "And anyway, I am certain he is only waiting for the right time to speak and for Georgie to be settled. It is inevitable that I will be mistress of Pemberley soon. But I tell you, Mrs. Reynolds did not take my warning, as kindly as it was given. Like a royal duchess confident of her position in the world, the old woman stood firm. She informed me that until she heard otherwise from Mr. Darcy directly, Georgie was the mistress of Pemberley. I have tried for the past few years to find some upstairs maid to help me with my… requests for information, but they are all fiercely loyal to Mrs. Reynolds. Well, the old woman will be singing a decidedly different tune once I take my rightful place as Mrs. Darcy. Perhaps I can send the old bat to Netherfield and bring the compliant Mrs. Smythe to Pemberley."

Louisa laughed and stirred another lump of sugar into her cup. "Oh, I almost forgot. I took tea with my sister-in-law yesterday, and one of the young ladies, I think Lady Derby's daughter, said she saw Miss Darcy on Bond Street a few days ago. While of course we cannot visit until the knocker is on the door, perhaps we might send over an invitation to dinner this week after all. If Miss Darcy is here, Mr. Darcy must also be here, for why would his sister come all this way without him?"

"Louisa! How could you forget to tell me this? I swear sometimes you vex me quite beyond measure. I will make the note immediately." Moving with haste to her desk, Caroline catalogued what dinners she had planned already for the week. "Will Thursday work for you? I do not want to wait too long but must give Mr. Darcy at least two days' notice. Really, if you had told me yesterday, as you should have, we could have entertained him tomorrow."

"It simply slipped my mind, dear, and I did not know you were so keen to have him to dinner. But no matter, Thursday will be just fine for myself and Mr. Hurst."

When Caroline finished the invitation for Darcy and his sister to dine with the Bingley family on Thursday, she looked back out of the window. A few strollers were still out at this unfashionable hour, on their way to numerous errands and calls. Caroline promised herself that this would be the year. She would no longer wait for Darcy to speak.

She would promote her match with Charles, Hurst, Georgiana, and anyone else who would listen. With luck, the expectation created by gossip would finally prompt Darcy to act. He would not want his reputation as a gentleman to falter by jilting his best friend's sister. And if social persuasion was not enough, Caroline would have to orchestrate another solution next summer at Pemberley.

The season always ends officially on the last Friday of June. Most of the best families take their leave of town by mid-June and spend the last few weeks of socializing at the country homes of their friends, before tucking into their own estates for the fall and winter. While Almack's and Vauxhall Gardens provided a pretty background for flirtations, most serious proposals were conducted in the more private setting of the end-of-season house parties or private balls. Any debuting lady would be the envy of the entire season if she could manage to procure prestigious acceptances to an end-of-the-season house party given by a member of *le bon ton*. Caroline would introduce the idea of hosting a small end-of-season house party at Pemberley, in honour of Georgiana's debut.

Oh yes, Caroline would be Mrs. Darcy by the end of this next season.

Her first act as mistress would be to rid the south garden of the wild and unruly rosebushes she saw being pruned on her last trip to Pemberley. Roses were far too common to be grown in such abundance and in so prominent a location. She would have them all removed before the house party. Perhaps, once she finally got an audience with Georgiana, she would mention the matter.

Just as Caroline was pressing the seal into the wax on her dinner invitation to the Darcys, Anna came back into the parlour with the post. Looking over the stack, Caroline saw several letters from the Hurst's Brighton housekeeper and nearly a dozen from Netherfield. Finally, she would learn whatever had happened to the Bennet family. Reaching for her small, engraved letter knife, Caroline went to work.

# Chapter 5

## Hidden Strength

***Wilton Row, Belgravia, London***
***22 September 1812***

Charles Bingley stood silently next to the large fireplace in a very ill-suited room at the back of the Bingley townhouse. The room faced north and west, which made the morning hours very dark, and the only window looked directly onto the stables. Before Bingley became master, it was used as the still-room. It would be very difficult for anyone to understand why Bingley had turned the room into a small sitting room, unless you listened very carefully while standing by the fireplace. This room happened to be directly below Caroline's favourite upstairs drawing room and the two fireplaces shared a flue. Bingley could hear every word said in his sister's drawing room from his place by the mantle.

Many of their shared acquaintances would recognize the stoic and strained demeanour on Bingley's face, as one often found upon the face of his good friend, Darcy. But only Bingley's loyal valet, Grayson, had ever seen the outwardly congenial man with such an expression upon his visage.

The happy demeanour Bingley presented to the world was not a total farce. He was naturally easy going and engaging. Never admitting to possessing a firmly held opinion was also easy, as he did not have many firm opinions on the frivolous things Caroline and other members of society constantly fretted about. But the weak façade was a coping mechanism developed long ago to deal with his sister's machinations. Caroline believed that she was the only Bingley sibling with any intelligence or ambition, but she was misinformed. In truth, Bingley was exceptionally intelligent, like his grandfather, but had enough compassion to realize the elderly man had been cruel and uncouth.

Bingley had listened to their grandfather, as often as Caroline. However, he had a different reaction to those lessons than his selfish sister. The young boy had loved his father very much and always felt angry at the way Grandfather Bingley treated him. After learning of their father's tragic death, young Charles went into the library to hide and cry alone. Shortly after he had quieted, Caroline and Grandfather Bingley entered the room without knowing Charles was hidden behind the sofa and began to speak poorly of their departed father and son. Charles's anger soon turned into fear as they began to discuss himself. Grandfather Bingley and Caroline agreed that they would have to keep Charles in line, now that he was the legal owner of all the Bingley family's wealth. Grandfather Bingley still controlled the minuscule amount of cash he had amassed through his salary as a foreman in the wool mill, but all the property and profits associated with the mill and the cloth manufacturing business had technically been owned by Richard, and now were passed to Charles. His relations spoke at length how the young master must be controlled and guided to make the most advantageous decisions. At the age of only seven years, Charles vowed never to trust his Grandfather Bingley or sister Caroline.

Since Bingley was often a boisterous child, when he decided to hold his tongue, he was often overlooked. Bingley would quietly enter the library and sit undetected in the large wingback chair, while Grandfather Bingley was instructing Caroline. Many of Grandfather Bingley's lessons were relatively neutral or could be employed without his cruelty. Indeed, servants often knew more of what was going on around the gentry than the master of the house. Loyalty and candid communication from one's servants could produce much valuable information. Unfortunately, Caroline insisted that, as the mistress of the house, she must hire all the servants. Thankfully, she had never challenged Bingley on his choice of valet. Grayson had been recommended to Bingley during his first year in Cambridge by Darcy, and was the son of the Darcy house stable master. Caroline would never dare go against a recommendation by Darcy, even though she was unable to influence Bingley's man. Shortly after taking on Grayson, the two men had a candid discussion about the state of Bingley's house. Both agreed they should never trust any of the other servants with sensitive information. Grayson took on a silent demeanour, only speaking to the others in the house to request necessities for his master.

In a stroke of genius, Grayson recommended that Bingley confide in Mrs. Reynolds, the elderly housekeeper at Pemberley. So, during his first trip to Pemberley, Bingley spoke with Mrs. Reynolds. He confided that his own house was populated with his sister's informants, and Caroline's sole goal in life was to climb the social ladder as high as she could reach. Mrs. Reynolds promised the young man that he could always contact her through Grayson with sensitive requirements and needs. After Caroline's interest in Darcy became apparent, they hid their communication inside letters to Grayson from one of the downstairs Pemberley maids. Caroline might have opened letters from the Pemberley housekeeper, hoping to learn information about the Darcy siblings' movements, but she would completely ignore letters from a low-ranking maid.

In fact, Caroline's belief that only the highest of female servants could be of any real use was one of her largest mistakes. She believed that men were generally clueless to the real value of gossip and would miss those details that were truly important. Bingley found that the stable boys were as knowledgeable as the housekeeper, and often more likely to move about undetected. With more help from Darcy, Bingley was able to get several stable boys from Pemberley instilled at both the Bingley and Hurst townhouses. Only one young man was involved in the information being passed back to Bingley. As another relation of Grayson and Mrs. Reynolds, Bingley was assured of his discretion.

This morning, Bingley had received a multitude of letters, sent express from his small but valuable network. Like Caroline, his correspondence had been interrupted by all the last-minute changes to their travel plans.

In addition to the routine information regarding his house and holdings, Bingley had received two letters of significant importance.

The first was from Mrs. Reynolds. That Caroline had been trying to engage her in passing information for several years was not surprising to Bingley. However, Caroline's behaviour during their latest visit was worrying. Caroline had blatantly lied to Mrs. Reynolds about her relationship with Darcy to try and force the housekeeper's cooperation. This escalation in his sister's behaviour gave Bingley significant pause.

Bingley had tried to protect his friend as best he could, but he had not made any overt steps to control Caroline for fear of her retaliation. Now, he hoped he would be able to salvage the situation once whatever she concocted came to a head. Long ago, Darcy told Bingley he would never marry Caroline regardless of the situation, but pressure from the Hursts or Darcy's uncle, the Earl of Matlock, might change Darcy's tune if she forced the matter. With Georgiana coming out in the spring, Darcy would not want to damage his sister with a scandal of Caroline's making.

The second important letter was unexpected and heart-breaking. The steward of Netherfield had sent him updates on the harvest along with news of the Bennets. His newest servant was a competent estate manager and another recommendation from Darcy. The man was also a keen observer and had immediately seen Bingley's interest in the angelic Jane Bennet. He rarely sent information not related to the Netherfield holdings, but each time he had, it was only one line and never failed to break Bingley's spirit.

The first was last February. *"Miss Jane Bennet is visiting relatives in Cheapside, London for the spring."*

At first, he believed that her decision not to call on the Bingleys during her stay in London was further proof of Darcy's contention that she did not care for him, and so he stayed away. Later, after much thought, he wondered if she *had* ignored him. It would be improper for her to call on a single man, so if she had visited, she would have called on Caroline or Louisa. His manipulative sisters would have never reported the visit to Bingley. Also, if the London servants were unaware of Jane's importance to the master, her visit would have garnered little attention below stairs. Grayson may have never heard of the visit either.

The second such note about the Bennets was received on his last day at Pemberley in August and read simply, *"Miss Lydia has eloped with an officer from Brighton and Miss Jane Bennet is distraught."*

It arrived express but was originally delivered to the Pemberley stables and then passed on to Grayson. The seal was intact when he opened the missive, and Bingley committed it to the fire the moment he understood the contents. Darcy would not say what caused Elizabeth and the Gardiners to leave for Longbourn so quickly, but Bingley was sure that they had received the same news.

Intent on keeping the intelligence from Caroline for as long as possible, Bingley had feigned indifference to the change in plans and continued on with their summer travels. With any hope, Jane's father and uncles would be able to remedy the situation before too much scandal could be created. Bingley had also asked Mrs. Reynolds to hold any post that came to Pemberley after their departure, until Grayson sent word that they were heading for London. Unfortunately, that meant he never received the third note from his steward, dated August 20, until today.

*"Mr. Bennet killed the officer in a duel but has passed of his own injuries, and the Bennet women have been turned out of Longbourn. Miss Jane and Miss Elizabeth go to London."*

His beautiful Jane was orphaned and living off the charity of the Gardiners. Lydia was never married to a dead man, and the Bennet women had lost all standing in society. If only that were the end, but a final missive arrived not an hour ago by express rider, independent of the bundle from Yorkshire.

*"Miss Lydia is with child."*

As Bingley was staring at that last sentence, Grayson knocked and motioned for Bingley to exit the room. Both men knew that if Bingley could hear every word of Caroline's conversations, she would be able to hear him. It was strictly silence inside the ill-suited sitting room.

Bingley followed his valet to the master's study.

"Sir, I am sorry to inform you that, though I intercepted the mail delivery and sorted your correspondence first, I was not able to delay any longer. Your sister has received a very large bundle of letters, many of which come from the housekeeper at Netherfield."

She knew.

Bingley sat heavily on the chair behind his desk and hung his head. It was certain. Caroline knew of the Bennet family's fall from grace.

"Whatever will save us now?"

Bingley had replayed every second with his beloved Jane, and he knew in his heart that Darcy was wrong. Elizabeth's words during their brief time together at Pemberley only confirmed his conviction. If Bingley was ever going to win Jane's heart, he would have to act carefully. He had always known that Caroline wanted him to marry into the aristocracy, but he was determined to be happy. Jane made him happy. What good was standing within the *ton* if it came with misery?

Tradesmen like Edward Gardiner had a comfortable living and friendly society amongst the other professionals in the merchant class. In contrast, many of the landed gentry were finding it hard to keep their coffers full from the profits born of only crops and sheep. When the inflated grain prices dropped after Napoleon's vanquish, they would find themselves in even worse shape. Bingley had been diversifying his holdings to continue to earn profit. Caroline never paid any attention to the business end of their wealth, as long as her allowance was substantial. Both the wool mill and cloth manufacturing business continued to make a profit every year. Bingley took all that profit and invested it in non-agricultural industries. Coal had been doing particularly well in the last three years.

With all his dirty trade money, Bingley planned to buy an estate far away from London and forget the *ton*. Darcy had been helping him look at properties near Derby for a few years and there was one north of Belper that was perfect. Once he figured out how, Bingley would sweep Jane away from all the turmoil caused by the gossiping harpies in London and live blissfully in Derbyshire. If his instincts were good, perhaps she would not even be too far from her favourite sister.

It was time to act.

"Grayson, have my horse saddled immediately, then come up and help me with my cravat. I intend to go directly to Darcy's house, before the storm erupts here. I know my friend has been in London these past six weeks and I have a standing invitation to be admitted through the back of the house. If I am lucky, I shall catch him before I must return to dress for our dinner tonight. If I could send Caroline away for some reason, I would, but I do not believe she will be persuaded to give up London if she believes Darcy's arrival is imminent. I know she means to trap him somehow. If only I could be sure that Darcy would not actually cave to any social pressure resulting from a compromising situation." Sparing a moment for the thought of Caroline trying to trap Darcy, Bingley smirked. "Her demise at her own hand would be poetic."

# Chapter 6

## Confrontations

***Darcy House, Mayfair, London***
***22 September 1812***

DARCY WAS IN SOME AMOUNT OF SHOCK. ELIZABETH WOULD FINALLY be his wife! He had wrestled with the decision for almost a year, and despaired of ever winning her love. Now, it was agreed, and he would become bound to her forever in a few short weeks. Edward came back into the room after finishing the inspection rather quickly. By 9:00 a.m., it was decided that Darcy would apply for a special license that very day at Doctor's Commons, and Edward's solicitor would draw up the marriage contract for both men to sign.

Edward insisted upon waiting until they could remove to Derbyshire before celebrating the marriage. It would be too much of a risk having the ceremony anywhere in town. At Pemberley, the only witnesses would be persons in the Pemberley employ and the vicar who owed his position to Darcy. Elizabeth would have to marry without any family present, but Elizabeth had already agreed that secrecy was of the utmost importance. Without Edward to give her away, they would have to wait until October

3, Elizabeth's twenty-first birthday, but that would only be a few days after the household reached Pemberley anyway.

They all agreed that if Lydia's fake marriage license ploy was to work, she would have to be removed from Meryton. Otherwise, she would likely crumble under questioning from her neighbours. If she moved to a place where she was unknown and introduced as the young widow of a soldier, no one would ask any uncomfortable questions. The only problem was where to take her. Edward had no close connections outside London and Hertfordshire. Darcy said he would consider the matter and come up with a solution, but, honestly, he was at a total loss. Perhaps Connor Grayson, Darcy's trusted valet, could find the solution. The Grayson family had served the Darcys for five generations. Mrs. Reynolds was the granddaughter of the original Mr. and Mrs. Grayson who served as butler and housekeeper to Darcy's great-grandparents. His family had always trusted a Grayson with their most sensitive needs.

When their conversation had come to an end, Edward searched the hall to ensure no one was in view of the offices, then he moved both Darcy and Elizabeth to his office at the end near the warehouse. They had an overly animated conversation about Darcy's supposed need for a social debutant companion for Georgiana, and Elizabeth's acceptance of such a position.

After their conversation ended, Edward asked Elizabeth to return to the house to explain her removal to her sister and aunt, then pack her belongings, as she would be moving into the Darcy house the next day. Before she disappeared beyond the view from Edward's window, Darcy was pulled back into the room by a startling question from the older man.

"Darcy, I am not sure the proper way to bring up this topic with you, but since you lost your father rather young, I am just going to come out with it." Edward straightened his waistcoat and adjusted his shirt-cuffs then cleared his voice and spoke without meeting Darcy's eyes. "Have you been intimate with a woman before?"

Darcy stared for a few moments as his colour rose. "I am not uneducated in the matter, but I have never ruined a young maiden or compromised any lady, if that is your meaning."

"While that is reassuring, in fact it is not quite my meaning." Edward looked about the room as if something would come to his rescue. Screwing his courage to the sticking place, he finally looked up. "I was more concerned about your education in the procurement of an heir, specifically, how quickly that event can sometimes occur."

Darcy's blank stare was followed by a slow look of horror. "Are you implying that a child could result from our union before Georgiana's debut?" Darcy's own parents had been married for nearly four years before Darcy had been born and then it took another eleven years before Georgiana came into the world. As a child, Darcy had heard about his mother losing children between himself and his sister, but he was unaware of how often such things normally happened. Thinking upon the matter now, it was obvious that his parents had difficulty begetting children, which could account for the long wait before his birth. And in fact, he had no idea whether his mother had suffered other losses before his birth.

"It is not set in stone, but Jane was delivered not a year after my sister and Bennet were married. Lizzy came before Jane was two years old and then each Mary, Kitty, and Lydia came about twenty-four months apart. Also, it is obvious that Lydia conceived with no trouble within a fortnight of becoming intimate with Wickham. It would be the ruination of all our plans if Elizabeth were to appear next summer heavy with child."

Edward could see the growing worry on Darcy's face and decided to be blunt once again. Putting on his best neutral businessman demeanour, Edward stood from his chair, clasped his hands behind his back and continued, "Have you heard of Jeremy Bentham the reformist? He has been promoting an item called a condom in some of his recent publications. It has been around in Italy and France for many years, but not in wide use here in England. Apparently, it is a sheath made of animal intestines that covers the male organ, used primarily to protect against the French disease. As a side observation, it also keeps a woman from conceiving. They are sold in bars, and at a shop near Covent Garden, to men wishing to engage female companionship of the variety to be found near the theatres. Also, our military has been purchasing them in bulk to try and stem the number of soldiers contracting disease in France. My services have been engaged twice to export such items to the troops in the last few years of Napoleon's war. I can discreetly obtain several for you if you wish."

Darcy could only nod without meeting Edward's eyes. To believe he could have compromised his beloved Elizabeth with a pregnancy simply by hoping it would not occur. How stupid! No one would ever believe that they had been married before the child was conceived even if they provided the special license as proof. Elizabeth would have been forever branded as his mistress that he took pity upon and married. His aunt would be seeking an annulment before the child was weaned. Thank goodness Edward was a man of intelligence, experience, and discretion. How much else would Darcy find himself unprepared for? It had been a long time since anyone had acted as Darcy's counsellor. It would be nice to have such a voice every now and again.

Thankfully, Edward accepted Darcy's non-verbal confirmation and decided to end their private interview. It was agreed that Darcy would return shortly before tea to the warehouse to sign the marriage settlement, then join the family for dinner.

❧

The minute Darcy stepped into his house, his butler informed him that Bingley was waiting in his study. After a quick shave and change of clothes, Darcy decided to see what his good friend wanted and try to hurry him out of the house quickly. He had to get to Doctor's Commons before 2:00 p.m. to apply for the license.

Darcy entered the study with as unaffected an air as possible, then spoke with feigned good humour. "Good morning, Charles. I am surprised to see you so early. Sorry you had to wait, but I was out for a morning ride when you arrived."

"Caroline knows, Darcy."

Confusion turned to realization as Darcy's mind raced. Whatever would they do?

"Stop staring at me like that and tell me what we are going to do about Jane's family. I know you have been working on the problem from the moment Miss Elizabeth and the Gardiners left Pemberley, and I have done all I could to keep Caroline in the dark, but if we do not act quickly, this whole thing will blow up before tea tomorrow."

Darcy noted Bingley's strong demeanour. The ever-affable young man, for once, was facing a problem straight on instead of allowing others to take the lead. "I do not know how you came to learn about the Bennet family's situation, but I will guess that the housekeeper at Netherfield was the one to inform Miss Bingley."

"Yes, yes, both my sister and I have servants who send us gossip." Bingley waved off Darcy's comments. "But that is not the point. The only thing that matters now is that Miss Lydia finds herself with child, and my beautiful angel is suffering! I will not stand by and let my sister ruin the love of my life like she has ruined so many others in the god-forsaken tea parlours of the *ton*. So I ask you again, what are WE going to do about it?"

For a moment, Darcy contemplated telling Bingley the whole story, including Darcy's intention to marry Elizabeth in haste. Bingley was obviously still in love with Jane and eager to protect her and the family. However, he and Elizabeth had agreed that the knowledge of their marriage was between only them, Georgiana, and Edward. Anyone else posed a risk to the exposure of their plans.

"I have indeed been in contact with Edward Gardiner since the untimely death of Mr. Bennet. He and I have agreed that the best plan is to purchase a fake marriage license for Miss Lydia and Wickham. She will be relocated to somewhere yet to be determined, and introduced as the widow of a soldier. Her relations and connections will be told that the ceremony took place before they reached London, and without her father present, which is why he still insisted on that blasted duel. You see, I have recently invested a large sum of money in Gardiner's import business, before Miss Lydia's elopement, that I would not like to see sullied by gossip and folly. Most of society will accept my word on the ceremony and will drop the gossip as the simple elopement with a tragic end of persons below their notice." Darcy cleared his throat and tried to keep his tone steady. "In addition to the fake license, I intend to hire Miss Elizabeth as Georgiana's social debutant companion as a show of faith in the respectability of the remaining sisters. With such a connection to the Darcy name, the gossip will die before the babe is even churched. With any luck, the remaining Bennet sisters will be marriageable after the full year of mourning for their father. Of course, none will even entertain a suitor until Mrs. Bennet's half mourning begins in February."

Bingley nodded his head. It was such a pity that Darcy would not transcend the scandal to take Elizabeth as his bride, but Darcy was in a completely different situation to the Bingleys. His uncle was an Earl! It was heart-breaking but understandable that the best Darcy could do was give Elizabeth a respectable position and protection. At least as Georgiana's companion, she would be exposed to the London marriage market, and someone like Bingley, with money from trade, may see her as acceptable. All hope was not lost.

"Well, old friend, this business deal sounds pretty good. I must have given a hefty sum to the Gardiner import business myself. In fact, now I recall us all discussing the same during our day of fishing at Pemberley."

"Charles, that is all well and good, Gardiner Imports does make sizable profits, but how can we say we came to such a conclusion at Pemberley? Your brother Hurst was with us while we fished, and he would surely have noticed if you committed several thousand pounds to someone's business."

"But we did discuss Gardiner's business while fishing, and Hurst can attest to that. I will simply say that you and I came to an agreement in the afternoon over billiards when Hurst went upstairs to drink a much-too-early glass of port and take a nap. We can even go so far as to say that we sent word to our respective solicitors to negotiate the deal, and they had reached an agreement before any of us learned of Miss Lydia's condition. This way, I can keep Caroline quiet. She will never want any of her precious money in jeopardy. Also, since I will say it was you who convinced me to invest, she will not question the initial connection either. Whenever I want anything in particular, all I need say is it was your advice to do so, and there is no argument whatsoever." With a self-satisfied grin, Bingley leaned back and took a sip of his coffee.

Darcy could think of no objection. "Alright. I will mention this to Edward tonight when I return to sign Miss Elizabeth's employment contract. I will give you the address to the Gardiners' house in Cheapside, so you can call on Edward and finalize the investment payment."

"Better yet, I shall join you in calling today and have it all done with." If Bingley dropped by the Gardiners', he might have the privilege of seeing Jane for a moment.

Darcy did not want Bingley to accompany him to Edward's warehouse where he might see the marriage contract. "I am invited to Edward's business office for tea then to dine with the family. Elizabeth is removing to Darcy house tomorrow morning, because we will be leaving for Pemberley in two morning's time. If you would like to call at the house for afternoon tea, I can bring Edward back to the house after meeting with his solicitor."

Just then, a bang was heard coming from the front foyer. "Damn-it man, you know who I am! Now, out of my way. I intend to see my idiot of a cousin before the day gets any brighter!" It was undoubtedly Colonel Richard Fitzwilliam, but Darcy was dumbfounded to know how he was in London today. He had sent word that he was removing to Rosings for his annual autumn summons from their Aunt Catherine, and had left for Kent only yesterday! Glancing at the clock, Darcy noticed the time was ten minutes before ten a.m. If Richard had left Rosings at first light, he would have had to nearly gallop full speed the whole way to Mayfair to arrive at this hour.

Both Darcy and Bingley startled when the bellowing began again, this time much closer to the study door. "Fitzwilliam Darcy, I know you are here, and I know you are hiding from the world! Bloody Hell!" BANG! The study door opened so fast that it left an indent in the plaster wall. "Why did you not tell me of Wickham and Miss…" Richard stopped short of naming the young lady when he noticed Bingley in the room.

"Hello, cousin. It is nice to see you. Would you please come sit down and have some coffee? I will also ring for some more substantial breakfast, as I am sure you have had none, riding out at first light from Kent. Additionally, Charles knows about Miss Lydia Bennet eloping with Wickham, but I'm at a loss as to how you know."

"Bullocks! Does your younger sister also know? And do not play nice with me, Darcy. You have not responded to over four letters I have written in the last month. I am forced to find out about Wickham's death from our aunt and her new idiot parson! Not to mention a host of other unfortunate things that have befallen our good friend's family. Does he know all?" Richard was still standing in the door frame, practically yelling.

With some of his usual humour restored at the petulant stance of a man dressed in full regimentals with a saber around his waist, Bingley responded to Richard. "Yes, I know everything, including Miss Lydia's delicate condition. I take it Mr. Collins has reported all via express to his former patroness? How lovely." Bingley wrinkled his nose and continued, with snide contempt in his voice. "It is wonderful to have such devotion from one's minions. Though one would hope a man of the cloth who now owns his own estate would consider his family before a woman who once gave him a position, but not everyone can be logical." Bingley turned to Darcy. "You will have to convince Collins of your plans and use his own intimate connection to the Bennets to carry your point. Maybe even make him fearful for his own future children's reputations or his sister by marriage, the young Lucas girl. What was her name? Marianne, Miranda …?"

"Miss Maria Lucas. Yes, I agree Charles. It was one of the stops I planned to make on the way to Pemberley. The sycophant has drooled all over my shoes, as well as Lady Catherine's, so I hope if I come to him and ask him on behalf of my investment and his family connection, to get in line, it will be all I need. Additionally, Mrs. Collins is a resourceful and intelligent woman. She is also an intimate friend of Miss Elizabeth's, so hopefully she will be able to keep her husband under control."

Richard finally moved into the room to take a seat when a maid entered with a breakfast tray and coffee. He was dreadfully hungry; he had fled Kent with only liquid and some toast in his stomach. When he had gone down to find coffee, his cousin, Anne de Bourgh, had been sitting in the breakfast parlour enjoying her tea in quiet. Lady Catherine had joined them a few minutes later. Richard had been able to take his leave as the sun was rising. Two horse changes later, he was pulling into Mayfair with a blinding headache from all the terrible brandy he had consumed last night after hearing the terrible tale of Elizabeth's family and toasting to Wickham's death. "You mentioned a plan? Is something going to be done to help the Bennets? Miss Elizabeth could have been your wife if only you would have taken your head out of your horse's arse and asked her to marry you! Your pride will be the ruination of all your happiness, mark my words!"

"Richard, what has gotten into you this morning? I've never heard you talk such!"

"Well, you best acquaint yourself with my talking such because you are going to hear much more of it from now on. I have mollycoddled you since your mother died, but no more! I will now be telling you when I disagree with your decisions, and you shall learn what makes the new recruits to His Majesty's Army fear your fierce cousin! As a side note, I threw you to the wolves with our aunt. She was not happy."

Bingley failed to contain his mirth. "Colonel, I do believe you are nearly drunk!"

"Of course, I am, man! I had enough brandy last night to send either of your pampered gentlemanly arses to an early grave." Richard covered his eyes as he sipped his coffee. "Now, tell me this plan of yours, and let me decide if you have any value as military strategists."

After listening to the plan, Richard agreed that it was solid, and even provided the final piece to the puzzle. "We shall take Miss Lydia, now Mrs. Wickham, and we should all practice calling her such so we do not slip in company, to our great-aunt, Lady Gwyneth Fitzwilliam in Scarborough. She would be happy to have the company and would be sympathetic to Mrs. Wickham's situation. The two might even find solace in confiding with one another."

"I remember mention of Lady Gwyneth, but I cannot now fully recall her situation. Why would she be good for Miss Lydia, … excuse me, Mrs. Wickham?"

"Lady Gwyneth Fitzwilliam is the youngest sister of the former Earl, our grandfather. She was born to the second wife of our great-grandfather late. In fact, she is younger than your mother by nearly eleven years. Her mother was the buxom younger daughter of another Earl, and was basically given to Great-Grandfather Fitzwilliam as payment for some land deal between the two. There was a minor scandal because the marriage took place only one month after our grandmother was dead and Lady Gwyneth was born in a short seven months as a healthy and robust young babe. After the old Earl's death, the Dowager Matlock went to live with her sister, and was rarely heard from again. She even left Lady Gwyneth with our Grandmother Fitzwilliam to raise. Your mother was furious about the marriage and Lady Gwyneth's birth." Richard refilled his coffee cup and speared another piece of ham onto his fork like a kebab.

Darcy wrinkled his nose. "Can you not use a plate?"

"Be grateful that I am not using the end of my long knife, as I would in camp." Richard took a large bite, then continued around his breakfast. "When Lady Gwyneth was sixteen, a man began courting her. Grandfather Fitzwilliam was elated to have a man willing to take his baby sister, younger than his own children who were all married and having children of their own, and he did not do much in the way of vetting the young man. He simply handed over her twenty-thousand pound dowry and wished them luck. But he was a polygamist and left her with less than one-thousand and pregnant after six months. She sent word to my father of her situation, and he went to retrieve her at once and placed her in one of the remote Matlock holdings near Scarborough. She was delivered of healthy twin boys, a Geoffrey and Malcom Fitzwilliam. After our grandfather passed, my father placed the Scarborough estate in the name of her older son, Geoffrey. She has lived in the sea town ever since. Her sons are now about twenty-three years of age. The younger, Malcom, is the vicar in the town parish. The estate is relatively prosperous and supports a house in Scarborough town, as well as a generous allowance for the younger brother. My father visits her at least once a year, and I make an additional trip every time I am ordered to Newcastle for brigade training."

Darcy listened, wide-eyed, to the whole of the tale. He was vaguely aware of his grandfather's youngest sister, but the circumstances causing her to be estranged from the greater Fitzwilliam family were completely unknown to him. How extraordinary that his family had shunned such a person as the daughter of the old philandering Earl, simply because her mother was used by men in power as a plaything to replace the beloved Countess. It also did not escape Darcy's notice that her mother was not some low-born woman upon whom the Earl had taken pity after getting her pregnant. In fact, there was a line of those kinds of women from the time even before his first wife's death. Nearly twelve known Fitzwilliam bastards had been placed with respectable merchant class families during the old man's reign. No, this woman had been the daughter of an Earl herself, which is likely the only reason she had been "saved" with a marriage upon the death of their great-grandmother. Darcy was brought back to the conversation by Bingley.

"How sad to hear of a real tale so much like Goldsmith's tale of *The Vicar of Wakefield*. She would likely be a wonderful companion for Mrs. Wickham. Young enough to commiserate and comfortably guide the young mother through her confinement, but experienced enough to provide the steady hand of a mother." Hearing the Colonel's tale only reinforced Bingley's desire to take his beautiful Jane far away from the expectations of the *ton* and live like simple, upstanding Englishmen. Like Mr. Bennet had lived.

"Yes, Richard," Darcy said. "I believe that situation would suit all admirably. Will you please send our aunt, Lady Gwyneth, an express with the request?"

"I will certainly send her an express, but we should not wait for a response. I shall accompany you to Hertfordshire to spread the news about Mrs. Wickham's new living situation, then I shall take the young lady to

Scarborough myself. As luck would have it, Mrs. Marshall, the Housekeeper of Lady Gwyneth's Scarborough house, and her daughter Miss Marianne Marshall are in town now, trying to find Miss Marianne employment as a lady's maid. They arrived six days ago and plan to return shortly. They can accompany myself and Mrs. Wickham all the way to her new home."

"Is Mrs. Marshall one of the Grayson grandchildren? Cousin to my Mrs. Reynolds?"

"Yes. Miss Marianne is a wonderful young girl, but has had no luck finding a position in London. She will be kept on in Scarborough until something can be secured for her."

Darcy thought about the connection for just a moment before deciding to offer the position of lady's maid for Elizabeth to Miss Marianne Marshall. She would need one as Georgiana's social companion anyway, so the additional hire would not give away their true situation. Also, Elizabeth deserved a quality abigail to care for her. Darcy always preferred to hire house servants from families already serving the Darcys, and there was no family with more persons serving than the Graysons. "Do you think Miss Marianne would come to work for me as an upstairs maid, with the added responsibility of preparing Miss Elizabeth for Georgie's social functions?"

"Yes, I believe that would be a wonderful position. I shall mention the situation to her upon my return to Matlock House." Richard stood, setting his teacup down on the breakfast tray. "Now, I must go. I am tired and smell of horse. This afternoon, after I take a much-needed nap, I shall discuss the position with Mrs. Marshall and Miss Marianne, then contact a man I know about the fake marriage license, as I certainly do not expect either of you to know where to find such things. When do we leave for Hertfordshire?"

"I plan to leave at first light in two days, on the twenty-fourth. I have several errands to run today as well, before going back to Cheapside to sign Miss Elizabeth's contract with Edward. Perhaps we should all say farewell for now." Darcy rose to see his guests out. He needed to ride directly to Doctor's Commons to ensure he was able to apply for the special license today.

Bingley also stood. "Yes, gentlemen, I must also be going. I told my servants I was going to my club this morning, and I had best put in an appearance, so as to keep Caroline from suspecting my true location. Would you mind if I lied and told her I met you on the street and we had drinks at White's to discuss the situation with our investments? I know you want to keep your house closed to callers, but a trip to the men's club is hardly an invitation to call before the knocker is replaced. If you leave by the twenty-fourth, surely she will not barge in, like the good Colonel did, before you remove to Pemberley."

"Yes, Charles. I believe one trip to White's today is an acceptable lie to placate Caroline. Good luck with the storm that I am sure is brewing in her upstairs parlour. Shall I meet you back here at four p.m. so we can call on the Gardiners for tea, or would you rather the address to come directly?"

"I will come back here. That way I can again tell Caroline that you asked me to accompany you on a trip to the Gardiners' home to remedy the situation, instead of going alone. I shall be here, dressed to call at four p.m. sharp. Good day."

# Chapter 7

## No More Foolishness

***Law Offices of Hamilton Phillips, Esq., Meryton, Hertfordshire***
***24 September 1812***

Lydia had to escape the house for a little while. Her mother was unbearable with all the wailing and calling out to no one for smelling salts. Kitty was a giggling fool and always running off to see Maria Lucas. Do not even ask about Mary. She had not so much as looked at Lydia since the day the physician confirmed she was with child. How had everyone she had ever known and loved turned on her so quickly? Her mother always bemoaned their entailed estate and instructed the Bennet sisters to marry as soon as possible. On the day she left Brighton, Lydia really thought her mother would be proud of her for eloping with Wickham. He was handsome, had an officer's position in the militia, and wanted to take Lydia with him for an immediate marriage. To be married before any of her older sisters would have really been an accomplishment. But Lydia was no longer naive.

When Wickham first took her to his bed, she was totally ignorant of the marital relations between men and women, including that it was the physical act that resulted in pregnancy. She understood now why so many older women bemoaned their wifely duties. It was embarrassing, uncomfortable and sometimes, downright painful. Wickham had at least never tarried long, and rarely came to her more than twice in one week. It was more often when they were alone in London, but still not every day, thankfully.

By the time her father burst into their dreadful room, the grime of their accommodations and Wickham's evening activities had begun to wear upon Lydia. However, she had stayed hopeful that the London interlude was merely a detour, and their life together would soon be filled with parties and frolicking, with Lydia as the envy of all the young women vying for the attention of the officers. When he demanded ten thousand pounds for a dowry, and refused to marry without money, the situation and Lydia's thinking changed immediately. She had been thoroughly shocked! He was supposed to be an officer and a gentleman.

The next morning, Lydia had followed both men to that unassuming field an hour north of London and watched the duel which eventually cost both men their lives. Watching Wickham bleed out on the field had been traumatic, but trying to get her father back to the Gardiners' residence and find a doctor to tend his wounds still gave Lydia nightmares. However, Lydia had maintained, even after the whole family had been turned out by Collins because of her foolish behaviour, that she had done nothing truly wrong in the decision to elope. Now, in the week since the confirmation of her condition, Lydia had been forced to face the fact that, as an unwed mother, she would be the complete ruination of all her family.

Especially her sisters.

Jane and Elizabeth were getting to be old for women without a dowry. At 22, Jane was nearly a spinster, but she was extraordinarily beautiful and serene; perhaps there was hope. Elizabeth would be 21 in a few short days. She was attractive in her own way, but slight of build and without the curves most men appreciated. She was also too intelligent for her own good. Their father had always treasured her intelligence and wit, but their mother had warned her repeatedly that her sharp tongue would be the end of all her chances for a husband.

Elizabeth would probably never marry.

Lydia hung her head and a few tears fell from her eyes. She had never been close with her second oldest sister, but she did love all her sisters. Elizabeth had always been the strong one of the family. Whenever their mother was overcome with some nervous fit, and their father retreated into his library, Elizabeth made sure Kitty and Lydia were reading their books and behaving. Elizabeth always took the younger girls out into the garden to play games when their lessons became too much a bore.

After years of hearing their mother's daily complaints about Elizabeth's bookishness and impertinent tongue, Lydia came to believe them. Elizabeth was too headstrong and would never be attractive to a man. She should read less and pay more attention to her ribbon trims. Lydia and Kitty had laughed and laughed at Elizabeth's rejection of Collins, saying how stupid their intelligent sister was for refusing the only offer she would likely ever receive.

In the immediate aftermath of their father's death, as they were forced to leave their home, Lydia had joined in with their mother's verbal abuses of Elizabeth. If only she would have married the ridiculous Collins, they could have stayed in their home. Lydia had joined in cursing Elizabeth, complaining about how unfair it was that Uncle Edward was taking her to London to have all the entertainments available in town, and to introduce her to eligible young men.

Now, however, Lydia could not be upset with Elizabeth. Collins would have made her sister miserable, and he might have thrown the rest of the family out of the house anyway, due to Lydia's folly. In the last week, her mother had turned on her. Mrs. Bennet would not even look at Lydia without yelling about how stupid she was and how terrible a thing she had done. Funnily enough, her mother's censure, experienced for the first time, was the eye piece that finally brought her entire life into focus. Elizabeth and Jane had frequently been embarrassed by their mother, and now Lydia could see why. It was, in fact, probably their mother's outlandish pursuit and loud vocalizations of the impending marriage between Jane and Bingley that had caused the gentleman's hasty departure from Netherfield.

Mrs. Bennet was also not a good parent. Lydia had been totally unprepared for the real world. She was told to flirt, be silly, chase after men, and snatch one as quickly as she could. Lydia had followed her mother's instructions to the letter. And now, she was ruined. If only she had listened to Elizabeth more.

Eventually, Lydia's thoughts turned to how much she wished to apologize to her second oldest sister and to ask the most intelligent member of their family what she should do now. The last time she had seen Jane and

Elizabeth, she was crying and pouting about being left behind in boring Meryton. Elizabeth had come to say goodbye and to give her a kiss on the cheek, but Lydia had turned her head and walked back into Uncle Phillips's house. Oh, how she wished she could take back the hurtful things she had said! After musing on how she could ever adequately word such a letter, the object of her mind walked into the room carrying a tray of fresh tea and sweet breads.

"Lizzy!" She jumped out of her chair. "Whatever are you doing here? Is everyone alright in London?"

Elizabeth put down with tray and held out her hands to her youngest sister. "Yes, Lydia. Everyone in London is doing fine. I have stopped here on my way north to see our mother, and discuss something of import with you, specifically."

Lydia ushered her sister into the chair she had been occupying and pulled up a new seat from their uncle's desk. Then, she poured tea for both of them, a courtesy she had never before performed. "Whatever you have to say, I am sure I will be delighted to hear it. I have been sitting here in the quiet thinking about all of the wise things you have said in the past, to which I should have paid much more attention."

To say that Elizabeth was stunned would be a gross understatement. "I'm glad to know that someone welcomes my presence. I fear mother's reaction when she learns I am in the house. But, tell me sister, are you well? Have our mother and uncle been treating you kindly?"

Lydia folded her empty hands in her lap and hung her head. "I would not say that my recent behaviour merits anyone treating me kindly, but they have not been cruel. Our mother is quite upset with my condition, and I am at a loss as to what to do to ease the situation."

Placing her cup and saucer on the tray, Elizabeth took both of Lydia's hands in her own and bent down to catch her sister's eye. "This is what I have come to speak to you about. I hope you will not be angry. Uncle Edward and I have been making plans for you, but they will require you to be very brave."

Lydia looked up, her wide eyes brimming with tears. "Lizzy, if you have come with a solution for my situation, I will be brave."

"I know you will, sister. You have been through a lot recently and I do not want to add to your worry, but both Uncle Edward and I feel it would be better if you were removed from Mamma and our connections here in

Hertfordshire. Mr. Darcy has recently invested a significant sum with our uncle's imports business and, in the interest of protecting his investment, he has taken a position of support for our family. He and his cousin, Colonel Richard Fitzwilliam, whom I met while visiting Charlotte in Hunsford last spring, have procured a forged marriage license for you and Mr. Wickham. Mr. Darcy explained all the complicated legalities to Uncle and me, but simply put, your having participated in a churched wedding ceremony combined with your pregnancy, will now make you Mr. Wickham's widow."

"But, Father was not there to give me away, and I am underage. Also, they both died in duel! How is anyone to believe this?"

Elizabeth placed a comforting hand on Lydia's arm. "Sweet sister, in truth, your elopement is not so surprising to our friends and family. If Mr. Darcy and his cousin, the Colonel, say there was a wedding ceremony, even a deficient one, most people will take them at their word."

"But everyone here in Meryton dislikes Mr. Darcy so, and it is well known that you and he are not on good terms. Why should they take his part?"

"Because he is rich." Elizabeth shrugged and picked up her teacup again. "And also because he is such a proud and aloof person, who is not known to take the part of another readily. Perhaps if someone like Mr. Bingley or Sir William Lucas were to insist, many would roll their eyes behind flapping fans and say that he was just being naive. But in this instance, Mr. Darcy's proud manner and direct speech works much to our advantage."

"Do not forget his large purse."

Elizabeth chuckled. "Heaven forbid we forget that. So, even though the elopement would be a slight scandal, no one will care for long. The license is dated August 2, the day after you left Brighton, and says the marriage was celebrated in Croydon, south of London. We do not want too many unanswerable questions, so it would be better if you were not around to have to face the inquisition from our connections."

Lydia stood and wrapped her arms around her middle, moving to stare out of the window. "Where am I to go? I do not know if London is the best place for a confinement, and our Aunt Gardiner is so busy with her children. I cannot impose this on them."

Placing her cup on the tray, Elizabeth looked at Lydia with new eyes. She was impressed that her most selfish sister was finally thinking of others before herself. "Mr. Darcy and Colonel Fitzwilliam have a great-aunt, the Lady Gwyneth Fitzwilliam, who lives in a comfortable home in Scarborough. She is willing to take you into her home and help you through your confinement. She has twin sons herself who are twenty-three years old. She also suffered from the deceit of a disreputable man. Her husband was a bigamist and took her twenty-thousand pound dowry after only six months of their invalid marriage, leaving her pregnant and penniless in Scotland. Mr. Darcy has never been to Scarborough, but Colonel Fitzwilliam says it is lovely, and Lady Gwyneth lives on the side of the cliff near Scarborough Castle. I am told that one can see the sea from the breakfast parlour. They will protect you and your child, I promise. It may also be possible for you to keep the babe, if that is your choice, after he or she is born. If you choose to place the babe with an adoptive family, we can discuss that arrangement after you both are churched."

"Move all the way to Scarborough?" Lydia was shocked at the length that Darcy and his family were willing to go to support an investment with Gardiner Imports. "Just how much money did Mr. Darcy invest with our uncle?"

"A considerable amount, for sure. In addition to your new living situation, Mr. Darcy is showing society that he supports our family by hiring me as the social debutant companion for Miss Georgiana Darcy. That is why I am here. The Darcys are relocating to Pemberley for the winter and I have already taken my position in their household. You will travel with us until we reach Mr. Darcy's estate in Derbyshire. Then, Colonel Fitzwilliam will escort you the rest of the way to Scarborough. I know this is a lot to consider all at once, but do you believe this plan to be one with which you would be willing to cooperate? It is you who has to relocate most of the way to Scotland and live with people none of your family has ever before met. What are your feelings?"

Lydia stared at her sister with mouth agape. To think of the cost and inconvenience so many people had incurred because of her selfish stupidity. Her uncle was even worried about the reputation of his business. And to be welcomed into a stranger's house on nothing more than the word of her great-nephews? But worst of all, Elizabeth had taken a position. She was no longer a gentlewoman, but a servant. Granted, companions and governesses were in the highest class of servants and were often gently bred, but she was a servant nonetheless.

Now Elizabeth would never marry. It was nearly written in stone.

Lydia would be able to present herself as a respectable widow, while her older, wiser, compassionate sister would live her life as a servant. Once Georgiana married, Elizabeth would find a new family to serve and so on, probably staying with one family for only five years before moving on again. Hopefully, the connection with the Darcys would ensure she always found work with the most respectable families.

The tears filling Lydia's eyes spilled over, and when she spoke her voice was barely above a whisper. "Lizzy, how can you ever forgive me?"

Elizabeth moved to the window where Lydia was still standing. "Lydia, come now. Mr. Wickham promised to marry you and our mother has always said that marriage was of the utmost importance. I could never blame you for that rogue's dishonesty. Come here, dear, it will all be right in the end." Elizabeth reached for Lydia to give her a comforting hug, but Lydia put up her hands.

"No, Elizabeth, I will not let you take all of the burden for this. I was foolish. I was selfish. You and Jane tried to tell Kitty and me that we were not behaving properly nearly daily, but I never listened. And now, you have taken a position, degrading yourself while I am elevated to the position of widow. I may remain a gentlewoman and go to live with the daughter of an Earl, while you are reduced to merely a gently bred servant. I do not believe I will ever be able to repay you this kindness."

Elizabeth thought for a moment and considered what to tell her baby sister, so grown up in this moment and so close to having a baby of her own. She gently took Lydia's hands and guided them both back to their seats. "Lydia, tell me truly, what has happened to you? Who has been unkind?"

A look of shame took over Lydia's face. She looked away, refusing to meet Elizabeth's eyes. "Do you remember Benjamin Millner?"

"The haberdasher's son?"

"Yes." Lydia played with a frayed spot in the seam of her sleeve. "He and I have always been on good terms, since I love ribbons above all else, and we are of an age. Well, the other day he asked me if I would... come to his rooms."

Before Elizabeth could contain her fury enough to even gather herself for a response, Lydia continued.

"He also offered to give me some of the best silk ribbon in any colour I fancied for my time. He said that I would have to consider how I would now support my child. But the worst part is, I sat on the bench outside the churchyard and actually thought about his offer." She furtively met Elizabeth's eyes, then looked once more at the fraying fabric. "He is not wrong that I will need to support myself and this child. And I am unfortunately familiar with the act of intimacy, as distasteful as it may be. If I leave and break from the family, perhaps Mr. Collins will be kinder to Mamma and my sisters. Maybe someone will marry Jane."

Elizabeth gathered Lydia into her arms and they both sat in silence for several minutes.

"Lydia, I cannot promise you much in this world. You are already facing the consequences of flirtation with Mr. Wickham by bearing his child, but I will do absolutely everything in my power to save you from that fate."

"No Lizzy, you have to think of yourself now. How long can Miss Darcy need a companion? You must distance yourself from me if you are going to be able to make a life beyond Meryton. I appreciate all that you and Mr. Darcy have done for me, but is this wise? What if he regrets the association and dismisses you?"

Elizabeth debated telling Lydia about her planned marriage to Darcy. No matter what decisions were made today, she was going to first birth then perhaps raise a baby. There were never certainties in childbirth. She may not survive. A few well-placed words from Elizabeth could relieve her conscience and help her move on to a more peaceful life.

"Lydia, I am going to tell you something, but first you must promise never to repeat it. Not to Mary, not to Kitty, certainly NOT to Mamma, and not even to Colonel Fitzwilliam or Lady Gwyneth, if you choose to go to Scarborough. Can you make that promise?"

Lydia's eyes widened at Elizabeth's tone, but she nodded her head.

Elizabeth took a deep breath. "I love Mr. Darcy. I have for some time. He is the best of men. He made me an offer of marriage in April that I refused, based in part on lies from Mr. Wickham and my own misinterpretation of his character during his stay at Netherfield. We have mended our mutual miscommunications and come to an understanding. It is our intention to marry as soon as our sisters are secure. Uncle Edward has already signed the marriage settlement contract and Mr. Darcy applied for the special license before we left London. You need not worry about my welfare. I do all this to protect you, Kitty, Mary, Jane, and my newest sister, Georgiana. I will see all my sisters happy and secure before Mamma takes the grey trim from her last widows' frock."

Lydia giggled behind her handkerchief in a moment reminiscent of the silly child she had been. "Truly, Lizzy? You love Mr. Darcy, and he wants to make you his wife? Will you be happy as Mrs. Darcy? Not as mistress of Pemberley with jewels, and furs, and fine carriages, but as Mrs. Darcy, who warms Mr. Darcy's bed and speaks of nothing over morning coffee? Will he buy you books and share them with you as Papa did? Will he allow you to walk in the morning dew and become brown skinned from refusing to wear your bonnet in the sun? You were right to refuse to Mr. Collins. That man would have made you miserable. I do not want you to sacrifice yourself to a more financially advantageous match simply to buy a solution to the problems I have created."

Elizabeth smiled and took Lydia's hands between her own. "Lydia, William and I truly love each other, and we enjoy each other's company. Yes, I believe William will share his books and intellect with me and not mind one bit if I wish to walk bare headed in the sun. And I hope that we will always have important nothings to discuss over our morning coffee."

Lydia re-folded her handkerchief and smiled through drying tears. "I am glad. You have eased my mind, considerably. I shall now be more than content to pack my things and travel to parts unknown, going to live my new life as a widow with distant cousins by marriage. When do we leave?"

***Longbourn, Hertfordshire***
***24 September 1812***

While Elizabeth spoke with the Bennet women, Darcy rode up to Longbourn house and requested an audience with William Collins. It was difficult to come calling on the Bennets' old home. It might seem odd, since Darcy spent so little time in this house while visiting the area last fall, but the manor felt empty to him without the boisterousness of the Bennet family. A quiet parlour was not at all what Darcy had anticipated and it caused him to shudder a little.

Hardly a minute after being shown to the east parlour, Charlotte Collins walked into the room carrying a beautiful tea service from which he remembered Elizabeth serving guests previously. Seeing the pained look on his face, Charlotte easily interpreted his discomfort. "Please, Mr. Darcy, have a seat and I will pour you some tea. I know it is a bit disconcerting to be in this house when all is quiet, but I assure you it will become easier with time. Milk or sugar?"

Darcy recovered his composure and joined his hostess in a chair near the side table. "Two sugars, please. Thank you for seeing me on such short notice, Mrs. Collins. It is a pleasure to speak with you again. I trust you have heard that Miss Elizabeth is in town for today and visiting her family. Though you would likely rather be visiting with her, what I have to discuss with you and your husband is of great importance, and I appreciate you taking the time away from your good friend." Darcy was about to thank the heavens for his good luck to find Charlotte alone, when Collins walked through the parlour door.

William Collins was the distant cousin of Mr. Bennet and, as the next closest direct line male relative of Mr. Bennet's grandfather, who started the entail, he became owner of Longbourn upon Mr. Bennet's death. He was also an ordained minister in the Anglican Church, with a rather inflated opinion of himself. Oddly, his self-importance did not overcome his extreme sycophancy. When Lady Catherine de Bourgh appointed him as the rector for Hunsford Parsonage, he transferred all his loyalty to that lady and her family. In Collins's opinion, no one was more learned, more generous, or more worthy of praise than Darcy's heartless aunt and her exalted relations. Perhaps not even the master a clergyman was supposed to serve, Christ.

Darcy said a silent prayer for patience and hoped that Collins would continue to take everything he said as near gospel.

But Collins didn't give him a chance to speak. "Mr. Darcy, how delightful that you have chosen to visit our humble estate! I hope you have not been waiting long. I was out in the garden; you will remember how much I enjoy the activity from your visits to our modest parsonage. When your express arrived requesting an audience, I hurried to make myself presentable. I do hope that your family is well, especially your esteemed aunt and cousin de

Bourgh. I have sent Lady Catherine several dozen communications since taking on my new position as a landowner, asking for her advice with certain matters, and she has condescended to respond twice. I have also taken her advice regarding my wayward family, setting them aside from the estate, but not completely without means. My dear Charlotte has been able to improve the efficiency of the house in a substantial way, which allows us to send my pitiable cousins some money annually, for their needs, and in hopes of attracting some form of husband. It is unlikely any gentleman of land would ever consider them now, but some of the shopkeepers in Meryton are yet unmarried, and of course, their Uncle Gardiner has connections within the merchants and tradesmen in London. Perhaps someone will find Miss Bennet's serene beauty compensation enough for the family's poor connections. Miss Elizabeth is much too strong willed to ever make a good wife, but I believe Mr. Gardiner could find her a position as a governess. Miss Lydia is, of course, worse than dead, and as your aunt has wisely advised, we do not acknowledge her in public as a fallen woman. Charlotte, did you ring for a fresh pot of tea? I'm sure Mrs. Hill could also bring some of her lemon cakes." Darcy was finding it difficult to maintain his composure. He wanted to throttle the ridiculous little man for saying such terrible things of his Elizabeth, but only detached propriety would suit his purpose today. Thankfully, Darcy was a man practiced in hiding his true feelings from all but the most proficient of observers.

Charlotte was one such observer. She moved to quiet her husband with tea and allow Darcy an opening to begin his discourse. "Yes dear, I have tea and shortbread here on the side table. Please, sit, and we shall hear what Mr. Darcy has come to discuss."

"Thank you, Mrs. Collins. I have indeed come to speak of a matter of great importance, which centres on exactly the topic of Miss Lydia, or I should say, Mrs. Lydia Wickham."

"What?" Collins nearly dropped his teacup. "She is married? Who…? Wait. Is not Wickham the man she eloped with from Brighton? But they were never married. My cousin Bennet found them living in great sin in London without the benefit of a churched wedding! Is that little harlot now trying to pass herself off as a respectable widow, since she can no longer hide the reality of her shame? Well, I will not have it! I am sorry you have had to be privy to such outlandish lies…"

"Mr. Collins, will you sit down!" Darcy was finally at the end of his patience and used his most commanding voice several notches louder than usual. Collins sat heavily on the chair he had recently vacated. Taking a deep breath, Darcy continued. "I am sure you will agree with me regarding Mrs. Wickham once you hear what I have to say. It is not she who is distributing the ***truth*** of her marriage, but, in fact, me."

"I do not understand. Why would you do such a thing?" Collins's red face looked as if he were about to explode, and he was holding enough breath inside his lungs to make him look quite round.

Setting his best stare upon Collins, Darcy explained. "There are a number of reasons for this, but the first one is that it is absolutely true." Though deception of any kind was an abhorrence to Darcy, he and Richard had discussed the necessity of keeping the forged license as quiet as possible. If they were to restore the Bennet women's respectability, everyone must believe it was true. "You see, my cousin, Colonel Fitzwilliam, is very well connected in both the regulars and the various militias around London. When he heard that Wickham had deserted his post from Brighton, he became involved in the search for him. Richard was not as fast as Mr. Bennet, unfortunately. However, he was the one to retrieve Wickham's belongings and remains after his death. Richard looked through Wickham's papers and found the common marriage license issued by a minister in Croydon. Apparently, Lydia Bennet and George Wickham participated in a church marriage ceremony on the second of August in Croydon. That is, the day after the couple fled Brighton."

Collins smashed his teacup into the saucer with such force, it was astounding that both were still intact. "This is an outrage! Neither was a resident of that place. What kind of vicar would sell a common license to two persons of such unknown character?"

Charlotte patted her husband on the hand. "I know this pains you, but many such men, when provided with ready coin, would marry two young people professing to be in love."

Darcy cleared his throat and continued. "Yes, well. My cousin also knew that before we learned of Mrs. Wickham's elopement, I had made a significant investment in Edward Gardiner's imports business. Now that the young lady is with child, the shame will reach every member of her family. And I do mean EVERY member. You would do well to consider your own reputation as we continue this discussion." Collins turned instantly white, when a moment ago he was so red. "If it became known that one of Gardiner's wards was so wholly ruined as to have a child out of wedlock, his business would suffer, and my investment would be in jeopardy. When word of Mrs. Wickham's situation reached myself and Richard, we sought out Gardiner to provide him with the marriage license and any additional support he might need. Mr. Bingley also invested at the same time as I, and we both are interested in helping salvage Mrs. Wickham's reputation in order to secure our money. So, I have come here to inform you about the plans that Gardiner, Bingley, and I have made for the Bennet women. I would very much appreciate if you would consent to promoting the truth of Mrs. Wickham's marriage. As I said, it would be in your best interest as well, since you are so closely connected with the ladies. You wouldn't want Miss Lucas or any future daughters you may have to be tainted by such pernicious gossip."

"How does this change her position? She is still sixteen and pregnant, without a husband."

Charlotte sighed. "Mr. Collins, were you not listening? Lydia is a widow, not a fallen woman. Granted, an elopement is not the most propitious of actions, but it was an act of young love. The remaining Bennet sisters are marriageable, and the child Lydia carries will be a legitimate of Lydia and Mr. Wickham's marriage. Mr. Darcy, you have saved us all!" Charlotte's eyes were shining with unshed tears. Hope, so far from any reality Charlotte could have imagined before Darcy walked in, was beginning to grow. Perhaps Jane and Elizabeth could find happiness with the men who loved them. If Bingley and Darcy were investing in Gardiner Imports, they must have a desire for the connection and an excuse to visit their business partner at his home. Unfortunately, Darcy's next words froze the smile on Charlotte's face.

"I, of course, would not want to see Gardiner Imports suffer from the foolishness of a sixteen-year-old child and a rake. Additionally, to show my support for the family's respectability, I have taken Miss Elizabeth into my household as Miss Darcy's social companion. My sister's debut will be in the spring, and she will need a chaperone and friend during her many social engagements next season."

"Mr. Darcy, are you sure you have adequately thought through this decision?" Mr. Collins blustered. "Miss Elizabeth is a quality young lady to be sure, but she is much too opinionated for superior society. Why, you observed her behaviour in your aunt's parlour. She voiced her mind as if she was capable of having such thoughts, even as a woman of low birth. She did not even have a governess! I am sure that your cousin, Miss de Bourgh, would be a much better companion than Miss Elizabeth. Once you are married to Miss de Bourgh, she will be able to perform as Miss Darcy's chaperone with ease. Perhaps it is time to solidify your relationship, as your aunt wishes, and prepare both Miss Darcy and the new Mrs. Darcy for the London season together."

Charlotte had been too wrapped up in thoughts of her poor friend moving into the position of paid employee to stop the foolish words coming from her husband. It was obvious that Darcy loved Elizabeth but now considered her much too tarnished for marriage. It was more obvious that neither Darcy nor Anne de Bourgh wished to marry.

Darcy was done being polite. He stood, handed his teacup to Charlotte, straightened his waistcoat and levelled a glare at Collins. "Mr. Collins, I have said my piece about Mrs. Wickham. I will repeat, it is in ***your*** best interest to get in line with the events as I have stated them here. I have also already sent a communication to my aunt about the matter so she may include the most relevant details of their hasty marriage when she visits with her circles. Before I take my leave, I will give you one last piece of advice:

"I rarely listen to my aunt or do as she bids, because Lady Catherine is foolish. She listens to no one and believes only what she wishes, despite all evidence to the contrary. I have no desire to marry my cousin, nor does Anne desire to marry me. In fact, my cousin does not even like me all that much. I am not now, nor have I ever been, nor will I ever be, engaged to my cousin. You should start thinking for yourself and listen to the advice of your intelligent wife over the ridiculous things my aunt chooses to say. Good day." He nodded curtly. "I shall show myself out."

# Chapter 8

## Truth Hardly Ever Acknowledged

***Pemberley, Derbyshire***
***3 October 1812***

Elizabeth Bennet sat at the vanity in her room staring at the wedding ensemble gracing her bed. It was too much. She had never owned anything so beautiful. She would never be able to be simple Lizzy in such a gown. Then again, less than an hour after donning the silk masterpiece, she would forever cease to be simple Lizzy and instead become Mrs. Fitzwilliam Darcy, mistress of Pemberley and Darcy House London, even if only a select few people would know her as such.

"Come, Miss, do not look so severe. Today is your wedding day! I know what you need, a nice warm bath with rose water and soft petals. Let me call the kitchen and we shall have you feeling better in a trice."

Looking behind her to the young maid brushing out her hair, Elizabeth smiled. "Thank you, Marianne, you are correct, of course. I was just wool-gathering. And a hot bath sounds lovely. I should be looking and feeling my best for Mr. Darcy."

Marianne Marshall had been a wonderful new addition to the household. Elizabeth was introduced to the young woman in London the day before they all left for Hertfordshire. Marianne had been told by Richard Fitzwilliam that she would be an upstairs maid and would also prepare Georgiana's new social companion for her important social gatherings, but upon removing to the Darcys' employ, she learned that the position was as Elizabeth's exclusive lady's maid. It was strange to Marianne that Darcy would hire a full time abigail for a social companion, but she had been brought up not to question the Fitzwilliams or say anything to anyone that could violate the family's trust. During the ride to Derbyshire, she again found it odd that Elizabeth and her sister, the young and pregnant widow of the former Pemberley steward's son, rode with the Darcys and Richard in the family's carriage, instead of in the second carriage with the other servants. The final oddity proved too much for the quiet young maid. Elizabeth was given a large suite of rooms in the family wing that connected to the rooms that Georgiana had always occupied. Marianne went to her great aunt, who also served as the housekeeper of Pemberley, Mrs. Reynolds, and asked if such treatment was common for a paid companion.

Mrs. Reynolds said flatly that it was not, but if Marianne wanted to stay with the Pemberley staff, she would make no other inquiries about the Darcys' personal decisions. All information about the family was to stay inside her lips, and not venture forth where anyone could overhear. Not two days later, after the carriage taking her mother, Richard, and the young widow back to the beautiful seaside town had gone past the bridge near the park gate, Mrs. Reynolds called together all the inside house staff and the head grounds staff for an important meeting.

*"I have some wonderful news. We shall be having a wedding here on the third of October. Mr. Darcy is going to wed Miss Elizabeth Bennet by special license in a private ceremony, presided over by our kindly old vicar, and celebrated at the Pemberley family chapel. This day also happens to be our new mistress's twenty-first birthday. I will have a special breakfast prepared to commemorate the wedding, and a cake for the lady's birthday. For reasons that I will not share generally, the Darcys' wish is for this marriage to be kept secret from society at least through to the next London season, even from certain members of Mr. Darcy's family, including Lord Matlock, Lady Catherine, and the Fitzwilliam Cousins.*

*"I am relying on each of you to protect them. We must not let one word of this slip to anyone, especially our own family members who serve the Fitzwilliams or de Bourghs. If servants from other employ ask questions about the family, shun them and report it to me, so that I may warn Mr. and Mrs. Darcy. I shall entertain no questions, nor will I tolerate anyone speaking of this after this moment."*

Since that moment, absolutely no one had spoken a word, even to each other, about the abnormality of the Darcys' marriage, especially not Marianne. She was now the Head Lady's Maid of Pemberley. Personal servant to the soon-to-be mistress of the house, and she now reported to no one except the mistress and master. She was a young girl of only nineteen, and had only ever played lady's maid to a few female visitors who came to the Fitzwilliams' Scarborough estate. Her total experience consisted of a handful of days that could be counted without utilizing her toes. Panic began to build inside her.

After Mrs. Reynolds had dismissed them to their duties, Marianne fled the servants' quarters to find Lilian Grayson, Georgiana's lady's maid and Marianne's cousin. Lilian would know what to do.

Lilian had been extremely supportive of Marianne in the last three days and had spent many hours teaching her the ways of the house. But Marianne had been terrified of offending her new mistress and had said hardly one word to Elizabeth while performing her duties. Finally, the day before the wedding, Elizabeth could take it no more.

*"Marianne, are you unhappy here at Pemberley? I know it is a long way from your family, but you will be able to visit them if you wish and if this situation is too much, you will be welcomed back into Lady Gwyneth's employ until a position you prefer can be secured for you."*

*"Oh no, my lady! I am perfectly happy here. I have little experience being the personal servant to such a grand lady and would not want you to suffer from my mistakes."*

*"Well, I'm certainly no grand lady. That honour I will reserve for Mr. Darcy's aunt, Lady Catherine, and similarly, I have little experience with having a personal servant. So far, we are equals. You may relax, for you shall not offend me in any way, I am sure. Perhaps we shall learn how to navigate this new life together."*

Since speaking so frankly the morning prior, their subsequent interactions were much easier. They even giggled together over the mess of tangles that was under her bonnet while Elizabeth dressed for dinner last night.

This morning, Marianne had laid out her new gown and was simply effusive over the fineness of the silk. She asked Elizabeth who had made such a wonder, and the stunned young bride could not even begin to guess.

It was now Elizabeth's turn to panic.

After Marianne left to fill her bath, Elizabeth turned her attention back to the gown on her bed. It was made of fine, ivory Chinese silk and trimmed with soft pink Indian ribbon. Lying next to the gown were matching gloves, a new bonnet, silk slippers, and a new warm pelisse.

How in the world did she think she was worthy of being Mrs. Darcy? How was she going to fit into this world of wealth and responsibility? How was she ever going to put on that fabulous dress, which probably cost more than her usual annual allowance and then some?

Marianne came back into the room to find Elizabeth with tears streaming down her face.

"Miss! Whatever is the matter?"

"I do not know if I can do this. I am just a simple country gentleman's daughter with no dowry at all. I have only eight dresses to my name, now nine with the one on the bed. No one knows my family; we were not very well off and now my mother and sisters are scattered to our various relations, relegated to genteel poverty. How am I to take over the position of mistress to this beautiful estate, and entertain the highest of society in London?"

Marianne came and picked up the hairbrush again, trying to soothe her mistress. "I know that I am not an authority on the workings of high society, but it seems to me that a rich gentleman like Mr. Darcy, who has connections to the Matlock Earldom and I am sure many other high society persons, could have married any one of the titled, dowered, and perfectly snobbish women of the *ton* if he cared one bit about such nonsense. But he did not. He has chosen a delightful young woman from a good gentleman's family with character and wit, because he loves you. Lady Gwyneth is always going on about how the persons of the *ton*, and especially the women, are not to be trusted and only ever look out for themselves. It seems to me a much better thing to be born in the country and live a simple, happy life. I am sure that the people here at Pemberley shall be much happier with a mistress who cares for them, rather than one who is always worried to get her petticoats dirty."

A little bell sounded from Elizabeth's dressing room.

"Now, that will be your bath all ready and hot! Let us get you into it before it cools too much. If we hurry, there will be plenty of time to wash some of the rose water into your lovely hair and let it fully dry before the ceremony."

Elizabeth soaked in the tub until the water cooled. Marianne helped her thoroughly wash her long dark hair, then produced a soft, small pillow to place on the edge of the tub. Her hair was pulled over the edge to drip dry while she relaxed. After she got out of the bath, Marianne brought in fire-heated towels to finish drying her hair and some large tin rollers to make nice, manageable curls. As the final pins were going into her incredible coiffure, there was a knock at the door connecting her rooms to Georgiana's. Elizabeth bid her soon-to-be sister to enter, and welcomed the young lady with a soft smile.

"Hello, Lizzy, I hope I am not interrupting your preparations, but I wanted to give you these things before you finalized your dress for the ceremony." Georgiana presented Elizabeth with the most beautiful natural pearls comprising a necklace, bracelet, and earrings. The tears Elizabeth had been crying on and off since seeing her new dress started to fall again.

Georgiana worried her lip and wrung her hands. "You certainly do not have to wear them today if you would rather not, but they are rightfully yours to do with as you please. They have been in the Darcy family for four generations. Usually, the mistress of the house presents them to her son's bride on the morning of their wedding, but since my mother is not with us to perform the honour, I have come. Each new mistress has added to the set before giving them to her new daughter-in-law. The original stock of pearls was obtained in India by my great-grandfather when he went as a young man with the East Indian Company. He made the necklace as an engagement gift for my great-grandmother and gave her the rest of the pearls to do with what she wished. When my grandfather became engaged to my grandmother, Great-Grandmother had matching earrings made and gifted the set to the new bride. Similarly, my grandmother had the bracelet made for my mother. Unfortunately, I was not able to make anything new to be ready for today, but I sent one of the largest left in the stock to our jeweller in London and commissioned a ring as your wedding present."

Elizabeth was now crying in earnest. "Sweet Georgie, of course I would be honoured to wear your ancestor's pearls on the day I join their ranks as mistress of Pemberley. I am sorry to distress you with my tears, but I cannot imagine the expense that you and your brother have gone to for my attire today. The dress waiting for me is of such a quality that I have never seen its equal. How I shall ever be worthy of all you and William have given me?"

Kneeling beside the vanity chair, Georgiana took Elizabeth's hands and looked imploringly into her eyes. "Lizzy, William is incredibly lucky to have become worthy of your affections. We have lived a life full of privilege, envied by many in society, but none of the money that pays for fine clothes or precious jewels has ever made either of us happy. My happiest moments are of sitting in my mother's rose garden while my father or William read me a simple child's book."

Georgiana turned her head to look out the window. Though she could not see anything from her position on the floor, she knew that beyond the glass was the south lawn and her mother's beloved roses. "Our money could not save my mother from the dangers of childbirth, or bring my father back after suffering a stroke. My Aunt Catherine has lived her life in pursuit of nothing but rank and money. She has always been miserable, suffering marriage to a man she hated, with no real friends to which she could turn for compassion. Think of Miss Bingley, who is so unpleasant, chasing after my brother's money without any consideration for what might make either of them happy."

Looking back to the vanity, Georgiana gestured to the pearl jewellery. "These trinkets, they are nothing compared to the worth of your gift. You have brought joy back into this massive, empty house. There are many days I wish we lived as many of the respectable gentry, instead of paragons of *le bon ton*. Then, no one would try to use us ill for their own financial gains."

Another knock at the door brought all three young women gathered around Elizabeth's vanity out of their thoughts. Marianne opened the door to Mrs. Reynolds who was carrying a small, wrapped package.

"Miss Darcy, Marianne, I am sorry to interrupt Miss Bennet's toilette, but I must ask you to leave us. I require a few moments alone with our beautiful bride." Mrs. Reynolds smiled kindly at all the young women as Georgiana went back to her own toilette and Marianne went to help the downstairs maids complete arrangements for the wedding breakfast.

Mrs. Reynolds then placed the package on Elizabeth's vanity. "This is a gift from Mr. Darcy."

Shaking her head at the generosity of her new family, Elizabeth joked, "How could I need anything else? He has already procured me this extraordinary dress and Georgiana has just now given me the Darcy family pearls. I do not know what else is left to be given, unless he has a miniature tiger as my new pet wrapped in that box."

"While I cannot say for sure what is inside the box, I'm sure it is not some kind of animal." Mrs. Reynolds chuckled. "But my lady, your Uncle Gardiner was the one to procure the wedding costume. Mr. Darcy did ask him if he knew of anyone in London who could make a dress for you for today, but I believe that the material came from your uncle's warehouse, and the dress maker was one of your uncle's friends."

Elizabeth's eyes widened. "You mean that Mme. Devy made this dress for me? She has made many of my best dresses over the years, and she is a highly sought after modiste, but I have never seen something so wonderful! If only I could thank her! I shall have to write to my uncle and ask him to pass along my thanks if he believes it would not jeopardize our situation."

"I am sure you shall get your chance, dear. Miss Darcy and you shall be having your season wardrobe made by Mme. Devy upon your return to London. Miss Darcy usually has most of her dresses made by the dressmaker in Matlock and has only purchased a few dresses a year from Mme. Devy while in London. But since she will be debuting in the spring, she will require a full wardrobe of the best and latest fashions. I sent the letter myself requesting appointments in early April for you both just yesterday. She is notoriously difficult to get into in advance of the season. But now, I believe you should open this beautifully wrapped box."

Elizabeth picked up the box and let out a large breath before taking off the ribbon and opening the top. Inside lay a beautiful silver hair comb with mother of pearl inlaid. There was a note.

> *My dearest Elizabeth, this was my mother's favourite hair comb. I remember her wearing it to the most important social functions and always on my parents' wedding anniversary. I hope you love it as much as she did. Happy Birthday, Dearest. I shall dream of all the future birthdays we shall share while I await your entrance into the church.*

"Mrs. Reynolds, will you place this into my hair?"

"Of course."

The comb was nestled into the pile of curls coming out of Elizabeth's coiffure. It was luminous against her dark hair. The motherly housekeeper then helped Elizabeth into the rest of her clothes. At ten minutes to eleven, the bride was ready to proceed to the chapel two floors below.

Before turning to leave, Mrs. Reynolds gave Elizabeth one last parting gift. "Miss Bennet, I know you have come here to marry without your mother or any close female relation to prepare you for this event. I must say you have handled all of this with aplomb and grace. Now, I shall ask your indulgence for my imprudent words, but tonight should be a joyous joining. There may be some discomfort at first, but trust Mr. Darcy to guide you and be gentle. He is a good man, as his father was before him. It is a much better thing to perform your wifely duty with a man who loves you."

With no more words to be said, Elizabeth walked out of the door, down the stairs, and to the entrance of the Darcy family chapel. Once the vicar was in his place, Mrs. Reynolds opened the double doors, and the ceremony joining Fitzwilliam Darcy and Elizabeth Bennet as man and wife began.

# Chapter 9

## A Peaceful Winter

***Pemberley, Derbyshire***
***13 March 1813***

"CHECKMATE! THAT IS THE THIRD TIME I HAVE BESTED YOU THIS week, brother."

Darcy frowned down at the chess board where Georgiana had indeed painted him into a very neat corner. The final move had been a pawn trapping his knight and blocking any move to salvage the game.

Elizabeth laughed from her place in a chair by the fire. "Do not look so shocked, William. Your sister is improving every day. I believe she will be a truly accomplished lady by anyone's measure before her presentation in May."

"That is no thanks to me, my dear. It is her almost nightly games against you which have provided all improvements to her skill at chess. I have been thoroughly bested by my two favourite ladies."

"I will remind you that it was your idea for we three to hold this little daily chess tournament." Elizabeth pointed a small finger at her husband and her eyes sparkled with mirth. "I believe your pride was showing a bit, thinking that it would be you who would reign as the daily victor, while Georgie and I would have to play each afternoon for the *honour* of challenging your superior skills after dinner."

Darcy ducked his head to hide the small blush that formed at his wife's teasing. Five months had not made him immune to her wry smiles and witty words. Before Darcy knew Elizabeth, he would never have believed that his greatest joy in life would be a woman taking him to task for his hubris, but in the short time since their marriage, Darcy had become addicted to her archness. Even Georgiana had picked up some of her sister-in-law's confidence and humour. Life at Pemberley this past winter had been livelier than any year since their mother had passed away nearly sixteen years ago.

However, loving something, and walking deliberately into a conversation guaranteed to make light of him, were two different things. Looking for any escape from continued teasing, Darcy changed the subject.

"I see we have finally received the mail after the recent snows. Is there anything of interest in that pile Mrs. Reynolds just delivered?"

Elizabeth sighed. "I would not say there is anything particularly interesting. Your aunt, Lady Matlock has sent a large letter for Georgiana which I fear includes several invitations we cannot refuse. I know we are leaving for London within the next few weeks, but since Matlock is only a few hours away, and the roads have cleared, I believe we will be required to attend another dinner party before we travel south."

Darcy stood from the chess table and sat in the chair next to Elizabeth. He took the mail from her and set it on a side table, then held both of her small hands in his own. "Elizabeth, I will not subject you to my aunt's discourteousness again. When we travelled to Matlock for the Christmas holiday celebrations, I expressed my displeasure to my uncle, in no uncertain terms, at your treatment and accommodations. To have you placed in the servant's quarters was absolutely unconscionable. Even if you were really a companion, it would have been customary to place you in an adjoining room to Georgiana's."

"I also talked to my aunt, Elizabeth." Georgiana had called for some fresh tea and handed both Darcy and Elizabeth a cup. "I was very distressed to have you below stairs."

Elizabeth shook her head. "I am sure that Lady Matlock did not mean any specific disrespect. The house was very full with her other relations. The

Earls of Nottingham and Derby have very large families, and my accommodations were not uncomfortable. We will have to get used to this treatment as we remove to town for the season. I shall be treated as a servant at the social gatherings we attend. You must socialize without hovering over me all night, especially with such close connections as Lady Matlock's relations."

Darcy scoffed. "My aunt only held that ridiculous party to play matchmaker. I have, of course, met the Earls of Nottingham and Derby before this past winter, but I do not believe we have ever been such a cosy family party before. It is certainly not the tradition my aunt spoke about so adamantly." Darcy sipped his tea and stared into the fire. "Lord Nottingham may be Aunt Matlock's brother, but I have never been much impressed with him. He is very high-handed with his children. The youngest, Bernard Finch, who was not at the party, is a barrister in London and a very good friend of mine. His father was not well pleased when he foreswore the army for a law apprenticeship. Even now, as he works with members of parliament drafting legislation, Lord Nottingham bemoans his profession and has said on more than one occasion that he would be more handsome if he wore a red coat."

"Well, my dear husband, of course he would be more handsome in a red coat." Darcy looked back to Elizabeth and she batted her eyes coquettishly. "Are not all men who soldier for our king and country the most attractive to young ladies and middling earls alike?" Elizabeth waved her handkerchief about with a toss of her curls.

Darcy caught his wife's hands again and gave her a stern look for her teasing, while Georgiana spoke through her laughter. "I cannot speak for most young ladies, but I would say that my brother's lack of a red coat did not take away from his handsomeness to the earl's daughters in attendance. It seemed that our aunt was very interested in providing plenty of time for you to become acquainted with Lady Fiona, and to a lesser degree, Lady Miranda." Georgiana had tried to speak with both young ladies about her brother's apathy for courting during their two days stay in Matlock, but it all came to no avail. Both the young ladies of marriageable age had decided they would not mind becoming Mrs. Darcy one bit.

"Yes, it does seem that Miss Bingley shall have some competition for your attention this season. Heaven forbid either Lady Fiona or Lady Miranda have the chance to observe the evenness of your penmanship. I am sure one or the other shall swoon." Elizabeth chuckled again into her teacup while Darcy scowled into his own.

Lady Fiona Finch, daughter to the Earl of Nottingham, and Lady Matlock's favourite niece, was tall, handsome, and heiress to fifty thousand pounds. At twenty-two, and facing her fifth season, Lady Fiona was tired of dancing with spendthrift dandies and impoverished lordlings at Almack's. Darcy was certainly not a spendthrift, and managed to be handsome without wearing a cravat that had a ridiculous number of knots. Lady Fiona was friendly with Caroline Bingley and knew that lady considered herself practically engaged to Darcy, but the reports of Caroline and Darcy's 'understanding' seemed to be greatly exaggerated by the upstart. Lady Fiona had decided during the Christmastide celebrations that she would use her close relationship with her aunt to secure more time with the ultimately eligible Darcy.

Lady Miranda Stanley, daughter to the Earl of Derby, was only out in society this past summer. Barely a woman at eighteen, she had been friends with Georgiana since they were young girls. Several autumns during their youth, the two had spent much time together while their fathers gathered for the hunt. The last time they had all been together was during Darcy's final year at Cambridge, the year before the elder Mr. George Darcy passed. At the end of the last London season, Lady Miranda had been able to secure several dances with Darcy at both Almack's and Matlock House, but her native shyness, combined with his general social unease, made for silent encounters. She had watched Lady Fiona make conversation with the handsome man with envy. She had as much dowry money and connections as the Nottinghams, and just as much right to be considered a good match. Lady Miranda took comfort that Darcy always appeared anxious when talking to the Lady Fiona. Lady Miranda understood his desire for quiet company. She was sure that, given the choice between the two women, she could be Mrs. Miranda Darcy before the fall.

"At least Richard was being helpful, instead of his usual habit of just laughing at my attempts to escape such tiresome situations. He was always right under foot to take me away for billiards and brandy when either Lady Fiona or Lady Miranda became too enthusiastic for my company."

"While I do not particularly like watching other women vie for my husband's attention, I cannot say I fault their taste." Elizabeth raised one eyebrow and took a sip of her tea, hiding her smile.

The arch look achieved her real goal, to make Darcy chuckle and lighten his countenance. The entire situation with the Matlocks had been very stressful, and Darcy had been in a dour mood for days following their return to Pemberley.

What Darcy had not told Elizabeth or Georgiana was that just before they all departed Matlock, Lady Matlock had issued another round of mandatory invitations to Christmas Eve. That invitation had specifically not included Elizabeth, since Lady Matlock assumed she would be spending her holiday with family. Instead of confronting his aunt in company, Darcy had gone to his uncle to say that in no way would Georgiana be returning without her companion, since Elizabeth did not have plans to be away from Derbyshire during the holiday. Lord Matlock had been a bit confused by the forceful way Darcy had spoken on the matter, but Richard again intervened on his cousin's behalf. He had said that they absolutely understood, and of course Elizabeth should not be left alone on Christmas. Georgiana's particular friend would always be welcome at Matlock. He also went on to say that she would most definitely be given rooms adjacent to Georgiana on her next visit.

Thankfully, a massive snowstorm three days before Christmas had made travel to Matlock impossible. This allowed the new family to have a peaceful and private holiday. Instead of having to pretend again that Elizabeth was Georgiana's companion, Mr. and Mrs. Darcy slept late in their massive bed and enjoyed the holiday as all newlyweds should.

A knock on the parlour door caught the attention of all three Darcys. "Excuse me, but an express rider has come with correspondence for Mrs. Darcy from Scarborough." Mrs. Reynolds handed over a letter with lovely, but unfamiliar handwriting on the outside. The wax seal was a crest from the Earl of Matlock used by immediate members of his family.

"It must be from Lady Gwyneth. I hope nothing is wrong with Lydia." Elizabeth looked up at Darcy with apprehension in her eyes.

Darcy took the hand not clutching the express note and ran his thumbs across the back of it. "My dear, by the physician's original estimate, your sister should have been delivered very shortly. It is most likely good news."

Elizabeth nodded and looked back down at the letter in her hand but made no move to read the missive.

Georgiana stepped up and held out her hand. "Shall I read what our great-aunt has to say?"

Elizabeth handed over the paper, immediately.

> *"Miss Elizabeth Bennet, please forgive the impropriety of my writing you without a prior introduction, however I wanted you to know, as soon as may be, that your sister has been successfully delivered of a fine, stout baby boy on 11 March 1813. Both mother and son are recovering well and will be churched by my son, Reverend Malcom Fitzwilliam in three Sundays. Lydia has named her son Thomas Anthony Bennet Wickham in remembrance of your father. Though we understand if Mr. Darcy is too busy to travel, it is Lydia's wish that you might be able to join us here in Scarborough for the christening. She wishes for you to be the child's godmother. Of course, I would welcome my relations as well.*
>
> *Yours etc.*
> *Lady Gwyneth Fitzwilliam."*

Elizabeth sniffed and wiped away tears from her eyes. "She is really safely delivered? And my nephew has been named for our father. I am so relieved."

Darcy looked back to Mrs. Reynolds. "Please have the express rider fed, and prepare him a bed for tonight. We shall pack our things and leave for Scarborough by the end of the week in order to be present for Master Thomas's christening. Will you please alert the staff to our change in plans?"

"Oh William, no! We are to be on our way to London before the christening. I would not have us change Georgie's plans. There is much to do for her coming out. Perhaps I might just go for a few days and come back before our original travel date."

Georgiana interjected before Darcy could argue. "Elizabeth, I would much rather go to meet my new nephew than spend a few days on Bond Street. We have our appointment with the modiste in one month and six days. There is plenty of time to travel north, witness Thomas baptised into the church, and have a leisurely trip to London. We must not miss these moments. Also, there is a postscript here on the bottom which is written in a different hand. Do you recognize it?"

Elizabeth took the letter. "Yes, this is Lydia's writing. Oh!" Elizabeth looked up, startled, and handed over the letter to Darcy, which he took with some confusion.

He read the last few lines and then looked up to his wife and sister, delighted. "She asks me to be Thomas's first godfather. I am very honoured that I should fulfil this role in his life."

Elizabeth chewed on her upper lip. "What do you think your Fitzwilliam relations will say at your acceptance of such a large role in his life? True, your father was Wickham's godfather, but is that enough of a connection to continue the tradition into another generation?"

"I am sure none of my relations will resent the connection. Except for Richard, most of them are unaware of my estrangement from Wickham, and will instead remember that my father loved him well enough during his lifetime. Besides, it will not be that much longer until our marriage is known to all our relations, so of course I am the best choice as a godfather. All will be well. I promise."

"Come, Lizzy, we shall go find Marianne and Lillian, so we may plan for all our upcoming trips."

"You go, Georgie. I need to sit and write a return letter for Lady Gwyneth, letting her know that we all shall come. My current letter to Lydia is also nearly finished, so I shall add a few lines of congratulations then close them to be taken back by the express rider."

Darcy placed a quick kiss on the top of Elizabeth's head. "Do not seal Lydia's letter just yet. Please leave me a few lines to accept her invitation to be Thomas's godfather. I shall find you in the library after talking with Connor."

Elizabeth walked across the hall and to her desk in the large library. There was both a master's and mistress's study at Pemberley, however, Darcy's mother and father had preferred to sit together when working on their respective duties and correspondences. So, a large corner of the library near the south facing windows overlooking the rose garden had been taken up with matching ebony desks. Elizabeth and Darcy decided to continue the tradition of working together whenever possible, and found great joy in sharing the responsibilities of Pemberley with the other.

After finishing her letters, Elizabeth looked up to the large calendar hanging on the wall behind Darcy's chair.

It was seven months to the day since her father had died.

Elizabeth thought of her father often, but not with true sadness. He had lived a simple life, full of mirth, and always enjoyed laughing at the folly of himself and his fellow man. Elizabeth believed that the worst offence she could commit against her father's memory would be to grow despondent and forget to laugh. So, she had always tried to remember his wit, then laugh at something he would have found amusing.

Today though, she was sad.

Somehow, the realization that her nephew had been named in his memory meant he was truly gone. Thomas Anthony Bennet had a grandson he would never meet. There would never be another new book lovingly selected by her father for her specific enjoyment. And one day, when she was hopefully blessed with children, they would never know the gentle humour of the man who did not take himself too seriously. Today, it hurt so much.

Elizabeth stood from behind her desk and walked to the newest bookshelves, erected just this past Christmastime. It had been a beautiful and snowy Christmas day. The three Darcys had taken their sleigh to the Pemberley parish church for the traditional afternoon service, then upon their return, Darcy had directed them all into the library to eat a cold luncheon and exchange gifts. While this seemed perfectly innocent to Elizabeth, Georgiana was confused as to why the presents were in the library instead of by the wooden crèche in the east parlour like always. When she was about to comment on the oddity, Darcy raised his finger to her lips out of sight of Elizabeth, and silently implored his baby sister to play along.

Darcy had a specific purpose for hosting Christmas in the library instead of the east parlour.

When Elizabeth walked into the library, she was curious about a new set of stacks positioned by the windows on the north side of the room. Not only were they newly constructed, they were not quite full. She went over to investigate but nearly fell to the floor when she realized what the shelves contained.

Mr. Bennet's books! Nearly every single one.

Her father had placed a small etched 'B' into the leather on the spine of every book he had ever owned, and the shelves were lined with them. She ran her fingers along the small, indented letters and wept.

Darcy had purchased many of the most beloved books of Mr. Bennet's collection after the ever industrious and intelligent Charlotte Collins had sent a letter to Elizabeth warning of Collins's desire to burn all the "immoral" books. Elizabeth had been beside herself. Darcy told her not to fret, he would contact the Meryton book seller immediately and tell the man of the travesty about to take place.

In reality, Darcy wrote to Collins directly. He told Collins that he desired to purchase many of the most collectable books, having heard of the quality from Elizabeth and knowing his inclination to rid Longbourn of many in the collection. Darcy had his London solicitor go to Longbourn and pay Collins a good sum for any of the books he wished to sell. While most would have considered the amount paid for a country squire's book collection insanity, upon inspection, Darcy realized he had paid well under what the books were worth. Along with the expected classics from his days at Oxford, Mr. Bennet had first editions of most of Wadsworth's poems, as well as Mrs. Radcliff's novels. There was also a rare specimen of the Elliot Bible, the only modern book translated into the language of the native peoples in the Americas, in fantastic condition. One would think that a clergy man would not have parted with a version of the Bible, but Collins did not even know what the book was, only that it was written in the language of the godless American natives.

The collection's most valuable item by far was *Fugitive Pieces*, a poem written by Lord Byron at the age of fourteen, but recalled due to the sexual imagery. There were only five copies known to have survived the burning. One each at Queen's College Oxford Library, Magdalene College Cambridge Library, St. Andrews Library, University of Bologna Library in Italy, and the Sorbonne. Several additional copies were believed to have survived in the hands of private collectors who had managed to purchase a copy within the short time it was for sale around Nottinghamshire and in a few exclusive bookstores in London, but none had before been confirmed. Darcy was amazed to find it amongst Mr. Bennet's books. That one edition alone, at a private auction in London, could fetch the entire sum Darcy paid Collins, likely more. But these were not purchased for their investment value, they were purchased to make Elizabeth smile.

Now, with the memories of Christmas and the loss of her father fresh in her mind, Elizabeth ran her fingers over the spines of those books. She could smell his favourite tobacco in the pages, and see the notes he had made in the margins. His life's work was right before her on the shelves. It was as if he were present again.

Elizabeth was still standing in the middle of the shelves nearly an hour later when Darcy came to find her. "Elizabeth? Darling, are you truly well? You seemed sad at the news from your sister."

Accepting his proffered handkerchief, Elizabeth dabbed at her eyes. "I must admit that the news of little Thomas's birth has brought to mind the loss of my father. I fear that I miss him a great deal more today, though it makes no sense."

Darcy drew Elizabeth into his arms and guided her to the couch by the fire. "It is natural to find yourself missing him today. I am often surprised by those things that remind me of my own parents, like every spring when the foals are born. My father loved our horses and took great pride in the quality of our stables. He would personally oversee the mares as they neared their foaling. I too am greatly proud of our thoroughbred lines but admit that every spring I find myself in a melancholy mood for missing my father. It is the same with the blooming of the roses. They always remind me of my mother."

"Does the pain lessen with time?"

"I do not think it does." Darcy sighed and pulled Elizabeth back into his side then reclined against the back of the couch. "I have heard many say that the pain of loss becomes better with time, but I do not think it is the intensity which lessens, only the frequency. Often, with the foals and the roses, I am just as taken with grief as the first time I learned of their passing."

"Is there anything which helps?"

"Before I knew you, I would have said no. But now I know better. I cannot replace my parents' love, but yours has come to remind me that there is much in life still to cherish."

# Chapter 10

## Determination

***Wilton Row, Belgravia, London***
***1 April 1813***

"I have heard that she is very beautiful and with the best of manners, but her father's estate was not able to provide large doweries for all four sisters. It was kindly of Mr. Darcy to support the eldest sister through the loss of the father."

Caroline barely restrained herself from rolling her eyes at Lady Elizabeth Shrewsbury, the Countess of Shrewsbury, in the middle of her sister's morning parlour. Lady Shrewsbury was the biggest gossip of the whole *ton*. She had to keep tongues wagging about someone else, or the conversation was likely to turn to how the last five Earls of Shrewsbury had failed to produce a male heir, which resulted in the loss of three baronies, a marquessate, and a dukedom. At least there had always been a cousin or nephew of close enough relation to take the earldom at each failed progeny. Lady Elizabeth herself, the current Countess of Shrewsbury, was still childless after more than twenty years of marriage, and barring some kind of divine intervention, the earldom would again go to the Earl's sister's son. Caroline understood why this made the lady so very nervous, but she envied her position. Lady Shrewsbury was able to enjoy her status as a highly placed person in society without having to face death or, worse, the loss of her slim figure, in childbirth.

Today's tea party for the ladies newly returned to town was a much-needed reprieve from the monotonous winter season in London. Caroline had been stuck indoors for much of the last few months, gazing out her parlour window, silently mocking her fellow city dwellers, the rich and the poor who had no proper country estate in which to escape London's sleet and smog. She was resolved: she would not be amongst them for much longer. However, her entire winter social schedule had been an absolute waste.

Darcy and Georgiana had spent the entirety of the winter months in Derbyshire without one trip to town or invitation for the Bingleys to Pemberley. Usually, Darcy would invite Bingley and her brother-in-law, Hurst, for a country hunt in early November. The year before last was an exception, due to Bingley taking the Netherfield lease. But this past November there had not even been an apologetic letter telling Bingley why the Darcys were indisposed to host their friends. It was absolutely maddening.

London had been no better. There was no true upper-level society anywhere to be seen. Only second sons and recently ascended tradesmen, like Bingley himself, could be found in the dance halls and theatres of town. Even many of the elderly dowagers, with whom Caroline and Louisa were friendly, had taken their winters at their son's estates instead of staying in London.

Finally, *le bon ton* had started to reappear in London and Louisa had quickly put together tea with several countesses, a viscountess, and other wealthy, but untitled, ladies. It would have been perfect if the talk had not centred almost entirely on the subject of the Darcys and their new, gently bred servant.

"But *dear* Miss Bingley and Mrs. Hurst, I have been led to believe that you are actually well acquainted with the lady. Pray, tell us what she is truly like."

Thankfully, Louisa Hurst interjected before Caroline had to come up with a response. "Oh, my, Lady Shrewsbury, I would not say that we are *well* acquainted with Miss Elizabeth Bennet, but we do have a passing connection. While Miss Elizabeth, who is the second daughter of five, is homely in her looks, she is not really refined in her style. Her older sister, Miss Jane Bennet is the true beauty of the family. Why, my sister and I once saw Miss Elizabeth after walking a distance of more than three miles through the morning roads after a large rainstorm. She arrived with petticoats and boots absolutely caked in mud." Louisa tittered behind her teacup while the assembled ladies all sported various shocked looks.

"And what of the widowed sister? Is it true that the Misses Bennets are related to the wife of Mr. Darcy's late steward?" Another countess piped up with questions about the Bennet family.

Caroline had to suppress another eyeroll and a huff. As if being forced to dance all winter with second sons studying at London University to become a barrister or clergyman was not dreadful enough, Caroline had to spread the ridiculous lie about Lydia Bennet being married to Lt. Wickham to save her brother's and Darcy's investment with the uncle from Cheapside. Caroline did not believe for one minute that there had been a wedding ceremony, no matter how many marriage licenses the Bennets put forward. It was revolting to have to repeat the little harlot's name in public and hope that the useless persons abandoned in London for the winter would repeat the gossip to their more important family members. She was sick from her bright red hair to her perfectly proportioned toes with being complimentary of the Bennets generally, and compassionate toward Lydia specifically.

Again, Louisa answered in a perfectly neutral and disaffected tone. "I am quite unsure of the full connection, but I believe that Miss Elizabeth's youngest sister did marry the godson of Mr. Darcy's father, or something like that. We did meet him once or twice when he was serving as a Lieutenant in the _____shire militia last fall."

"Her youngest sister?" An older lady from nearer the pianoforte spoke up. Caroline looked over her tea for the first time and noticed that Lady Sefton, the most prominent patroness of Almack's Assembly Rooms, and Hurst's great aunt, had joined the conversation.

"Yes, my lady," Caroline simpered. "I am quite sure that Miss Lydia, that is, Mrs. Wickham, is Miss Elizabeth's *youngest* sister. She could not have been much older than sixteen when she married, and I believe the Bennets are anticipating she will be delivered this spring of a baby, if it has not already occurred."

Several ladies around the room mumbled, "*Oh my,*" and "*Well,*" behind teacups and fans at learning that this new companion to Georgiana Darcy had a sixteen-year-old younger sister with a baby.

Lady Shrewsbury, who could always be counted on to get the juicy heart of any gossip, opened the door for which Caroline had been waiting. "Why ever was a younger sister married at sixteen if she had older sisters still at home?"

"It is of course not my place to speak ill of the dead." Caroline paused for a sip of tea and to make sure she had the attention of every lady in the room. "But Lt. Wickham and Mrs. Wickham eloped from the militia's summer encampment. Her father was not present to give away his daughter, so their marriage was a bit defective at the beginning, though now I am sure it does not really matter. As to why the older Miss Bennets were not yet married, well, as Lady Shrewsbury said earlier, they have little fortune and not many accomplishments. They did not even have a governess growing up."

Another round of soft exclamations prompted Caroline to quickly hide her smile behind her fan.

Louisa brought the conversation back to mild compliments towards the Bennet sisters. Their purpose, after all, was to help their brother and his investment by keeping out harmful, pernicious gossip. "I am truly quite astounded that Mr. Darcy brought Miss Elizabeth into his house as companion to Miss Darcy, however she is kind and lively. Also, I am sure he regards her as no competition compared to his sister, which is important in a social companion. As long as she helps Miss Darcy feel comfortable in society, I shall not worry for her dresses being out of season."

Caroline stood up to refill several teacups and was very satisfied with the way the ladies were speaking of the Bennets, and Elizabeth specifically.

Caroline smile and mused to herself, "*At least that little chit is now so low as to be unmarriageable by any man of land or wealth. She may be part of Darcy's household, but she is forever now beyond the reach of any gentleman of consequence.*" Caroline nearly laughed while pouring Lady Sefton another cup, which caused the older lady to give her a searching look. Too amused with her own thoughts, Caroline just continued with her internal monologue. "*It is unlikely Elizabeth has even spent any time in Darcy's company. She has likely been more in the company of the kitchen maids than Georgiana and Darcy this past winter. She probably has her rooms in the servant's wing!*"

Silent thoughts aside, Caroline was still upset with the situation regarding the Bennets. Another worry for Caroline had been Bingley's frequent visits to Cheapside. He went to keep an eye on Edward Gardiner and his investments. Darcy felt the oversight was necessary, so she was resigned to the visits, but it was worrisome that Jane was within easy reach of her dim-witted, rich brother. She would have to review the guest lists for the upcoming dinner party at Hurst's townhouse after Covent Garden's Shakespeare theatre opening night. There were bound to be a few titled young ladies in attendance.

Caroline was startled out of her thoughts by another question from Lady Sefton. "Miss Bingley, do you know when the Darcys will be coming back to town?"

This was another sore spot for Caroline. "No, my lady, unfortunately I have not yet heard back from Miss Darcy regarding their travel plans for the season."

If only she did know when the Darcys were coming back to town. Caroline had sent several personal invitations to Darcy House for various dinners and teas, but none had yet been answered. Unfortunately, for the sake of civility and proprietary, the invitations had to include Elizabeth. But as soon as Caroline was formally engaged to Darcy, Elizabeth would be dismissed. Perhaps she could convince him to marry by special license within a few weeks. Then she could take her place as mistress of his home before the end of the season. She would even be able to welcome everyone to Pemberley for the summer house party which she was determined to help Georgiana plan as hostess, instead of being relegated to the guest wing yet again.

With the discussion of the Darcys fully extinguished, Caroline allowed Louisa to steer the conversation to other topics while Caroline retreated again into her thoughts.

The only question in her mind was how best to ensure her marriage to Darcy took place. It would be much too forward and a horrible breach of propriety to speak openly to Darcy about what was holding him back. Caroline suspected that it was a mixture of caring for Georgiana and his belief that she would be there once *he* was ready. If indeed that was the case, she must remedy both situations. She would not only orchestrate meetings between eligible young men for Georgiana, but also spend some time flirting with those men herself. If Darcy no longer feared for his sister but instead feared losing Caroline, he may make his move.

And if sisterly stability or jealousy would not induce action, she would have to orchestrate a different kind of situation. Darcy had always come to Bingley's house for dinner at least once a week during the season in the past. There was no reason to lessen the frequency of those invitations. Also, now that Georgiana was out, perhaps there would be dinners at Darcy House that included both genders. Either house's library would be a fine location for a liaison. As long as a well-timed maid came to find them. Honour would induce Darcy to church, of that Caroline was sure.

***Rosings Park, Kent***
***1 April 1813***

Anne de Bourgh sat quietly in the music room of her grand estate of Rosings, reading the newest gothic novel from Mrs. Radcliff. Her mother would never approve, but she did not monitor the purchases Anne made from the bookseller in town. Since Richard had left abruptly in September, there had been little in the way of excitement at Rosings. The Bennet family situation had lost its interest after learning of the marriage license. Deficient though it had been, at least there had been an attempt by the couple to wed. That both father and son-in-law had died over such a silly dispute was unfortunate, but not worthy of more fuss. In addition, Darcy had made a substantial investment with the Bennets' uncle, and Lady Catherine would not want any of the Darcy holdings to suffer from such tragic connections.

Suddenly, but not so unexpectedly, a loud crash came from the direction of Lady Catherine's study. Once a sennight or so, the grand lady would become enraged at something or the other and throw one of the porcelain Chinese vases at the wall. Now that Lady Catherine's eyesight was beginning to fade, and she could not tell the difference, the steward had taken to purchasing cheap fakes to place in the mistress's study for exactly this exercise. Anne sighed then put her book on the side table, preparing for a rant on whatever had her mother furious with the pottery today.

She did not have to wait long.

"Hobbs! We must leave for London immediately. Get the carriage ready and send me Mrs. Baker. Anne and I must be packed at once!"

Anne merely looked up to her mother's loud entrance to the music room.

"Anne! There you are. Come, you must get up now. We are going to London." Once Lady Catherine stopped in front of Anne, her daughter could see the large vein in the side of her mother's temple, which would bulge during a particularly energetic session of ceramic hurling. In fact, often when Lady Catherine got this overexcited, she would manage to break something of actual value during the rampage. Since everything in Rosings actually belonged to Anne, and not her mother, Lady Catherine's nasty habit of destroying the de Bourgh family china was a serious annoyance to the young mistress. One day, the daughter would be able to stand up to her fierce mother, but that day was most likely to be the day she laid her mother to rest in the de Bourgh mausoleum.

Anne sighed. "Yes, Mother. I heard you telling the staff. Might I ask why we are removing to London in such a hurry?"

Lady Catherine never stopped pacing as she responded. "I have received a letter from Darcy. Neither he nor Georgiana are coming for Easter in two weeks. They are staying in London to obtain Georgiana's new wardrobe. Apparently, an appointment with some French modiste is much too important to reschedule, despite his familial obligations to your late father!"

"Mother…"

"And do not get me started on the shirking of his duty to you! I have given that boy plenty of time to make his addresses to you directly, but, really dear, you are not getting younger."

"I know how time works, Mother." Anne pinched the bridge of her nose.

"Do not take that tone with me, young lady! Darcy must honour your particular engagement." Lady Catherine stopped for a moment to open the sideboard and get a small glass of sherry. "I have tried to make the arrangements easy for him since my own dear sister is not here to help guide him in matters of a marriage, but really, he must be the one to run the engagement announcement. I cannot run it."

"Please tell me you did not send The Times a notice of our engagement!" Though Anne did not really fear London society, she did not want to be publicly jilted.

"They would not take it! I tried to have the announcement run, but the editor wrote back and said it is their practice to accept notices from the groom or the guardian of the bride. Either my brother or Darcy will have to run the announcement, which is why I sent it to Darcy in my last letter." Pulling several pages of paper out of her pocket, Lady Catherine started to wave around what appeared to be the letter from Darcy, which started this whole diatribe. "Look here! Look on page two, where he dishonours you and me and his own mother, my dear sister, who did wish to have our houses and fortunes joined with your marriage. From your cradles we planned it! Look for yourself!"

Lady Catherine threw the pages at Anne, and Anne was obliged to lunge forward from her chair to grab the letter. After pursuing the pages, she found what was most likely to have caused her mother such outrage.

> *Aunt, I must be firm here. I will never run the announcement you enclosed in your last letter, and I must insist that you do not run such an announcement. As I have told you in the past, I will never become engaged to my cousin. The overly wordy announcement that details the particularity of our cradle made arrangement must therefore be discarded. I will marry only a lady of my own choosing, rather than bow to the unrealistic expectations from my family. Though I was only 12 at the time of her death, I do not remember my mother ever saying a marriage with Anne was her particular wish. She may have believed that if our temperaments and inclinations were in the direction to make our union a happy one, she would have welcomed Anne as her daughter-in-law. But Lady Anne would never have wanted her children to have anything less than a fulfilling marriage. In addition to my mother's ambivalence to such a union, my father was outright hostile to the idea in the last years of his life. Father told me that I was not bound to my cousin, either by contract or honour, and he wished me to make a happy marriage instead of a marriage of money.*

Anne was elated to hear, once and for all, that she would not be required to marry her dour cousin Darcy. But her elation was short lived. Lady Catherine had other ideas.

"How DARE he make a fool out of my Anne while he gallivants around with that little low-born harlot?" Lady Catherine bellowed to no one in particular, even though she was not two feet from her daughter. Anne tried to suppress a smile at this. It seemed her mother was not as blind to the romantic leanings of her cousin as everyone thought.

Anne had been certain Darcy had affection for Elizabeth last spring when they were both visiting Kent. She had hoped he might ask for her hand during one of their morning walks through the Rosings grounds, which would have put an end to her mother's ridiculous marriage schemes. But alas, there had been no such understanding, and now Elizabeth's family was tainted with the elopement and pregnancy of the youngest sister. Surely, Anne's haughty, disdainful, self-righteous cousin would never degrade himself with such a wife.

While Anne was musing on the Bennets, her mother continued to rail at the tapestries. A final declaration from Lady Catherine brought Anne back to the room.

"I shall now know how to act! You and I are going to London for the season. I wonder how quickly I can terminate the lease on our townhouse? They are tradesmen, rich off of the barbaric east China trade route. Do you know that the son of my current tenant has actually *been* to China? Now, going to India with the East India Trading Company and staying within the British society of Bombay is one thing, but traveling to China with such savages, that is just barbaric! I would have cancelled their contract right then and there, but they have always paid on time, and it can be hard to find such diligent tenants. Oh, never mind, we shall stay with my brother for the season."

"Oh, that is lovely, I have wanted to see my Fitzwilliam cousins…"

The end of Lady Catherine's walking stick thundered on the floor in a motion Anne knew was meant to silence her. "And I will carry my point with the Earl. He will surely be in support of your match and shall make sure that Darcy sees reason. A few well-placed words with my good friends will have your engagement all over town with or without an announcement. You will be seen at all the premier society events looking positively regal, to let him know what he would be giving up, were he to jilt you."

This time, Anne did not try to interject any thoughts. This was not a conversation.

"Once Darcy sees that he must either marry you or make his family look ridiculous, he will likely purchase a special license. We shall have a fantastic wedding to cap the season at St Margaret's Church, with a reception at Matlock House in St. James Square. It will be as your father and I were wed. We shall have to order your gown right away if it is to be ready before June. What was the name of that modiste Georgiana was going to? Mme. Devro or something? Your Aunt Matlock will know. Do not worry about the arrangements, dear. I shall talk to the staff at Matlock house and the bishop of St Margaret's once we arrive in London. All will be ready."

With that declaration, Lady Catherine swept out of the room with as much force as she had swept into it, leaving a bewildered Anne in her wake. Perhaps now would be a good time to retire to her room with a headache. That should delay their departure to London by at least a fortnight. Her mother was solicitous of Anne's fragile health, if not of any of Anne's other desires.

# Chapter 11

## Sewing the Threads of Support

***Darcy House, Mayfair, London***
***19 April 1813***

On the morning of their second full day in London, Elizabeth and Georgiana dressed for their ten a.m. appointment with Mme. Devy. Both ladies were nervous for the first social outing where they would have to pretend Elizabeth was merely Georgiana's social companion. At least it was acceptable for the women to publicly call each other by their Christian names so there would be no inadvertent slips, but there would still be introductions and inquiries. Each hoped that there would not be an irreversible mistake so early in the season. Darcy joined the ladies for a later breakfast than was his wont, to give the small family one last bit of communion before the whirlwind of the next nine weeks commenced.

"William, when did you say Mr. Bingley would be coming by today? Georgie and I shall be at Mme. Devy's until at least luncheon, but perhaps we should take our meal in one of the tea rooms instead of coming home if he is to be by at that time." Elizabeth would have loved to see Bingley, but was worried about having Caroline in the house for too long. She was inevitably going to have to suffer the lady's company throughout the season, so she wanted to avoid contact when possible. If Caroline called with her brother, like she would no doubt try to do, but found the ladies of the house out shopping, she would not be able to stay for more than a quarter hour. She may not stay at all, as the butler knew to request she leave her card. Bingley was coming to discuss business, and Darcy was not home to callers.

"Charles is scheduled to come about eleven a.m., but he will likely arrive earlier, and Miss Bingley would never come calling before the fashionable hour. We will spend our time in the study then remove to White's for luncheon and further men's socializing. I shall be home for tea but promise to issue no invitations. You ladies are safe from Miss Bingley if you return for your meal, but do take your time and enjoy one of the fine tea houses if you wish. Do not forget to have Georgie carry the money and make any payments for you both. The dressmaker's bill should come to the house, as well as any other clothes shops at which you choose to stop. Georgie, promise me you shall take your sister to look for some dancing slippers. I know you believe your old ones are adequate Elizabeth, but you should at least get ones that match the ball gowns you choose." Darcy spoke with a smile, hardly concealed behind his coffee cup and snorted into his drink when he lifted his eyes to his wife's scowling face.

Georgiana was also laughing without any attempt to hide her mirth. Since their wedding and the many gifts Darcy had obtained for his wife at Christmas, Elizabeth had been loudly protesting the number of gowns and accoutrement both her husband and sister felt necessary for this season. "Do not worry, brother!" Georgiana chimed in. "I shall drag poor Lizzy to all of the accessory shops and see to it that she acquires new dancing slippers, a set of summer riding boots, and at least two sets of day gloves. She shall be properly burdened with boxes before we make it to tea."

"Fine! I shall cease my arguments about your spending money on totally unnecessary items for me *if* you will allow me to bring home at least one book of my sole choosing and promise to read it with me, *sans* complaint!" That sparkle in Elizabeth's eyes was the greatest joy of Darcy's life.

"My dear, I consent. Even if you bring home the most atrocious gothic novel full of sappy romance tripe, I shall read every word aloud to you and even modulate my voice with the characters if you come home with all the purchases Georgie deems necessary."

Husband and wife shook on the agreement and Georgiana let out a bark of laughter at their officiousness. Shortly after they had all drained the last of their morning refreshment, Marianne and Lilian entered with their ladies' outerwear, reporting that the carriage was ready at the front entrance. Darcy gave his wife one last chaste kiss on the forehead.

"I love you dearest, and I am so proud of the strength you have shown in supporting our family. No matter what anyone says to you or about you, we are married. No one can take that away."

A short quarter of an hour later, Elizabeth and Georgiana walked through the door to Mme. Devy's shop, already full with ladies of the *ton* desperately trying get an appointment with the famed modiste. Immediately upon presenting themselves to the front attendant, the Darcy women were accosted by Georgiana's acquaintances. Most of them were women who had been introduced to the young miss in Lady Matlock's parlour but actually wanted an audience with her brother. Each in turn came up to the pair, greeted Georgiana as if they were the best of friends, and ignored Elizabeth. Unnoticed by either sister, Caroline Bingley was watching from a corner of the shop with a wicked look on her face: Elizabeth was being snubbed by London's elite. That look faded with one word from the back of the shop.

"Lizzy!" Mme. Devy emerged from behind the curtain separating the fitting area from the front of the shop and pushed through the parting crowd to embrace the previously invisible woman. Every eye was now positively trained on Georgiana's companion.

"My dear, let me look at you! You are as beautiful as the last time I saw you. Now, introduce me to your delightful friend." Mme. Devy turned towards Georgiana and waved her hands looking the younger lady up and down. "Miss Darcy, I understand you are debuting this season, yes? Well, do not worry. I shall have you both looking like princesses before your coming out ball, just you wait."

Caroline could take no more. "Miss Darcy, Miss Eliza, how wonderful to see you both again."

Elizabeth barely contained a frustrated groan at the sudden appearance of Caroline. Thankfully, Georgiana had spotted her upon their entrance and was prepared to respond with some civility. "Hello, Miss Bingley. How good to see you again."

"I had no idea you were returned from Pemberley. Mr. Darcy hardly ever comes to London before the first week of May. I shall have to call as soon as possible, and you must come to dinner at our townhouse as soon as Mr. Darcy's schedule will allow. I know he is busy with business in the next few days before the season officially starts, but it is refreshing to take dinner with good friends before the hectic social agenda begins, don't you agree? I shall have the invitation to your house before the day is done." Anticipating that the dressmaker knew Elizabeth's tradesman uncle, she asked her next question with a wide smile. "Now Eliza, you must tell us how you know Mme. Devy so well."

Mme. Devy hated the Caroline Bingleys of the world. Superiority and snobbery from the daughters of royal dukes, she could stomach. They had made her family very well situated over the years, and what was the point of a title except to over-inflate the ego? But tolerating women whose money was as 'tainted' as her own, who were coming into her establishment for no purpose but to look down upon others, was not worth the profit she made from their purchases. She also knew Caroline's ploy was to get Elizabeth to admit that the Devys were friends and business partners with the Gardiners, thus exposing the Bennet family connections in trade. But Mme. Devy was prepared for such an attack. Her parents had bought the house next to Mr. Edward Gardiner, Sr. only a few years after coming to London, and quickly became friends, then business associates with the gruff old tradesman. The Devy and Gardiner children had all played together when they were young, and Mme. Devy was fond of her old friends. Fanny Gardiner had married Mr. Thomas Bennet and moved into the country, then the younger sister had met and married the town solicitor near her brother-in-law's estate, but Edward Gardiner Jr. had stayed in the family home and continued to run the family business. Mme. Devy's brother had taken a position as a footman with a respectable family many years ago and was now the butler to a great house near Kensington. So Mme. Devy and her family lived in the house her parents bought all those years ago next door to the Gardiners. Now that Mme. Devy was one of the most sought-after dress makers in all of England, and Edward Gardiner was among the largest importers of fine fabrics, their families' business relationship was invaluable. Nearly all the most exclusive fabrics every season, sewn into fashionable creations at

Mme. Devy's shop, worn by the highest of the high of London, came from Gardiner Imports.

"Why, Miss Bingley, I thought you knew! Miss Elizabeth Bennet is the daughter of a well-respected gentleman from Hertfordshire, God rest his soul. But since your family is from trade, I understand that you do not keep track of such things as the important landed gentry outside the London scene. Tsk tsk."

Mme. Devy turned from Caroline and led Elizabeth and Georgiana to the dressing rooms in the back, continuing to speak about the Bennet family to all the assembled ladies.

"But no matter. I have known Lizzy and her sisters their entire life. My father was a long-standing gentleman's tailor here in London and also the official tailor to Oxford University. He made all the school robes and attired many of the gentlemen who attended school there. Mr. Bennet was an Oxford man and began coming to my father when he was at university."

For dramatic effect, Mme. Devy turned around and tapped Elizabeth on the arm with her measuring tape. "I do not know if even you know this Lizzy, but your father met your mother through a shared connection with my father."

Elizabeth's surprise was real. "No, madam, I do not believe I have heard that before. I thought my parents were introduced at my mother's coming out ball."

"They may have been introduced at a ball, but they first saw each other in my father's shop." Mme Devy spoke to Elizabeth and Georgiana but her strong voice could be heard by the whole shoppe. "Your mother's father was also a client of my father's, and one day, while Mr. Bennet was being fitted for his last term senior robes, your mother came by to retrieve an order. In addition to the suits, I had just finished your mother's ball gown for her debut. Even though I had not established my own shop yet, a select few of the wives and daughters of my father's clients had allowed me to make them dresses. Your mother's was my first ever ball gown. She looked absolutely *magnifique*. Before your mother was out of sight of the window, Mr. Bennet turned to my father and asked how he could secure an invitation to her ball. I believe they were courting before the end of the night and engaged during Oxford's first term break. The rest is history and five beautiful sisters. Since then, I have made at least one gown a year for each of the young Bennet ladies, and often more."

The whole store was silent.

Caroline seethed inside from the modiste's snub, but she could not let her anger show. She still had not secured an appointment with the woman despite being in town all winter, and it would be unacceptable to wear a ball gown from any other establishment at Georgiana's debut in a short nineteen days. "How lovely. I am sure Miss Eliza has always cherished such finery as can only be obtained in London. I know that the Meryton dressmaker leaves something to be desired." Caroline looked at the dress Elizabeth was wearing for the first time and noted the superior cut and fine quality of the dress. Where in the world had she gotten such an ensemble?

"While I never wanted for acceptable clothing in my old home, I must say that Mme. Devy's creations have always been my best pieces. In fact, one dress she made for me before I left for Pemberley last September is undoubtedly without equal." Elizabeth looked upon the older lady with gratitude in her eyes and hoped she understood.

Mme Devy's eyes sparkled. "It was nothing, my dear! I knew you would love it and it is my pleasure in life to make clothes for those who are grateful and look splendid wearing them. Now come, come! We must begin." Turning around, Mme. Devy clapped her hands and sent her assistants scuttling off into the back of the shoppe.

"Miss Darcy, Lizzy, I hope you will not mind but I have already started your collections. For Lizzy, of course, I could make a dress that fit like a second skin without even consulting her measurements, but I took the liberty of asking your housekeeper to have the Matlock modiste send your measurements, Miss Darcy, dear. I have chosen a few fabrics that are of the finest quality and made them into my most fashionable patterns. We can always adjust the sleeves and necklines if you do not like what I have chosen and I have left the trims for you to decide, but seeing you both here today, I am sure you will love the silks I have already started. This way, you can each have a ball gown, two evening gowns, and five day dresses before the official season even starts. Oh! And Hannah dear, bring out the matching gloves, slippers, and shawls."

The stunned silence continued as two young assistants brought out eight dresses each, mostly finished, for Elizabeth and Georgiana. When the assistant named Hannah returned with armfuls of accessories in matching fabrics, the tittering began. Many of the women in the shop were curious about Elizabeth, who obviously came from a good family, even if they had never heard of her. It was also generally noted that Georgiana was not being given dresses of noticeably higher quality than her companion. From the perspective at the modiste's shop, the two were equals.

Caroline had slunk back into the corner of the shop during the flurry of activity. Once Elizabeth and Georgiana were standing hostage in front of the assistants with pins in their dresses, Caroline decided to once again bring up the topic of Elizabeth's inferior family. "Miss Eliza, how is your ***youngest*** sister? Has she been safely delivered?"

Technically, speaking of such an indisposition in public was not the best of manners, but since this was a woman's establishment such topics were not outright banned. And the reaction from the watching crowd was as Caroline had wanted. With the mention of a younger sister with a babe, the titters stopped to hear whatever details would be divulged. Amazingly, it was the usually shy Georgiana who came to Elizabeth's defence.

"Oh yes, Miss Bingley. Mrs. Wickham has been safely delivered and her son is the sweetest babe I have ever beheld! He is so pudgy about the cheeks and has crystal clear blue eyes. I know both Lizzy and Mrs. Wickham were glad to see each other before we had to leave for London."

This was definitely not what Caroline was expecting. She tried to soldier on. "Miss Darcy, you have been to visit the young, widowed mother?"

"Of course, Miss Bingley. Did you not know that Mrs. Wickham is living with my great-aunt, the Lady Gwyneth Fitzwilliam, in her house in Scarborough? My great-aunt had been looking for a new companion to come live with her, since both of her sons are now grown and out of the house, and Mrs. Wickham was delighted to join her after both her husband and father passed. Lady Gwyneth was even more excited to have the young widow once her condition was confirmed, and she adores having a babe in the house again. We all visited in late March since Fitzwilliam had been wanting to visit her ladyship anyway. Even my Fitzwilliam cousins, Colonel Fitzwilliam and the Viscount joined us for a few days."

Mme. Devy joined the conversation once more to put any negative gossip to rest. "Yes, my dear. I was so heartbroken to hear about little Lydi's husband and then to lose her father in less than a sennight! How terrible.

But that is what sometimes happens when one is married to an army officer. They do not all last through the wars. At least she has her son to remember his father and provide love on lonely nights."

Elizabeth was extremely grateful to both her sister and her long-time friend for deflecting Caroline so effectively and with so much of the truth. The insinuations were only slightly left of completely accurate. "I do believe that Lydia took our father's death the hardest, since it came so swiftly after the loss of Mr. Wickham, but she is content with her situation in Scarborough and has enjoyed living with the Fitzwilliams. Mr. Darcy was generous to be named as my nephew's godfather. His own father had been godfather to Mr. Wickham, and it seemed only right that the next generation continue that connection between the families. It was indeed a joy to celebrate the new life after so many losses this past year."

Caroline decided that no good could be achieved in the dressmaker's shop, especially since the renowned Frenchwoman was so obviously biased in favour of the little chit and her disgraceful family. She would have to have an exclusive tea party at Louisa's townhouse in the next few days. Then she would be able to give the real gossip behind the Bennets, telling everyone that the 'army officer' and Mr. Bennet both really died in a duel over an elopement. For now, she would bow out, but not before she reminded everyone of Miss Elizabeth's position.

"Well, I'm glad to hear that both your sister and nephew are healthy and well settled in the north. It is a shame she will miss the season, as I remember how much Mrs. Wickham loves to dance, but you will no doubt be able to give her many delightful details of your time chaperoning Miss Darcy. It was very kind of Mr. Darcy to give you the opportunity to join his household after your father's estate was entailed to your cousin. I am sure you will enjoy the entertainments for as long as Miss Darcy has need of your services."

With a kind smile and more truth in her words than Caroline could ever fathom, Elizabeth replied, "Yes, Mr. Darcy is very kind, and I have never been happier than this winter as a valued member of the Darcy family household. I am sure that Georgie and I will have a wonderful season and enjoy each other's friendship for many years to come."

# Chapter 12

## The Best of Intentions

***Gracechurch Street, Cheapside, London***
***25 April 1813***

"AUNT, DO YOU THINK THAT WE HAVE DONE THE RIGHT THING WITH tonight's entertainment?"

"How do you mean, Jane dear?"

Jane Bennet fiddled with the ribbon on her evening gown as she stood in the doorway to Madeline Gardiner's dressing room, watching the maid finish her aunt's coiffure. "I know that Uncle has been opposed to us making introductions for Lizzy to suitors. I do not know why, but I am sure that he must know something that I have not considered. Do you believe we are right to move forward with these plans?"

Madeline's maid tapped her shoulder, indicating that she was done with the lady's hair. "You may retire, Taylor. I will require some help after dinner, but please take some time to rest now." Madeline waited until her maid left before speaking again to Jane. "My dear, men are not equipped to deal with marriage. My husband is the best of men, and I do love him, but he can provide no reasonable explanation for his resistance other than his belief that Lizzy is not desirous of a husband."

"But Lizzy has always said that only the deepest love would move her to matrimony. Is it right to thrust men into her acquaintance with expectations?"

Picking up Jane's hands to still them from mussing her dress, Madeline sighed. "I know my dear. And we both know your sister can be quite stubborn at times. I have not broached the subject with her directly, but I suspect that these past six months, living as a gently bred servant, might have changed Lizzy. She gave up so much when she left with the Darcys. Perhaps she might now see the value in marriage to a moderately wealthy man, with a home of her own and a return to polite society. I cannot say exactly what her reaction will be, but we owe her the opportunity to choose that life over the life of a servant."

"I know you worry for her situation, but Charles has promised that he will care for my sisters after we are wed. Lizzy need not marry to return to gentility."

"Are you having second thoughts about this path? It was your plan originally."

Jane considered the question. In truth, Jane Bennet was feeling guilty. It was a silly thing for which to feel guilty, and she was sure Elizabeth would tease her to no end if her sister knew, but it could not be helped. Last September, when Elizabeth had told them that she was taking a position with the Darcys, Jane and Madeline had protested to no avail. Elizabeth would not be moved. She had said that it was best for everyone, and that Jane must stay in London so she may find a good husband. Now it seems her sister might have known that Bingley would be coming to call. He had come the very day that Elizabeth had agreed to be Georgiana's companion.

Three days later brought another visit from Bingley. After nearly two weeks of regular of visits, he asked Jane if she would step out with him for a stroll through the nearby church gardens. It had been one of those vividly bright fall days with enough warmth from the shining sun to make the everyone forget that the winter was nearly upon them. He had led her to a bench on the south side of the abbey overlooking the peaceful courtyard where two apple trees miraculously grew in the middle of London. Then, he had professed his love and promised Jane that if she would marry him, he would take care of her entire family for as long as any of them should live.

Since that day, Jane and Bingley had shared many more walks about the quiet church yard. They talked of his sister's constant scheming, which he hated. She spoke of how her mother's expectations had always felt like a burden and that since her father's passing, she had been blaming her reserved nature for the Bennet family's demise. He told her how he longed to make a quiet life in the country and forget the London elite. She told him that sounded wonderful. He told her that her mother and all her sisters, including Lydia and her child, would be welcome in his home. That he would do everything in his power to make her family whole and happy again. If her younger sisters never married, they could live with the Bingleys for all their days. At this, she had only joyful tears.

Two weeks ago, a letter had arrived for Jane from Elizabeth. This particular letter had outlined the Darcys' plans for traveling to London and Georgiana's debut. Elizabeth wrote of appointments to visit Mme. Devy's Bond Street shop and all the planned activities surrounding Georgiana's official court presentation. She gave certain days when she would be able to come visit. and a list of invitations that were being extended by Georgiana for Jane and Mary to come to Darcy House. There was even a night that Darcy was allowing Elizabeth to use his theatre box for her relations. The Gardiners, Jane, and Mary were to join Elizabeth for a showing of *Romeo and Juliet* the first week of June. The box could hold a total of nine persons, but it was unclear from Elizabeth's letter if the other four available seats would be occupied. Perhaps they would see Bingley there and could invite him to join them.

And there was the basis of all Jane's guilt. Elizabeth had surrendered her status to preserve Jane's. While Jane was entertaining the suit of a wealthy man whom she genuinely loved, Elizabeth had taken a position as a paid companion so that the Gardiners could take in Jane and Mary long enough to observe their father's full mourning period. Long enough to make them marriageable. Now, Elizabeth was creating respectable opportunities for Jane and Mary to be seen in society.

Even though Elizabeth would be dancing with eligible men at every major society event this coming season, the chances of her meeting someone who would consider marrying a gentil servant were nearly none. The men at the events Elizabeth would be attending were looking for a wife with at least a twenty-thousand pound dowry, and preferably a title. If she were to ever have a chance at marriage, she would need to meet men with fewer expectations and more heart.

Tonight was the night that Jane was going to finally put her plan to secure Elizabeth a good husband into practice. Jane and Madeline had carefully considered all the men of their acquaintance for those suitable to introduce to Elizabeth. Once she had mustered the courage to ask Bingley, he too had supplied a list of men he thought would welcome meeting the lovely and intelligent Elizabeth. So, three men of trade and two recently ascended gentlemen were coming to dinner tonight, as well as several of their mothers and sisters.

The only slightly unwelcome guests for the night were Darcy and Georgiana. Not that anyone in the Gardiner house was at all unhappy to see the Darcys, but Jane hoped that Elizabeth would not spend the entire night attending to Georgiana instead of speaking with the eligible men brought in to specifically seek her attention. The Darcys' inclusion in the party was somewhat of a surprise, since the invitation had been insisted upon by Edward.

Madeline had been nearly at the end of her patience, trying to explain why they should not invite Elizabeth's employers to the party. Never in all their years of marriage had Edward ever looked at the guest list for a dinner party, let alone insist on particular invitations. But he would not be moved. The Darcys were investors in his business, they were good friends to Bingley, and they were Elizabeth's employer. He insisted that failing to issue them an invitation would be atrocious manners.

Jane had penned the invitation and given it to Georgiana when Elizabeth and Georgiana had called at the Gardiners a few days ago. Both Madeline and Jane had been sure that the Darcys would decline, given the late notice of the invitation and that none of their station would be in attendance. So, when Georgiana accepted immediately upon receiving the invitation, both ladies were shocked. Even more so when Darcy sent over a confirming reply with his warm regards for anticipation of the evening.

"No, Aunt, I am still sure that we should introduce Lizzy to men who might marry her. I am just worried about Uncle's reaction to the situation.

I wish I had been able to talk to Lizzy before this evening without Miss Darcy around."

Madeline sighed. "You are right about that, dear. It would have been better not to surprise your sister with attentions from men, but I hope she will be practical about this. In any case, there is no real time now. Perhaps you might take Lizzy into the dining room to help with the floral arrangements if they arrive early, but we must now make the best of the evening."

"Of course, Aunt. That is a good idea."

Jane and Madeline were descending the final stairs just as the door was opened to the first guests. Thankfully, it was the Darcy party.

"Lizzy! I am so glad to see you!" Jane rushed to her sister and enveloped her in a hug before the housekeeper could even take her shawl.

Elizabeth chuckled and patted her sister on the back. "I am always glad to see you too, Jane, but we were here just a few days ago for tea." Pulling back, Elizabeth looked at Jane's face. There was something in her expression that Elizabeth could not place.

Madeline and Edward stepped forward to greet the Darcy siblings. "Mr. Darcy. Miss Darcy. We are so happy to have you tonight. I hope you will not mind that Jane and I were still working on the flower arrangements and final touches to dinner."

Darcy bowed to his hosts. "Of course, we understand. Please, continue with your preparations."

"Oh yes! Maybe I can be of some help. I like arranging flowers more than most other tasks. Do you have need of me?" Georgiana's eyes shone.

"Miss Darcy, that is a kind offer. Perhaps you might join me in the parlour while Lizzy helps Jane in the dining room." Madeline sent Jane a pointed look, which Elizabeth did not miss.

Elizabeth accompanied Jane into the dining room to finish placing the various vases filled with flowers upon the table and to light the candles about the room. Feeling the weight of the silence, Elizabeth waited until Jane was ready to speak.

Finally, Jane took the opportunity to speak. "Lizzy, I'm so glad you have been able to come this evening. I believe that it will be a wonderful opportunity to make new friends."

"Of course, I shall always have time for my family, Jane," Elizabeth replied, without looking up from her flame. "The Darcys may have a busy social schedule, but all are agreed that making time for one's close friends is much better than sitting through a dinner party given by mere acquaintances who only want the wealthiest guests gracing their table."

"I am glad to hear it. We were actually surprised that the Darcys decided to accompany you tonight. Surely, they will not find equals amongst tonight's guests."

Elizabeth looked up at this remark. "Whatever do you mean, Jane? Mr. Bingley will be here, and he is Will… eh… Mr. Darcy's closest friend. Also, I believe Mr. Darcy said he is friendly with Mr. Bingley's friend, Mr. Tannerbaugh." Elizabeth turned back to her task quickly, to cover her faux pas. "They were all at Cambridge together, were they not?"

Jane looked at the back of her sister's head with a furrowed brow. Did she really hear her sister nearly call Darcy by his Christian name? And a shortened version of it at that? Perhaps it was nothing. Elizabeth was on such intimate terms with Georgiana, and they certainly seemed to be as close as two unrelated women could be. Maybe Elizabeth was used to hearing Georgiana address him informally, or maybe Darcy was less formal in his home than Jane would have imagined. But, perhaps there was something else going on between her sister and her handsome employer. Jane decided not to press that issue tonight with a house full of guests set to arrive any moment, but she stored it away to discuss with Madeline and Bingley.

Jane continued with her plan. "Yes, of course, Mr. Darcy is friendly with several of the guests tonight, but I do hope that you will be able to relinquish your post as companion for the night and take the time to make an impression upon the young men in attendance."

Now it was Elizabeth's turn to furrow her brow. "Why ever would I need to make an impression upon the guests? Are they not Uncle's business associates and potential new investors brought by Mr. Bingley?"

"No, Lizzy." Jane flushed. "While perhaps they are also those things, each young man has been invited tonight with the specific purpose of meeting you."

"But, what interest can they have in me?" Elizabeth flushed, beginning to suspect her sister's purpose. "You do not mean to bring me suitors, do you Jane? When did you turn into Mamma? Please tell me that Uncle's guests have not been so bluntly spoken to as to expect my attentions tonight!" Elizabeth was near a panic. Darcy would not be happy with this expectation for the evening, and the last thing she needed was for her protective and slightly jealous husband to betray their affection in mixed company.

Jane could see the worry on her sister's face but could not fathom from where it came. Elizabeth had always been the one of them that was able to laugh in the face of their mother's schemes and continue as if nothing was amiss. Panic was not an emotion Jane was used to seeing in Elizabeth's expressive eyes. "Calm yourself, Lizzy. Of course, no such suggestion has been made to the gentlemen. That would be highly inappropriate. But each has been chosen specifically for his suitability for you." Jane decided a little equivocating was in order. "And Mary, of course."

"And what of their suitability for you, dear Jane?" This question was to go unanswered as the front door knocker was clearly heard before Jane could find her voice.

Back in the parlour, the whole party began to assemble. Instead of allowing Jane to steer her towards the gentlemen who had arrived with Bingley, Elizabeth made her way directly to Edward and Darcy. They were sitting in a conveniently secluded section of the room.

"Uncle, I have yet to greet you properly. It is good to see you again. Have you been having an enjoyable talk with my husband?" Elizabeth kept her voice low, since the possibility of being overheard was great, but speaking the truth with one of the few people who knew their situation eased her worry considerably. Uncle Edward was her guardian, and he would protect her publicly, even when Darcy could not.

"Yes, my dear. William and I have been having a nice chat. Did you and Jane have any time to catch up before the guests arrived?" Edward had been trying to gently dissuade Jane and Madeline from their matchmaking schemes, but it was hard to do without giving away too much.

"Yes, Uncle, we had a most enlightening talk just now." Before Elizabeth could continue, Jane, Bingley, and a Mr. Andrew Tannerbaugh came to greet their host and be introduced.

"Darcy, old man, how amazing to find you here! It has been an age since we last met. I am sure it's been three years if it's been a day. How are you?" Tannerbaugh came straight up to shake Darcy's hand and get a better look at Jane's beautiful sister. Bingley had spoken in the carriage of his courtship of the eldest Miss Bennet, but also mentioned that two of her younger sisters would be in attendance tonight. Jane was certainly beautiful in a classic and serene sort of way. But Tannerbaugh enjoyed a livelier disposition, and he was interested in the description Bingley had given of a young woman of wit and humour.

"Tannerbaugh, I was not about to miss this evening once Bingley mentioned your inclusion in the invitations." Darcy smiled genuinely at his old friend from university. Tannerbaugh was a man close to Bingley's disposition and had always been able to lift Darcy's mood. However, if Darcy had been able to hear the thoughts running through the younger man's head, he likely would not have made the introductions so readily. "I am well, very well indeed. Let me introduce you to our host for the evening and a good friend of mine, Mr. Edward Gardiner. Edward, this is Andrew Tannerbaugh. He, Charles, and I were at Cambridge together."

After the men bowed and shook hands, Darcy turned to Elizabeth. "Also allow me to introduce one of Edward's nieces, Miss Elizabeth Bennet. Miss Elizabeth is also a good friend to my family and currently a member of my household as companion to my sister." Darcy delivered the introduction, which had been carefully crafted and practiced over the last several weeks, for the first time. It was still a bit awkward, but no one suspected it was a lie.

This was the opening Tannerbaugh had been waiting for. "Miss Elizabeth, it is a pleasure to make your acquaintance." He bowed low over Elizabeth's hand and ghosted a kiss over her knuckles.

Elizabeth withdrew her hand as soon as politely possible. "Thank you, Mr. Tannerbaugh. I understand that you are a long-time acquaintance of Mr. Darcy and Mr. Bingley. I would not want to burden your reminiscing. I believe that I shall provide some entertainment while we wait for dinner to be announced."

With that, Elizabeth curtsied and quickly retreated to the pianoforte. She played softly while the remainder of the guests filtered into the parlour, effectively ensuring that there would be no more introductions before the dinner call. Jane was mildly annoyed at her sister's uncharacteristic retreat, but she reasoned that Elizabeth was uncomfortable being introduced to eligible young men with expectations. Perhaps she would become more accustomed to the idea during dinner. Jane had carefully chosen the seating so that Elizabeth was placed between Tannerbaugh and one of Edward's business associates, Mr. Carter. A third young man, Mr. Slaughter, who was a respectable London barrister, was seated directly across from her sister. Elizabeth would have the opportunity to converse with as many of the eligible men in attendance as possible.

So, it was quite a surprise when Jane looked down the table and saw Elizabeth sitting directly between Darcy and Edward! Jane was sure that she had placed Georgiana in that seat, thinking that the ever-protective Darcy would not want his baby sister, newly out in society, to be sitting near young men not of his intimate acquaintance. But clear as day, Elizabeth was sitting in a seat so far removed from any of the eligible guests that she would not be able to even hear their conversations, let alone participate in them. In Elizabeth's intended seat resided Mary, and in the seat originally designated for Mary sat Georgiana, across from her brother and next to the sister of Mr. Carter.

Elizabeth chanced a look down the table and met her sister's annoyed glare. She knew that Jane had put in a lot of effort to this party, but Elizabeth was in no mood to entertain suitors. After Jane revealed her intentions for the evening, Elizabeth had switched the place cards for herself, Mary and Georgiana. Catching a glimpse of Jane's countenance for himself, Edward chuckled at his nieces' respective scheming.

At least not all of Jane's effort would be wasted. Mary would get the chance intended for Elizabeth. Their younger sister had changed dramatically in the last few months. No longer subjected to their mother's constant references to Mary's plainness, the most conservative Bennet sister had found her own beauty. It also helped that Madeline was gently teaching Mary about dressing her hair in conservative but appealing fashions. Their aunt had also taken Mary shopping and found several styles that suited Mary but were more flattering than those she had sewn herself. All in all, the "plain" Bennet sister was not looking so plain in the glittering candlelight.

Dinner progressed slowly but with lively conversation all around the table. Mary found a fellow music lover in the kind Mr. Slaughter; Georgiana and Miss Elaine Carter spoke of the activities surrounding their formal debuts, both of which would be taking place in early May. Elizabeth, Darcy, and Edward had a lovely talk about all kinds of topics.

The only conversation which was stilted was between Madeline, Jane, and Bingley at the opposite end of the table from Edward, Elizabeth, and Darcy.

The former three kept an eagle eye on the conversation of the latter, especially on the interaction between Elizabeth and Darcy. None could say that they crossed any lines of propriety, but their friendly banter and frequent mild laughter was a sign that the two were comfortable in each other's presence. Jane began to worry about the implications of Elizabeth's earlier slip in the dining room, while Bingley mused that he had never seen Darcy so at ease during a dinner party with persons unknown. Madeline worried about another scandal for the Bennet sisters. At least Edward was continuously involved with their conversation and could observe them from a close vantage point. Madeline resolved to ask her husband about his impression of their relationship that evening after all the guests had gone.

When the last of the plates were cleared away, Madeline invited the ladies to the parlour for tea while Edward invited the men to stay for brandy and cigars. With the ladies departed, most of the men gathered closer to Edward's end of the table and spoke at length of the imports business. Darcy especially was fascinated with the tradesmen in attendance who had been to China or India during their early years working for their fathers or the East India Trading Co. It was a long time after the last of the cigar butts were extinguished before Bingley could introduce the idea of re-joining the ladies.

As the men filed out of the dining room, Bingley held Darcy back. "Darcy, you must not monopolize the male conversation in the parlour. Jane and Mrs. Gardiner have put a lot of thought into this night, and you are getting in the way of the introductions."

Darcy was taken aback. He thought the night had gone on swimmingly so far and was contemplating a few new investments with the tradesmen to which he had been introduced. "What introductions are you talking about? I have already been introduced to each of the men here tonight and cannot see how my conversation with them has hindered the evening."

"Surely you know why these ***eligible*** men have been invited to dinner?" A blank stare was all that answered Bingley. "They are here to meet Miss Lizzy and Miss Mary, not to talk business with a potential investor. Your sister will not need a companion forever, and then what do you expect Miss Lizzy to do?"

"You cannot be serious. What does Edward have to say about all this?" Darcy's panic and anger battled for dominance. His first impulse was to storm into the parlour, grab his wife, and leave immediately.

"Jane confided that her uncle is not at all concerned with Miss Lizzy's prospects. In fact, she feels he is oddly opposed to making introductions for her." Darcy let out some of the tension in his shoulders at this. Of course, Edward would not be supporting schemes to marry off his wife to someone else. "But nevertheless, both Jane and Miss Lizzy are now over twenty-one and can make their own choices about whom to marry. I have assured Jane that any or all of her sisters are most welcome to live with us forever, but would you not rather Miss Lizzy be happy with a home of her own?"

"I can assure you, Charles, I spend a great deal of time considering Elizabeth's happiness and marital felicity every day." Darcy rushed out of the room without even noticing his mistake in speaking about Elizabeth in such a familiar tone.

But Bingley noticed.

# Chapter 13

## Questions and Answers

***Gracechurch Street, Cheapside, London***
***30 April 1813***

Edward Gardiner sat in his study with a terrible headache. Andrew Tannerbaugh had been to call on his wife and nieces nearly every day since his introduction to the Bennet sisters at Jane's dinner party the prior week. The young man's goal was to catch a day where Elizabeth was visiting with the family. This morning was likely to be the day for that unpleasant occurrence.

Elizabeth had sent word early to Madeline and Jane that she was free for the morning, since Georgiana would be visiting with her good friend Lady Miranda. Elizabeth would see Georgiana to the Stanley townhouse then come to the Gardiner residence for a nice long visit. Little did she know that Tannerbaugh was likely to intrude on her precious family time.

After the dinner party last week, as soon as the door had closed on their last dinner guest, Madeline and Jane had turned on Edward, demanding to know what was going on with Elizabeth and Darcy. Apparently, Elizabeth's lack of cooperation in meeting any of the eligible men and the obvious familiarity between them did not go unnoticed. It was all Edward could do to dissemble about their relationship and insist that he had seen no evidence of impropriety.

Seeing the evening through the eyes of his wife and niece, it was easy to guess at the true affection Elizabeth and Darcy felt for each other. However, that open affection in their situation as employee and employer would ruin Elizabeth.

Edward had sent a warning letter to the Darcys early the next morning, detailing both the schemes and concerns swirling around the Gardiner residence. A reply had been sent with their thanks and a plan by Elizabeth to only come on mornings that were not Madeline's calling day to minimize the possibility that she would meet any would-be suitors. Unfortunately, Madeline and Jane could not be stopped, and Tannerbaugh was focused on having his chance with Elizabeth. One could only pray that the situation did not devolve into a debacle.

At the sound of the heavy front door knocker, Edward rose from his desk and proceeded into the parlour. If he could not stop the uncomfortable situation, he would at least be present to mitigate the damage.

***Darcy House, Mayfair, London***

The Darcys' London house staff were in a state near panic. They had not witnessed such a scene as what took place this morning since the day, nearly two years ago, that had brought news of an alarming nature concerning Georgiana and a Mr. Wickham. Having long ago relieved themselves of that particular worry, and spending the last six months receiving letters from Pemberley detailing, then seeing for themselves, the marked joy in all three Darcys since their master's wedding, many had forgotten how incredibly fierce Darcy could be when provoked.

And Caroline Bingley had certainly provoked Darcy.

"Connor! Have my horse saddled, and bring my riding coat and hat!"

The provocation had come in an innocent enough package, just a small, folded invitation delivered shortly after ten a.m. by one of the Hurst footmen. It was an invitation to a dinner party that night at the Hurst townhouse in Kensington. It was even addressed in Mrs. Louisa Hurst's hand instead of Caroline's. But the inside revealed Caroline's overly ornate script. More in the style of a letter than an invitation, Caroline ruminated on how wonderful it would be to have one last, quiet *family* dinner before Georgiana's court presentation in the morning. If it had stopped there, perhaps Darcy would have rolled his eyes at her stressing of the word 'family,' since the Darcys were not family to either the Bingleys or the Hursts. But the final line made Darcy's blood boil.

Elizabeth was not invited.

Not only was she not listed on the front of the invitation, either by name or by position as would be expected for a social companion, she was, in fact, specifically called out in the body of the note as unexpected. Even though Caroline used some flowery language about giving 'Miss Eliza' a night off to dine with her 'Cheapside relations' before her duties consumed her waking hours, the message was clear. No lowly servants allowed. The Hursts were expecting only two Darcys to dinner.

Additionally, Lady Sefton was expected, along with Hurst's older brother and sister-in-law. It would be rude to bring an unexpected guest. Darcy did not want to insult the most influential patroness of Almack's the very week he was expecting his sister's application for membership to be reviewed. His first reaction had been to decline outright, but Bingley knew he did not have dinner plans for the night, which meant that Caroline likely knew. And if he refused an invitation from such close friends when he had no other obligation, he again risked insulting the Bingleys and the Hursts, including Lady Sefton, by association. No, he would have to go to dinner at the Hursts, without his wife, and probably endure the not-so-thin barbs to Elizabeth's person from their de facto hostess. Perhaps he could orchestrate an early departure, since they must be formally dressed and in the palace presentation hall early the next morning.

But, despite his forced pleasantries that evening, he still planned to express his fury with Caroline to Bingley.

Darcy still had not quite forgiven his friend for the intervention at the Gardiner's dinner party last week. Even if Darcy could understand Jane and Bingley's intentions, he still did not like having other men look at his wife with an appraising eye. Elizabeth had taken the whole event with her usual aplomb, though she had admitted later that night in their bed that she had been uncomfortable all evening, knowing about the schemes being advanced by her own family. The mothers and sisters of the eligible men present had not been subtle during the ladies' social time, asking Elizabeth and Mary many personal questions. The only saving grace was knowing that Edward would never let anything get out of hand in his home.

Now, the Bingleys were once again getting in the middle of the Darcys' affairs, and Darcy was not going to take it quietly! Intellectually, he knew that Bingley had nothing to do with the invitation to dinner tonight nor Caroline's direct snub to his wife, but he had allowed his sister to chase after the Darcy fortune for long enough.

"Your outer things, sir." Connor appeared with Darcy's riding apparel.

"Yes, thank you. One moment please." Darcy hastily scribbled an acceptance for the Hursts and thrust the note into the hands of one of his footmen. "Make sure this gets back to the Hurst townhouse as soon as possible."

The young footman nearly tripped trying to get the note from the master's hand and take it to Kensington.

"Mr. Simpson, I need you to inform my sister and wife of the evening's plans as soon as they arrive home. Miss Darcy and I will be going to the Hursts for dinner. Unfortunately, Mrs. Darcy will not be joining us, and I expect the staff to take every care of her in my absence."

Simpson, the long-time butler for the Darcy family, bowed low. "Of course, sir. Mrs. Darcy shall be in want of nothing all evening."

"Good. Please also have Mrs. Simpson direct Cook to prepare some lemon biscuits. They are her favourite."

"Absolutely, sir."

Darcy glanced at the clock in the entry. It was now nearly eleven a.m. Wanting to leave before the calling hour, he turned and walked out of the back door to the mews. With a flurry, Incitatus was taking the first strides away from the Darcy stables as the grandfather clock in the vestibule began to chime the hour and Caroline rapped on the front door knocker.

Connor was standing on the landing of the stairs leading to the family wing when Simpson opened the front door.

"Good morning, Miss. May I help you."

Caroline turned up her nose at the Darcys' butler. She did not like the man's officious manner. "I would like to call upon Mr. and Miss Darcy."

"I am sorry, Miss, none of the family is home. If you would please leave your card, I will inform the family of your visit when they return."

Caroline's expression turned sour, and then the lady actually stamped her foot. "That cannot be true! I know for certain that he intended to be home today. You know who I am! I expect you to let me in the door this minute and tell your master that I have come to call. He will certainly see me, even if he is declining general visitors. I am not just any caller but one of his closest friends!" Caroline was practically yelling by the end of her tantrum.

"I am sorry, Miss, as I said, none of the family is home. Mr. Darcy left for his club, and the ladies of the house are out this morning, visiting. But if you would leave your card, I will place it on the silver tray for when the family returns."

Several servants abandoned the pretence of doing their duties to blatantly stare at the confrontation in the doorway when Caroline began outright shouting at the stone-faced butler. "What do you mean, he's left for White's? How can he have decided to change his plans and leave in under an hour? I do not believe you. Let me in this minute!"

"Madam, I assure you that the master has left and is not at this moment in this house. I cannot speak to his change of plans, as Mr. Darcy comes and goes as he pleases. It is my job as his butler to accommodate every whim he chooses to entertain in an efficient manner. Now, it is not the practice of the Darcys to allow guests during their absence. If you would please leave your card, I will gladly let the family know of your visit when they arrive home." Simpson stood like a statue in the doorway, giving the annoying woman no room to look into the house or push past him into the foyer.

"You had better start thinking about your situation and asking for introductions to gentry in need of a butler, for when I am mistress of this house, you will not spend one more day in its residence!" Caroline's face now sported a very unattractive shade of red that clashed with the colour of her hair. Connor bit his knuckles to keep from laughing out loud.

Simpson was in no way intimidated by this display. Secure in the knowledge that Elizabeth would, God willing, be mistress of Darcy house for a long time after the elderly butler departed this life, he replied evenly, "Should you ever become mistress of this house, I will gladly walk out its front door and follow the Darcys to wherever they have chosen to relocate, for you cannot seriously believe my master would ever marry you. Good day, madam." And with that, Simpson closed the door with a loud thud, turned the heavy lock so that it would be audible from the outside, and strode off towards the servants' quarters for a much-needed glass of brandy.

Connor decided it was time to take a trip to Belgravia. Despite the general rule that what happed inside the Darcys' residence stayed there, he was certain his brother and Bingley needed to know about this confrontation. Besides, even though Simpson had told Caroline that Darcy was at White's, in truth he was on his way to the Bingley townhouse. It would not do for Caroline to go home and find her brother and Darcy having words. If he took a fast horse and kept to the alleys, avoiding the crowded fashionable streets of Hyde Park, he could arrive before Darcy and convince Bingley to head to White's. Then they would both be out of reach of the red-headed shrew before her carriage could make it back to Wilton Row.

Dashing out of the back door, Connor found that his father, Darcy House's stable master, already had a horse saddled and waiting for him.

***Gracechurch Street, Cheapside, London***

Andrew Tannerbaugh was the first to arrive at the Gardiner residence promptly as the great clock in the foyer struck eleven a.m. He knew from Madeline's note that Elizabeth, or Miss Lizzy as her family called her, would be calling sometime just after eleven. Upon confirming that only Madeline, Jane, and Mary were seated in the parlour, Tannerbaugh decided to take the opportunity to speak with Edward privately. Even though Elizabeth was of age, it was a good idea to speak to her uncle before coming to an understanding in his home.

"Mr. Gardiner, thank you again for allowing me to grace your home. I was hoping to speak to you for a moment before joining the ladies."

Edward was surprised at the young man's request, but he saw this as an opportunity to head off the coming confrontation before it began. "Mr. Tannerbaugh, I would be happy to entertain you in my study. Please, come this way."

Tannerbaugh mistook Edward's inviting demeanour as confirmation of his acceptance as a suitor for Elizabeth and began speaking before the door to the study was fully closed. "Mr. Gardiner, you can make no mistake as to my purpose today. I know your wife and niece have encouraged my intentions, and the only thing left is to come to a formal understanding. As a man of twenty-six, I have waited for a while to find a woman worthy of my affections. While I have not known Miss Lizzy for long, I am convinced that we would make a wonderful match. She is beautiful and poised with a lively spirit. Her status as a gentlewoman would ease my introduction into society, and our sons would be the grandsons of a gentleman. I have a generous inheritance coming to me when my father passes and I intend to purchase an estate in Kent as soon as an agreement can be made with the seller. In fact, marriage to a gentlewoman may expedite those negotiations. So, sir, I ask for your blessing to speak with Miss Lizzy privately, today, with the intention of proposing marriage."

Edward took a moment to gather his thoughts while he poured two glasses of scotch from the decanter. "Mr. Tannerbaugh, I have many things to say about your purpose here today, and none of them are what you likely wish to hear. First, I would refrain from addressing my niece so informally. She would take offense to someone outside her intimate circle calling her any variation of Lizzy, and she most definitely hates to be called Eliza, so do not try that either. Second, while I am aware of my wife and Jane's desires for Elizabeth, I do not share them. My niece is perfectly happy with her situation, and I happen to know that she is not looking to alter her position at this time."

Edward took a fortifying sip of his scotch before continuing. "Finally, my niece is a passionate young woman and has often said that only the deepest of love could induce her to matrimony. You speak of a marriage of convenience, mostly your own convenience, which offers her only wealth and an upscale London neighbourhood address. While many women of her station might jump at such an offer, Elizabeth will not. Since you have only been introduced to the lady once at a crowded dinner party, I do not believe that Elizabeth will be receptive to your suit. I cannot give you my blessing to ask for her hand, and I would advise you not to make such an offer."

Tannerbaugh was at a loss. "I understand your concern about your niece's feelings. Perhaps I should change my offer to one of formal courtship, so that we may become better acquainted before we become engaged. You are right that the last week has not afforded me the opportunity to keep company with Miss Elizabeth that I would have wished. I must admit that I am a bit surprised that you would not welcome a suitor for one of your orphaned nieces. Their care must be costing you a great deal with the loss of revenue from their father's estate."

"I assure you, young man, I am more than able to care for all of my family. The expense is not a burden on me at all." Edward swirled his drink in his glass then met the younger man's eye.

Tannerbaugh huffed and set aside his tumbler of scotch. "Then why would you allow Miss Elizabeth to take a position with the Darcys and risk losing her status as a gentlewoman?"

Edward was not in the mood to have his decisions questioned by this young social climber. "My niece was determined to find a position and was two weeks from her twenty-first birthday when Mr. Darcy and I signed her employment contract. If I had not agreed, she would have left on her birthday and taken the first position offered to her." Edward set his glass down and put his hand on the doorknob. "Now, I believe that we have exhausted this topic. I suggest that we join the ladies."

But Tannerbaugh was not going to let Edward have the last word. He stood and faced the older man with hands on his hips. "As you have rightly pointed out, Miss Elizabeth is of age. She no longer needs anyone's permission to marry and can entertain any suitor she wishes. If she was so determined to take a position, then she might be more inclined than you believe to be securely married and mistress of her own home. I regret that you are so dismissive of your niece's welfare, but I shall not be deterred. My purpose stands. We shall see what Miss *Lizzy* thinks of my offer." With that, Tannerbaugh picked up his glass, drained the remaining scotch in one gulp, then left the study, slamming the door behind him.

Edward picked up his glass and also drained the last drops. *Oh, lord,* he thought, *help us all survive Lizzy's reaction to this.*

***White's Gentleman's Club, St. James Street, London***

Darcy strode into the front parlour of White's with a determined look on his face. He had been turned away at the Bingley residence by the butler, saying Bingley had left for White's to meet another gentleman acquaintance for a few hands at the gaming tables. Before turning back to his horse, Darcy caught a glimpse of who he thought was Connor in the back hall talking to his older brother. Connor had definitely been at home when Darcy left over thirty minutes ago. Surely there was no way his valet could have beaten him here. The streets of London had been an absolute mess given the hour and the fact that much of the *ton* had finally arrived in town with the official start of the season tomorrow. Darcy had been forced to speak to several acquaintances strolling along Rotten Row before finally making his way to the south entrance of the park.

Oh well. It did not really matter what his valet was doing since his services were not needed for several hours. Turning from the house, Darcy quickly headed off towards St. James Street. Bingley was indeed in the front parlour, where non-member visitors were admitted to wait for their party to arrive. He had given Darcy's name as the member upon whom he was waiting, since he was truly not meeting anyone else, and the staff was accustomed to seeing him in Darcy's presence. But he at least feigned surprise at Darcy's arrival, mere seconds after he had taken a seat in one of the great wingback chairs.

"Darcy, what a pleasant surprise. Care to join Bristol and me for cards and luncheon?" Bingley reasoned that it did not matter whose name he threw out, since Darcy was likely to demand a private audience in one of the smoking rooms.

"No Charles, I do not plan to entertain the tables today, and I must insist that you disappoint our good friend as well. I have some important, private, business to discuss with you."

"All right. I am sure I will not be much missed, as there was going to be a group playing. If anyone asks after me, the staff will surely tell them that we've gone upstairs to discuss business in private." Bingley nodded at the footman in the room, who gave a curt bow in acceptance of the message that would never be delivered.

As soon as a waiter set two tumblers of scotch down on the table in a private parlour between the two men, Darcy rounded on his long-time friend and began to vent his frustrations. "Charles, what is the meaning of your sister excluding Elizabeth from the dinner party tonight? It is completely ridiculous and extremely rude! Georgiana will be most uncomfortable all night, knowing that her best friend and companion is not at her side, besides being embarrassed at the snub directed at a lovely young woman who has every right to be recognized by our friends and family. It is not to be born!"

Bingley had only met Darcy's aunt, Lady Catherine de Bourgh, once, but the experience had been memorable. He was suddenly struck with the family resemblance. "Darcy, do you not think that a night off to see her family might be nice for Miss Elizabeth? She cannot live her life at your beck and call all the time."

"She is not at my beck and call! She is a valued member of my household and treated with respect. If she wants to visit her family, she is always welcome to take the carriage, and Georgiana enjoys visiting with the Gardiners as well. We would never demand so much from Elizabeth that she should feel the need for a night off." Darcy was so infuriated from the events of the last week that he was beginning to forget himself.

Bingley had always been suspicious of Darcy's admiration of Elizabeth. Perhaps it was time someone blatantly asked him about his intentions. "Darcy, do you love Miss Elizabeth? Will you ever marry her, given that much of the *ton* will assume she was your mistress before becoming your wife?"

Darcy stopped short and all the fight drained out of him. Trying for a nonchalance he did not feel, he replied, "Why would you ask such a thing?"

"Come off it man, you have been in love with Miss Elizabeth since we all danced at Netherfield. If you had done something about that a year ago, perhaps the Bennets would not be in such a poor position now. Or if I had not listened to you and Caroline at the time, I would have been in a position to help their family after Mr. Bennet's death. You cannot tell me today, after spending all evening mooning over her at the Gardiners in full company last week, that you do not love her. The question I have for you is what are you going to do about it?"

Darcy sat and stared at his best friend, second to only his cousin Richard. It was easy to forget that Bingley was such a bright and observant person because he played the flippant fop so well. *Now what should I say?* Darcy wanted nothing more than to run to Elizabeth's side so that she could tell him what to do. This was a decision they really should make together, but he did not have that luxury. Bingley was waiting. Since it was unlikely that he was going to completely fool his friend, he decided something of the truth was the best option.

"Yes Charles, I love her. I have never wanted to deny it, but think what Lord Matlock would say if I married the sister of a woman ruined by George

Wickham. And I know what Lady Catherine would say. She still holds the delusion that I will marry my cousin, Anne. Until Georgiana is well settled, I cannot risk the Darcy name. After my sister is happy with a good man, I shall turn to my own happiness."

"And will Miss Elizabeth wait until such time as Miss Darcy is settled? How many years must she wait while her reputation becomes more tenuous? Today, she is the daughter of a deceased gentleman. She can use her upbringing to attract a man of at least modest wealth who wants an introduction into the gentry. In a few years, she will be nothing but a gently bred servant, unsuitable for marriage by any man in the *ton* and most of the wealthy merchant class. If you will not, or cannot, marry her, what will she do?" Bingley's words were pointed, but his tone was soft.

Darcy looked up from his glass, directly into Bingley's eyes and spoke with passion. "I will marry her. Elizabeth Darcy will be my wife and I will be truly happy for the first time since my mother died. Until the day I can make this known to the world, I shall provide her a home and the respectability that comes from the protection of the Darcy name. I will never look at another woman or offer for another. Georgiana and I treat her as a member of our family and already show her the respect due as my wife. I understand how this may look to the members of our social sphere, but I cannot find the desire to apologize."

"Have you spoken of this to Miss Elizabeth?"

"Yes, and her uncle Edward." Darcy nodded his head and stared into his scotch. "We have kept out intentions from the rest of her family to protect her other sisters. Additionally, Elizabeth fears her mother's demands if our understanding were to become known. I have been supplying Edward with money, Elizabeth's 'salary,' for the purpose of establishing a new home for Mrs. Bennet and some dowry for Miss Bennet, Miss Mary and Miss Kitty."

"What possible excuse can you provide for keeping all this from Jane, especially after learning of her fears for her favourite sister?"

Darcy shifted in his chair and cleared his throat. "Elizabeth did not want to ask her gentle and good sister to keep such information from their mother. Perhaps you are right and given the new revelation of Jane's fears for Elizabeth's future, we should reconsider that decision."

Bingley blinked several times and shifted in his seat. After a long moment there was only one response he could make. "I see. Very well."

# Chapter 14

## Adding Injury to Insults

***Gracechurch Street, Cheapside, London***
***25 April 1813***

ELIZABETH WAS LOOKING FORWARD TO THE DAY WITH HER FAMILY. This would be a whole day without having to deal with scheming ladies trying to win her husband's money or mildly insulting questions about her family. She planned on finally interrogating Jane, in a nice way, about her relationship with Bingley and perhaps taking her young cousins to the park after luncheon to feed the ducks. As the carriage pulled up to the Gardiners' residence, Elizabeth looked forward to her boisterous cousins' greetings.

What greeted her instead was an overly familiar Andrew Tannerbaugh and a scowling Edward.

"Miss *Lizzy*, how wonderful to see you. It has been far too long since we have been in company." Tannerbaugh managed to secure Elizabeth's hand before she could respond, and bowed low. His lips made decidedly more than a brushing touch to the back of her knuckles.

Finding her voice, Elizabeth responded with a mildly scolding tone. "Mr. Tannerbaugh, it has been barely a week since my uncle's dinner party where we were initially introduced. I would say that is not long at all for persons of such little acquaintance." Finally breaking from Tannerbaugh's grasp, Elizabeth moved to Edward. "Uncle, I am so glad to see you. I have been looking forward to seeing my family for an extended visit. I was unaware that you had business associates to entertain today." Elizabeth emphasized *business*.

"Oh no, Miss Lizzy, I am not here to discuss business with your uncle. I have been invited by your aunt to spend the morning in the company of good friends." Tannerbaugh tried again to separate Elizabeth from her recalcitrant uncle by taking her hand to lead her into the parlour, but Elizabeth was not about to be handled by this man.

"I am delighted to hear you have become so acquainted with my aunt in merely five days. Perhaps you should enjoy your friends without my interference. I shall speak to my uncle for a few moments." Elizabeth and Edwards were about to head back to the study when Madeline finally came into the hall to stop her niece and husband from ruining Tannerbaugh's plans.

"Now, Lizzy, what nonsense is this? Mr. Tannerbaugh would not see your inclusion in our party as interference at all, I am sure. In fact, we were all saying the other day how much your lively presence would brighten the entire affair."

"Why, Aunt Maddie, how nice of you to include me. I see I must ask you for news of my mother, as it is obvious you have been exchanging letters with the lady. Tell me of the news in Meryton." Elizabeth's normally soft eyes were hard and cold as she sent the barb in her aunt's direction. Both Jane and Mary cringed, but could not disagree that their aunt's words sounded much like what their mother would say in the same situation. Perhaps it was as Mrs. Bennet had always said: finding good husbands for five daughters could change a person.

Elizabeth made a beeline for the empty seat on the settee by Jane, that their aunt had recently vacated. She safely placed herself between her sisters and took each of their hands in her own. Edward, Madeline, and Tannerbaugh entered shortly after Elizabeth, and each was at a loss as to where to sit. All the other seating in the room was designed to be slightly separated from the settee and slipper chair where Jane, Madeline, and Mary had previously been sitting to provide Elizabeth and Tannerbaugh some private conversation. Elizabeth had immediately noticed the re-arranged floor plan and was becoming more and more uncomfortable with the situation. Perhaps she should outright ask that her carriage be brought back around and invite her family to visit at Darcy House when they would be free from other social obligations. Jane and Madeline glanced at each other and inwardly sighed. This was not going well.

After a moment of awkward standing about, and overly enthusiastic questions from Elizabeth of her sisters, the maid brought in a lovely tea service. Jane hopped up to serve their guests and invited Tannerbaugh to take a seat. Never one to miss an opportunity, Tannerbaugh sat close to Elizabeth on the settee. Elizabeth's alarmed expression caused Edward to ignore his wife's invitation to sit with her on a sofa a bit removed from the young people. Instead, he dragged a chair across the floor to a position near his nieces and his guest. Madeline had to stop herself from stamping her foot in aggravation.

Mary was extremely confused, but could tell her sister Elizabeth was alarmed, her aunt was frustrated, her sister Jane was concerned, and her uncle was resigned somehow. Madeline had been so sure this morning that Elizabeth would welcome Tannerbaugh's presence, and perhaps there would even be an understanding of some kind between the two. Mary reasoned that if there was ever going to be any understanding, the fewer people witness to it, the better. She excused herself to go and check on the Gardiner children in their nursery.

Madeline also excused herself to check on the kitchen arrangements for dinner that evening. Jane decided to stay, since Elizabeth looked near a panic, but she placed herself on a seat closer to her uncle instead of taking the slipper chair, which had been vacated by Mary. Tannerbaugh decided that now was his opportunity to speak to Elizabeth.

"Lizzy, I…"

Elizabeth cut him off, immediately. "*Mr.* Tannerbaugh, I am sure you are a welcome friend to my aunt and uncle, but I have never given you leave to address me so informally. Please remember that I am a gentlewoman and will not tolerate being disrespected in such a way."

Some of the irritation of the morning seeped into Tannerbaugh's façade, and it is well known that angry people are not always wise. "Miss Elizabeth, I believe you will find that you are no longer a gentlewoman, but simply a gently bred servant. I have been trying to change that situation, but I will not tolerate such insolence from you when you are my wife."

"And when exactly do you believe that I shall be your wife, sir? So far, you have been barely introduced to me at a crowded dinner party, you have taken extreme liberties both with my person and my name on the second day we have ever been in company together, and now you have insulted me most grievously. I should like to never see your face again after this moment, and I can assure you that I shall never agree to be your wife!"

Elizabeth was shouting now, properly shouting. It was as if both the egotistical assurance from Collins's proposal and the insulting barbs from Darcy's first proposal were combined into one especially insulting moment. At least this delusional man had not taken forever to state his purpose.

Jane and Edward stared open mouthed at the couple sitting on the settee. It was unimaginable that Tannerbaugh had said such a thing. Perhaps he had been given too many assurances of her acceptance. Jane doubted again whether she and Madeline were correct to introduce Elizabeth to eligible men, when Tannerbaugh suddenly reached out and struck Elizabeth across the cheek.

The next moment lasted an eternity. Tears formed in Elizabeth's eyes as she held her palm to her face, but the ice and fire in her stare never faltered. Edward pulled the younger man to his feet roughly by the back of his cravat, choking him. Madeline, having entered the room just as Tannerbaugh's hand connected with Elizabeth's face, wheeled on her heels and opened the front door so her husband could throw the ruffian down the front steps without so much as one word.

Once her family was back in the parlour, Elizabeth spoke. "Aunt, if you will have a cold compress sent to me, I require a few minutes of rest before continuing with our visit. Perhaps, when I return, we can put all this scheming to rest. Uncle, I trust you to handle this in any way you see fit."

Elizabeth ascended the stairs without even a cursory glance back to her family.

Jane was nearly drowning in her own tears. "To think, we introduced Lizzy to that horrible man, not knowing his character! He struck her during their first conversation. Think what she might have endured had she actually been inclined to marry him!" Jane was shaking now and worrying a hole into her handkerchief.

"Calm yourself, Jane. Elizabeth was never in danger of marrying that man. She does not desire a suitor, and perhaps it is time that you both begin to trust me on this matter. I know what is best for Elizabeth, and it is not a man like Mr. Tannerbaugh," Edward gently chided his wife and niece.

"Yes, Edward. It seems that Lizzy is better off as she is now. I will let you handle this from now on. Jane, would you take Lizzy a cold compress while your uncle and I retire to the study for a while?"

"Of course, Aunt. I will go now."

Elizabeth was laying on the bed shared by Jane and Mary, silently weeping into Jane's pillowcase. The elder sister came to sit on the bedside and laid the cold compress gently on her younger sister's face. "Lizzy, I am so sorry for what has happened here today. I know that you have been unhappy about our attempts to find you a suitor, and we should never have encouraged Mr. Tannerbaugh against your wishes."

"No, Jane, you should not have. You know I have never wanted a husband simply for the sake of security, so why would you encourage one so much as to be expecting my acceptance?" The betrayal stung.

"I am worried about your future happiness and feeling guilty about your choice to take a position to save me from such a fate. I am the oldest. I should have been the one to become a governess and lose my position in society for the sake of my sisters. Instead, I entertain a courtship with Charles while you have lost everything to save us all." Jane couldn't stop herself from shedding sympathetic tears.

Elizabeth smiled at the inadvertent admission by her sister. "I have been hoping to hear confirmation of your understanding with Mr. Bingley. I am very glad for you! You will make a beautiful bride. If you do not think that the Pemberley garden is too far from London for the affair, I might say that the rose garden in the fall is quite picturesque."

"Lizzy! You cannot offer the use of someone else's house for such a thing as a wedding!"

"You are right, Jane, and if I was merely Georgiana's social companion, my offer would be highly inappropriate. But in truth, I am more than a servant in the Darcy household. I have kept this from you, believing it was better, but I can see I have only brought you pain." Elizabeth took a deep breath and sat up on the bed. "You must never tell anyone else, but I am not Miss Elizabeth Bennet any longer."

Jane's confusion turned to astonishment. She sat heavily on the hope chest at the end of the bed and was unable to find any words.

Reaching for her sister's hand to comfort her disquiet, Elizabeth continued. "William and I were married in a private ceremony in the Darcy family chapel on my birthday last. Uncle Edward signed the marriage settlement before we left London. Only he, Georgiana, Lydia, and the Darcy house servants know. We have come up with the story about my taking the position as Georgiana's companion to protect Georgiana during her coming out season. I am sorry I did not trust you with this earlier."

Suddenly, all of Elizabeth's, Darcy's, and Edward's previously baffling behaviour made much more sense. "Are you happy, Lizzy? Please tell me you have not sacrificed your own happiness still for our sakes. Especially after the regrettable events of this morning, I would have you do anything but marry without affection."

Elizabeth smiled from behind her cold compress. "I am happier than I have ever been."

A wide smile creased the corners of Jane's usually serene face. "Then, that is all that matters."

# Chapter 15

## Interference

***Gracechurch Street, Cheapside, London***
***30 April 1813—Immediately Following Mr. Tannerbaugh's Expulsion***

As soon as the door to Edward's study was firmly shut, Madeline turned on her husband. "I demand that you divulge whatever you and Lizzy have been keeping from me."

Edward sighed and poured himself another glass of scotch and his wife a glass of sherry. Elizabeth had given him permission to handle the situation 'as he saw fit,' and it was obvious that keeping secrets was only causing problems for them all. Madeline would understand the need to keep this information from their sister Bennet, and if Edward's instincts were correct, Elizabeth was having a similar conversation with Jane upstairs.

"My dear, Elizabeth and Darcy have been married since October."

Madeline sank to the settee, her face white with shock. After a moment, she took all of the sherry in her glass in one large swallow then handed her glass back to her husband to be refilled.

Edward continued, as he poured her another drink. "We knew it would be a scandal, and my sister Bennet would never be discreet enough to protect the family's reputation, so we have kept this from most of our family and acquaintance. As far as I know, only myself, Miss Darcy, and the Darcys' house servants, whom I am assured are all very loyal, have been trusted with this information. Now you know, and I presume that Lizzy is telling Jane at this moment."

"I see." Madeline was quickly regaining her colour. "That certainly changes the Bennets' situation."

Edward took another large sip of his own drink. "Although it does change the trajectory of their situation, it does not change the immediate future. Not until Miss Darcy is married or at least engaged. And hopefully, Jane will be married to Mr. Bingley before the end of the summer, so he may also help in the restoration of the family."

"I can certainly understand their desire for some privacy, but many young women marry soon after the death of a father for obvious financial reasons. Did Mr. Darcy truly fear his relations and peer connections so much that he demanded they keep this arrangement a secret during the season?" Madeline had no fewer fears for her niece now than when this conversation started, they were just different.

"No, Lizzy insisted." Edward shook his head. "She believed that Darcy's sister would be irreparably harmed by Lydia's situation. Darcy preferred a short engagement and the announcement of a *fait accompli* to his family, but she would not be swayed. Even now, with the difficulties in maintaining the facade, she has not wavered."

Madeline pinched the bridge of her nose. "Yes, that certainly sounds like our Lizzy. So, what are we to do now?"

"*WE* are going to allow Darcy to lead his own household, and listen to Lizzy when speaks of her wishes. Other than that, there is nothing we can do."

"Of course, you are right." Madeline smoothed her skirt, rose, and rang for the housekeeper. "One of the mews boys should go to find Darcy and bring him here. His wife being struck across the face is not something that should be kept from him."

The poor boy ran nearly all the way to the Darcy's townhouse, only to be told the master was at his club. When he had made the run to White's, he was told Darcy had left for his solicitor's office some thirty minutes ago. Another dash about town and the solicitor's page told the lad that Darcy had concluded his business quickly and already left for home. Knowing that it was important Darcy come to the Gardiners' home immediately, the boy once again made his way to Mayfair. For the last time, he found himself arriving right after his prey had left, but at least this time the gentleman had left for Cheapside. Simpson had informed his master of the summons from the Gardiners as soon as he crossed the threshold, and Darcy had turned right around, calling for a new horse to be saddled. The kindly old butler took pity on the poor boy, who nearly collapsed on the doorstep, and sent him down to the kitchens for a kip and something to eat.

Darcy was nearly sick with worry by the time he completed his mad dash to the Gardiners' home, fearing whatever had happened for them to send a summons. He did not wait for the Gardiner's butler, opening the front door himself in an attempt to get to Elizabeth all the sooner. Edward came out of his study at the sound of the front door and encountered a very agitated Darcy.

"Darcy, I am glad you have come. Please, let me pour you a brandy, or perhaps a scotch, in my study."

"I came as soon as I could. What has happened, Edward? Is Elizabeth well?" Darcy was in such a state, he did not realize that Madeline was in the room.

She stepped forward with a full glass of scotch. "Yes, Mr. Darcy. Lizzy is well but she has had a rough day today. She had an… unpleasant encounter this afternoon, which was in a large part my fault, for which I am very sorry indeed."

Darcy looked up at Madeline as he took a seat. "I do not understand. What happened?"

Edward and Madeline eyed each other warily. Neither was sure how to start the conversation. Madeline continued. "Well, do you remember Mr. Tannerbaugh?"

"Of course. He is an old acquaintance of mine from Cambridge. We only were there at the same time for two years, but I remember he was a capital fellow."

Edward cleared his throat, attempting to hide a snort.

Darcy looked at from Edward to Madeline.

"Yes, I am sure he is… a capital fellow… generally. However, today, there was a misunderstanding, and… well, he… you see… I am not sure exactly why, but he… well, he…" Madeline was twisting a handkerchief between her hands. The words would not come.

Edward placed his hands on her shoulders and she fell silent. "Mr. Tannerbaugh came here this morning for the express purpose of courting Lizzy. I tried to stop him from pursuing that purpose, but he would not be deterred. Their conversation did not go as he had planned, and Lizzy gave him an angry retort. He then struck her across the face."

Darcy launched out of his chair and walked back toward the front door before Edward could register his movement. Thankfully, Madeline caught up to him before he could leave.

"Mr. Darcy!" Madeline cried. "Where are you going?"

"I believe my first destination is to the sword chest in the Darcy House study to retrieve my grandfather's rapier, then I am going to kill Tannerbaugh without even the courtesy of first striking him with my glove!"

Edward was finally able to get around the displaced chairs and into the hall. "Darcy, please take a moment and breathe. I understand that you are enraged, and rightfully so. But engaging in a duel is what got us all into this precarious position. If my brother had not acted rashly, he might have lived and we could have saved Lydia, and the whole Bennet family, much grief."

"How can I allow this insult to go unchallenged?"

"I believe that Lizzy would rather you go upstairs to comfort her than commit murder for her honour. It would be more prudent if you did not end up in gaol."

"Fine. I insist on seeing her this instant." Darcy marched up the stairs to the bedchamber where Elizabeth and Jane were resting.

Both sisters had fallen into a doze, after their respective revelations, from the stress of the day. They were laying on the bed, facing each other with hands clasped, the compress resting on Elizabeth's cheek. Darcy stormed into the room, crashing the door against the wall, which jolted both sleeping sisters to wakefulness and sent Jane tumbling to the floor.

The alarmed expression on his wife's beautiful face finally penetrated Darcy's half-mad mind.

"Miss Bennet, please forgive me. Here, let me help you up. My interruption of your rest was inexcusable. I shall let you both return to sleep."

Jane waved him off. "No, no, Mr. Darcy. We were just dozing, and you must take some time to speak with your wife. I will return downstairs."

As Jane slipped out of the door and closed it, leaving only Elizabeth and Darcy inside, her words finally registered. Darcy made his way to the bed and took Elizabeth in his arms, feeling only relief at finally having her small frame resting against his larger one.

"My dearest love, I am sorry that I was not here to protect you today."

"Really, William, it was not your fault. While I am not happy with my sister and aunt for arranging the meeting with Mr. Tannerbaugh, I cannot fault them their hopes and fears for my future." She sighed and settled further into his warm embrace. "It is a dim reality, but many men view women just as property. I fear for Mr. Tannerbaugh's future wife. Then again, maybe today has changed the course of his mind."

"I wish to see him punished for his actions."

Elizabeth looked up at him and moved an errant curl away from his eyes. "Oh, no, my love. You cannot. And really, there is no need. I am not so fragile as to break. He will be banished from our thoughts, and after a night in your arms, I shall be fully well."

The grandfather clock down the stairs struck a much later hour than Darcy had realized, and he groaned. "I must apologize again, but Georgie and I are expected at dinner with the Hursts tonight." He took a deep breath. "You are not invited."

Elizabeth's eyes grew wide. "I am aware that Miss Bingley has a distaste for my company, but I did not know that Mrs. Hurst holds me in such contempt."

"I fear that this is all Miss Bingley's doing. It is to be a very small party, but also includes Lady Sefton. Georgie is not even officially out until tomorrow morning and has not had her invitation to Almack's. I fear offending the most influential patron by bringing an uninvited guest to the party."

"I agree, dear, that you did what you had to do. I shall be just fine at home tonight." Elizabeth's eyes danced. "Perhaps Marianne will consent to play some cards with me. I am supposed to be one of the servants, and it is high time I started acting like it." Elizabeth stroked Darcy's face and smiled, trying to dispel the pained look in his eyes.

"Are you sure that we cannot stop this charade before anyone else tries to harm you? I believe your sisters here and aunt are now in our confidence. Perhaps we can weather this storm together."

Elizabeth sighed and sat up from the bed. She considered his proposal but was ultimately unconvinced. "No, I do not think we should change course yet. Although Jane and Madeline are in our confidence, Mary is yet unaware. Besides, we have already weathered my introduction on Bond Street. It will be just a few weeks until we can put this all behind us. I heard from Jane today that Mr. Bingley has spoken up. He hopes to marry Jane as soon as my mother's year of mourning is over. When they are safely married, we can reveal the truth. Until then, I will have to endure treatment as a servant, and you must endure the solicitous attentions of Miss Bingley and the other ladies."

"Very well, but there shall be no more conditions on this." Darcy placed both hands on Elizabeth's shoulders and his eyes searched hers. "The minute Bingley signs the register, we will announce our marriage. Even if Georgie is not yet secure or something else happens with one of your sisters or mother, I will wait not one moment later."

"Yes, dear." Elizabeth laughed. "I am sure that Jane will be very happy to share her wedding breakfast with us. Perhaps you shall serve as Mr. Bingley's witness, so that as soon as the ink is down you can turn to the congregation and shout it out, or will you at least allow them to make it out of the church?"

Darcy's eyes twinkled in response. "Impertinent woman! You understand my meaning, but just as punishment I believe I shall make a formal, loud announcement in front of the church following the Bingley wedding. Your sister and my friend are the most generous of souls, and I am sure they will not mind. Now, let us ask your most kind sister to accompany us home so that you need not play Vingt-Un with the servants. I will have you safe and well entertained this evening."

Elizabeth stood and took his proffered arm. "Lead the way, Mr. Darcy."

***Hurst House, Kensington, London***
***30 April 1813—The Dinner Hour***

If Darcy's day had been stressful, his night was outright rage-filled. The Hurst dinner party was indeed small, only ten individuals in all, including Louisa and Reginald Hurst, Reginald's brother the Elder Mr. Hurst and his wife Mrs. Hurst, Charles Bingley, Caroline Bingley, Lady Sefton, Lady Sefton's companion, Darcy, and Georgiana. With so few persons, it was impossible for either Darcy or Georgiana to avoid Caroline. Immediately upon their arrival, she attached herself to them. She prattled on about Georgiana's presentation in the morning and the ball in two days, asking far too many questions than was strictly polite in mixed company. Finally, she came to the crux of her extended dissertation on the subject: Caroline offered, in the most dissembling way possible, to help with the last-minute details for both events.

"I am sure that your aunt, the Lady Matlock, has everything well in hand, but it is always nice to have *experienced* help when executing such important events. I am sure that she is feeling the stress of having naught but Miss Eliza to help her." Caroline waved her hand about and nearly struck Georgiana in the face. "I doubt Eliza has even seen St. James's Palace, let alone been inside for presentations."

Georgiana's ire at the treatment of her sister reared in full force at Caroline's degrading comments.

"In matter of fact, you are quite wrong, Miss Bingley. Miss Elizabeth was presented at court when she was sixteen by her father's aunt, the Lady Hershel, whose husband had been a Naval Captain and knighted for his distinguished service to the Crown. After their great-aunt died, the younger Bennet sisters, Miss Mary and Miss Catherine, were fortunate enough to have Lady Lucas do the honour upon each turning sixteen. Mrs. Wickham is the only Bennet sister not to have been presented, since she was married before the event could take place. I am sure that Miss Elizabeth has adequately prepared me for the event tomorrow, and has managed to procure anything I may need for both the presentation and the ball."

All during her speech, Georgiana was looking about the room, with her fan lazily wafting cool air over her face to keep the angry flush from becoming too noticeable. After another pause, Georgiana turned to Miss Bingley, snapped her fan shut, and tapped the harpy on the arm. In a placating voice, and with a small smile on her face, she said, "But I do *appreciate* the offer to help retrieve the items I will require before entering society."

Caroline's eyes flashed at the information that Elizabeth had been presented by family who had a bestowed title, and at such a young age. Caroline had not been presented until well after Louisa's marriage and only grudgingly by Hurst's sister-in-law. The other women in the *ton* had snickered behind their feathered fans at her tenuous introduction into society, no matter how much money she had spent on her gown. With a titled aunt, Elizabeth was accepted as a moderately well-situated gentlewoman, regardless of what she wore, and promptly dismissed as a threat to any of the heiresses in the London marriage market. Well, as soon as Caroline procured an offer from Darcy, the chit would be out of a situation, and Georgiana would have to get in line behind the new Mrs. Caroline Darcy.

Dinner was not much better, since it was obvious that Caroline had personally selected the seating arrangement. Darcy was seated directly to the right of Caroline and across from Lady Sefton. The entire meal was spent in conversation initiated by Caroline about some lovely part of Pemberley, or an inane question related to Darcy's noble family connections.

Georgiana was faring little better with a continual string of questions from the elder Mrs. Hurst about the Darcys' new gentil servant. She had heard about the extraordinary service she was given at Mme. Devy's establishment and the quality of the clothing purchased. It seemed an unnecessary expense to the older lady, spending such sums on even the best of companions. Georgiana was embarrassed, not just for herself, but also for the young woman sitting to her other side who served as Lady Sefton's companion. The lady's servant was dressed appropriately, but plainly, and using not nearly the quality of fabrics that Darcy had purchased for Elizabeth. No matter how many times she tried to deflect the questions, Mrs. Hurst would come right back to the topic.

Once the ladies separated from the men for refreshments, it got worse. First, Georgiana had to endure repeated barbs directed at Elizabeth from Caroline and Louisa. She tried to defend her sister but was afraid of going too far and betraying their secret. Lady Sefton kept looking strangely at her during the conversation and Georgiana finally lost her nerve and held her tongue entirely. When the men joined the party, Caroline was eager to set up tables for whist, but the game would only allow four players to a group, leaving two guests out of the games. Knowing that Darcy never played at cards, she stole a private moment with him during the games.

"Mr. Darcy, I know you must be concerned for Miss Georgiana's coming out, since your esteemed aunt has only Eliza to help with the planning. Your sister is much too loyal and naive to believe that her companion is unsuited to the job of planning such an event, but surely you would welcome a more appropriate guide to ensure Georgiana's debut is a success."

Darcy merely shrugged his shoulders and continued to watch the card game.

But the lady would not be deterred. "And, not to speak ill of the poorly situated, but are you not concerned that Eliza is a poor influence on your sweet sister? She is much too bold in company, acting as if she were one of Miss Georgie's friends instead of a paid servant. I know it is a change for the poor dear, being thrust into the life of a servant, where she used to be a gentlewoman, but if someone does not take a firm hand with the young woman, she will be an embarrassment. Perhaps, if you wished, I could accompany Miss Georgie and Eliza to their first few events." This, of course, meant that Darcy would have to procure her an invitation to many of those same events, since she had neither the popularity nor the standing in society to garner such invitations personally. "I could instruct Eliza on the proper behaviour for someone of her station. It would not do for the *ton* to see how poorly she performs her duties."

If Caroline was more familiar with Darcy's facial expressions, she would have seen the thunder in his eyes and the rise in colour to his cheeks. Unwisely, she continued.

"In fact, if there was to be more of a connection between the Bingleys and the Darcys, Miss Georgie would have no need of a companion at all." Caroline went so far as to brush her palm over Darcy's arm and lean forward slightly to give him a better view of her décolletage.

Repulsed, by both the intrusion upon his person and the demeaning things she was saying about his beloved wife, Darcy pulled his arm from her reach. Drawing the attention of most of the rest of the room, he put the lady in her place.

"Miss Bingley, I'm sure I don't know to what you are referring. Charles and I are as connected as two unrelated men can be, and neither of us have immediate plans to increase our connection. As for your opinion on how Miss Elizabeth is performing her *duties* in my household, all I can say is that I am very satisfied." Darcy sported a small blush and barely contained a smile at his own inappropriate innuendo, praying only after the words left his lips that no one else took his words at their true meaning. "She does not need further instruction in how to behave in her new station. Thank you for your offer to serve my family, but no thank you. In the future, if I ever have need of your opinion, I shall supply it to you."

# Chapter 16

## A Ball Full of Mischief

***Matlock House, St. James, London***
***2 May 1813—Georgiana's Official Debut Ball***

*HOW HAS MY LIFE BECOME A LIVING TORTURE?*

Darcy stood broodingly on the periphery of the Matlock House ballroom. He watched closely as both his wife and his sister were squired about the dance floor by dandies and rakes! Or, at least that was how it felt. In fact, most all of the men present were either family, close friends of the Fitzwilliam and Darcy families, or men of the best breeding with impeccable reputations. Elizabeth and Darcy had discussed dancing partners with Georgiana before the ball, and each man had asked her imposing older brother for permission before securing the guest of honour's hand for a set. While there was no such need to gain Darcy's permission for anyone to dance with Elizabeth, so far, many of the eligible men seeking an introduction had also extended Darcy that courtesy. Only Richard and Bingley had asked for a dance from Elizabeth without seeking Darcy's permission. But this did not keep Darcy from hating every minute that either his baby sister or his wife was in the arms of other men.

Richard sauntered up to Darcy, who had been hiding in a corner of the ballroom all evening with a sour look on his face.

"Come, old man! Tell me what has you in such a brooding mood? Georgiana has performed flawlessly, and everyone is speaking of how well she looked yesterday at her presentation. There is nothing I can see to have you acting so foreboding."

Darcy huffed and crossed his arms. "I do not like the way these so-called gentlemen are looking at her, as if she was some horse on sale at Tattersalls."

Richard took another drink of his wine. While Darcy's words implied he was speaking of Georgiana, his eyes were glued to Elizabeth. "I am sure it will get better as the season goes on."

"Humph." Darcy continued to follow Elizabeth across the dance floor. "And while Georgiana acquitted herself well in front of the queen, I would not say that yesterday's presentation was at all enjoyable. My aunts were absolutely atrocious!"

"How so? Mother came home saying the entire affair went well."

"Of course your mother was pleased, but did she tell you what Aunt Catherine did to Eliz… Miss Elizabeth? Neither Lady Catherine nor Anne was expected, but both were in the carriage when it rolled up to our house at ten a.m. Then, Lady Catherine nearly had an apoplexy when Elizabeth began to enter the carriage, and said she was not fit to be riding with the titled ladies to such an important event. She even said, at a very injudicious volume, that Georgiana's companion should not come inside the palace as she was not needed with so many family members to chaperone, then she insisted Miss Elizabeth ride in the servants' carriage which was following." Darcy's voice was rising, unsarcastically loud, and he threw his arms frustratingly into the air. "Do not give any mind to the fact that she is there for Georgiana's social comfort, as much as her chaperone. I believe that at least three of my neighbours walked by just to hear the commotion coming from the Matlock carriage."

Richard chuckled. "Did you expect Aunt Catherine to be reasonable?"

"I expect her to have basic manners in company!" Darcy stuck his finger in Richard's face. "Your father should not let her out if she cannot keep her tongue."

"I assure you, Father has no ability to curtail Lady Catherine. She is a bitter old lady who has been hiding from London society these twenty years, Darcy. No one will take what she says with any sincerity."

"Do you know what she tried to do when the ladies came home from the presentation?" Darcy levelled his cousin with another intense look. "She tried to dismiss Elizabeth from the luncheon. As if she had not helped Georgie design the table and menu. Aunt Catherine said that Elizabeth should take her meal in the servants' dining room! It was infuriating!"

Richard's eyes had grown large at Darcy's passioned speech and informal references to Elizabeth. He looked around to ensure that their conversation was not being overheard by anyone then placed his hand on Darcy's forearm and spoke under his breath. "I understand you are angry, but this is not the forum for discussing your ire at our aunt. Please try to calm yourself."

Darcy grumbled, but ultimately relaxed his stance. It would not do to act like a jealous husband in front of the entire *ton*.

Richard let Darcy have a few moments of silence to recover his composure before changing the subject. "Have you taken a turn around the dance floor yet, other than your opening dance with Georgie?"

Another scowl fixed itself on Darcy's face and he recrossed his arms. "I have no intention of entertaining the ladies present. This is about Georgiana's debut, not my prospects."

"Nonsense! Tonight has been carefully orchestrated to cater to both Georgie's coming out and my mother's unwed sons, nieces, and nephews."

Darcy took another look around the ballroom with little enjoyment. Both Lady Matlock's eligible niece and cousin were present, Lady Fiona Finch and Lady Miranda Stanley respectively, along with their families. The Earl of Bristol and his family was also amongst the numerous guests.

Mr. Goodwin Hervey, the Honourable Earl of Bristol, was a young man newly into his inheritance. In fact, Bristol was originally the second son and had studied to become a clergyman before his father and older brother were killed in a carriage accident nearly two years ago. Bristol had studied alongside Bingley at Cambridge and had been good friends with the Darcy and Fitzwilliam boys all his life. The change from aspiring man of the cloth to Member of the House of Lords had been a massive undertaking, and the bookish young man was anything but ready for the assault from the marriage-minded ladies of London. Lady Matlock and the Dowager Bristol both hoped that Georgiana and the young Bristol would make a good match, due to their shy and quiet natures.

Bristol's younger sister, Lady Grace Harvey, was also looking for a connection to the Darcys but could not care one fig about her brother and the mousey Georgiana. She had her sights squarely on the master of Pemberley, or more accurately, on the ready cash in the bank account of the master of Pemberley. In her first season last year, Lady Grace had little luck, along with the rest of London, securing any time with the elusive bachelor. But now, with her brother expected to court the sister, she had her chance at Darcy.

With Richard making the first foray into drawing out Darcy, other young men followed. Many were, no doubt, hoping to get a chance to dance with Georgiana or Elizabeth, but several were friends of Darcy looking for some conversation.

Amongst the group were Bristol and the Finch boys: Oswald Finch the Viscount Finwell, second son Army Captain Thurston Finch who was a good soldier but a spendthrift, and third son solicitor Bernard Finch. While Darcy had been playmates with Finwell and the Captain since they were all barely out of their cradles, it was Bernard who had always been a true friend. A quiet, educated, and kind young man, Bernard was his grandmother's favourite, his father's disappointment, and often picked upon by his older brothers. He had earned top marks at Oxford, then went to clerk for one of the most sought-after solicitors in all of London. At not quite twenty-four, he was poised to become a partner in the exclusive London practice, and last year had purchased a lovely five-story townhouse facing Russell Square Park. Darcy had dined with Bernard at his home last season after visiting the British Museum and was quite impressed with the size and comfort of the place.

With such a large crowd of unmarried gentlemen forming, it did not take long for the match-minded women to intervene. Just before the end of the fourth set, Lady Matlock came over to the group of eligible men with a gaggle of young women in tow. She intended to break up the stag party and personally ensure that her ridiculous son and nephews danced with each of the titled young women in the room.

Although not initially invited by the Countess to join the invading ladies, Caroline Bingley attached herself to the group. The Bingleys had been invited only due to Bingley's friendship with Darcy and the hopeful inclusion of Lady Sefton. It seemed the older lady showed up wherever Caroline

went, so Lady Matlock put aside their questionable background and allowed the two social climbers inside Matlock House for Georgiana's big day.

Caroline made a beeline for Darcy the moment Lady Matlock interrupted the men. Putting her fingertips lightly on his arm, Caroline drew him away, trying to engage Darcy in a semi-private conversation away from the crowd. "Mr. Darcy, how lovely to see you tonight! Georgiana looks absolutely radiant in her ball gown, and I am sure you are so proud of her presentation."

Before he could even contemplate how to reply, Lady Matlock stepped in, separating Caroline from Darcy. "Of course, we are all so proud to finally have Georgie out in society." She then turned her back to Caroline and spoke only to Darcy. "I know it has been since before Christmas, but you remember my niece, Lady Fiona, and my cousin's daughter, Lady Miranda, Fitzwilliam?"

"Yes, Aunt, of course. Ladies, are you enjoying the evening?" Darcy replied, stiffly and generically, since he was honestly having a hard time remembering which blonde lady was which. The one in the green dress had blue eyes like Lady Derby, and the one in the blue dress looked more like Lady Matlock, so perhaps the first was Lady Miranda and the second was Lady Fiona, but he was not sure. Richard would know. He would have to ask him to identify the ladies before addressing either one.

From somewhere to Darcy's left, another young woman abruptly made her presence known. "Brother, aren't you going to do the courtesy of introducing me to your good friend?" The lady was addressing Bristol with a hard gleam to her eye and a fake smile plastered on her face.

"Of course, Grace. Darcy, may I present my sister, the Lady Grace Hervey. Grace, this is Mr. Fitzwilliam Darcy of Pemberley and Derbyshire."

Lady Grace quickly curtseyed then extended her hand for Darcy to bow over. The gentleman performed the expected pleasantry, then found himself with Lady Grace somehow attached to him, having maneuvered herself to twist her arm under his elbow. Before Darcy was done staring at her hand gripping his arm, the audacious lady began speaking again. "Mr. Darcy, it is such a pleasure to finally be able to meet you properly. I know that we were introduced when you visited with my brother several summers ago at our estate, before I was out in society, but now we are all able to enjoy such sophisticated company. This is truly a fabulous event for Miss Darcy;

she must feel every bit a princess today. Goodwin, have you had occasion to dance with the guest of honour yet? No? Well, you should not wait too long, or her dance card will be completely full. And what about you, Mr. Darcy, have you had your fill of dancing this evening?"

Still baffled at how the young woman was maintaining her physical attachment to him, and developing a plan to disentangle himself without doing her bodily harm, Darcy was completely at a loss to follow her incessant rambling.

Not even waiting for a reply from her captive, Lady Grace went on. "I am sure that you have not, since you have thus far only danced four dances with ineligible women in your family. Do you have a specific lady chosen for the quadrille, sir?"

"No, I have not engaged any specific lady for the quadrille," replied Darcy automatically, still attempting to make space between them.

"Wonderful! I would love to accompany you for the next set. Thank you, sir." And with that, Lady Grace began to drag Darcy towards the dance floor. He was doubly confused by her actions until he heard the beginning stanzas of a quadrille and had to stifle his moan. She had tricked him into dancing with her for one of the longest sets of the entire night.

Elizabeth watched as her husband was dragged onto the dance floor by a young woman whom she had never met. Once she arrived at the grouping of men, and now women, where Darcy had been standing for half the night, she observed the sour looks on many of the women's faces. Given the general mood of the group, Elizabeth decided not to comment on Darcy's current dance partner. Instead, she located a cup of punch and headed to the terrace for some fresh air. The dark corner of the space was the only place one could find any significant air movement, so Elizabeth moved into the shadows opposite the massive ballroom doors.

After only a few minutes in the cool late evening breeze, Elizabeth heard and saw her husband help a theoretically faint young woman onto the terrace. It was the same women he had been forced to dance with moments ago, and her ploy was so ridiculous that it was almost comical.

Almost.

She was not about to have her husband caught up in some scandal, so Elizabeth made to go assist the young woman and free Darcy from her grasp. Interestingly, Caroline beat Elizabeth to the young woman's aide.

"Lady Grace, are you alright? I saw you have a dizzy spell on the dance floor and Mr. Darcy escort you outside for fresh air. Can I be of assistance?"

"Yes."

"NO."

Darcy and Lady Grace answered at the same time in the opposite. Darcy cleared his throat and finally freed himself from the distressed woman's clutch. "Yes, Miss Bingley. That is most kind of you to look after Lady Grace while she recovers from her spell. I must get back to the ball and ensure Georgiana is well. Excuse me, ladies." With that, he jerked his head in a motion that might have been a strange attempt at a bow, then spun around and strode back into the ballroom.

Caroline turned to Lady Grace the second Darcy was across the threshold. "Do not think for one moment that I believe you had a fainting spell in there! I know exactly what you were trying to do, and it will not work. He cannot be trapped by the likes of you. And even if he were found in a compromising position, who would make him marry you? Your pathetic brother, the Cleric Earl? Do not make me laugh! Bristol may be an earldom, but he has no sway over Fitzwilliam Darcy."

"As if you ever had a chance with anyone in that entire ballroom. You with your dirty trade money and a brother dressed up like a gentleman but running a mill in Yorkshire! And do not tell me that marrying your sister to the younger Hurst brother gives you any standing in society. Just because Lady Sefton graces your sister's table does not make you a gentlewoman. You have failed for nigh on five seasons to catch the master of Pemberley, but that does not mean others will similarly fail. We shall see who makes the match and whose family will force the issue if necessary." Lady Grace flipped open her fan directly in front of Caroline's face, giving her the cut direct, then strode back into the ballroom, her chin lofted into the air.

Caroline stomped her foot then counted to one hundred before smoothing down her silk skirt and heading back inside. Elizabeth shook her head. Scheming ladies were generally harmless, but such flagrant acts where anyone could see were dangerous. Both ladies could have caused a significant scandal if anyone but Elizabeth had overheard such admissions. Surely if any of the numerous countesses in attendance had been in Elizabeth's spot enjoying the cool air, both young women would now be packing for exile from London Society.

After re-entering the room, Elizabeth spied her husband on the dance floor once again, this time with Lady Fiona. It appeared that Lady Matlock had taken over the male socializing corner and was now practically lining up the young ladies, making Darcy dance the rest of the evening. Georgiana was dancing with Bristol and not immediately in need of Elizabeth. So, she decided to chat with Richard, who was deep in conversation with Anne de Bourgh.

After the set was finished, Darcy brought his dance partner back to the small grouping including Elizabeth and his cousins. Although it was proper to escort a young lady back to her guardian after a dance, he was drawn towards Elizabeth's twinkling laughter and Richard's booming voice telling some embellished anecdote about the cadets newly joined to his regiment.

Forgetting himself for a moment due to the stress of the last hour, Darcy addressed the whole group informally. "Now Elizabeth, you must remember that whatever Richard tells you, it is a lie. Do not believe one word. Anne, tell her how poorly our wayward cousin represents the truth."

Richard snorted. "I am sure I do not know what you mean, Darcy. I am one of the king's finest. See how many shiny medals they have given me?" He dramatically pointed to the pins and medals displayed on his bright red dress uniform, all shined to a high polish for the formal event. "Such a man would not lie to gentil ladies, would he?"

Richard winked at his cousin Anne then stepped forward to bestow a low bow over his other female cousin's hand and handle the introductions. "Lady Fiona, may I say you look lovely tonight, and you dance wonderfully. Let me introduce you to my other Fitzwilliam cousin, Miss Anne de Bourgh, and you already know the lovely Miss Elizabeth Bennet. Ladies, may I present Lady Fiona Finch, cousin to me by my mother's brother, the Earl of Nottingham."

After cursory curtsies all around, the group returned to their humorous discussion of Richard's inept soldiers, boys not yet eighteen, who may well go to war in France before they were able to grow beards, unless Britain could capture Napoleon and finally put an end to this bloody war. It was an easy conversation and for the first time in nearly thirty-six hours, Darcy started to relax.

When the strings of the band announced the supper set, Darcy decided to continue being selfish and acquire his wife's hand for a dance, then sit with her during the midnight meal. To everyone looking on, it appeared that the master of Pemberley overlooked his heiress cousin and his aunt's favourite titled niece to dance the all-important supper set with his employee. Lady Catherine nearly tripped on her hemline trying to stop the tragedy before the couple made it to the dance line, but she did not make it in time. With a loud huff and a stomp of her cane, she marched in the direction of Anne. Intent on giving her daughter a piece of her mind for allowing Darcy to get away, she was once again thwarted, this time by Richard making a dramatic show of securing Anne's hand for the supper set.

If Darcy had been paying attention to the room instead of focusing exclusively on his lovely wife, he might have seen the fury etched onto one aunt's face and the disapproval on the other's. Many of the matchmaking mammas were sporting an outraged countenance and their daughters looked as if the refreshments table was supplied with nothing but lemons. Several faces belonging to Darcy's lifelong male friends showed varying degrees of suspicion. And one kindly old face, who had seen enough of the London marriage mart to know what loved looked like on a dance floor, looked on with a mixture of pity and hope.

The other thing Darcy missed, that would have certainly been of the utmost importance to him, was that Georgiana was again paired with the youngest son of Nottingham, Bernard Finch. They talked and laughed as they danced and seemed to share the same slightly dazed look whenever the dance required that they clasp hands for a few moments.

All three Darcys plus Bernard managed to find each other inside the massive dining room, and soon they were blissfully surrounded, or protected, depending on the perspective, on all sides by Bingley, Richard, and Anne. Lady Fiona took the seat next to her youngest brother and Caroline was forced to sit next to her own brother, too far away to politely converse with Georgiana or Darcy. At least she was seated only one chair away from the hostess and could easily converse with Lady Matlock.

Caroline decided that now was the time to introduce the idea of a June house party at Pemberley. She would need Lady Matlock as the driving force for such an event, since Darcy would certainly never agree to such a thing on his own.

"Lady Matlock, this has been the most delightful evening. Thank you for including my family in the invitation. Seeing such a wonderful friend officially become a member of society has been truly an honour." Caroline tried to put on her most deferential expression, even though she bristled inside at the knowledge that it was only her connection to Lady Sefton which won her the invitation. "Such a beautiful debut deserves an equally stunning end cap. Have you and Miss Darcy given any thought to an end-of-the-season house party at Matlock? Or better yet, at Pemberley? It would give Miss Darcy a chance to play hostess, and the Pemberley gardens are particularly lovely in the summer."

Elizabeth was two seats from Caroline with Bingley sitting in between. The two listened in, one with amusement and one with dread, but neither could intervene in the conversation since they were not seated close enough to Lady Matlock to politely address the Countess.

"You make a good point, Miss Bingley. There have been few opportunities for Georgie to host guests at Pemberley since becoming of an appropriate age to do so. And heaven knows, my recluse of a nephew only ever invites hunting parties devoid of eligible women to his estate. I shall think on the matter and discuss it with Georgiana." In reality, Lady Matlock was already mentally going through the available cardstock she had seen at the stationer's last week and deciding whether they should plan to leave a full two weeks before the official end-of-the-season or stay for the Regent's ball on the last Friday of June. Her brother, Lord Nottingham, liked to attend every year, but if missing this year meant his daughter could become engaged to Fitzwilliam Darcy of Pemberley, he would be willing leave town early.

Darcy was blissfully unaware of the conversation between Caroline and his aunt, since he was deeply engaged in conversation with Bernard and Georgiana over the Charter Act, newly introduced to parliament this season. The Act would renew the East India Company's charter but reduce their monopoly to only Indian Tea and goods from China. Bernard had been involved in drafting some of the humanitarian provisions intended to provide money for the education of Indian children and for advancing native literature in both Hindi and English. Darcy was mostly interested in the economic impacts of the new Charter, both as an investor in the East India Company and a consumer of imported goods. Perhaps he should pay Edward a visit for the express purpose of discussing how this might impact Gardiner Imports.

Georgiana cared little for the long-term viability of the East India Company. Instead, she was entranced, hearing of Bernard's passion for using his career to the betterment of society and the benefit of children half the world away. With a dreamy look in her eyes, Georgiana asked several pointed questions about how such laws were consummated and when they could expect that actual schools would open their doors to Indian children. Elizabeth recognized the look of adoration on Georgie's face. It was the same expression often looking back at her from her vanity seat. Perhaps the Darcys' farce would come to an end much sooner than any of them expected. Lord help them all when Darcy figured out the truth.

The evening eventually turned into night and the night gave way to the first rays of the sun, and Georgiana's official debut ball came to a close. Darcy had been forced to dance with several additional eligible ladies after supper, but never extended a second dance to anyone other than Elizabeth and Georgiana. In fact, he would not have even extended that courtesy to his sister if Elizabeth had not stopped him from taking her onto the dance floor for the final set. The end to the evening was a waltz set and Darcy was certainly not inclined to share such a dance with anyone other than his fetching wife. As that would have been their *third* dance of the night, Elizabeth knocked some sense back into him before she shooed him away to claim Georgiana.

As the Darcys were waiting for their carriage, Lady Matlock told Darcy that she intended to plan an end-of-the-season house party in Derbyshire for Georgiana, but divulged no specifics. It was only through the overheard supper conversation that Elizabeth was able to give actual details on their way home. Darcy was none too happy about being forced to continue their farce into the late summer. After the events of the last few days, he was ready to forget the whole ridiculous affair and run a wedding announcement in the London Times. And he was certainly not going to allow anyone to treat his wife as if she were a servant in her own home! But Elizabeth placated him like she had each time before. It would only be for a short while, and they would not place any guests in the family wing so at least they should have their private sitting room as an escape in the evenings and early mornings. Besides, she was sure that Georgiana's debut was a wonderful success. In fact, Elizabeth mused silently, she would not be surprised if Georgiana and Bernard Finch came to an understanding much sooner than expected.

# Chapter 17

## Jealousy and Introductions

***Theatre Royal, Covent Garden, London***
***15 May 1813***

THE FRONT STEPS OF THE THEATRE ROYAL WERE FLOODED WITH people. The entire population of London seemed to be at the theatre to see the new Italian opera by Carlo Cocchia, *Arrighetto*. Most of the *ton* had been excited to see the production because it was rumoured that the famed Italian tenor, Tommaso Berti, who originated the leading role at the opera's premier in Venice, would be performing for London's opening night. Darcy was excited to attend their first high society function where he would not be required to watch Elizabeth be treated poorly.

As soon as the carriage carrying the Darcys stopped at the front of the line, Darcy jumped out, grabbed the step and handed out first Georgiana, then Elizabeth. He offered each lady an arm and then the three made their way up the imposing steps towards the entrance. Less than two minutes later, they were accosted by Lady Grace.

"Mr. Darcy, Miss Darcy! What a pleasure to see you out tonight." Lady Grace curtsied very low. Then she smiled coquettishly and looked up at Darcy through her dark eyelashes as she leaned to the perfect angle for viewing her décolletage on his ascent. "Goodwin! Come here. Look, it is the Darcys."

Darcy gave a curt bow to Lady Grace then turned his attention to greeting Bristol. Georgiana was left to take up the mantle of speaking to Lady Grace and make the necessary introductions.

"Lady Grace, how lovely to see you as well. May I introduce my companion, Miss Elizabeth Bennet? Elizabeth, this is Lady Grace Hervey, sister to the Earl of Bristol. Lady Grace, this is Miss Elizabeth Bennet, formerly of Longbourn."

Lady Grace turned her eyes to Elizabeth and became instantly irate. Elizabeth was wearing a gorgeous full length evening gown with matching gloves and shawl, in the most delicate pale green silk. Lady Grace knew that fabric. She had fallen in love with the silk the moment she had seen it in Mme. Devy's shop window, but by the time she got an appointment with the dressmaker there was not enough for a full evening gown. Lady Grace had settled for a short hem, slim summer calling dress with a contrasting fabric for the bodice and no matching shawl. Now this servant had HER dress! How in the world had she been able to convince Darcy to spend such an exorbitant amount?

"Well, Miss Elaina, that is such a beautiful gown. You are certainly lucky to have such a generous employer to spend nearly half again your annual salary on one dress."

Georgiana observed the look of derision on Lady Grace's face with confusion. Elizabeth was dressed in a fashionable gown that was not exorbitant, with no added lace or embroidery. "My brother is exactly as generous as ***Elizabeth*** deserves, given her place in his house, and gladly pays the modiste's bill. Lizzy, was not the green silk for this particular dress a gift from your Aunt and Uncle Gardiner? I believe it was one of the gowns already mostly finished by the time we made it to our appointment last month."

Elizabeth nodded and patted Georgiana on the arm. "Yes, dear. I believe this was one of the fabrics my uncle sent over as a gift. As was the lovely pale blue silk used for one of your evening gowns."

"And who exactly is your Aunt and Uncle Gardiner? I have surely never heard that name spoken in the *ton* before. From the quality of the silk you are wearing, I am sure that only the wealthiest of the nobility could afford to *legitimately* purchase such items. How is it that the daughter and sister of the Earl of Bristol cannot get a full evening gown of the same silk used to make dresses for servants?"

A smile graced Elizabeth's face. "My uncle is Mr. Edward Gardiner, the third generation, sole proprietor of Gardiner Imports which supplies the London market with a variety of goods from India, China, Spain, France, before the war of course, and most recently Italy and Greece. An expansion that was financed by investments from Mr. Bingley, Mr. Darcy, and the Duke of Grafton. Every bolt of silk ever used in Mme. Devy's shop, and her father's tailor shop before her, has been bought from Gardiner Imports. If you think that the only people in London with enough money to access the finest Chinese silks have titles, then you are sorely misinformed."

Before his sister could reply, Bristol intervened. "Miss Darcy, it is lovely to see you again. I must congratulate you on your presentation. I hear it was a delightful success."

Lady Grace decided to take the change in conversation as her opportunity to engage with her real prey, however, when she turned around, she was thwarted again: Darcy was greeting a large group of newcomers.

"Edward, Bingley, I am glad we caught you before we entered. Mrs. Gardiner, Miss Bennet, Miss Mary, may I say how lovely you look tonight."

Madeline, Jane, and Mary curtsied their greetings while Lady Grace took a moment to critically inspect the women. Though she would never have asked to be introduced to such low people, this was apparently Elizabeth's family. The aunt and uncle in trade plus some sisters, perhaps. The aunt of Georgiana's companion was an attractive woman of a slightly older age than Darcy, though not much older, with an extremely fashionable evening dress made of the highest quality silk. Elizabeth's sisters were both wearing well-made, fashionable dresses of silk in flattering colours for each sister's particular complexion. Convinced that the family of Georgiana's companion was somehow leaching off Darcy, Lady Grace decided to try again with Georgiana.

"Miss Darcy," Lady Grace started abruptly, "did you accompany your companion when she shopped for her clothes this season, or did she go on her own for her fittings?"

"Lady Grace, I'm not sure of the purpose for your question, but Elizabeth and I always go to Mme. Devy's shop together."

"And you are certain that you received all of the items ordered? None were directed to a different address?"

"Why would our dresses be delivered to a different address?" Georgiana looked between Lady Grace and Elizabeth in confusion.

Elizabeth was not blind to the insinuation being made, but was keen to avoid any confrontation in the full view of the whole of the *ton*. "I am sure that Lady Grace is just inquiring about our experiences with Mme. Devy. Have you had some trouble with your own modiste, my lady? We could made an introduction if you are looking to change to Mme. Devy's shoppe." Elizabeth patted Georgiana's hands to try and calm her nerves.

"Excuse me! I have been frequenting Mme. Devy's shoppe since my own coming out several years ago. I certainly do not need an introduction to get an appointment."

Snapping her fan shut, Elizabeth put on a relieved expression. "That is well, then. I am sure you are quite well-acquainted with her exemplary level of service, and not implying that something unsavoury has occurred."

"I believe you know exactly what I am implying, Miss ***Emma***." Lady Grace gave Elizabeth a look of loathing and glanced pointedly at Jane and Mary.

Georgiana was starting to wring her hands together in distress. "Dear Georgie," Elizabeth said, "is that not the Earl of Nottingham's carriage just there? Shall we go say hello to Mr. Finch? Please excuse us, Lady Grace. Enjoy the performance tonight." Georgiana was too distressed, then distracted with Bernard Finch, to make a polite exit.

Turning back to her brother and the Gardiner party, Lady Grace found that Darcy was engaged in a business discussion with several men. Unwilling to request an introduction to any of the other people, Lady Grace moved away.

"My lord, I am sorry to say, but I believe your sister has abandoned you." Mary Bennet quietly directed Bristol's eyes to the top of the stairs, where indeed Lady Grace was greeting acquaintances at the entrance to the building.

"I dare say she has. Well, with so many people milling about, I am sure that she cannot have need of me just yet. But I really should follow her to our box. Will I see you again, Miss Mary?"

Mary started at this question. She was not the kind of person whom many remembered or asked for extended discourse. Having been told her entire life she was plain, and being of a quiet disposition, most tended to forget Mary was even present. Bristol, however, had been immediately impressed with the Bennet sisters, Mary in particular. From the moment they arrived, it was obvious that the eldest Bennet sister was attached to Bingley. But what was most intriguing to Bristol was that none of the Bennet sisters had immediately taken up simpering to either himself or Darcy.

Since taking the title to Bristol, the elevated younger son had only felt as if he were the fox hearing the horn when in the presence of young unmarried ladies. It had not always been such. For nearly his entire life, Goodwin Harvey, aspiring clergyman, had been invisible. The contrast was quite disconcerting.

In fact, this phenomena of ascension in the eyes of the *ton* was a common topic of conversation between himself, Bingley, Darcy, and Richard Fitzwilliam. During their university days, Goodwin and Richard had been overlooked by the ladies due to their obstacles in inheriting, while Bingley had been overlooked because of his heritage. Darcy had been pursued constantly by the most beautiful and wealthy ladies of the *ton*, even before his father's untimely death. The other three had shown little sympathy for Darcy's plight. They understood the need to help protect their friend from attempts to entrap him, but true sympathy had not come until three days after the funeral for Bristol's father and brother. The young man, now the Earl Bristol, had accompanied his mother to the modiste, for a private appointment to have several of her dresses turned into mourning attire and to obtain black lace for trimming the others. Suddenly, he was accosted on Bond Street by several young women wishing to 'pay their respects' to the Dowager and new Earl. Bristol was so unaccustomed to such treatment that he merely stood in the street, gaping at the growing mass of ladies and matchmaking mammas.

Since then, he had been unable to go to any social event without constantly having to fend off women. Every simple morning call turned into rumours of affection and courtship. Thankfully, his good friend Darcy did not laugh at his change of circumstance. Instead, Darcy had clapped him on the back and given him sound advice for avoiding the matchmakers.

When the Gardiner party arrived with three beautiful ladies in attendance, Bristol initially hid himself behind Darcy to avoid unwanted attention. After observing that none of the ladies were vying for Darcy's special attention, Bristol decided to be polite and request an introduction. Instead of the usual fawning, the Bennet sisters continued their conversations after the pleasantries were observed. Bristol, feeling an odd sense of peace in the countenance of Mary Bennet, asked her how her season was progressing. They spoke on a surprising range of topics for the short duration of their conversation. They discovered that they both shared a love of scriptures, both preferred the poetry of Edward Perronet to Byron, and both believed that they should like nothing more than to spend their lives working for God's church.

Mary had not fawned over him. She did not agree with everything he said, and in fact she had challenged him on the true meaning of one of Perronet's most famous pieces. Bristol had to be honest in that she was not as beautiful as her older sisters, but he found her modesty attractive, and she had beautiful features with a pleasing look in her eyes. She had even laughed at something he said, really laughed, instead of tittering like so many ridiculous ladies of the *ton* were wont to do. This Mary Bennet had no pretence. She was genuine, and it appeared her sister was as sweet and genuine in her interaction with Bingley.

"I cannot say for certain if I will see you again, my lord," Mary replied, "but we are frequently in the company of the Darcys, and my aunt has accepted several generous invitations from them this season. I certainly hope that we will have the opportunity to speak again."

Bristol smiled brightly. "Excellent! I shall look forward to it. Now, I really must follow my sister." Bristol bowed low over Mary's hand then bounded up the stairs, taking two at a time.

Elizabeth and Georgiana returned in time to see the final exchange between Mary and Bristol, but there was no opportunity to ask questions. Bernard Finch had also joined the group as well.

"Finch, it is nice to see you this evening." Darcy extended his hand to his long-time friend. As he was not completely blind to the moods of the women in his life, from Georgiana's slightly blushing countenance and Elizabeth's wide eyes bobbing between Georgiana and Bernard, Darcy decided to issue the intelligent, well-mannered solicitor an invitation for their last box seat. "Will you not join my sister and our guests for the performance. I believe we have exactly one seat left."

Georgiana exclaimed, with much more feeling than was usual, "Oh, yes, Mr. Finch. Do join us! We have such a merry party this evening. And after, we are all having supper at Darcy House. We could easily include one additional seat at the table."

"I am most grateful for the invitation. My family has no set plans for this evening, so I am happy to join you."

Elizabeth snapped her fan shut and clasped her hands together in delight. "That is most wonderful indeed. But I believe we should move off the stairs now and make our way to the box. Come, Mr. Darcy, will you not help my aunt up the stairs?" Darcy immediately offered one arm to Elizabeth and the other to Madeline Gardiner. Jane and Bingley were already several steps ahead, with Edward escorting Mary. With no other man left to attend her, Bernard happily offered Georgiana an arm and followed the Darcy party into the theatre.

Just as the Darcys moved out of sight of the carriage lane, a beautifully liveried landeau stopped in front of the theatre. First to step out was Reginald Hurst, who promptly held out his hand for his great-aunt, Lady Sefton. Next out was Louisa Hurst, and finally came Caroline Bingley.

Arriving in such a stylish equipage, with one of the most recognizable and elevated ladies in the whole *ton* brought exactly the attention Caroline had hoped for. Smiling and waving at titled persons simpering towards Lady Sefton, Caroline pretended that she was already a highly placed lady. And soon she would be, in truth. Tonight was a calculated attempt to increase the pressure on Darcy.

Since his father's death, Darcy had always taken his operas with his Matlock family. The Darcys' traditional box was still maintained by the Darcy family, but it had been let back to the opera house to sell for the past five seasons. Caroline had meticulously planned her introduction into the Matlock box this evening, which she hoped would end with an accepted invitation to the Darcys to join their party in Lady Sefton's nearly-empty box.

It would have been easier if her useless brother had accompanied them tonight, as Darcy was more likely to come with his best friend, but Bingley had insisted he already had an engagement this evening. No matter, Caroline planned to push Darcy to accompany them with the opportunity for Georgiana to converse with Lady Sefton ahead of the Almack's invitations, expected next week. Naturally, Darcy would not allow his baby sister to accompany them alone. So, both brother and sister would end up relocating to the more spacious position conveniently devoid of any meddlesome aunts and rich, attractive cousins-by-marriage.

Unfortunately, for Caroline, when she finally managed to elbow her way into the Matlock box, there was only Lord and Lady Matlock, their second son, Colonel Richard Fitzwilliam and their daughter, Lady Marianne, with Lady Catherine and Miss Anne de Bourgh: all people Caroline did not want to see. After false pleasantries from the ladies and hearty welcomes shared between Hurst and Richard, Caroline asked about the whereabouts of Georgiana and Darcy.

Lady Catherine's shrill voice rose above the group. "Darcy has taken back his box on the other side of the theatre. I cannot imagine why, though he says that with Georgiana out, they should maintain their own box and invitations. But I still insist that it is rather ridiculous to have just the two of them in a huge box all alone when their closest relations and dearest friends are all over here with plenty of seats to accommodate them, and even the companion, if Georgiana insists on bringing her. I wrote Darcy a note about this yesterday but did not receive any reply. Their party should look positively empty."

The assembled group looked towards the opposite set of boxes where Lady Catherine was pointing, just as the Darcy box curtain was pulled back to reveal a rather merry, large party. Caroline, Lady Matlock, and Lady Catherine all looked sourly at the cast of persons entering one of the most exclusive and visible set of seats in the whole theatre. Darcy's tall frame could easily be seen holding back the curtain. Lady Marianne was the first to voice the question everyone was thinking:

"Who is that beautiful blonde lady in the dove grey dress?"

Caroline was having a hard time holding in her ire, so Louisa spoke up. "That is Miss Jane Bennet. She is Miss Elizabeth Bennet's eldest sister. The rest of the party appear to be the Bennet's Cheapside relations and of course, our brother." She turned to Caroline. "How strange that he did not tell us he would be here tonight as a guest of the Darcys."

"Yes," Caroline practically snarled. "How very strange."

A ringing sound came from the stage, which signalled to everyone that the show was about to begin. Hurst directed his family out of the Matlock box. "Come, Caroline, let us take our seats. Have a lovely evening, Lord Matlock, Lady Matlock. Fitzwilliam, nice to see you again."

Caroline took a seat in the back of the box near the railing. To an outside observer, she was calm and presented the appropriately disinterested visage which was so popular amongst the young ladies of London. Inside, however, she was seething. The Darcy box was forward of her own accommodations, so the last row of seats inside the box, where Darcy and Elizabeth sat, were invisible to all but the one or two boxes at the very front of the theatre. For the first act, Caroline stewed in her seat, sending curses towards her brother for not getting her an invitation to Darcy's box. With only low people connected to Elizabeth otherwise invited to the evening's party, Caroline was sure she could have been the one sitting next to Darcy in the last row, nearly invisible to the rest of society. But instead, she was on the other side of the theatre, not even able to catch his eye.

Ever since Georgiana's debut ball, Caroline had been trying to get an audience with Darcy. However, she had been thwarted at each attempt. The Darcys had not accepted any dinner invitations to the Bingley or Hurst homes, and she was being outmanoeuvred by Darcy's aunts. Lady Matlock and Lady Catherine both had their own agenda for Darcy's future bride and had been making it difficult for any lady, other than Lady Fiona, Lady Miranda, or Anne de Bourgh, to get more than a few seconds of private conversation with the man. At three events where Caroline and Darcy had been in company together, they had not even shared a formal greeting.

It was time to adjust her plans.

As soon as the curtain fell on the first act, Caroline rose from her seat. "Sister, Lady Sefton, I believe I need some refreshment. Please excuse me."

In the hall, after she grabbed a glass of wine from a passing servant, Caroline found her intended prey. "Lady Elizabeth Shrewsbury! How lovely to see you this evening."

Lady Shrewsbury waved at Caroline and walked toward her. "Oh, Miss Bingley! Yes, it is a lovely night. I see your brother is entertaining the Darcys and their party this evening. Tell me, is one of those lovely ladies the companion about whom we have heard so much this season?"

"Of course, my brother is always happy to entertain our good friends. In fact, the lady in the green dress is Miss Elizabeth Bennet. The other young ladies, other than Miss Darcy, are Miss Elizabeth's sisters. It is such a kindness by Miss Darcy to host her companion's family tonight. I am sure they would otherwise not be able to enjoy such a refined evening."

"I am sure Mr. Darcy and Miss Darcy are nothing if not kind. Why did you not join them?"

Caroline took a sip of her wine, then leaned in as if she was going to give Lady Shrewsbury some secret. "I would always be happy to be in company with Mr. and Miss Darcy, but you know how men are with gossip. Mr. Darcy does not want too much attention paid to the connection between our houses before formal announcements can be made."

"And is an announcement expected soon?"

Sighing, Caroline put on a sorrowful expression. "It is a woman's burden to wait, my lady. Mr. Darcy is fully devoted to Miss Darcy's debut season, and my own brother is not inclined to press the issue. I have only my absolute belief in his honour and our long-standing friendship to sustain me. Though, if Miss Darcy's season is a success, I would expect an announcement before the Regent's ball."

# Chapter 18

## Offenses

***Matlock House, St. James, London***
***30 May 1813***

"Come, please, gather a plate of cake and find a seat. The musical performances are about to begin. Lady Jersey, you are first at the pianoforte." Lady Matlock directed her guests for the after-dinner entertainment. The scheduled musical exhibition by various ladies, and even a few gentlemen who were so inclined, was an annual event at Matlock House, going back at least two generations. Lady Matlock drew up a schedule of performers and it went much in the order of rank. First came any of the married ladies who wished to participate, then the titled unmarried ladies, and then the sisters and daughters of wealthy gentlemen. The men were sprinkled throughout to give the party some variety. Those who were not included in the invitation to exhibit were the companions to Lady Sefton, Anne de Bourgh, and Georgiana, although all three were lovely pianists with significantly more natural talent than several of the 'accomplished' ladies in the room.

Darcy took a seat near the back of the room, far from the pianoforte, next to Bristol. Neither man had a particular interest in the musical talents of the exhibiting ladies. But Lady Matlock was not satisfied with this seating arrangement.

"Come, William, Lord Bristol. Two such fine bachelors must not occupy such disadvantageous seats. There are two comfortable places very near the instrument that I insist you take." Lady Matlock waved at one of her footmen. "Peters here will arrange for a location which affords a better view of the pianoforte."

Darcy was firm in his answer. "No, Aunt, that is not necessary. Bristol and I are perfectly well situated here and can easily hear the performances at the front of the room. Save those closer seats for the brave men who might serve to turn pages for the young ladies. You know I am never the best suited for that employment."

There was little Lady Matlock could do, short of making a scene, to encourage Darcy's attentions towards the young ladies. Soon after the first pianoforte notes began to fill the room, Richard and Viscount Huntley also joined their cousin. Except for during Georgiana's performance, the four gentlemen generally carried on a conversation about the ongoing conflict with Napoleon, parliament's latest acts, and fund stocks.

Approximately five participants into the evening, Lady Fiona was scheduled to perform her selection. In a final attempt to persuade Darcy into reasonable action, Lady Matlock called for a short intermission so that everyone could refresh their drinks. When Darcy returned to the coffee table, Lady Fiona and Lady Matlock pounced, together.

"Nephew, I know you jested when you said you cannot turn pages. I have seen you perform such a service for your sister countless times."

Darcy stiffened. "Aunt, I do sometimes turn pages for Georgiana at home, but I promise you I am not dissembling when I say that I have no talent for the occupation unless I am very familiar with the piece, which is not often."

"Come now, I am sure you are being modest, Mr. Darcy," said Lady Fiona. "Please, do come turn the pages for me as my turn is next. My brother, I fear, always misses the turn on purpose to make me look the fool. You would not like me to look foolish, would you, Mr. Darcy?"

And so it was, Darcy found himself at the pianoforte turning pages for the rather scandalous Italian aria, *Voi che sapete che cosa è amor*, performed by Lady Fiona. It was extremely uncomfortable for Darcy, who spoke enough Italian to understand the meaning of the piece, and for everyone else who watched the gentleman slowly become as stiff as a statue and the colour of a tomato. As soon as the last page was turned, Darcy bowed woodenly toward the piano and returned to his seat in silence.

Following the end of the scheduled exhibitions, more coffee, tea and cake was placed around the parlour. Lady Sefton, who had been keeping a watchful eye on the assembled guests, stood to refill her tea and took a seat next to Elizabeth.

"Miss Elizabeth, I hope you have been enjoying the evening."

"Yes, my lady. It is always enjoyable to hear such lovely music from the accomplished young ladies."

"I fear that your young lady, Miss Darcy, was the only truly accomplished musician in the bunch. I am sure that Mr. Darcy is quite proud of his sister's skill at the pianoforte."

Elizabeth smiled and looked over to Georgiana who was deep into a conversation with Bernard Finch. "It is an easy thing to be proud of Georgiana's musical skill. Though I have often heard that a truly accomplished lady must have, in addition to musical talent, skill at drawing, painting, dancing, netting purses, arranging flowers, and the modern languages."

"Pish Posh! I cannot believe any lady fits the bill of such an exhaustive list. No, I have never seen such a lady who excels at more than one of those tasks. Truly, we saw the evidence this evening with our very own eyes that, of the accomplished ladies assembled here tonight, none, save Miss Darcy, gave a truly skilled exhibition." Lady Sefton's eyes had a hint of laughter.

"I am glad that I have never been subjected to such harsh criticism of my accomplishments." Elizabeth reconsidered. "Though there was one day when Miss Bingley enumerated the many flaws in my education. I had no governess, you see, and was left to the education of my father's extensive library. It was a most unfortunate education for a truly accomplished lady, I understand."

"It does not surprise me at all that you have extensively read from a wide variety of well-reasoned books. No one who has had the pleasure of your conversation could have any doubt that you have employed your time wisely." A friendly tap on Elizabeth's arm punctuated the sincerity in Lady Sefton's voice.

Elizabeth's smile was genuine. "Thank you, my lady."

"Besides, Caroline Bingley would not understand what makes a lady truly accomplished if she studied all the books in Christendom. I fear that child is hopelessly ignorant and dull."

With bulging eyes, Elizabeth struggled to form an immediate reply. "But, my lady, you often are found in the company of Miss Bingley, her sister and brother-in-law Hurst. I believed you enjoyed their company."

"Heavens, no! I tolerate Miss Bingley because I quite like my great-nephew Hurst. Reginald is a kind boy and Louisa is a fine enough lady when she is not kowtowing to her younger sister. No, I mostly keep Miss Bingley close because I do not trust her." Lady Sefton took another sip of her tea, completely unconcerned with the inappropriate direction of her conversation.

Elizabeth took a moment to look around the assembled guests and ensure that no one was eavesdropping on their conversation. Though there was no love lost between Elizabeth and Caroline, it would not do to be overheard having such an unflattering conversation about the lady.

"I was, frankly, glad to have an evening without Miss Bingley," Lady Sefton said, with a serene smile. "She and the Hursts are off to some event at Vauxhall this evening. Knowing Mr. Darcy and several other prime gentlemen whom Miss Bingley insists on chasing would be here, I originally declined to attend. But Lady Matlock's musical engagements have been something I have enjoyed since I played in this very room my first season. Of course, the hostess then was the current Lord Matlock's grandmother, but it was a virtually identical night to this one."

"Now, you must be exaggerating. You are not old enough to have been a guest of Lord Matlock's grandmother, unless you came out when you were still in nappies."

Lady Sefton gave a small snort into her teacup. "Admittedly, the lady in question was getting on in years and did not survive many more seasons after my first, but I debuted many years ago now."

"I would have liked to have known you then, as a bright-eyed debutant." Elizabeth tapped Lady Sefton on the arm with her fan. "I wager you were still just as self-assured and interesting back then as you are today."

"Though I was definitely self-assured, I do not believe you would have liked Maria Margaret Craven very much. I was brought up to have a very high opinion of myself, prioritizing wealth and connections above anything else." Lady Sefton used her spoon to stir a few sugar crystals still at the bottom of her cup. "My marriage to William Philip Molyneux, the second Earl of Sefton made me very highly placed indeed. When we married, I thought that I had made the best match possible and was unabashed in my effusive boasting to anyone who would listen. My husband is a personal friend of the Prince Regent, after all." Lady Sefton sighed and looked around the room, wistfully. Elizabeth sensed that this story was not all happy and waited patiently for the noblewoman to continue.

"I came to really understand what it means to be a close personal friend of the Prince Regent after a few years. My husband is a gambler, spendthrift, womanizer, and never looks upon me with any kindness. Now that I am an old woman, secure in my fortune and place in society, I have made a happy life without Lord Sefton. We keep separate residences, and my greatest joys are my family and overseeing Almack's." Turning to look back at Elizabeth, the wistfulness and pain had already left Lady Sefton's eyes. "It is a particular pleasure of mine to watch the young people meet and dance during the season, even more so when there is obvious affection between the courting couples." Lady Sefton gave Elizabeth a look that seemed to both ask and answer the important questions surrounding her own future happiness.

Abruptly, Lady Sefton changed the subject. "I must say, though, that I have also heard you play on occasion, and I was sorry that you were not included in the exhibition earlier."

Elizabeth blushed and looked down. "I am no great proficient at the pianoforte. I do not take the time to practice that I should. Georgiana has asked me on occasion to play duets, but I am sorry to say that I do not use my own time on the pursuit."

"I have not found any fault in your performances thus far. Why do you not play something for me? I would be very grateful if you would play that lovely Scottish lullaby you performed a few days ago during tea at Darcy House."

Elizabeth dissembled. "I believe that Lady Matlock was not expecting any more performances for the evening." Looking around, Elizabeth caught the eye of their hostess, who was unexpectedly watching her conversation with Lady Sefton. The sour look on Lady Matlock's face caused Elizabeth to start.

Lady Sefton was not blind to the mood of Lady Matlock, but as the reigning paragon of society, she boldly looked Lady Matlock in the eye and walked Elizabeth to the seat at the pianoforte. Nearly all of the other guests had become involved in partaking of the coffee and cakes, so Elizabeth played the sweet tune softly as pleasant background music.

As if drawn by some unknowable force, Darcy walked over to the pianoforte until he was standing next to the instrument with one hand on the lid and both eyes trained on Elizabeth. He always loved listening to his wife play, and this song was a particular favourite of his. She sang softly to the melody flowing from her fingers. Part of the song she sang in English and part in Gaelic. Darcy was always amazed at how she could make the northern language, so full of harsh consonants and guttural noises, sound as lovely as any French love song.

With his attention so fully engaged with the vision of his wife, Darcy missed the veritable smoke rising from his aunt's ears and Lady Fiona's actual stomping foot. He also missed the satisfied smile upon Lady Sefton's face while she observed the young couple at the piano.

At the conclusion of her song, Lady Matlock swept over to the pianoforte and nearly caught Elizabeth's fingers in her swift motion to close the fallboard. "I believe we have had enough music for the evening. I would not want the strings of my instrument to be worn out with so much excessive playing."

Several of the other guests had followed Lady Matlock over to the pianoforte and Elizabeth was embarrassed that her playing had offended their hostess somehow. Darcy held out his hand for Elizabeth to stand from the bench when Lady Fiona decided to engage with her aunt's haranguing.

"Miss Elizabeth, you look peaked, all of a sudden. Are you sure you are not fatigued from such a long day of performing your duties to Miss Darcy?"

"Yes, dear. I quite agree that Miss Elizabeth looks flushed. I have a room down the servants hall available to you for a short rest while my nephew and niece enjoy the company of their friends." Lady Matlock began to wave over one of the footmen.

"That will not be necessary, Aunt." Darcy scarcely kept the rage out of his voice, but it showed on his face. "We have all had a busy couple of days and I find that I, also, am fatigued. Thank you for a delightful evening. Please have our carriage brought around."

Several minutes later, Darcy had collected Georgiana away from her conversation with Bernard Finch and bundled his family into their carriage for Darcy House.

As soon as they had dressed for bed, Elizabeth sat on the chaise by the fire in Darcy's bedchamber. "Come here, my love. We must have some conversation before we retire."

Darcy sighed. "I know what you are going to say. I should not have become so angry at my aunt. But she was so very rude to you, and for no reason other than some prejudice against your position."

Elizabeth patted the seat next to her on the chaise again and Darcy reluctantly took a seat. He was immediately wrapped in Elizabeth's slender arms. "William, you know that she has plans for your marriage which include one of her favourite relations. Perhaps if it was just your indifference to Lady Fiona, your aunt would not be so forceful in her offenses. But I suspect it has more to do with your change in character recently."

"Whatever do you mean?"

Running a soothing pattern against his chest, Elizabeth continued. "Your character, perhaps not in essentials, but in outward expression, has changed much since our argument in Hunsford. You are less prideful around those who are of lesser rank than yourself. You more openly associate with tradesmen, such as my uncle, and you are not as stoic in company as you were before. I do not mention these changes to imply that I do not approve, I very much approve of you. But I wonder how much of the change your close relations also perceive and how that has affected their attitude towards you… and me."

"What do you suggest I do about this?"

"I am not sure." Elizabeth sighed. "Perhaps you might try going back to your stoic mask in company. And also, you must take care to perform those little pleasantries that are expected of the gentlemen, like turning pages for the daughter of an Earl, without looking as if you are being tortured. Perhaps you should practice arranging such little elegant compliments as may be adapted to ordinary occasions, to give them as unstudied an air as possible."

Darcy knit his brow together. "I am at a loss to your meaning. Practice elegant compliments? Where in the world you would get such an idea?"

Elizabeth laughed. "Do not worry yourself, dear. It was something I heard once before as a means of being pleasing to other people. But you are right, this is not your way. Social distance and haughty disgust served you well in Meryton at keeping unwanted attention away. Perhaps we should return to that repose."

"Minx!" Darcy laughed. He turned and dug the tips of his fingers into Elizabeth's side, making her shriek. "You will not get away with such insolence."

"You like my insolence. And besides, I am not wrong."

"No dear, you are not wrong, about anything."

# Chapter 11

## Rumours

***Darcy House, Mayfair, London***
***3 June 1813***

THE DAY TO DEPART LONDON FOR PEMBERLEY WAS SEVEN DAYS AWAY. One week. One-hundred sixty-eight hours. Darcy had seven peaceful family breakfasts, seven enjoyable luncheons at home or White's, and seven terribly stressful dinners at some notable townhouse where there would likely be at least one lady trying to get his attention or, worse, some dandy trying to engage Georgiana.

If only he could cancel the bloody house party which would follow them for an additional two weeks.

His aunt decided that Georgiana would host the most perfect house party for all their most dear relations and friends. So, naturally, nearly sixty people would be invading his home for the last two weeks of June. All six Nottinghams, four Derbys, three Bristols, five Matlocks plus Anne de Bourgh, two Bingleys, two Hursts, one Lady Sefton, plus companions and servants would be coming together in a large caravan to Pemberley. At least Georgiana had been able to issue her own invitations instead of allowing

Aunt Matlock to order them. The Darcys were able to include Jane and Mary Bennet in the party without the countess vetoing the ladies' inclusion.

Now Darcy needed to figure out how to orchestrate a major catastrophe somewhere on the estate so he could disappear for the entire event.

This morning was dedicated to making plans and writing letters detailing instructions to Mrs. Reynolds regarding the party. Elizabeth and Georgiana were organizing several picnics, outings to the local sights, and hopefully a traveling troupe of musicians for one of the last nights. Darcy's only suggestion so far for an activity was a chess tournament one evening after dinner.

Elizabeth had been making lists of instructions to Mrs. Reynolds for several days now, and was finally putting the finishing touches on her nearly five-page letter as the front doorknocker sounded loudly and was easily heard from the study where all three Darcys were working. As it was nearly one p.m., certainly not the calling hour, and a Thursday instead of Tuesday, the family ignored the interruption. That is until the interruption came barging into the room with the ridiculous thump-thump-thump of a cane and the shrieking voice of Lady Catherine.

***Wilton Row, Belgravia, London***
***3 June 1813—11AM Sharp***

The Bingleys' butler was used to many people coming in and out of the townhouse, and prided himself on knowing the relations of each person who graced his door. But this morning, he was sure he had never seen the supposed *lady* before, nor had he ever even heard of her from the tittering amongst the various guests who frequented the home. But her card said she was sister to the Earl of Matlock and widow of an unknown knight, so he let the lady into the parlour while he went in search of his mistress, Caroline Bingley.

At the mention of Lady Catherine's name, Caroline was thrown into a tizzy. Her normal day for receiving callers was Friday, not Thursday, and she was loathe to entertain this particular guest when she wanted to be sitting at her window watching the fashionable of London meander onto the

Rotten Row. But one does not ignore a guest with a title in their home, so she checked her appearance and proceeded into the parlour.

Lady Catherine had found the most ornate chair with slightly taller legs than the other furniture in the room and was sitting in it, as if she were the Queen ready to receive ladies for presentation. Already, Caroline was annoyed, because she usually sat in that chair. But you know what they say about 'great' minds. In order to hide her annoyance, Caroline curtsied deeply and greeted Darcy's aunt into her home, offering tea and cakes.

"No thank you, Miss Bingley. I would like no refreshment. You can be at no loss as to the reason for my visit this morning."

"Indeed, you are mistaken, madam. I have not been at all able to account for the honour of seeing you here." Caroline tried to remain sweet but strong in her conviction that this was her house, and she was not going to be bullied by a recluse, no matter her title.

"Miss Bingley," replied her ladyship, in an angry tone, "you ought to know that I am not to be trifled with. But, however insincere you may choose to be, you shall not find me so. My character has ever been celebrated for its sincerity and frankness, and in a cause of such moment as this, I shall certainly not depart from it. A report of a most alarming nature reached me last night. I was told that not only was your brother on the point of being most advantageously married to some titled lady, but that you, that Miss Caroline Bingley, would, in all likelihood, be soon afterwards united to my nephew, my own nephew, Mr. Darcy. Though I know it must be a scandalous falsehood, though I would not injure him so much as to suppose the truth of it possible, I instantly resolved on setting off for this place, that I might make my sentiments known to you."

"If you believed it impossible to be true," said Caroline, colouring with astonishment and disdain, "I wonder you took the trouble of coming to our home, which you have never before visited. What could your ladyship propose by it?"

"At once, to insist upon having such a report universally contradicted."

"Your coming to Wilton Row, to see me and my brother," said Caroline coolly, "will be rather a confirmation of it, *if* indeed, such a report is in existence." At this, Caroline flipped open her fan and began lazily fanning herself to try and cool the redness coming onto her cheeks.

"If! Do you then pretend to be ignorant of it? Has it not been industriously circulated by yourselves? Do you not know that such a report is spread to all of London?"

"I may have heard that it was."

"And can you likewise declare there is no foundation for it?"

"I do not pretend to possess equal frankness with your ladyship. You may ask questions which I shall not choose to answer."

"This is not to be borne. Miss Bingley, I insist on being satisfied. Has he, has my nephew, made you an offer of marriage?"

"Your ladyship has declared it to be impossible."

"It ought to be so; it must be so, while he retains the use of his reason. But your arts and allurements may, in a moment of infatuation, have made him forget what he owes to himself and to all his family. You may have drawn him in."

"If I have, I shall be the last person to confess it."

"Miss Bingley, do you know who I am? I have not been accustomed to such language as this. I am almost the nearest relation he has in the world, and am entitled to know all his dearest concerns."

"But you are not entitled to know mine; nor will such behaviour as this, ever induce me to be explicit."

"Let me be rightly understood. This match, to which you have the presumption to aspire, can never take place. No, never. Mr. Darcy is engaged to my daughter. Now what have you to say?"

"Only this; that all of London knows that to be a lie."

Lady Catherine hesitated for a moment, and then replied, "The engagement between them is of a peculiar kind. From their infancy, they have been intended for each other. It was the favourite wish of his mother, as well as of her's. While in their cradles, we planned the union: and now, at the moment when the wishes of both sisters would be accomplished in their marriage, to be prevented by a young woman of inferior birth, of no importance in the world, and wholly unallied to the family! Do you pay no regard to the wishes of his friends? To his tacit engagement with Miss De Bourgh? Are you lost to every feeling of propriety and delicacy? Have you not heard me say that from his earliest hours he was destined for his cousin?"

"Yes, and I had heard it before. But what is that to me? If there is no other objection to my marrying your nephew, I shall certainly not be kept from it by knowing that his mother and aunt wished him to marry Miss De Bourgh. You both did as much as you could in planning the marriage. Its completion depended on others. If Mr. Darcy is neither by honour nor inclination confined to his cousin, why is not he to make another choice? And if I am that choice, why may not I accept him?"

"Because honour, decorum, prudence, nay, interest, forbid it. Yes, Miss Bingley, interest. For, do not expect to be noticed by his family or friends if you wilfully act against the inclinations of all. You will be censured, slighted and despised by everyone connected with him. Your alliance will be a disgrace; your name will never even be mentioned by any of us."

"These are heavy misfortunes," replied Caroline. "But the wife of Mr. Darcy must have such extraordinary sources of happiness necessarily attached to her situation that she could, upon the whole, have no cause to repine."

"Obstinate, headstrong girl! I am ashamed of you! You are to understand, Miss Bingley, that I came here with the determined resolution of carrying my purpose; nor will I be dissuaded from it. I have not been used to submit to any person's whims. I have not been in the habit of brooking disappointment."

"That will make your ladyship's situation at present more pitiable, but it will have no effect on me."

"I will not be interrupted. Hear me in silence. My daughter and my nephew are formed for each other. They are descended on the maternal side from the same noble line, and on the father's from respectable, honourable, and ancient—though untitled—families. Their fortune on both sides is splendid. They are destined for each other by the voice of every member of their respective houses, and what is to divide them? The upstart pretensions of a young woman without family or connections, and with a fortune tainted by trade. Is this to be endured? But it must not, shall not, be. If you were sensible of your own good, you would not wish to quit the sphere in which you have been brought up."

"In marrying your nephew, I should not consider myself as quitting that sphere. I have been raised as one of the elite of London, and my brother was given a gentleman's education. My family in this generation is every bit the social equal of the Darcys."

"True. You brother has a gentleman's education but that does not make him a gentleman. Do not imagine me ignorant of your true situation."

"Whatever my connections may be," said Caroline, "if your nephew does not object to them, they can be nothing to you."

"Tell me, once for all, are you engaged to him?"

Though Caroline would not, for the mere purpose of obliging Lady Catherine, have answered this question, she could not but say after a moment's deliberation, "As of today, I am not."

Lady Catherine seemed pleased. "And will you promise me never to enter into such an engagement?"

"I will make no promise of the kind."

"Miss Bingley, I am shocked and astonished. I expected to find a more reasonable young woman. But do not deceive yourself into a belief that I will ever recede. I shall not go away 'til you have given me the assurance I require."

"And I certainly never shall give it. I am not to be intimidated into anything so wholly unreasonable. Do not think me blind. Your ladyship wants Mr. Darcy to marry your daughter, but would my giving you the wished-for promise make their marriage at all more probable? Supposing him to be attached to me, would my refusing to accept his hand make him wish to bestow it on his cousin? I must beg, therefore, to be importuned no farther on the subject."

"Not so hasty, if you please. I have by no means done. To all the objections I have already urged, I have still another to add. I am no stranger to the particulars of your family's assent into the *ton*. I know it all; that your father and grandfather were nothing but common mill workers who were able to secure financial gain by marrying into the merchant classes, and how your sister's marriage to the Hursts bought your brother a gentleman's education, but he still earns his money from trade! And is such a man to be my nephew's brother? Such a man may be a friend from university, but as a relation and then with connections to the honourable Earldom of Matlock? Heaven and earth! Of what are you thinking? Are the shades of Pemberley to be thus polluted?"

"You can now have nothing farther to say," Caroline resentfully answered. "You have insulted me in every possible method. I must beg you to leave my house."

She rose as she spoke. Lady Catherine rose also. Her ladyship was highly incensed. "You have no regard, then, for the honour and credit of my nephew! Unfeeling, selfish girl! Do you not consider that a connection with you must disgrace him in the eyes of everybody?"

"Lady Catherine, I have nothing farther to say. You know my sentiments."

"You are then resolved to have him?"

Caroline replied with steel in her eyes. "Yes. I shall have him."

"It is well. You refuse, then, to oblige me. You refuse to obey the claims of duty, honour, and gratitude. You are determined to ruin him in the opinion of all his friends, and make him the contempt of the world."

"Neither duty, nor honour, nor gratitude," replied Caroline, "have any possible claim on me, in the present instance. You can be assured that I plan to become Mrs. Darcy by the end of the summer. If his friends believe him ruined or trapped, I shall not be bothered."

"And this is your real opinion! This is your final resolve! Very well. I shall now know how to act. Do not imagine, Miss Bingley, that your ambition will ever be gratified. I came to try you; I hoped to find you reasonable, but depend upon it, I will carry my point."

At this last declaration, Lady Catherine swept her skirts around the legs of the chair she had been occupying and strode from the room as if she owned the whole row of houses. Her cane made violent strikes on the parquet flooring as she left through the front door without even acknowledging the butler.

***Darcy House, Mayfair, London***
***3 June 1813***

Lady Catherine was still shrieking at the top of her lungs several minutes after the inhabitants of Darcy's study had overcome the shock of the intrusion. Unfortunately, no one had yet to decipher what it was that she was carrying on about. From the decided sway to her stance and the redness in her cheeks, Elizabeth decided it was time to intervene.

"My Lady, please, take this seat and I shall fetch you a refreshment. Would you prefer tea, or perhaps a nice wine with which to calm yourself?" The large, overstuffed wingback chair from the side of the room was moved to directly in front of the large desk where all three Darcy's had previously been working on preparations for the coming house party.

Though she stopped her high-pitched speech, Lady Catherine's ire had not yet abated. "I never drink wine this early in the day. How ridiculous! A lady is liable to get drunk before she is even dressed for dinner. Whatever made you think this uneducated country maid was a suitable companion for Georgiana, William? Tea, Miss Elizabeth, and a strong brew with two lumps of sugar plus a measure of cream. Have the maid bring it and leave us. I must speak to my nephew without the help gossiping behind our backs."

Darcy and Georgiana were respectively furious and embarrassed by their aunt's treatment of the one person in the whole world who was kindly seeing to the comfort of the ridiculous woman. Elizabeth kept reminding herself that it was all for the sake of their sisters.

Darcy had just about had enough of his relation's demands this day and was fighting the urge to tell his Aunt to leave and never return. "Aunt Catherine, you can say your piece in front of Miss Elizabeth. She is more a member of the household than a servant, and my house staff is very loyal in any case. Besides, your tirade has already divulged whatever you wanted to keep secret to anyone inside the house and quite possibly the inhabitants of the next address as well. Now, please tell us calmly what has you in such a state."

"Tell me, nephew. Are you planning on offering for that awful Bingley woman? I will not have it, you know! She is wholly unacceptable!"

All three Darcys were so relieved that this easily-dispelled nonsense was what had Lady Catherine so infuriated, they each let out a surprised laugh. "Truly, Aunt Catherine, this is what you have become enraged about?" Darcy asked. "Some rumour, likely started by Caroline Bingley herself and believed by absolutely no one in the *ton*, that I am on the verge of declaring myself to her? Let me put your mind at ease: I do not now have plans to offer for her, nor will I ever entertain such a ridiculous notion. Caroline Bingley will turn into a bitter spinster waiting on my proposal."

Lady Catherine calmed somewhat, but she was not nearly done with her interrogation of her nephew. "While that is a relief to hear, I am telling you: watch that harpy. She is the kind that would try to entrap you into marriage, and if her sister's in-law decide to get involved with any perceived scandal, it shall take the total combined power of the Fitzwilliam, Darcy, and de Bourgh names to stop Lady Sefton."

"I assure you, I have known for quite some time that Miss Bingley is determined to have me, and I never allow myself to be separated from the company during social engagements. Richard and Charles Bingley have always been diligent to provide witness that I have never compromised any lady trying to entrap the Darcy fortune. These precautions have saved me from a number of plots since university, and I do not intend to stop now."

"If you would hurry up and marry Anne, none of this would even be an issue. There would be nothing to entrap. Georgiana could have a suitable chaperone, Miss Elizabeth could move on to more suitable employ, and Anne could be rightfully instilled at Pemberley as the new mistress."

Any humour in the situation drained from Darcy in an instant, and he was once again furious with his aunt. "Lady Catherine, I have informed you on multiple occasions that it is not my intention to marry Anne. She is neither inclined towards me nor am I bound to her. There will never be a union between us, so you should start looking elsewhere for her prospects."

"You cannot turn your back on her now! All of London expects your marriage! I have even ordered the invitations for a lovely August wedding in Kent. I had hoped for a June wedding at St. Margaret's with the wedding breakfast at Matlock house, but you have taken your time with the formal appeal, and my sister Matlock could not be bothered to make the arrangements. Then the new St. Margaret's bishop, who claims not to know me, refused to schedule the ceremony without confirmation from the groom! Well, my vicar in Hunsford was most obliging, and of course the Rosings Park servants could have the breakfast ready with hardly a day's notice. After the ceremony, you will take your wedding trip to the Lakes and return home to Pemberley before Michaelmas."

"Excuse me?" It was Elizabeth who found her voice first and exclaimed the question each was screaming inside their heads.

"Did I not already dismiss you, Miss Elizabeth? How unacceptable that you should speak to your employer's family in such a tone. Really, Fitzwilliam, you must let her go this instant. Publish the engagement announcement with the London papers to be run this week and let Anne welcome your guests to the house party as the expected mistress. She can even tour the family apartments during the party and plan updates to be completed before you finish your wedding trip."

It was Georgiana who spoke up this time. "Aunt Catherine, Elizabeth is my companion to dismiss or keep by my side, and in truth, she is a member of our family in such a way that we do not restrict her movements inside the house. I would never be so impolite as to send her away. You are not mistress of this house, and no matter your relation to the master, your place is not to direct the members of our home. Now, please apologize to Elizabeth for your unending rudeness." Georgiana spoke with a calm directness that none had yet heard from the young lady. The similarity to Lady Catherine's sweet, but determined, baby sister was never so apparent. She had never allowed anyone to abuse the Fitzwilliam or Darcy servants, from the most respectable upstairs staff to the lowliest stable boy. Lady Anne Darcy always said that each deserved respect and kindness for all their hard work.

The thought of her beloved baby sister whose life was cut tragically short by the whims of nature induced Lady Catherine to actually issue the demanded apology. "Forgive me, Miss Elizabeth. This is your home and I should not assume the role of mistress where I do not rightfully hold that title."

Elizabeth respectfully nodded her head. "Thank you, my lady, I shall think on it no more."

When the scene in front of him came to a close, Darcy finally regained his voice. "Lady Catherine, I must insist that you repeat your declaration regarding some invitations to a Kent wedding in August. Did I hear you correctly, that you have actually ORDERED invitations declaring my wedding to your daughter in two months?"

"Yes, Fitzwilliam. I was worried that if you proposed too late in the season, they would not arrive in time to have the wedding when the orchids are in bloom. You know how much Anne loves the orchids in her father's greenhouse."

Fitzwilliam George James Darcy stood from his chair, gathered his full height, straightened his jacket and waist coat, and then fixed his aunt with the most intimidating stare. "I will say this exactly one time more, then the subject shall be forever closed, and no one in this house shall even acknowledge you if you speak on it again. I will not marry Anne, ever. Nothing you do, neither rumours you have spread, nor invitations you have ordered, shall change my mind. I suggest you give up this fool's errand before you irreversibly hurt your daughter. Incidentally, I had no idea that Anne loves orchids. We are not overly fond of each other and rarely converse beyond mild pleasantries. Perhaps you were thinking of Richard. He is the gentleman who often entertains our cousin during visits to Rosings Park. In fact, I bring him along for most visits to provide a buffer between Anne and myself. Good day, Aunt. I hope you have a pleasant trip back to Kent." Without another word, Darcy left the study and walked straight up the staircase to the family wing, looking for relief in the one place even his overbearing aunt would not follow: the master's bedroom suite.

The three ladies left in the study watched Darcy ascend the stairs, quiet with their own thoughts.

Georgiana spoke once Darcy turned out of their collective sight. "Aunt Catherine, my brother is very serious on this matter. You should allow my cousin Anne to direct her own future. She is a young woman who deserves to make decisions that will increase her happiness. This season, she has danced with some eligible men and enjoyed the company of her Fitzwilliam family. Surely there is another gentleman of her acquaintance that you would find an acceptable suitor whom Anne prefers to my brother. I believe I can name several right now, and some even with titles of their own. Lord Captain Thurston Finch comes to mind."

Lady Catherine's affronted face would have been comical if not for the disgust evident in her features. "An army captain! How ridiculous!"

Georgiana tried with mild success to hide her eye roll. "A decorated army captain with a valuable commission who is the son of the Earl of Nottingham. The second sons and even third sons deserve to find happy marriages too."

"Well, perhaps I shall ask Anne what she prefers and allow her to produce a list of alternatives to Fitzwilliam. But if word of your brother's jilt of my Anne begins to damage her reputation, I shall know how to act! I shall insist he do the honourable thing!"

This time Georgiana did not even try to stop the eye roll. "Aunt, not one person amongst the *ton* believes that my brother and my cousin are engaged, even under such particular circumstances upon which you like to expound. She shall not be 'jilted' by rumours amongst our social acquaintances, rather, her reputation might be tainted by her mother's unseemly and presumptuous behaviour. I caution you to cease your proclamations about their impending marriage, for William is not to be moved here. He will not marry Anne."

"Humph." Lady Catherine set down her teacup, rapped her cane on the floor twice, and then rose from her seat. "I must be going. I've already spent much too long here. Thank you for the tea. Enjoy the rest of your afternoon, dear."

Georgiana rang for the doorman and accompanied her aunt into the foyer to issue a proper goodbye.

Just before the grand lady swept out of the front door, she paused and half turned her head and shoulders back towards Georgiana.

"Please let me say, my dear, how much you remind me of my dear sister, Lady Anne, every day. You have certainly grown into a beautiful and graceful young lady." Then, Lady Catherine was over the threshold, down the front steps, and ushered into her waiting carriage before the lone tear fell from Georgiana's cheek.

# Chapter 20

## Traveling and Interrogations

***An Inn off the Great North Road***
***10 June 1813***

A MOST EXTRAVAGANT CARAVAN AMBLED THROUGH THE STREETS OF London. Seven large equipages with full liveried coachmen plus three servant carriages and two luggage carts made up the party which transferred the guests of the Darcys' summer house party. Over the objections of Darcy, Lady Matlock insisted the whole party meet at Matlock House and depart together at ten a.m. Such a nonsensical departure hour ensured that the streets were filled with traffic and fashionable people strolling towards their morning calls. That was Lady Matlock's intention, of course: for everyone in London, from the lowliest street beggar to the Prince Regent himself, to see the grandeur of Georgiana Darcy's traveling party.

Inside the Darcys' converted stagecoach—an enormous, specially-made equipage which Darcy's father had purchased from the old posting station in Derby—the atmosphere was tense. Georgiana and Elizabeth were attempting to engage the other four ladies in some conversation, but Lady Grace,

Lady Fiona, and Caroline refused to speak. Only Lady Miranda made any attempt at civility.

Back at Matlock House, there had been a mild disagreement about who was to ride in which carriage. Assuming that Darcy would accompany his sister, each of the young ladies still vying for his attention tried to insinuate herself into the Darcy stagecoach. The four ladies nearly pushed each other down to get close to Georgiana and express their desire to travel with their *dear friend.* When the time came to load into the carriages, Lady Matlock loudly commented how lovely it would be if Lady Fiona and Georgiana could get some time to catch up with each other during the journey north. Before either Darcy or Georgiana could open their mouths to indicate the Bennet ladies had already been invited to travel with the Darcys, Lady Fiona had taken Darcy's hand and stepped into the coach. Not to be left out, Caroline instantly stepped in behind Lady Fiona. Lady Miranda and Lady Grace each all but tripped on their skirts to gain seats before the coach was filled without them.

So, with four simpering ladies seated inside, there was room only for Georgiana, whom Darcy handed in second-to-last, and then finally Elizabeth. The collective glare towards Elizabeth and audible groan of the other coach occupants would have been humorous except for the long day of travel ahead. And Darcy was left without a seat in his own transport! Thankfully, Bingley stepped up at that moment and offered seats in his well-sprung and recently re-cushioned carriage to Darcy, Jane, and Mary.

Now, more than two hours after setting out from St. James's Place, the Pemberley-bound caravan finally passed Hampstead Heath, and the traffic thinned into a reasonable flock of northbound travellers. The coachmen coaxed the horses into a nice canter and the passengers inside the Darcy coach let the calm of the countryside temper their sour moods.

Darcy was seriously displeased with his aunt for arranging the travellers in such a way as to deprive him of the pleasure of riding in his own coach. He had a mildly pleasant trip riding with Bingley, Jane, Mary, and Bristol, who had surprisingly joined Bingley instead of riding in his own carriage. Mostly, however, Darcy sat staring out of the window with a forlorn look upon his face. Darcy's actions and attitude were generally ignored by his sisters-in-law and best friend, each of whom were well acquainted with his more morose tendencies and also guessed at the true bent of his thoughts, wishing a certain set of fine eyes was amongst them. Unfortunately, Bristol was neither used to seeing his old friend so downhearted, nor was he privy to the true leaning of Darcy's heart.

"Darcy, my man, what has you so depressed this day? Are you not enjoying the company of these lovely ladies and your university comrades? Surely, if you prefer the attention of another young lady, your sister's companion could be made to travel with us once we stop to refresh the horses in a few hours. I have to say I was surprised that Lady Matlock did not object to her being handed into the coach after your sister. I know she would have preferred a more prominent figure sit near the window so as to be seen riding down The Mall."

Darcy's anger flared, instantly. He was about to demand an apology for speaking so disrespectfully about Elizabeth, but was saved by Jane's gentle, diplomatic voice.

"My lord, I am sure my sister considers it her duty to accompany Miss Darcy and provide the female companionship she has come to rely on in such social situations. Miss Darcy is the hostess for this party and the young women now sitting in the Darcy coach are her personal guests and friends. Our Lizzy provides guidance in female conversation and quiet strength while instructing Miss Darcy in her duties as hostess. Besides, Mr. Darcy, I am sure, would rather not listen to all the talk of fashion, gothic novels, and balls, that is likely to dominate the conversation of five young ladies straight from the London season."

"Yes, thank you, Miss Bennet," Darcy said. "I dare say you are correct in your assessment of my interest in the general companionship to be had currently in my coach, but I was dismayed by my aunt's interference with the travel arrangements. I am mortified that Georgie's invitation to you both was so abruptly rescinded. At least Lady Matlock knows enough not to question my decision about sending Elizabeth with Georgie. My sister is not well at ease in such demanding social situations without Elizabeth, even when she is with me."

This time, it was Mary who spoke up. "Yes, Mr. Darcy, your sister does seem to respond to ours very well. We are all so glad that our families have become so close since Lizzy took her position in your household. Thank you again for including myself and my sister Jane in the invitation to your estate for the summer." Showing a new grasp of social awareness since the start of the summer season, Mary smoothly changed the subject. "Lord Bristol, where exactly is your ancestral home?"

The remainder of the conversation in the Bingley carriage centred on the differences between Pemberley and the Bristol estates.

Unlike Jane's kind representation of the conversation likely to be taking place in the Darcys' coach, when the ladies did begin to speak, it was not about fashion and balls.

Shortly after passing Hampstead Heath, Caroline decided to take her disappointment of being without Darcy's company out on Elizabeth.

"Miss Eliza," Caroline sneered, "we are nearly to Meryton, are we not? Have you had occasion to visit your poor, widowed mother since taking your position with the Darcys? And what of your cousin who inherited your father's estate? Did he not marry your particular friend, the former Miss Charlotte Lucas? I dare say it is nice to have the option to visit your friend at your former home if you ever have time to take away from your duties. Perhaps once Miss Darcy marries, or more likely when Mr. Darcy marries, and your services are no longer required, you can spend a few weeks in between situations visiting your family and friends."

Elizabeth was unruffled. "Miss Bingley, I have had two occasions to visit my mother in Meryton and one trip to visit my youngest sister in Scarborough since joining the Darcy household. Mr. Darcy has been extremely kind to allow me such time with my close family. Neither trip to Hertfordshire allowed for time to visit with my cousin Collins at Longbourn, though I know Mr. Darcy personally paid Mr. and Mrs. Collins a call while we were on the road to Pemberley last fall. Perhaps someday I will again visit my childhood home, but I am content to live at Pemberley and Darcy House for now."

"Yes, I imagine that your new accommodations are far superior to Longbourn. It can be no surprise at your preferring even the Pemberley servants' quarters to your prior home." Caroline did nothing to hide the scathing tone in her voice, but Elizabeth smiled through the misguided woman's diatribe.

"While Pemberley is unquestionably one of the most beautiful estates in all of England, I imagine that the change is more one of scale than real substance. My rooms at Pemberley, in the family wing, have all the same basic accommodations as Longbourn, such as a dressing room, a lovely fireplace, a comfortable bed, and a private sitting area." Elizabeth readjusted the button on her new blue traveling gloves. "I am surprised that you do not know the layout of typical country homes, Miss Bingley. Netherfield boasted a nearly identical layout of the Longbourn family wing, as the two homes were originally built within five years, with the original wing of Netherfield being slightly older. The second wing and new public rooms at Netherfield were added less than twenty years ago. But, I understand that not all ladies, especially those raised in London, have the same education in running a country estate."

Georgiana attempted to redirect the conversation. "I do hope that you will all find the accommodations in the guest wing to be comfortable. We have redecorated many of the rooms over the past year in anticipation of my coming out and hosting of more varied guests. Many of the rooms had not been reviewed since my mother's passing."

Caroline turned her pinched expression into an artificial smile as she turned her attention to Georgiana. "Oh, my dear Miss Darcy! You should have let me know you were redecorating. I could have assisted in your efforts." Caroline grasped Georgiana's hand from her seat across the coach. "I know how demanding such work can be on one's own, without help from someone with a refined sense of fashion."

"Actually, Miss Bingley," Georgiana pulled her hand away from Caroline's grasp as discreetly as possible, "Elizabeth helped a great deal, as did our long-time housekeeper, Mrs. Reynolds."

"Of course, such an experienced servant like Mrs. Reynolds would have the skills to oversee the work, but truly refined taste can only come from attention to fashion at the highest levels." Caroline looked down her nose at Elizabeth as she spoke about refined tastes. "But do not fret, my dear, this is why you have included only the closest of friends and family in this first invitation. We shall not be offended at any of your choices. In fact, I shall be glad to take a day and tour the rooms with you, making suggestions for some additional renovations which will correct any… misjudgements that Miss Eliza has made."

The discourse in Darcy's coach did not improve over the day of travel.

The first night at the Huntingdon traveling inn was even worse than the day had been. Lady Matlock had chosen the accommodations for the trip and made arrangements with the inn keepers. The inn that first night was well-kept and clean, but small. It had limited rooms, forcing most of the married couples and several of the unmarried sisters, including Jane and Mary Bennet, to share a room for the evening. Lady Matlock had determined that Elizabeth, instead of having the room attached to that of Miss Darcy, should share a room with Anne de Bourgh's companion, Mrs. Jenkinson, in the servant's wing.

To say that Darcy was furious would be a gross understatement. All day he had been separated from Elizabeth, due to Lady Matlock's heavy-handed ordering of his affairs. Now he would not even see her during the night. If Mrs. Jenkinson was expecting Elizabeth to share her room, then an absence would surely be noticed and commented upon.

It was also not lost on Darcy that Lady Matlock, whether maliciously, or simply out of long standing and ingrained prejudice, had treated Elizabeth as if she had no standing in society at all. It would be absolutely unacceptable for an unmarried gentlewoman to share a room with another lady who was not her close relation. Also, no one would bat an eye at three unmarried sisters sharing a room in a coaching inn, and additional cots were certainly available for the evening. No, instead his aunt had singled out Elizabeth as the Bennet sister who had lost all respectability. Her sisters were still treated as the daughters of a landed gentleman, and offered the comforts of a generous room and a lady's maid.

The second day was poised to pass like the first, until Darcy made it clear that he would be riding his horse instead of riding in any equipage. This declaration prompted Lady Fiona, Lady Grace, Lady Miranda and Caroline to wander towards their own carriages instead of spending another day trying to intimidate the other unmarried ladies. While Darcy exhausted his body to distract himself from his anger, Georgiana, Elizabeth, Jane, Mary, Bingley and Bristol enjoyed pleasant conversation in the comfortable Darcy coach.

On the second evening, Darcy again found that his aunt had reserved a room for Elizabeth and Mrs. Jenkinson to share in the servant's quarters, even though this particular inn was more than twice the size of the previous establishment and such space-saving was not necessary. This was the moment that Darcy's physical and mental exhaustion overran his propriety. In a slightly louder voice than was necessary, he informed the inn keeper that his sister wished for her companion to share her rooms that evening, and the double servant's room would be unnecessary. Then he requested dinner for himself, his sister, and Elizabeth be taken to the sitting room adjoining their two rooms.

While the Darcys enjoyed the peace found only within their small party, many of the other travellers were decidedly less at peace. Lady Matlock followed Darcy's example and requested dinner for herself, her husband, and her sons be taken in a private dining room. She was determined to have a serious conversation with the men closest to Darcy concerning his inappropriate behaviour.

"Henri, this ridiculous preference for his sister's companion has got to stop! How is he ever to choose an appropriate wife if he keeps insisting on treating that servant as if she were still a gentlewoman. I am sure that if we were not heading to Pemberley right now for an exclusive house party, the Earls of Nottingham and Derby would be reconsidering their approval of Darcy as a suitor for their daughters. As the head of this family, you shall have to set that boy straight!"

Lord Matlock slowly sipped his wine and considered his wife's passionate speech. It was his opinion that his nephew was in no hurry to marry anyone, especially not any of the ladies currently fighting over his attention. And with such a beautiful companion to capture his thoughts, there would be nothing he could do to convince Darcy to give up his attentions to Elizabeth.

"My dear, I understand your desire to see our nephew advantageously situated in marriage, but you misrepresent my position within Fitzwilliam's life. Indeed, I am the head of the Fitzwilliam family, but not the Darcy family. Fitzwilliam Darcy, as did his father before him, has always conducted his business outside of my purview. Yes, our nephew comes to me for advice when he needs it, and he has always headed my concerns when I have brought them to his attention, but I assure you that I have no ability to demand anything of the master of Pemberley." Lord Matlock looked towards his son Richard, who knew Darcy better than almost any other person. "What do you think, Richard? Has William made any preference for a young lady known or even hinted?"

After taking a large gulp of his wine, Richard looked around the small parlour. He was convinced that Darcy wanted to marry the enchanting Elizabeth Bennet. His attentions to Lydia Wickham and the inclusion of her other sisters in invitations, both now to Pemberley for the house party and during the season, signalled to Richard the depth of Darcy's resolve to make Elizabeth the next mistress of Pemberley. But saying so to his mother was likely not the best way forward.

"No, Father. I do not believe Darcy has any preference for the high society ladies currently in our company, or any other lady from the *ton*. I am also unsure exactly what any of us shall accomplish by bringing attention to what you consider ill-advised attention to Miss Elizabeth, Mother. He is sometimes hard to read, but I do not believe he looks to his own matrimony plans now."

While his parents continued to argue about Darcy, Richard silently ate his meal, keeping the remainder of his thoughts to himself. All the Fitzwilliams from Matlock would have been shocked to know that the two persons at the centre of their evening discussion were, at that moment, indulging in a shared bath.

❧

The warm rays of the sun were beginning to peek through the curtains in the spacious, but sparse, rented room occupied by Darcy and Elizabeth. It was finally the last day of traveling for the large group of partygoers, and Darcy expected to arrive at Pemberley's grounds in time for tea that afternoon.

After a restful night spent in each other's arms, Darcy opened his eyes to see the sun highlighting his wife's dark hair with kisses of auburn. He knew that they should rise. She should leave his bed and go back to his sister. All the Darcys should prepare for their two-week ordeal where Elizabeth would again inhabit the bedroom connected to Georgiana's room instead of his. Should, should, should… All the 'shoulds' were pushed aside in favour of a few more stolen minutes in each other arms and tasting the spot behind his wife's ear that always made her sigh with pleasure.

Just as Elizabeth started to respond to his ministrations, the door to Darcy's room shook with the force of banging from the hallway.

Both Darcy and Elizabeth froze for a second. When the knocking sounded again, this time with a call from Viscount Finwell, the oldest son of the Earl of Nottingham, Elizabeth buried herself into the covers and Darcy rose to find his robe. He made sure that the bed curtains facing the door were securely closed and no part of his wife was visible before opening the door to the hall.

"Finwell, what in the world is so important before six a.m.? I was under the impression we had chosen a departure of eight a.m. for the whole party, and breakfast was to be available in an hour." Darcy barely opened the door and did not make any move that could be interpreted as an invitation for the Viscount to enter. Looking behind the man banging on his door, Darcy saw that his oldest Matlock cousin, Viscount Huntley, was also standing outside his door.

"I am glad you had enough time in company last night to be appraised of the traveling plans." Finwell fixed Darcy with a hard stare. "I thought you abandoned us all before dinner." The irritation in Finwell's expression stemmed less from any perceived slight on the part of his long-time friend, than from the hours he had endured of his sister, Lady Fiona's complaining. Last night, he had been subjected to all manner of vile accusations against his friend, and demands that as the next Earl of Nottingham, he must speak to the wayward master of Pemberley. Before he was allowed to rest, he had been conscripted into doing her bidding and thus was up and dressed before any coffee could be smelled coming from the kitchen.

Huntley had promised Lord Matlock he would warn Darcy about Lady Matlock's mood and suspicions. He also planned to caution Darcy not to provide too much ammunition during the party with which to assassinate Elizabeth's reputation and perhaps his own in the process.

Trying to diffuse this tension, Huntly addressed his cousin. "Truly, Darcy, we have decided to ride ahead of the caravan and take a bit of sport with our mounts. Plodding along at the speed of the carriages for two days has us all weary. Come with us, old man, and we shall reach Pemberley in time to take a few turns about your training track before we must once again be presentable for tea. We shall also call for Richard and Finwell's brothers. Perhaps even Bristol, but he seems to have taken a preference for riding inside the carriages these last few days. Oh, and I suppose Bingley would enjoy some sport too." Huntly reached into the door to grasp Darcy's shoulder in a friendly manner. "Come, let us leave the ladies and old men to the cushions, and escape to manly pursuits."

Darcy stepped back and closed the door slightly to dissuade any of his friends from entering his bedchamber where Elizabeth was still hidden under the bed covers. Though Darcy certainly enjoyed riding his horse, and would have welcomed a few turns about the track with his friends, fear for the safety of his wife and sisters was foremost in his mind. "I think not. We are out in the middle of the country and still nearly seven hours from Pemberley. The next section of road is often empty and rarely sees travellers. Leaving the traveling company so devoid of men could invite trouble from highway men and other troublemakers."

Finwell huffed and crossed his arms. Could Darcy not let go of his overwhelming sense of responsibility and be suggestible for once? "That is ridiculous. You have five coachmen atop your equipage alone. Each other carriage has at least two, and often three coachmen. The number of male servants outnumber the ladies nearly two to one. Add to that your uncle, my father, Lord Derby, Mr. Hurst—though I do not know how useful he would be in a crisis—and possibly Bristol or Bingley. The young ladies will not find themselves without proper protection."

"I would never forgive myself if anything happened to my family so I could engage in some sport. No, I believe I shall stay with the caravan."

Finwell was frustrated. He needed to separate his friend from the group to have the conversation he had promised his mother and sister. It would be altogether too embarrassing to attempt the words in the hearing of the women. "Darcy! I insist that you come with us and that we find some separation from the group. Now, get dressed. I am going to demand coffee from the kitchen before this ridiculous affair begins." Finwell abruptly turned and stormed off towards the stairwell, leaving Darcy bewildered.

Huntly only shook his head and continued on with their request-turned-demand. "Darcy, Finwell is correct. The ladies will be well protected by our servants and fathers. We should not waste this opportunity to be in company with each other, since it will be expected that we all spend time with the young ***eligible*** ladies during the house party. Please say you will join us."

Perceiving something in his cousin's phrasing, though not comprehending exactly what unsaid message he was trying to convey, Darcy decided on a compromise. "Perhaps once we get to the outskirts of Leicester and the road has more regular traffic we can separate from the group. If we gallop all the way back to Pemberley from that point, we could arrive nearly two hours in advance of the carriages. This should be plenty of time to engage in some sport, and my three-year-old horses should be ready for racing. We have had good stable classes these last five years. This year's racing class was being broken as we left Pemberley for the season last spring."

Knowing that this was the best they were going to get from his immovable cousin, Huntley clapped Darcy's shoulder. "William, I believe that to be a grand compromise. Additionally, we will now have time to enjoy some much-needed breakfast before taking off. I shall leave you now to your toilette and inform the other riders of the day's plan."

Darcy nodded and turned to close the door. When he heard the viscount's footfalls moving away from his door, he locked it firmly and went back to his beloved wife. Elizabeth had been hiding under the bed covers throughout the entire conversation, moving as little as possible and even breathing only as much as was necessary for fear one of their early morning visitors would hear her. Once Darcy climbed back under the covers, she released her death grip on the sheets, snuggled into his offered embrace and hid her face in his neck. Neither spoke for a few long moments.

Finally, Darcy broke the silence. "Dearest, are you alright? I am sure neither of the viscounts had any idea you were here, as they could not even see the bed from their viewing angle. Please, Elizabeth, look at me. Let me know you are well." Darcy gently placed his finger under Elizabeth's chin to lift her face to his. He had been prepared for embarrassment due to the situation and even perhaps anger at him for allowing such a risky event to take place, but he was not prepared for tears.

"William, we have been so blind to how others see us. My reputation will surely be ruined, and all our sisters shall come down with me. How could we let this happen?"

"What are you talking about? I am sure no one suspects anything untoward is happening between us. None of my friends could have possibly seen you here and you have been in the company of either my sister or yours during both days of traveling. Why do you fear for your reputation?"

"Oh, my sweet love, do you not see why your friends, each with either an unmarried sister vying for your attention, or, as in the case of your cousin, a matchmaking mother hell-bent on seeing you advantageously married, have come to separate you from the traveling party? Did you not catch Lord Huntley's emphasis on spending time with '***eligible*** young ladies,' or how Lord Finwell desires to have a private conversation with you before we arrive home, likely regarding his sister's ambition to become the mistress of Pemberley?" Elizabeth took Darcy's face in her hands and rubbed his chin with her thumb. "I fear you shall be subjected to questions regarding your intentions towards the unmarried ladies in our party and perhaps even warnings about engaging in inappropriate activities with your sister's companion."

This revelation was most unwelcome. Darcy replayed the last two days in his head, including the most recent conversation with the two viscounts. He began to see his aunt's manoeuvring in a much different light. Going back even further through the events of the last eight months, he thought about how many of the times he had been offended at the way Elizabeth was slighted by Lady Matlock followed immediately behind some overt act of attention paid to her by him.

Now, in the warm embrace of his wife, with the morning sun full in the sky and two whole weeks of company ready to invade their sanctuary, Darcy began to fully appreciate the precarious position in which they found themselves. Oh, if only he had not allowed his aunt to bully him into this ridiculous house party! When he turned his attention back to Elizabeth, all the anger flew away with the sight of tears still streaming down her lovely face.

"Do not fret, dearest. I will not allow your reputation to suffer. I promised you last September that I would protect our family and I shall keep that promise." Darcy wiped her tears with the edge of the coverlet and kissed each of her eyes. "Today, once the caravan enters the road to Leicester, I will lead the young bucks in a race to Pemberley and submit myself to whatever conversation they wish to have. I will not lie if the conversation turns to my intentions regarding their sisters and cousins, but I will not hint at the true direction of my affections. Furthermore, I promise to behave for the next two weeks."

Elizabeth laid her head on Darcy's shoulder and wrapped her arms around his middle. "We have only these two weeks to bear and then we shall become like hermits, accepting no invitations and issuing the same."

Darcy brushed back a few stray hairs from Elizabeth's forehead. "Hopefully, Jane and Bingley will come to a final understanding soon."

"Yes, and I will stand by my promise to allow our marriage to be announced during the exchanging of Bingley's ring."

Though Elizabeth loathed being tickled, Darcy loved the way her little shrieks of laughter lightened her whole countenance. And tickling was always a well-deserved punishment for such teasing.

"You, my dear, are a menace! I will certainly wait until the register has been signed and no one can stop the legality of the ceremony." Both laughed and snuggled back down onto the pillows. "I am also hopeful that Bernard Finch may approach me as to an understanding with Georgiana. Even if he is not in a position to marry for another year or so, a formal courtship during the little season this winter, followed by a respectable engagement would bring them close to a year before their marriage. With Jane and Georgiana so well situated, we need not fear what our high connections might say."

Darcy sat up and took Elizabeth with him. Situating her on his lap, he kissed her with reverence and passion.

"I promise you my dearest, loveliest Elizabeth, all of your sacrifices and all of your enormous patience shall not be in vain."

# Chapter 21

## Duty and Honour

***Pemberley, Derbyshire***
***13 June 1813, Early Morning***

EARLY MORNING RAYS OF THE SUN SHOWERED ELIZABETH IN A BRILLIANT warmth through the curtains of her temporary bedchamber. Though the massive Donisthorp longcase clock chimed only eight times, the manor house had been busy with activity for nearly three hours. The servants had begun preparations for the first full day of the Darcys' house party even before dawn broke above the woods surrounding Pemberley. With the rising of the sun, so too did Darcy and Elizabeth rise from their cold, lonely beds. Neither slept well without the other, and they found that attempting sleep after the sun invaded their bed-chambers was a lost battle. It was a happy accident that they met on the stairs leading from the family wing to the breakfast dining room.

"Good morning, Elizabeth! You are up earlier than I would have imagined."

"Yes, I found I could not sleep in this morning. I also decided that I should take some time with Mrs. Reynolds today before the party starts in earnest to review any requirements or items she has been unable to obtain."

"I am sure Mrs. Reynolds has everything well in order. Even if there were shortages of requested items, alternatives have most assuredly already been provided."

"Of course, you are correct, I just hate to leave it all on her shoulders. I have forever been an early riser, so there is nothing bothersome about the task. What has you awake so early this morning? Did you not adequately tire yourself out with racing horses yesterday?"

Darcy made a frustrated face before schooling his features. "I cannot say that my body was over tired after the men's horse sport yesterday, but I was definitely left in poor spirits and tired of mind."

After leading the young men in a race to Pemberley the day before, Darcy had dutifully listened to his cousin and friends regarding the wishes of their mothers and sisters. Finwell had bluntly repeated the accusations of Lady Nottingham and Lady Fiona. Lord Asbury, the eldest son of Lord Derby merely stated his sister, Lady Miranda, had a long-standing admiration for Darcy. Finally, his cousin, Huntley, noted that Lady Matlock was becoming impatient with the unmarried state of all three of the Fitzwilliam male cousins. Darcy was as contrite as he could muster but defended himself, declaring that he was not inclined to marry any of the young ladies in their party. While none of the viscounts had been happy with the news, they were not particularly surprised. After hearing of the scheming and gossip circulating through the ladies of their party, it became difficult to keep his promise to Elizabeth to be a gracious host.

"Do not think on it anymore. Let us enjoy the entertainments set out for these days."

"Yes, I am looking forward to many of the planned activities. This morning I must ride out with the steward and check on a few of the tenant farms. I shall be back in time for luncheon, I am sure."

This first morning for Darcy and Elizabeth, spent in familiar surroundings, in familiar conversation at their sunny table, continued for another quarter hour with only their own servants in observation.

Or so they thought.

In actuality, the personal servants to Lady Matlock, Lady Nottingham, Lady Derby, Lady Grace, and Caroline Bingley all observed at least some portion of Elizabeth and Darcy's morning repast. So, before any male guest had even begun to stir, and with the primary parties engaged with estate business and therefore insensible to the storm brewing inside their guest wing, all the matchmaking mammas and the scheming ladies were being regaled with some version, mostly exaggerated, of the Darcys' early morning movements.

It was purely blind luck that Elizabeth's abigail, Marianne, was stocking Lady Matlock's bath with fresh linens at the exact moment the countess's own abigail burst in with the morning gossip. As personal servant to the mistress, Marianne was considered on equal footing with Mrs. Reynolds and above such tasks as moving the laundry about. But with so many guests all arrived at the same time, it had been difficult for the upstairs maids to fulfil all the requests for specific comforts. This morning, it was a good thing Marianne did not consider herself too high to help the household generally, as there was no one better suited to deliver this message to Elizabeth than herself.

Marianne stayed long enough to get the full story of what Lady Matlock's abigail was relaying before racing down the servants' staircase to find Mrs. Reynolds. Along her way to Mrs. Reynolds's office, she passed through the servants' dining room where Lilian and Connor Grayson, Georgiana's and Darcy's personal servants, were both having breakfast. She paused long enough to beg that they both leave immediately to the upper floors and keep their ears open for any gossip amongst the visiting servants and gentry. With only one glance between the Darcys' personal servants, all were off in a dash to gather what information they could.

Marianne knocked on the door to Mrs. Reynolds's office but did not wait for an invitation to begin. "Mrs. Reynolds! Mrs. Darcy, I must have your attention! I am sorry to bring this to you, but Lady Matlock's maid had some awful things to be saying this mornin'."

"What are you talking about, Marianne? We have not been here above five hours awake. What disaster could have already befallen us all?" Elizabeth was in a very good mood after her comfortable breakfast with Darcy and inclined to waive away the young servant's fervour. "Is there something wrong with the wallpaper in her ladyship's room? I have already heard much from Miss Bingley about how *unrefined* the new papers are in her rooms even though that is the exact paper I saw on the walls in the music room at Lord Grafton's home when we were there for dinner three weeks ago."

Shaking her head, Marianne stumbled over her next words. "No, I do not know what to say. It is most… indecent and… ungenerous."

Elizabeth patted Marianne's hand comfortingly. "I shall not think less of you for having to say that which others are guilty of gossiping about. It is better we know what problems may arise than become surprised."

"Yes, yes of course." Marianne fumbled with her apron. "Well… I mean… Lady Matlock's maid saw you at breakfast with the master, and then Lady Matlock discussed where she expected you might have slept last night to be up so early with Mr. Darcy."

This got Elizabeth's attention quickly. "Oh." It took several moments for Elizabeth to be able to gather her thoughts. "That is certainly less than ideal. However, eating breakfast together in a public room is not strictly outside of propriety."

"No, of course, ma'am. I am glad I have got here before her ladyship. It is a miracle, as there was talk of coming straight away down the stairs in her dressing gown."

Elizabeth chuckled. "I am not so sure that God's miracles extend to keeping lies and secrets from Mr. Darcy's family and other peers of the realm, but I do appreciate the warning."

Before any of them could decide how to handle any fallout from this situation, Lady Matlock barged into Mrs. Reynolds's office without evening knocking.

Just as Marianne had predicted, the enraged countess had donned her dressing gown and little else before storming out of her rooms. She initially demanded to speak with her nephew. When the guest wing footman informed her that the master had left early to inspect the fields, she turned her anger towards Elizabeth whom, she was informed, was meeting with Mrs. Reynolds.

Not waiting for directions to the housekeeper's office, Lady Matlock veritably flew down the stairs and rounded into the servant's corridor. She opened the first door on her right with all the confidence of a woman who had daily run two households and overseen the operation of three others for more than thirty years.

"Miss Bennet! How dare you act in such a vile manner with a house full of quality guests! I am heartily ashamed to even know your name, let alone to have had you as a guest in my own homes. What have you to say for yourself?"

"I am sorry, Lady Matlock, but I do not take your meaning. What actions do you disapprove of?"

Lady Matlock was nearly purple, she was holding herself so rigidly. "Cavorting with my nephew for a start! You are not a stupid girl, so do not pretend to be ignorant now of the bounds of propriety."

Elizabeth sat up straighter in her chair and raised one eyebrow. "Is taking breakfast in the public rooms at the same time as Mr. Darcy a breach of propriety that I was unaware of?"

"And exactly how did you *know* when Darcy would be at his breakfast if you were not with him before descending the stairs?"

"Excuse me, madam, but you are frank and entirely insulting. While I cannot stop your outbursts and idle gossip, I can choose not to grace certain questions with an answer."

"How dare you speak to me with such insolence, you, you, you *adventuress*?" Lady Matlock took a menacing step towards Elizabeth's chair, but Elizabeth just maintained her place without flinching. "I demand you leave immediately. Go back to your mother and take your baggage hooks out of my nephew. He is a nonpareil catch and will have his choice of the ladies once he is free of your Jezebel allurements! If you do not desist, you will be the ruin of both William and Georgiana. Have some decency!"

Lady Matlock's diatribe hit too close to many of Elizabeth's own fears for her family's reputation. While the rightful mistress of Pemberley would not be bullied into admitting wrongdoing where there was none, she did start to shed silent tears at the thought that they would be unsuccessful at protecting all the Bennets, Darcys, Fitzwilliams, and Gardiners.

"Josephine Finch Fitzwilliam! You will stop this madness, at once!"

The four women in Mrs. Reynolds's office looked back at the door and were very surprised to see an angry Lord Matlock bellowing at his own wife.

"Henri! What are you doing here? I would not need to take this hussy to task if you had spoken to William like I had asked."

Lord Matlock had spoken to Richard and Huntley the night before regarding the outcome of the young men's separation from the traveling party and the conversation that necessarily took place. While Richard had relayed that Darcy vehemently denied anything illicit regarding his relationship with Elizabeth, he had also decided to shared his private knowledge of Darcy's love for Elizabeth before her father's death, and Richard's belief that, once Georgiana was well settled, Darcy planned to marry her.

Before retiring for the night, the earl had decided that he had seen enough misery amongst his family members in regards to forced or arranged marriage. His own older sister had been sacrificed to Sir Lewis de Bourgh to pay his father's losses from a failed horse breeding investment. Lady Gwyneth had been neglected, due to the circumstance of her birth, and sold to the first man to look in her direction. While he and Josephine were tolerably happy, Lord Matlock personally knew of only one couple, Lady Anne and George Darcy, who had been truly in love during their marriage. If his nephew wanted to be happy with the sweet tempered, intelligent daughter of a gentleman, he would support the boy when the time came. He never imagined that time would come before breakfast next.

Standing in the Pemberley housekeeper's office, having heard several of the vilest things ever uttered by a lady come from his wife's mouth, Lord Matlock decided that he had to put an end to his wife's machinations.

"Josephine, you will desist abusing the young lady, this instant! She has done nothing except rise at an early hour to attend to her duties before the rest of the guests begin demanding her attention." He raised his finger and pointed a menacing finger at Lady Matlock. "This is NOT your house! I have allowed you too much latitude in your scheming concerning our nephew's marital state. Well, that ends today. If William is inclined to marry a woman you have deemed a good match, then bless them both. But if he is not so inclined, then when he does make HIS choice, you are hereby ordered to wish him joy and graciously accept the lady into our family. I do not care if she were to have been born a street urchin or sold flowers at Covent Garden before meeting William. The next Mrs. Darcy shall be given all the advantage of our connections and our support. Until that day, you are not to make one mention of his current state, you are to desist throwing young women into his path, and you are NEVER to abuse a member of his household again. Now, apologize to Miss Elizabeth and come back upstairs to right your appearance before we are expected to breakfast."

With a very sour look on her face, Lady Matlock turned towards Elizabeth. "Miss Elizabeth, it seems that this morning's gossip has been greatly exaggerated. I am sorry if my words caused you distress."

Lord Matlock took Lady Matlock's arm and forcefully escorted her out of the housekeeper's office, then back up the stairs to their suite of rooms.

Several long moments passed before any of the remaining ladies said anything. Finally, Marianne broke the silence. "I really must be going back upstairs. There are lots of towels and linens left to be sent around. Sally and Emily were having a hard time of it. I will keep my ears open for anything else, ma'am."

Elizabeth sighed. "Yes, I believe that is the best we can do for now. Thank you again for coming to me with the warning, even though we could not avoid the unpleasant discussion."

"Of course, ma'am. I shall see you when it is time to change for dinner."

Elizabeth nodded and turned back to the list of meat orders, which was still in her hand.

"Mrs. Darcy, as I was saying before, we are well in stock for the requested items. Please do not trouble yourself overly. If you would like to take some tea in your sitting room for a while, or perhaps even lie down again before the rest of the guests rise, I believe that would be a good thing. You seem a little pale this morning."

Elizabeth managed a smile. "You are right, of course. I slept poorly last night, and my stomach was upset this morning. I believe I will take some tea. Oh! I did want to ask, did Cook change the recipe for the lemon-dressed potatoes? They were not much to my liking last night."

"I am sorry, I do not believe the recipe has changed, but I shall ask." Mrs. Reynolds eyed Elizabeth with some suspicion. "Cook specifically included them last night as they are your favourite."

"They have always been the most excellent boiled potatoes with a hint of lemon and dill, and you are correct, quite my favourite. Perhaps it was just the traveling that has me out of sorts. No one else seemed to have any complaint about the potatoes. I am sure they were quite the exemplary vegetable." Elizabeth chuckled to herself with the memory of another dinner which seemed so long ago now.

Mrs. Reynolds gave Elizabeth a critical eye as she took her leave. Then, she went to the kitchen to personally prepare a special blend of tea with certain restorative and medicinal properties for her mistress.

By luncheon, which was to be taken on the large patio overlooking the extensive formal gardens, Elizabeth was feeling more herself, and Darcy was returned from the morning tenant meetings. Elizabeth was directing the final placement of chairs and tables as well as arranging the buffet table. Several of the guests, including Lady Matlock and Lady Nottingham, were milling about near the doors to the music room. Darcy was engaged in a discussion with several of the men just a few paces off from the ladies.

Elizabeth approached the gathered guests. "I believe that all of the food has been put out. Please come find a plate."

The friendly overture was met with stony silence from the countesses. Lady Matlock took the arm of her niece, Lady Fiona, and brushed past Elizabeth without looking at her directly. Lady Nottingham followed suit immediately. From inside the music room, most of the remaining assembled ladies headed outside without speaking to Elizabeth. Only Caroline Bingley interacted with Elizabeth on her way towards the buffet. Caroline smirked most ungenerously, then opened her fan directly in Elizabeth's face.

From ten paces away, Darcy saw all. He was just about to go demand what was wrong from someone, but Richard stopped him.

"Darcy, come talk to me for a moment." Richard led Darcy off to the far end of the terrace and directed them both to look out over the balcony.

"Why have you separated us from the group?" Darcy demanded. "Do you know something of Elizabeth's ill treatment just now?"

Lord Matlock had spoken with the other men before Darcy arrived home that morning and informed them that he would support his nephew and the members of the Darcy household against the vicious rumours regarding his relationship with Elizabeth. Lord Matlock, with help from Richard and Huntley, insisted that the only real evidence showed that his young, motherless niece had taken a particular liking to her witty, compassionate companion and Darcy was only guilty of allowing a sisterly, familial affection for the young woman. However, Lord Matlock's support for Darcy did not guarantee that Elizabeth would be treated with kindness. It just ensured that there would be no more public outbursts.

Probably.

"You must understand how disappointed some of the ladies are with your… lack of interest in the very eligible, very beautiful, very rich daughters of earls. It makes them talk. My mother was chastised by Father for her abuse of Miss Eli…"

"What do you mean, ***abuse***?" Darcy growled.

"Lower your voice, man! When did you lose your ability to stay stoic and silent for weeks on end?" Richard sighed and cleared his throat before continuing. "Yes, my mother confronted Miss Elizabeth this morning about some ridiculous gossip started by Mother's own abigail. Father was none too happy and took her to task for it. He has also spoken to the men, but you must be careful. Let Miss Elizabeth have some personal space. Be a little more hospitable to the ladies. Get this over with and then come up to scratch."

Richard did not wait for Darcy's response. He simply walked away to find his own plate.

While Darcy fumed across the terrace, Lady Sefton approached Elizabeth and linked their arms. "Come, dear, let us find a place to sit. I see you and I are not popular conversation partners this afternoon. I wonder why?" Lady Sefton's eyebrows rose with genuine questioning, but the effect was ruined by her large smile and laughing tone.

"Perhaps we frighten the other ladies with our taciturn natures."

Lady Sefton laughed. "Ha! My dear, I have never known a less taciturn young lady than yourself. Even when you have every right to be withdrawn. No, it must be our sharp wits. For neither of us suffers fools well, and who is more a fool than a woman chasing a man of good fortune?"

# Chapter 22

## Fun and Games

***Pemberley, Derbyshire***
***17 June 1813***

FOUR DAYS HAD NOT MADE MUCH OF A DIFFERENCE IN THE MOODS OF the guests at Pemberley, but at least the lovely activities kept everyone so well entertained that they did not display much open hostility towards Elizabeth. While it genuinely distressed her to know that Darcy's extended family may never fully accept her position as Mrs. Darcy, she was sure that she would never truly have any reason to repine. Darcy loved her completely. Georgiana was the most wonderful sister, and they would be happy together once all of the interferences left them. Elizabeth was also taking extraordinary pleasure in watching Jane and Mary enjoy the company, particularly the company of the gentlemanly son of a mill owner from Yorkshire and a certain earl from the south. As long as Elizabeth's sisters were safe from the scorn of society and Darcy loved her without reserve, she cared not what others said.

Over the last few evenings, Elizabeth had taken a particular joy in expressing many opinions not her own, especially related to politics, when conversing with one or the other of the earls. Even her staid husband had openly chuckled at her antics the prior evening. Elizabeth had been caught out when Lord Matlock heard her discussing the industrialization of the commons, playing the part of the Tory opposite to the staunch Whig ideals of Lord Nottingham. Earlier that day, she had discussed the exact same topic with Lord Matlock, only she had him convinced that she truly believed in Whig populist progressivism! When he heard his own words parroted by Elizabeth at his old friend and political rival, Lord Matlock was astonished. Even more so when the old bag actually listened to the young woman and conceded a point he himself had been trying to make for years! Lord Matlock nearly fell out of his chair with laughter and declared that all parliamentary debates were obviously useless. Instead, they should take turns speaking with witty, pretty, and intelligent women, because obviously that was where common ground could be reached.

Additionally, Elizabeth had taken a liking to the grand Lady Sefton. While Caroline often complained that her great-aunt by marriage was prickly and snobbish, Elizabeth found her to be a delightful conversationalist, and quick witted. In fact, Elizabeth believed that the distinguished lady held a similar disposition to herself, which may explain Caroline's dislike of both.

Yes, overall, this party was not nearly as unpleasant as Elizabeth had feared it would be. She was perhaps a bit overtired of late, but she was finding rest difficult without Darcy's comforting arms to surround her. The event was nearly half over and before anyone could blink an eye, most of the guests would be leaving for their own estates and Elizabeth would once again take her rightful place as mistress of Pemberley.

This lovely afternoon, everyone was enjoying the many joys of the Pemberley gardens.

Elizabeth and Georgiana had planned an easy afternoon of lawn games, garden tours and open carriage rides around the house grounds. Seating groups had been constructed near enough to the several games so that those who did not wish to play could enjoy watching the sport and speak to the other spectators. While Georgiana and Elizabeth battled Richard and Mary in lawn bowling, Darcy took up a seat under the large elm tree. He had just escorted Caroline, Lady Miranda, Lady Grace and Lady Fiona to the open Landau waiting to take guests on a tour of one of the more picturesque, and *long,* riding trails about the grounds. It would be over an hour before the horses made their way back to the formal gardens. Darcy had hoped to have Elizabeth and her sisters take the grounds tour with him, but he had been accosted by all four of his shadows the moment he mentioned a relaxing ride.

Bingley chuckled at the scene, but mostly at Jane's shocked expression watching four 'ladies' each try to take Darcy's arm. In the end, Bingley had forced Caroline to take his arm and leave Darcy alone. He then offered his other arm to Jane, and helped Darcy pile the women into the equipage. Just as all the ladies were situated, Bingley turned back to the game of lawn bowling and commented how well Georgiana was playing. When Darcy turned to observe the game, Bingley climbed in, closed the door, and called to the driver that they were ready to depart. Darcy did not even have to make an excuse as the carriage trotted off without him.

Not one to look a gift horse in the mouth, Darcy wandered to the seating area under the elm, anticipating the distinct pleasure of watching his wife's face flush a lovely shade of pink with the sporting exercise.

After a few minutes, Bernard took one of the other seats under the elm tree. The young solicitor would have claimed he did not have much of a reason for drifting under that particular elm, but his eyes were more often than not pointed in the direction of Georgiana. Now, Darcy would all too soon admit that he was not the best at reading the moods of women. Nor had he ever been the type of man to consciously observe those acts and attitudes of others which feed the gossip mills, but only a blind fool would have missed the way his old friend looked at his sister. It was also clear to Darcy that Georgiana had not been in as high of spirits recently.

Elizabeth had remarked to him during a rare moment of relative privacy that Bernard had been keeping a bit of distance from Georgiana during the house party, and they could no longer be found after dinner with their heads close, discussing some topic of mutual interest. In fact, as Darcy thought back over the last five days, he did not believe he had seen Bernard on the same side of the room as Georgiana since arriving at Pemberley. The only logical conclusion to Darcy was that the two had quarrelled over something and now were not speaking as freely with each other.

Whatever the reason for this new distance, it was making his baby sister unhappy, and Darcy was resolved to find some way to rectify the situation.

A private audience with Bernard under the elm tree seemed like the perfect time to take matters into his own hands.

"My sister looks well this afternoon, does she not, Bernard?"

Bernard jumped nearly into the top branches at Darcy's sudden and rather forced outburst. "I dare say she does, Darcy. Miss Darcy is quite the lovely young lady. You must be proud of her accomplishments."

"I believe I would be proud of my sister if all she had ever accomplished was a sweet disposition and a genuine smile, but yes, her education is quite complete. I only hope that a man worthy of her shall see her true value someday."

At these words, Bernard bristled inside.

Ever since their arrival at Pemberley, Bernard had been distant and uneasy. Georgiana had dared to hope that, perhaps, here, amongst friends and family, he would be more relaxed than when dancing in full view of London society and that they may come to an understanding.

Sadly, instead of moving towards an understanding, he had been distinctly avoiding her.

Darcy had very much hoped that he could have all three of his sisters currently under his charge well settled by the end of this house party. He had even entertained some musings about using the grand ball next week to announce all three betrothals and introduce Elizabeth to all of the Derbyshire gentry as his Mrs. Darcy. While he had positive knowledge that Bingley planned to propose to Jane before the ball, and it seemed that Bristol and Mary were often found discussing music or scriptures at the edges of the party, Bernard had not said one word about his intentions.

Bernard Finch was terrified.

Growing up the third son of the Earl of Nottingham, he had certainly lived much of his life in comfort and luxury, but it had always seemed transient. His older brothers never let him forget that he would have to make his own way in the world. Any stipend the estate could provide for him would not support a family, and he had never been particularly close to the viscount, so planning to live at the family estate was out of the question. His father had paid his way through school and supported him in his early days at the solicitor's firm, but since purchasing his own London town home nearly two years ago, he had received only a token allowance.

True, much of his season entertainments were funded by his family, and as a bachelor he was not expected to entertain, but he was still expected to at least dress the part. Silk shirts were terribly expensive. Knowing the cost of only enough silk to cover his thin upper torso, he did not even want to imagine the price of one of the fashionable dresses that ladies were expected to wear, sporting at least one layer of silk, and another of taffeta, plus lace trim and matching gloves. And the average lady of the *ton* purchased more than twenty such dresses every year!

If Bernard was honest and pragmatic about his situation, it really was not that dire. A successful London solicitor with personal accounts for members of the gentry could easily earn an income of over one thousand pounds per year. His house in town did not need to support tenant farms, or maintain the roads traversing his property. So, in terms of available money, this income was approximately equal to a well-positioned country gentleman. Plus, his mother's will set aside a significant portion of her settlement for him. But one thousand pounds per year would not purchase them the lifestyle of the London *ton*, and he would not see any of his maternal inheritance until after her death, which he hoped was an exceptionally long time from the present. Bernard was proud of his profession, but it would not support the lifestyle Georgiana enjoyed.

Logically, he knew Georgiana did not care about his annual income. Logically, he also knew that Georgiana had a large dowry and would be able to purchase her own personal items and support several of the additional staff which would be required if he were to marry. He was fairly certain, because he worked at the firm which handled the Darcy personal accounts where the men enjoyed gossip as much as any scheming lady of the *ton*, that there were some restrictions on the principal amount of her dowry and that at least a portion was set up as an annuity. However, this really mattered little. Even if the whole sum was an annuity, the annual interest on thirty thousand pounds invested in the funds would bring at least one thousand and two hundred pounds, more than doubling his annual income.

His head also told him that Darcy was a generous man who had little close family left, and who absolutely doted on his sweet baby sister. Darcy would forever purchase Georgiana whatever gifts she desired, would probably host them both and any children with which they would be blessed at Pemberley each summer for extended periods, and even supply them with an annual allowance, if needs be, to keep Georgiana and their children in the life to which she was accustomed. He would likely even pay for their sons to attend university.

All of this would be perfectly normal for a couple in their situation, even expected amongst the upper set. Many of his friends who were younger sons had such an arrangement with their wife's family. The only daughter of a wealthy family who enjoyed a close relationship to her oldest brother was a highly prized commodity with the younger sons. Often, in such a situation, it was more likely that the husband would become integrated into the wife's family than the traditional arrangement. Bernard surmised that his potential brother-in-law would actually be happy about adding a brother, especially when the alternative is losing his sister.

But no matter how many times his head told him that marrying Georgiana was the most logical decision he could ever make, his heart was holding him back. He loved her so completely and would never forgive himself if she lost the opportunity to marry a great man and take her rightful position as the mistress of a grand house. With her noble lineage, beauty, accomplishments, and dowry, Georgiana could easily become a countess or even a duchess. Arriving at Pemberley after so long a time living alone in his London townhouse brought Bernard out of the fantasy world he had built during the season. It was obvious, from the elegance of Pemberley's newly furnished guest wing to the extravagant sophistication of each formal dinner, that Georgiana was being raised to assume her place among the nobility.

How could he ever ask her to give up her rightful position in society because he was foolish enough to fall in love with her kind heart and passionate intelligence?

And he suspected Darcy did not believe that the mere *third* son of an Earl was good enough for his baby sister.

Turning back his conversation with Darcy, Bernard's anger infused his retort. "I suppose that only a man with lands and a mansion to match Pemberley would truly be ***worthy*** of Miss Darcy? What is the price that will secure such a beautiful lady? No less than five thousand pounds per year, I expect. Well, we cannot all be Mr. Fitzwilliam Darcy of Pemberley, you know."

This uncharacteristic outburst from his even-mannered friend caught Darcy off guard. He was now quite sure he knew what had kept Bernard and Georgiana apart, but he could not fathom how his friend had come to the conclusion that Darcy did not approve of the match. Not for the first time since his ill-fated proposal to Elizabeth in Hunsford, Darcy was grateful that he had learned how to control his own temper. Additionally, eight months of blissful matrimony with a woman who was frank and open had taught Darcy that sometimes a situation called for clarity of speech, propriety be damned.

"My friend, I believe that I shall count a man as worthy of my sister ONLY if he loves her truly and has managed to earn her love in return. Be he a duke, an under gardener, or even a solicitor. And do not be fooled, it is a much harder thing to find such a man than one who merely has an income of £5,000 per year. I have more than enough means to provide for Georgiana and any man she chooses as worthy of her affections. Though I must say, I do not believe someone owning a fine London townhouse with eight bedrooms and a valued position advising members of parliament constitutes a man in need of my support."

Stunned silence followed Darcy's all but explicit declaration that he would welcome Bernard as a brother. After another few minutes, Bristol joined Darcy and Bernard under the elm tree and Darcy called for a tray of lemonade. While some conversation did flow between the three relaxing gentlemen, the majority of their remaining time on the lawn was spent watching Elizabeth, Georgiana, Mary, and Richard play lawn bowling. Though, truthfully, none of the spectators took any notice of Richard.

Eventually, the games were packed away and the Landau returned from its grounds tour in time to see Darcy disappear into the manor house through the terrace doors with Elizabeth on his arm, laughing jovially at something she had just said. Four annoyed ladies and one content couple made their way back across the lawn to ascend the grand staircase and change for dinner.

Darcy was able to relay to Elizabeth his conversation with Bernard and she ensured that the dinner seating arrangement was adjusted so Bernard was seated right next to Georgiana. With any luck, they could finally come to an understanding, and perhaps even make a joyous announcement during the ball in a week's time!

❧

Georgiana was nervous as the end of dinner approached. As the hostess, it was her duty to signal the end of the meal and announce the entertainment for the evening. After not quite a sennight of performing the task, tonight was the first time that dessert would be served outside the dining room and the gentlemen and ladies would not be separating. This would require Georgiana to actually speak her invitation to adjourn to the drawing room instead of simply rising from her seat.

After the last of the meats had been cleared from the table, Georgiana looked to Elizabeth for support. Elizabeth's warm smile and encouraging head nod signalled it was time. Rising delicately from her chair, Georgiana had to start twice before being able to make her voice heard.

"This evening, we have planned some joint entertainment. For anyone inclined, we shall be having our dessert in the drawing room and a chess tournament. The winner shall earn a lovely prize to be sure, so there shall be lively competition. For anyone who does not wish to play chess, we have whist tables made up and Cook has made the most lovely fairy cakes. Please follow me to the drawing room."

Without much thought, Georgiana turned her smile upon her dinner partner, Bernard Finch. Bernard was so entrenched by her smile that he rose from the table without sparing a look for anyone else and offered Georgiana his arm. Most of the adults paying even minimal attention to the interactions of the young people could see how lovely a couple they made.

Now, the whole party made their way to the drawing room. Many of the older adults decided not to join the tournament, but most took seats near the tables to watch the young people. Of course, some of the more prominent figures in the room took their place among the players. When Lady Sefton took her place opposite Lady Miranda, the young woman looked as if she would be sick.

"Do not worry so, my dear. If you should beat me, I will only delay your admittance to Almack's next year by a few weeks. Hardly anyone comes during the little season anyway."

The wicked glint in Lady Sefton's eye told Darcy right away that she was merely teasing Lady Miranda, but then again, he was more than familiar with such teasing from a pair of fine eyes. The joke was completely lost on the young lady. Even though Lady Miranda was a well-practiced chess player, she failed to see Lady Sefton's bishop which took her queen within five moves, and the match deteriorated from there.

As the host, Darcy decided he should not play, but encouraged everyone else to take a place. In an attempt to tease him in the same manner as Georgiana or Elizabeth, Lady Fiona laid her hand on Darcy's forearm and said, "If you do not know how to play, I'm sure we could use one of the tables, and I can instruct you in the rules."

Darcy was quick to extricate himself from Lady Fiona's grasp and replied with his cold mask firmly in place. "I am perfectly well versed in the rules of the game, Lady Fiona, but I believe it would be poor manners if I ignored my guests in order to win a tournament in which the prize is something that I already own."

Before she could stop herself, Georgiana made a very unladylike snort and commented, "As if you would be the victor, dear brother, as Elizabeth has taken her place against Captain Finch."

Caroline chose this moment to interject herself back into the spotlight of the party. She had been seething all day and trying desperately to remain calm in this house where an unseemly outburst would not be covered up by her own loyal servants. First thing this morning, from her bedchamber window, she had spied Darcy walking out into the rose garden with Elizabeth and Lady Sefton before breakfast, but she had not been able to dress fast enough to join them. Then, she had been unlucky in choosing a seat too quickly at luncheon and could scarcely see Darcy, who was sitting between Lady Grace and Lady Fiona. But the final straw had been that ridiculous ride around the grounds.

*How dare Charles!*

She had successfully schemed such that the only available seat left in the Landau was directly across from her with a perfect viewing angle for her dangerously low-cut décolletage. Then, her idiotic brother took off before Darcy could even so much as glance at her ample assets.

Once she was back in the manor house, Caroline resolved to increase her offensive tactics, but she would have to tread carefully. These sorts of campaigns required precision and sharp attention to not squander any opportunity. Georgiana's remarks gave Caroline the perfect opening.

"My dear Eliza, do many of the *other* Pemberley servants play chess? I would not think that such a game lends itself well to someone without the *formal education* only available to the finest of society."

Darcy and Georgiana bristled at the implication that Elizabeth should spend her evenings in the company of the servants or that she was uneducated merely because she did not attend some expensive finishing school.

"Miss Bingley," Darcy replied. "I'm not sure Elizabeth has ever played chess against the multitude of Pemberley's staff who are educated in the game, but I believe my sister was referring to Elizabeth's winning record against myself and Georgie from this past winter and spring. At last count, I believe Elizabeth was winning nearly fifty games to Georgiana's eighteen and my dismal handful of wins."

Unlike Caroline, Darcy had enjoyed a glorious day. After breakfast with Elizabeth and a handful of other guests who were early risers, he had spent a few hours in productive meetings with his steward. Lunch had been enjoyable, even with the constant attentions of Lady Grace and Lady Fiona. His talk with Bernard meant that there were no more barriers to a wonderful match for Georgiana. He had noticed a new addition to Jane Bennet's left third finger. And the final crowing jewel to the day had been when Bristol had approached him before the dinner hour to ask permission to court Mary for the remainder of the house party, and if Darcy would do him the great honour of introducing Bristol to her uncle at their earliest convenience.

With three of their sisters nearly settled with respectful, thoughtful, and well-situated men, Darcy was feeling secure. Surely, if Jane, Georgiana, and Mary were all engaged or being formally courted by such men, Elizabeth would consent to announcing their own marriage soon. Perhaps even during the ball at the end of the next week. The stress of the situation was visibly wearing on his beautiful Elizabeth, and he was personally looking forward to demanding respect for his wife's position from all the mercenary, gossiping 'ladies' who would not even look Elizabeth in the eye this past season.

"Well, then," Caroline sneered, "I hope I shall have the pleasure of matching wits with Eliza before the tournament is over."

The night turned out to be wonderful fun for everyone involved. Darcy served as the tournament master, declaring match winners and drawing up the next pairs until the twenty or so players were reduced to four. Even though chess was considered a game of strategy and therefore more suited to a man's mind than a woman's, the final four players were Caroline v. Lady Fiona and Lady Grace v. Elizabeth. Never underestimate the cunning and strategic dominance of ladies, especially those in the marriage mart.

Lady Fiona was a fierce competitor, but lost her king to Caroline at the end.

Lady Grace and Elizabeth played a strained game. Even though there was no possible way that Lady Grace could have been mistaken as to Elizabeth's name, she repeatedly referred to her opponent as "Elinore" or "Emily" and once "Ashley." In Lady Grace's mind, it was a degradation to be playing opposite the paid companion—a *servant* for goodness sake—and the correct form of address to someone so wholly beneath herself was unnecessary.

Elizabeth was worried for Darcy's reaction to the deliberate disrespect and thankfully recognized Lady Grace's aggressive style of play nearly immediately. Even when the Lady was faced with an obviously losing board, she did not alter her attack style. She continued her fruitless campaign and aggressive stance even when Elizabeth moved in on Lady Grace's queen. Truly believing that power and connections made one superior in life, it came as a shock to the ill-mannered lady when, first her queen was taken by a pawn, and then Elizabeth got within two moves of taking her king. By the time Lady Grace decided to perhaps pay more attention to the game than to her attempts to degrade Elizabeth, it was too late. Elizabeth had quite successfully cornered Lady Grace into a trap.

After a break for some coffee and more cake, the final match between Caroline and Elizabeth was set up at a table in the centre of the drawing room. Some of the guests had retired, but the majority of Pemberley's inhabitants, including a larger number of upstairs servants than were strictly assigned to attend the drawing room, gathered to watch.

The game lasted for nearly an hour. Both Caroline and Elizabeth lost many pieces during the battle. Neither opponent spoke much, either to each other or the spectators, but the late hour did nothing to dampen the energy in the room.

Ultimately, Caroline made a surprising play and sacrificed her rook to thrust her queen, hiding behind, into play. Elizabeth was almost taken off guard, but managed to stop the attack by sacrificing her own queen. Without her most valuable piece, Elizabeth was unable to ward off Caroline's next attack, when she managed to sneak a pawn behind Elizabeth's defences and trap the king. At nearly midnight, Caroline was declared the winner.

Elizabeth herself presented Caroline with the evening's prize, a beautiful set of overlarge silk handkerchiefs finely embroidered with a scrolling **P** for Pemberley and the Darcy family crest.

And with the evening's entertainments ended, all of Pemberley's inhabitants headed to their beds.

Caroline ascended the grand stairs towards Pemberley's guest wing and made the decision to wait no longer. Looking upon her newly acquired handkerchiefs and taking them as a sign of her continued success, Caroline decided her new life would begin tomorrow. She pulled a long chain out of her pocket and looked down at the small but powerful object secreted away in the folds of her silk evening gown. Her maid had performed magnificently in procuring the item, and now nothing would stand in Caroline's way to getting everything she deserved.

# Chapter 23

## Check Mate

***Pemberley, Derbyshire***
***18 June 1813—Early Morning***

Jane Bennet could not claim to be an early riser, having lived her whole life with Elizabeth and Mary. In fact, Jane could only recall a handful of times in her life when she rose before her sister Elizabeth, and at least three of those times were due to Elizabeth taking ill. But, when compared to the ladies of leisure who kept "town hours" even while in the country, Jane was certainly up and about well before the fashionable hour.

This morning, Jane woke early. She must write several letters regarding her engagement to Charles Bingley.

During their stay at Pemberley, Bingley and Jane had been enjoying the relative freedom of courting openly with the blessing of her family under the guardianship of Darcy. The morning before, Bingley had invited Jane on a lovely, private walk around the lake before breakfast.

Bingley had been looking for an opportunity to tell Jane about the estate Darcy had found for him. At slightly under thirty miles to the north of Pemberley along well-maintained roads, it would be an easy distance from her favourite sister. Holdworth Hall was a modest estate with only four tenancies, but the house was reportedly in fine shape and about the size of Netherfield. Bingley did not need the money from farming since he still made nearly three thousand pounds each year from the wool mill and cloth manufacturer in Yorkshire, and an additional two thousand pounds from interest on his investments, but he wanted to provide Jane with a lifestyle to which she was accustomed. The estate was near the hamlet of Holdworth, right on the edge of the Peak District and less than two hours from the city of Sheffield.

Bingley and Darcy planned to meet with the estate's owner the week following the house party and negotiate a purchase price, if the property was in as good shape as they had been told. Bingley wanted to bring Jane and her sisters with him to determine whether she would have any pleasure in living there.

Just as they had reached the westernmost edge of the lake and turned back towards the manor house, a glorious sunrise crested the Pemberley woods and created a glittering display upon the surface of the water. Bingley had turned to comment on the beauty of the day to Jane and was rendered mute by the even greater beauty of his angel bathed in the morning sun. Her golden hair was glowing, and her pale skin shimmered with the healthy flush of their exercise. Off in the distance, a flock of birds cast fluttering shadows across the lake and solidified Bingley's resolve. Heaven was here, right in front of him. Bingley had dropped to one knee, taken out his mother's emerald ring that had been living in his waistcoat pocket for more than a month, and proposed.

Now, Jane's mother needed to know of their plan to wed at Pemberley near the end of August, and hopefully accommodations could be made for the rest of her family to join the Gardiners on their northern journey.

Another reason Jane rose early that morning was her fervent desire to speak privately with Elizabeth before the rest of the guests woke. The past week had been a trial for Jane. This was Elizabeth's home, the place she was rightfully mistress, but the others treated her with such distain. Without disclosing Elizabeth's secret, Jane had spoken to Bingley about the protection of her sisters after their marriage, and her fiancé had assured her that the Bennet family would be well cared for. Even Lydia and the baby. If they wanted to live with the Bingleys for the rest of their lives, he would support them. He would always keep his home open to the Bennet women.

Jane wanted to speak to Elizabeth about being able to finally call an end to her secret marriage. Even if Elizabeth was not yet ready to come clean with all of society, surely their families and close friends should be told. If the interactions between Georgiana and Bernard last night were any indication, she need not worry about her newest sister's future happiness. From now on, Jane was going to help shoulder the worry for the three youngest Bennet sisters.

After completing the letter to her mother, Jane asked the maid who had been attending her at Pemberley if the mistress was awake yet. It had been a small pleasure of Jane's to be able to speak freely with the young maid, Amy. Since the Pemberley staff all knew of the Darcys' wedding last October, Jane felt comfortable acknowledging her sister's position while in the privacy of her own rooms. Additionally, Jane had gleaned many comforting details of her sister's life in Derbyshire. Amy relayed that the master and mistress seemed much in love and had spent a great many happy days together over the winter and spring.

Amy replied that she had not seen the mistress's maid in the kitchens yet, which would indicate that her mistress had not completed her morning toilette, but that she was sure to be awake soon. Jane asked if Amy would bring her a tray with tea, toast, and some fruit to take to her sister's room, as she desired a private audience.

Several minutes later, Jane was walking down the family wing corridor with a lovely tea service and some light edibles when a blood curdling scream issued from the door behind her, at the top of the family staircase. Jane whipped around in time to see the door to the master's suite thrown wide by an unfamiliar maid. Colonel Richard Fitzwilliam and several footmen were barrelling down the halls towards the door, and Jane could see Bingley's red hair pop out from around the corner leading to the guest wing.

With bile rising in her stomach, Jane took a few steps towards the open door she knew led to her brother-in-law's bedchamber. From her position in the hall, she was the first to see the sight of Caroline Bingley sitting up in Fitzwilliam Darcy's bed, obviously unclothed and clutching the bedsheet to her breast, a most wicked smile gracing her usually stoic features.

After the whole of the house, including the servants, had gone to bed the night of the chess tournament, Caroline quietly took out the small treasure she had secreted away in her dress. It was a rather tiny piece of brass for something so powerful—the spare Pemberley master key pilfered from Mrs. Reynolds's office by her maid. It had taken her servant five whole days to find her way into the old housekeeper's private office, and Caroline had to supply the girl with lessons in picking a lock the evening before, but Caroline finally had her true prize. This key could open any door in the whole of the house, including the bedchambers of the family wing.

Winning at chess had been child's play to the confident, educated, moneyed, Caroline. Taking the title as the best player amongst the guests had been satisfying, but beating Elizabeth in the final match had been pure poetry. That no-class chit could never compete with Caroline. It was absurd! And more than a little obscene. All the ladies had been whispering behind their fans that Darcy had taken her as his mistress, and with Georgiana still in the house, no less! Did the penniless ***servant*** think that just because she had bedded him, he would deign to actually marry her? It was such a grand joke!

The irony of Caroline's own plan to secure the position of Mistress (with a CAPITAL M, thank you very much) was totally lost on the lady.

In the dark of night, Caroline made her way across the house to the ornately carved door which led to the mistress suite. Perhaps it was a bit naïve and somewhat romantic, but Caroline wanted to come to Darcy for the first time from the mistress's bedchamber instead of from the hall or the sitting room. She would act as if she was already mistress of this house, instead of some conniving harlot. Her plan was to open the adjourning door, come into the room, and when he asked what she was doing in his bedchamber, she would remove her nightshift and join him in his bed. If even half of what the young ladies tittered about was true, no man would be able to resist the invitation of a bare, beautiful woman in his bed.

Alerting the rest of the house to her whereabouts would again fall to her maid. Caroline did not like giving such an important task to a servant, but she must appear as if she was innocent in the seduction and embarrassed of her actions. She could not boast about her conquest as the men are said to do in their clubs. Therefore, it was necessary to have her maid go about spreading the word.

Upon entering the mistress's chambers, Caroline noticed that the room had been redone recently, certainly since the passing of the late Lady Anne Darcy almost seventeen years ago. For a moment, Caroline paused to consider her actions. If Darcy had gone to the expense to have the mistress's rooms updated, then surely, he intended to take a wife soon. Since Caroline could not fathom he would choose another, she briefly thought that tonight's deception was perhaps unnecessary. But, then Elizabeth rose to the front of her mind, and she continued.

Caroline's last thought as she unlocked the door between the mistress's and master's bedchambers was that, while the furnishing had been done in attractive and expensive fabrics, Caroline preferred a much more ornate style, so it shall need redoing again.

An annoyed huff was all that escaped Caroline's well-honed control upon finding the master's chamber devoid of her prey. How was she to seduce an empty bed? Well, no matter. It would have been a much better thing to secure her position by allowing Darcy to bed her immediately, but she did not actually need Darcy to be present for her plan to work. Being found in his bed would be more than adequate to ensure she was thoroughly compromised, and Darcy would have no choice but to marry her with haste.

Caroline discarded her dressing gown and nightshift onto the floor, then crawled into the massive bed. She decided that there was no need to disturb her sleep while waiting for Darcy to come up from whatever business he was tending, so she drifted off into a deep, peaceful sleep shortly after closing her eyes.

❧

Elizabeth woke to the startling sound of crashing dishes in the family wing corridor. She had been sound asleep much later than her usual wont, but it had been a late night for her and her husband.

After the chess tournament, Elizabeth, Darcy, and Georgiana said goodnight to their guests and headed up the family wing stairs together. Darcy noticed that Elizabeth leaned a little heavier on his arm than usual and the dark circles under her eyes concerned him greatly. They may be maintaining the facade of employer and employee for a bit longer, but he was not going to shirk his duty as her husband. After escorting his wife and sister to their adjoined bedchambers, he went to his dressing room and quickly changed for bed. Then Darcy traversed the five doors between his room and his wife's temporary room, careful to lock all of the doors behind him, to inquire after her health.

Contrary to his expectations, Elizabeth was not angry with her husband's presence in her bedchamber. She had been having a hard time sleeping through the night recently and overly tired during the day. She conceded that the chances of being discovered were low and asked Darcy to stay with her that night, a request which he was more than happy to oblige.

The master and mistress of Pemberley slept quite soundly wrapped in each other's arms all night.

Just as the first hint of light started to fill the sky, Darcy's valet, Connor, knocked loudly on the bedchamber where his employer slept. An urgent note had been delivered by the sixteen-year-old son of the Darcys' nearest neighbour, Elisha Masters. A fire had broken out at one of the tenant homes during the night and Elisha's father was in Scotland on business. The young man had never handled such a disaster on his own before and called on his nearest neighbour for help. Mr. Masters had been a very great help to Darcy when he was twenty-two and had the whole responsibility of Pemberley dropped on his head following his father's death, so of course, Darcy rose immediately, calling to have his horse saddled.

Connor knew that his master had shared his wife's bed that night, so he did not even bother going into the master's bedchamber that morning. Connor had retrieved work clothes from Darcy's dressing room and entered the mistress's temporary chamber through the servant's entrance. Darcy was dressed and in his saddle as the sun started to rise.

Elizabeth went back to sleep for a few hours. She was sleeping deeply, but she briefly opened her eyes when she thought she heard someone yell. She closed her eyes again, when a loud crash in the hallway made her sit straight up in bed. Then the sound of voices grew steadily outside her door. Elizabeth was donning her dressing gown when her abigail, Marianne, burst into her room looking quite wild in the eyes.

"My God, Marianne, whatever is the matter?"

Marianne had left her mistress before Darcy had come to his wife the night before and was unaware of their sleeping arrangements the night prior.

Having heard only that one of the unwed young women had been found in the master's bed, she was at a loss as to what to tell Elizabeth. "Mistress, I must beg you not to go out into the hall. Something dreadful has happened! Please, you must wait here in your rooms until Mrs. Reynolds can find the master."

"Whatever are you talking about, Marianne? Mr. Darcy left early this morning to help young Elisha Masters deal with a fire on one of the tenant farms. It is unknown when he shall return, but I do not expect he shall appear until the last of the flames are put out and the family has been situated in a temporary home. Now, tell me immediately what has happened to have you in such a state."

"Mistress," Marianne quaked as she spoke, "please excuse my unpardonable rudeness, but do you know where Mr. Darcy slept last night?"

Elizabeth was now too angry to even become embarrassed at such an inquiry. "Though I cannot imagine why it should be anyone's business but our own, Mr. Darcy spent the night in the bed, here, with me."

"The whole night, madam?"

"Yes! The whole night, Marianne! Have you ever known Mr. Darcy to leave me in the middle of the night? Now, I demand once again that you tell me what has happened, or I shall march straight out that door and find someone who WILL tell me."

The commotion in the hall and in the bedchamber adjoining her own had drawn Georgiana out of bed. Elizabeth's raised voice brought Georgiana barging into her sister's room in time to hear Marianne's explanation.

"Forgive me, mistress, but while I was fetching fresh towels for you this morning, I saw Connor and Jon Grayson huddled together and sayin' something about a horrid scandal to be had. Then, in the servants' stairs, I heard the screamin' that surely woke the devil himself. A moment later, one of the guest maids, I believe Miss Bingley's personal maid, came barrellin' down the back staircase saying quite loudly that some young miss had been found in Mr. Darcy's bed this morning. I could hardly believe my ears, but when I arrived in the main hallway, there was a crowd gathered about the master's chamber door, and your sister, Miss Jane, dropped Lady Anne's best china tea set after seein' into the room. I rushed right here and that is all I know. I swear it, my lady."

Elizabeth paled, but kept her head, which was a good thing, for she barely heard Georgiana's gasp behind her before the younger lady started to swoon. Elizabeth was just able to make it to Georgiana before she hit her head on the hard floor.

# Chapter 24

## Consequences

***Pemberley, Derbyshire***
***18 June 1813***

Colonel Richard Fitzwilliam was in shock. This could not be happening. It was unthinkable. His stoic, uptight, morally untouchable cousin could not have taken a maiden into his bed with a house full of respectable guests and the lady's own family under roof. There was something terribly wrong with this picture, but Richard could not readily figure out what it was.

Jane Bennet quickly regained her equilibrium after dropping the breakfast tray, and decided that only quick action by someone who knew the Darcys' secrets would save them now.

"Colonel Fitzwilliam, we need Mr. Darcy immediately. Go find his valet and bring him here at once. Charles, escort Caroline to her rooms and ensure that she dresses appropriately for the morning. And someone fetch me Mrs. Reynolds at once!"

Sparing one small glance for Caroline as Bingley forcefully dragged his sister from the room, Jane muttered, "Oh Caroline, what have you done to yourself now?" only loud enough for Caroline herself to hear. It was a bit unnerving to see the pity in Jane's usually kind eyes, but Caroline resolved to put it out of her mind. She held her head high as she clutched the sides of her dressing gown and walked back towards her own rooms.

Turning to an upstairs maid, Jane ordered the broken dishes and mess to be cleaned at once. Another maid was ordered to rush to the kitchens and have breakfast redistributed between the master's study and the yellow parlour, each which should be hastily prepared to receive the Darcys' guests.

Soon after both maids rushed off to their tasks, Bingley, Richard, the Grayson brothers, and Mrs. Reynolds appeared back in the family hallway outside the master suite.

"Mrs. Reynolds, is there somewhere we might speak with more privacy?"

"Of course, Miss Bennet." Taking out her chatelaine, Mrs. Reynolds unlocked the door to the sitting room between the master's and mistress's chambers. Richard and Jane followed her inside.

Connor was the first to speak up. "I know for certain that Mr. Darcy did not sleep in his rooms last night." Looking around, Connor decided to use a partial truth to cover for Darcy. "He has been working very late in his study these last several days and resting on the long couch in front of the fire there. This morning, before dawn, there was a fire on a neighbouring tenant farm and young Mr. Elijah Masters begged for his help. I took Mr. Darcy work clothes and saw him out of the back door myself before six a.m. I am certain he did not touch that harpy and is most certainly still ignorant of her intrusion into his bedchamber."

Jane had often been teased by her sisters and father for looking upon the world with rose coloured glasses, always ready to think the best of people. However, the last year, and Mr. Tannerbaugh's encounter with Elizabeth especially, had tempered Jane's faith in the goodness of people. While last fall, Jane would never have believed that Caroline was capable of such deceit, all doubt of Caroline's guilt in this situation was gone.

Jane nodded. "Thank you, Connor, for your defence of Mr. Darcy. I fear that Miss Bingley will find herself very disappointed in this instance, and while I would save her that unpleasantness, nothing we do here will hold weight until Mr. Darcy is returned. How shall we get him back? I hate to think of leaving others to deal with the fire."

"I will go and fetch him," Richard spoke up. "And I shall leave my brother with young Elijah. We are acquainted with the Masters family, and Huntley will know how to help."

"That is an excellent solution, thank you, Colonel." Jane sighed deeply. "Has anyone seen my sister or Miss Darcy this morning? They should be apprised of what has happened."

Mrs. Reynolds answered. "Neither of those ladies had called for their maids before I was summoned, but I believe I saw Marianne in the upstairs hall earlier. I will check on them and ensure that all the preparations for separate breakfast have been made." Mrs. Reynolds looked back to Richard. "Colonel, might you also talk with your father and have the men gather in the study for now? I think it best to control the discussion, and Lord Matlock is the best person to do so while Mr. Darcy is out."

"At once, of course. I shall leave now to my tasks." Richard saluted the group as he exited.

Mrs. Reynolds set out to find Elizabeth and Georgiana, and make sure that all the ladies were brought to the yellow parlour for breakfast, and to await further instructions. Upon entering Elizabeth's bedchamber, Mrs. Reynolds transferred her internal household tasks to Lillian and Marianne, who already had the two Darcy women fed and dressed for the day. Elizabeth and Georgiana, still looking pale after the morning's shock, descended to the first floor to greet any guests who came down the stairs looking for breakfast.

In all the confusion and chaos, no one noticed Mrs. Reynolds slip out of the door leading to the side of the house, or her subsequent brisk escape down the lane towards the servants' hamlet village of Pemberley.

With Darcy gone, helping his neighbour with a tenant house fire, Lord Matlock tried to take control of the men's discussion in the master's study, but the room was in a complete uproar! Richard had relayed the basics of the situation before taking Huntley to find Darcy. Before the Earl had been able to shake the sleep from his eyes and call for his valet, his wife had come bursting into his bedchamber to shriek about how every one of the guests' maids knew that Caroline had been found in Darcy's bed that morning.

Now, Lord Matlock sat behind Darcy's massive ebony desk and tried to make plans with the other Earls, but no one would stop shouting over each other.

*"Cannot let the Darcy name get a scandal! He must be made to marry within the week."*

*"The wedding must take place as soon as possible."*

*"The bishop in Nottingham can issue a special license today, if necessary."*

Lords Nottingham and Derby generally agreed that a marriage must take place within the sennight, but each disputed who should be the bride. The Darcy name was what was important, and the Darcy money. As long as the master of Pemberley married quickly, it would not matter that he had compromised some little social climbing trade chit. Caroline would be the one scandalized. The only thing that seemed to be of agreement was that, no matter what, the upstart could never be the mistress of Pemberley and should be sent back to her father's Yorkshire mills where she belonged. Darcy should marry one of the more appropriate daughters of the nobility present. They could easily hush up all this unpleasantness, so long as Caroline never came back to London.

Lord Matlock was not inclined to completely ruin a young woman, especially one with ties to Sefton. "Come, gentlemen, some consideration must be given to the lady in question. I am sure Darcy will have much to say on the matter when he arrives."

"Lord Matlock!" Bingley had joined the more illustrious men and made his way to front, relying on his position as the brother of the ruined lady in question. "My sister deserves none of your consideration. I am fully willing to remove her from all polite society, immediately. I will not sanction her marriage to anyone at the moment, least of all to Darcy. She constructed this whole situation, and with Darcy off helping the young Mr. Masters with an estate fire, he cannot even know what has happened. Surely, he need not be pressed into any marriage now."

Lord Derby spoke up. "I do not doubt that your chit of a sister is to blame here, but that does not mean Darcy can forego marriage."

"I quite agree!" Bellowed Lord Nottingham. "He should have been contracted to my Fiona years ago, but without his father here to advise him on the issue, he has continued to be stubborn. Darcy is too old and too rich to continue as a single man. This incident proves that he is too much in danger. Thankfully, we are all close friends and family here now. I shall have my brother, the Bishop of Nottingham, come here as soon as may be, with a special license. Darcy and Fiona can be married in two or three days."

"And why exactly do you think he would choose Lady Fiona? My Miranda is the better choice by far for Darcy's temperament."

"Lady Miranda is still a child!"

"And you think tha…"

This argument continued in spite of Lord Matlock's efforts to keep the peace.

Unnoticed, Lady Sefton sat quietly in a chair by the window, watching the men act like headless chickens. She had wanted to come with the men to ensure that Caroline did not receive what she wanted by so shameless a manoeuvre. Much to her surprise and delight, her great nephew's brother-in-law was holding his own.

Nearly one hour after the shouting had begun, the lords in the room still had not made any progress. Finally, the door to the study opened with a loud BANG! For a few blissful seconds, all the commotion ceased while everyone turned their heads. There stood the man himself, Fitzwilliam Darcy, covered in soot and singed around the edges. Slowly, he took a step into the room. In a blink, the cacophony of voices started again, louder this time, shouting out directions and demands to the master of Pemberley.

The noise of the master's study was a staggering contrast to the absolute silence in the yellow parlour. Lady Nottingham, Lady Darby, and the Dowager Bristol had given orders to have their trunks packed and ready to leave immediately. Their daughters' trunks were also being packed, under much protestation from the hopeful ladies who each believed that their father or brother would get them installed as the next Mrs. Darcy instead of the unworthy trade trollop. When each titled lady finally appeared in the makeshift breakfast room, dressed in traveling clothes instead of morning dresses, no one said a word. Georgiana had no idea how to handle the situation and Elizabeth felt it a much better thing to keep her head down until she could speak to Darcy.

More than three quarters of an hour after the breakfast things had been laid out on the side table in the parlour, Caroline and her sister, Louisa

Hurst, made an appearance at the door to the yellow parlour. Caroline was dressed in her finest day dress, wearing not one, but two jewelled silver combs in her orange hair and an emerald drop pendant neck choker with matching earrings. It was totally inappropriate for breakfast, but what did Caroline care? Today was to be her finest triumph, and she was going to enjoy every minute. With her head held high, Caroline marched straight to the head of the table, typically reserved for the hostess, which had a chair but no table setting. Caroline sat down and asked the nearest footman to bring her some fresh tea and a place setting. The startled footman looked to Elizabeth for direction and rather than start a new fuss, Elizabeth gave a short nod allowing the servants to proceed, catering to Caroline's rude and presumptive behaviour. At least Louisa had the good manners to look properly embarrassed.

Caroline proceeded to give demeaning and often nonsensical orders to the servants. "Gracious me! You there, bring in a whole new spread of morning bread. There is not nearly enough for the calibre of persons at the table. And this béchamel sauce is far too salty." (It most certainly was not.) "Have Cook make a new batch at once."

After taking a sip of her fresh tea, Caroline turned to the guests at the table. "Good morning, ladies. I trust everyone slept well." Everyone at the table continued in angry, resigned, or mortified silence. "At least as well as you could in such unfashionably decorated rooms. I will be certain to have the best decorator here at the earliest convenience."

Caroline buttered a scone and added a healthy dollop of cherry preserve before taking a large bite, completely ignoring the piercing stares of the other guests. In such a situation, most women of quality would have left the table the moment Caroline walked into the room, but each was too hell-bent on seeing the ridiculous woman put in her place to move one inch away from the yellow parlour.

Elizabeth prayed silently in her seat that Darcy would be back soon and this whole ridiculous event would be put to rest. With the security and assurance of a woman who loved and trusted her husband implicitly, Elizabeth spared a few sad thoughts for Caroline's pitiable future. Perhaps Darcy and Bingley would be able to find someone to take her for her dowry, preferably far away from the *ton* and Derbyshire.

Caroline's absurd behaviour, combined with the hostility of the room, was beginning to wear on Elizabeth's continued fatigue. Apparently, one night of mostly uninterrupted sleep was still not enough to dispel her lingering tiredness and nausea. Only a moment before Elizabeth decided to escape the parlour and search for Mrs. Reynolds, Lady Sefton, who had been absent all morning, made a grand entrance. She came in with a flurry, boasting a bright, cheerful smile, strolled right up to Elizabeth's chair, and took Elizabeth's hand between her own.

"My *dear* Mrs. Darcy, how wonderful it is to finally be free to acknowledge your position in company. I cannot tell you how lovely this house party has been, and so much excitement! You simply must let me tell you that I have not been so entertained in many years."

Darcy and the men of the master's property had barely managed to extinguish the flames which destroyed one home and were threatening at least two more when Richard and Huntley arrived at full speed. Darcy's stomach dropped at the look in Richard's eyes. He knew that look. It was the same look Richard had sported when he rode up to Darcy House in London personally carrying the express letter announcing the death of Darcy's father.

All of a sudden, Darcy was running towards his cousins, desperate to learn what could have possibly happened in the less than four hours since he had left the manor house.

"Good God! Richard, what's the matter? Is Elizabeth alright? Has something happened to her or Georgie? Please tell me they are both well!"

Huntley, the oldest of the three cousins, and more than a bit tired of playing peacemaker between his mother and his cousin responded before Richard could even open his mouth. "You should concern yourself less with the servant you hired to provide social companionship to *your sister*, and tell us what in the world you were doing taking CAROLINE BINGLEY into your bed last night! Does not your paid bint keep you satisfied? Was it the excitement of potentially getting caught? Well, now you will have to answer truthfully to all of the questions you have been avoiding this season."

Darcy blinked once. Then the stress of the past nine months, combined with the particular stress of this past week and the morning fire rose to a blinding rage. Taking Huntley by the lapels of his riding coat, Darcy unleashed his stress.

"YOU WILL NEVER AGAIN SPEAK SO DISRESPECTFULLY OF *MY WIFE*! Elizabeth is rightfully the mistress of my home, and I will not have one word spoken against her. Do you understand me! I can take you apart bit by bit with a rapier, and I certainly will not give you the choice of weapon in a gentlemen's duel the next time you unleash that acerbic tongue of yours against my wife. DO I MAKE MYSELF CLEAR?"

Richard's superior strength and experience dealing with hot-headed soldiers subdued Darcy before the Fitzwilliam gentlemen provided any more of a show for the gathered tenant farmers and Elisha Masters, but only just. "Darcy, now is not the time to brawl in the field like children. Miss Elizabeth and Georgiana are fine, but my brother and I came here to take you back to Pemberley, urgently. Miss Bingley was indeed found in your bed this morning, wearing naught but the bedclothes, and she means to trap you into marriage. Your valet has adamantly declared that you were not in your bed at all last night, but that will matter little to the earls, who are most likely gathered at this moment to try and force you into some kind of action. If you are not married by the end of the day, I am certain you shall be married by the end of the week. If you do not come with me post haste, you will likely have no say in the eventual bride."

The gravity of the situation finally penetrated Darcy's rage, and he looked between his cousins, taking a moment to calm his breathing. "Since I married Elizabeth by special license in the Pemberley Chapel last October with the blessing and consent of her Uncle Gardiner, I am not at all worried about what marriage schemes might be brewing inside Pemberley's walls. But we must contain this scandal and find some hole in which to hide Caroline Bingley for the rest of her natural life. She was in my bed, you say? Unclothed? Perhaps an Irish nunnery will take her. At least the Catholics know what to do with unbalanced, manipulative women."

Huntley and Richard looked at Darcy with nearly identical expressions of shock. Huntley recovered first. "Did you say you married Miss Elizabeth *last October*?"

"Yes, and we had our own reasons for keeping that information from being generally known outside a very select few persons. Today, that secrecy ends. Someone must stay with Elisha and help get the family settled in a new dwelling. The tenant house is a total loss. At least it is summer and the rains have not yet started. Richard, I would prefer you accompany me back to Pemberley."

"Do not worry, Darcy," Huntley said. "I came specifically for the purpose of staying with the young Mr. Masters. I have no intention of returning to your house until well after the supper hour. I may even ride back to Matlock and hide in my rooms until Mother's rage cools. Perhaps I shall see you again at Christmas… next year." With a final nod, Huntley strode away from Darcy and Richard to offer his assistance in relocating the unfortunate family whose entire lives had been destroyed by a fire.

Without another word, Darcy mounted his horse and headed for home with Richard close behind.

Upon re-entering the house, Mrs. Reynolds was met with a barrage of reports from the various maids and footmen trying to contain the situation. Caroline's outrageous behaviour was noted, but quickly dismissed as unimportant. Elizabeth would handle her soon enough. That Darcy had returned five minutes ago was very good news. Motioning to the new guest she had retrieved from the village, Mrs. Reynolds climbed the main staircase to the master's study.

Unfortunately, Darcy's appearance had not settled the storm or brought any kind of order to the assembled earls.

In fact, for the full five minutes that Darcy had been standing in the doorway to his own study, he had been able to say no more than two words and could only barely keep up with the myriad of voices calling for him to alternatively marry Caroline, don't marry Caroline, marry Lady such and such, or tell them the truth.

Mrs. Reynolds, with the help of two large footmen, cleared the doorway and made an entrance path for her guest.

"Silence!" The elderly vicar of Pemberley parish walked into the study and used his clear voice, accustomed to commanding the attention of men of wealth, to finally bring the room under regulation.

Everyone in the room, from the earls to the footmen carefully monitoring the situation, and the one lady nearly forgotten in the back, looked directly at the kindly man of God who had graced the Darcy family with his words of wisdom for nearly forty years. Each man present had listened to his sermons during summer holidays from school spent with friends, or social calls that turned into weeklong visits. The old vicar commanded the respect the cloth rightfully bestowed onto his person and took a moment to look each man of wealth and status in the eye before taking the massive book tucked under his arm to the centre of Darcy's equally massive desk.

Each and every man could hear the hearty paper rustle as the vicar opened the book to the current date then proceeded to go backwards, showing Lord Matlock that each page was dutifully filled completely, without even one line left empty. When he came to the page detailing October 3, 1812, he merely stopped turning pages and allowed the earl to read.

Just as Lord Matlock's eyes alighted on the line in the ancient book that stated Fitzwilliam George James Darcy had wed Elizabeth Francine Bennet by special license, the second shrill scream to reverberate against the halls of Pemberley that day rent the silence.

Lady Sefton had figured it all out the second the vicar had ambled into the room carrying what could only be the church's official book of records. Combined with the mixture of relief and nervousness on Darcy's face, she was sure that Darcy and Elizabeth had been married since well before the London season had even started, and they did not want to announce their marriage for some reason or another. There were certainly reasons enough for such deception. His awful relations may have tried to stop the union. Her father's death was not yet a year in the past. The youngest Bennet had that patched-up affair with the officer and a baby. Georgiana's recent debut and the other Bennet sisters who have yet to secure husbands... The reasons mattered not to Lady Sefton.

At one time in her past, the lady was ashamed to admit, they would have mattered a great deal. However, in her middle-age, Lady Sefton kept mostly to herself and her family, except when overseeing Almack's. It was a particular pleasure of the grand lady to watch the young people meeting and dancing away the night during the season, even more so when there was obvious affection between the courting couples. And it had always been overly obvious to Lady Sefton that there was an immense amount of affection between Fitzwilliam Darcy and Elizabeth Bennet, now known to be Elizabeth Darcy.

Having experienced a marriage built exclusively on money, connections, and social selectiveness, Lady Sefton never wished such a life upon anyone. Even the ridiculous sister-in-law of her nephew, Hurst.

Caroline Bingley was the worst kind of money grabbing, social climbing, gossiping harpy that London society had to offer. She was unkind and insincere, even to her siblings. But Lady Sefton knew Caroline was a product of the harsh English society which valued land ownership and a connection to nobility above the things that truly mattered. Well, the misguided young lady was in for quite a shock and an uncomfortable lesson in exactly how cruel the London elite could truly be.

Entering the yellow parlour, she quickly took stock of the assembled noble ladies, Elizabeth, Georgiana, and Bingley's sisters. One well-placed statement would put this whole thing to bed almost immediately. Coming to Elizabeth's side and taking her hand in a clear sign of respect, Lady Sefton did her part in launching the newly revealed Mrs. Darcy to her rightful place.

"My *dear* Mrs. Darcy, how wonderful it is to finally be free to acknowledge your position in company. I cannot tell you how lovely this house party has been, and so much excitement! You simply must let me tell you that I have not been so entertained in many years."

Elizabeth quickly regained her composure after Lady Sefton's greeting. It came as no surprise that this lady, the highest and most grand person of their current company, was the one to break the news.

Elizabeth chuckled and shook her head. "Thank you, Lady Sefton. I am very glad that you have found the entertainment to your liking. Please have a seat. Can I offer you some tea and breakfast?"

Lady Fiona was the first to find her tongue. "What do you *mean* calling this *servant* by the name, 'Mrs. Darcy'?"

Lady Sefton settled herself in her chair with more care than was strictly necessary and smoothed out the creases in her morning dress before pinning the young woman with a withering look. "What I mean, Lady Fiona, is that Mr. Darcy wed the lovely Miss Elizabeth Bennet ages ago by special license here in Pemberley's chapel, and I, for one, am glad that they have finally decided to announce their marriage publicly. In fact, the vicar is in the study with all of the men right now, along with the parish records book, to testify to the fact of their marriage." Lady Sefton decided to play as if she had known all along, to quell as much argument as possible. "Of course, those of us who knew respected their request for privacy. With the unfortunate death of her dear father, it could have been a scandal if the *ton* knew how quickly they married. But, of course, it is no crime and with five unmarried sisters, I believe it was noble of Mr. Darcy to help his intended's family in their time of great need and mourning."

A small, but shrill noise drew all eyes toward Caroline at the head of the table. After Lady Sefton's declaration that Elizabeth was Mrs. Darcy, all of the colour drained from Caroline's face. The lady's insistence that the Pemberley vicar was with the men put a crushing weight in Caroline's stomach. All that fear turned to rage upon looking back to Elizabeth. She looked much too content, almost relieved, at Lady Sefton's words. And there was a particular sparkle in her eyes that Caroline had always absolutely loathed.

Caroline turned an unhealthy shade of purple, then screamed with all her might and lunged at Elizabeth.

# Chapter 25

## Some Number of Weddings and a (Belated) Funeral

***Pemberley, Derbyshire***
***20 August 1813***

MRS. REYNOLDS WAS SITTING IN HER OFFICE EARLY IN THE MORNING, finishing a sizeable order for the Lambton butcher before tomorrow's wedding breakfast. The triple wedding of Miss Jane Bennet to Mr. Charles Bingley, Miss Mary Bennet to Lord Bristol, and, the most surprising, Mrs. Lydia Wickham to Mr. Malcom Fitzwilliam was going to be a joyous event! Tonight, the Darcys were hosting a formal dinner with some dancing for the assembled family and friends. Then, tomorrow at eleven a.m., the Pemberley parish church would be filled to capacity with all of the well-wishers. While the family came back to Pemberley for the wedding breakfast, the assembly hall in Lambton would host a large event for all the Darcys' tenants and the surrounding community members. Darcy had insisted on observing all the expected celebrations upon the marriage of his wife's sisters as if they had each been born a Darcy.

The celebrations were a welcome change from the mood of the past few weeks.

Pemberley's inhabitants had a very sombre five days leading up to the one-year anniversary of the death of Mr. Bennet. The Bennet women and their close relations had observed a full five days of remembrance for Mr. Bennet, including daily services in the Pemberley family chapel and no formal entertaining. Though Mr. Bennet had not, in his whole life, set foot inside Derbyshire County and certainly not on the Pemberley estate, each of the Darcys' tenants paid their respects to the mistress out of genuine affection and respect.

On 14 August 1813, Mrs. Bennet put away her mourning clothes, donned her widows cap, and came to breakfast in a sweet yellow day dress. The dinner party held that night was certainly not the liveliest seen at Pemberley, but it was a nice evening with some lovely entertainment by all of the young ladies, and much welcomed by the Bennet family.

Mrs. Reynolds put down her quill, sprinkled a handful of sand over her paper and stood to attend to the day's duties. Before leaving her office, she performed her new routine, adopted in the wake of the "Caroline Bingley Incident." Since discovering that Caroline's maid had forced her way into Mrs. Reynolds's office to steal the spare family wing master key, Mrs. Reynolds began checking that the key-box was appropriately full each and every time she either entered or left her office. After checking the box and locking the office door, Mrs. Reynolds spared a thought for that poor, stupid young woman then shook her head and went about her duties for the day.

***Pemberley, Derbyshire***
***18 June 1813—Just past the Breakfast Hour***

Upon hearing Caroline's scream, two footmen who had been attending the breakfasting ladies dashed to the table to restrain her from laying a hand on their mistress. A third footman went to Louisa Hurst who had become much too lightheaded in the wake of Lady Sefton's revelation regarding the Darcy marriage. Both Caroline and Louisa were taken to their rooms, forcibly in the case of Caroline, and kept there until Darcy and Bingley could provide specific instructions. Caroline's temper had reached such a level that four footmen were required to guard the doors leading from her rooms. All the way from the yellow parlour to the guest wing she screamed about the treatment of the servants in what was surely soon to be *HER HOUSE*, profusely declaring that it simply could not be true that Darcy was already married to the *LOW-BORN CHIT*, and demanding to be brought to her brother *AT ONCE*!

All the assembled ladies sat silently in their chairs until the door to the parlour was firmly shut by the butler. No one moved, or even blinked, for what seemed like an eternity to Elizabeth.

Finally, Lady Matlock broke the silence. "My dear Georgiana, I do not believe that I have been properly acquainted with your new sister. Would you do me the honour of an introduction?"

As shocked as both Elizabeth and Georgiana were at the civility of the words spoken by Darcy's illustrious aunt, Georgiana readily jumped at the opportunity to formally introduce Mrs. Elizabeth Francine Darcy, neé Bennet, formerly of the Longbourn Estate in Hertfordshire and daughter to the deceased Mr. Thomas Bennet, Esq., to the women at the table. Following the example of Lady Matlock, all the other noble ladies swallowed their pride and requested an introduction. Even Lady Fiona and Lady Grace decided it was in their immediate best interest to bite their tongues, at least until their fathers and brothers could be interrogated.

All the commotion caused by Caroline's removal from the yellow parlour had the men in the master's study dashing down the hall towards the women. Darcy was the first to reach the doors. He flung them open as Georgiana was completing the formal introductions and barrelled into the room, still looking an absolute fright in his sooty and singed work clothes, with smoke smudges across his face and hands.

The sudden appearance of her husband in such a state startled Elizabeth, and she rose from her chair in such haste that she knocked it down onto its back. "William! What in the worl…?"

Elizabeth's exclamation was cut short as all the blood in her head could not follow the rapid ascent, and the mistress of Pemberley promptly fainted. Immediately, Elizabeth was swept into the arms of the nearest waiting servant and removed to the bed in the mistress's chambers before she could fully come back to herself.

The hours between breakfast and dinner passed in a blur. The earls of Matlock, Nottingham, and Derby followed the Darcys upstairs and requested that their wives and daughters attend them in their rooms. The Dowager Countess of Bristol requested her son escort her to her rooms, and Lady Grace followed on the heels of her mother and brother, leaving only Georgiana and Lady Sefton at the table.

In the weeks following the incident, no one would be able to accurately describe exactly how it had happened, but by dinner time, all the assembled earls had decided that the best thing was to support Darcy and his wife, and each ordered his family to get in line or skip the next London season. The wealth of Pemberley was too great to be shunned, and each had too intimate a connection to the Darcy family (or dearly wished for a much greater connection) to escape all ridicule if any of the events of the day reached the gossip mongers of the *ton*.

To Elizabeth's absolute amazement, all her guests (except a few who were newly departed for the north) appeared at the appointed dinner hour, dressed in their finery, and proceeded to treat Elizabeth with the respect due the mistress of Pemberley. That evening, Elizabeth and Darcy sat at opposite ends of their large dining table and entertained their guests with good humour and no small measure of private joy.

While the earls had been handling their irate wives and petulant daughters, Darcy and Elizabeth had consulted with the Lambton physician concerning Elizabeth's troubling symptoms and recent fainting spell. Mrs. Reynolds had taken the liberty of calling the doctor after her mistress fainted. Personally, she believed that the halls of Pemberley were shortly to be filled with the pitter-patter of little feet. After the family's return from town, Mrs. Reynolds had noticed a few pointed changes in Elizabeth's food preferences. Though previously, Mrs. Reynolds had never seen Elizabeth eat more than a few bites of sugared cakes, much preferring Cook's tart lemon bars, in the last week the mistress of Pemberley had more than once chosen and consumed a whole slice of cake with powdered sugar frosting and had turned her nose at the dish yesterday when presented with a lemon bar. Additionally, Elizabeth had not once eaten her formerly favourite dressed potatoes with the lemon-dill salad cream, though Cook had included them at three different meals with the purpose of pleasing her mistress.

Combined with her constant tiredness of the last few days and the morning's fainting spell, Mrs. Reynolds was fairly certain Elizabeth was with child.

The doctor also concluded as much and told the Darcys that he expected them to welcome a new addition to the house about the first week of February, but of course nothing was certain until the babe quickened sometime in the next six to eight weeks. He also relayed that the fainting spell was perfectly normal for a newly pregnant woman who was overtaxing herself, and to avoid strenuous activity for a while. The knowledge that his pregnant wife had fainted from overtaxing herself sent Darcy into a panic. He was convinced that they needed to dismiss all their guests at once and place Elizabeth on bed rest immediately. Thankfully, Mrs. Reynolds and the doctor were able to disabuse him of those ideas before he informed Elizabeth, who was napping peacefully in her bed, of his reckless plans.

The final resolution to the day's mischief came before Mrs. Reynolds could show the good doctor back to his waiting curricle. Caroline had been shoved into Bingley's carriage in the company of Louisa and Reginald Hurst and sent on her way to an estate near Carlisle in the far north of England, owned by one of Hurst's cousins (on the non-Sefton side of the family) who never came to London. Reginald Hurst had spent too many years living in a house filled with Caroline's spies, believing that Bingley would never exert any control over his sister. A great many days had seen Hurst escaping into alcohol to drown out Caroline's incessant gossip and demands. This morning, he had been awakened from his alcohol-induced sleep by his wife in a state of panic. After he derived meaning from Louisa's hysterical speech, Hurst had rushed to the master's study to try and stop a travesty from befalling Darcy, whom Hurst had always rather liked. Hurst was as amazed as his great-aunt to witness Bingley's assertiveness with the earls.

His brother-in-law was not so blind to Caroline's wicked nature as he had originally thought.

After the arrival of the elderly Pemberley vicar and his records book, Hurst had again mirrored his great-aunt's thoughts, this time regarding Darcy's current marital status, and he immediately left to see to the removal of his family party from Pemberley.

Informing the Pemberley staff to have their trunks packed and sent along, Hurst ordered Bingley's carriage to depart as soon as possible. A small valise each was packed for Caroline, Louisa, and Hurst, then the three left without taking any formal leave of their hosts or the other guests. Hurst and Bingley had managed a rushed conversation regarding the handling of Caroline's ruination, then Bingley relinquished all responsibility for his sister.

Caroline was given exactly two choices: Marry the first man with whom Hurst could contract and Bingley would give the full twenty thousand pounds of her dowry to her new husband, or establish herself with what was left of her inheritance after her years of overspending, which was considerably less than twenty thousand pounds. Bingley would never give Caroline one additional farthing, and Caroline was henceforth never to step foot in one of Bingley's or Hurst's homes ever again. While Louisa visited her sister at least once a year and Bingley and Jane managed to visit Caroline every few years, more due to Jane's forgiving and kind nature than any familial affection from Bingley, no other person at Pemberley that day ever heard from or saw Caroline Bingley again.

The remainder of the Darcys' summer house party was an overwhelming success. Although Elizabeth had been sure that their noble guests would leave Pemberley before the day was done and never again acknowledge any of her family in public, they did not. Thankfully, any awkwardness from the revelation of Darcy and Elizabeth's marriage was put aside during that first dinner. Elizabeth was altogether too fond of laughing at the folly of the world to hold a grudge against the women who had previously treated her with such little respect. Besides, the Darcys really had put on a fabulous holiday, and everyone was looking forward to the final week's scheduled entertainments, so why ruin a good holiday with a few dashed hopes?

As conversations of such an intimate nature were highly irregular amongst the upper set, only Lady Matlock ever directly addressed an apology to Elizabeth. On the morning of the second day following *the incident*, Lady Matlock requested a private interview with both Elizabeth and Darcy after breakfast.

Lady Matlock apologized for her prior treatment of Elizabeth and her interference in Darcy's private dealings. She revealed that she had been feeling pressure from her sister-in-law to secure Lady Fiona the match she desperately desired and the added stress of her own children's continued unwed states was beginning to take a toll on her poor nerves. Elizabeth nearly spat her tea all over Lady Matlock upon hearing her mother's favoured expression come out of the lady's mouth. First Aunt Gardiner and now Lady Matlock had exhibited ridiculous and hurtful behaviour when faced with the responsibility to secure marital felicity for five young people. Perhaps her mother was not so absurd after all.

Lady Fiona and Lady Grace were the only two guests that never quite regained their full enjoyment of the entertainments. With now five failed seasons behind her, Lady Fiona was feeling all the desperation and pressure of an old maid. Her aunt's connection to Darcy had been her last hope of catching a young man with a proper estate. Her father had given her until her twenty-third birthday to choose a man of her own before he contracted for her marriage. The leading contender was the old, fat, and generally unappealing Earl of Southwark, who was looking for a replacement to his first wife who died birthing his third daughter. With her twenty-third birthday coming shortly after the New Year, Lady Fiona would have to beg her youngest brother to let her stay with him in London all winter to attend every single society event between now and her birthday, in hopes of finding someone more appealing.

Lady Grace was less disappointed at missing out on Darcy's person than his pocketbook.

Additionally, after hearing of her brother's intention to court and marry Elizabeth's younger sister, Lady Grace was exceedingly worried that she would be sent to live in the Dower House, due to her exceptionally rude and demeaning treatment of the future countess's sister. Much to Lady Grace's confusion and relief, she found Mary and Elizabeth to be kind and forgiving.

The crowning jewel of the summer was a fabulous ball on the final night of the Darcys' house party, which included the assembled guests as well as all the prominent Derbyshire families. William was overjoyed to introduce his wife to the quality gentry in the area. Elizabeth donned her wedding costume for the first time since the day they were married, and welcomed her guests with all the splendour that Pemberley had to offer.

Since their marriage was no longer a secret, Darcy decided that as many members of their respective families as could make the trip should also be in attendance for Elizabeth's grand debut as the mistress of Pemberley. He had sent several express invitations to the Gardiners, the Phillipses, and Lydia.

The whole evening had been an unqualified success!

Everyone in attendance had been charmed by the new Mrs. Darcy, and more than one person mentioned that they had never seen Darcy in such a grand mood or dance so many sets. The first half of the evening was fully dedicated to revelling in the hostess's uncommon skills and her twinkling laughter.

At supper, the Darcys decided that the night was too wonderful, and such a grand occasion deserved even more felicity. So, before the dessert was to be set out, Darcy called for a round of champagne, then raised his glass to toast the engagements of his wife's three sisters. Just the day before the ball, Bingley, Bristol, and Malcolm Fitzwilliam had each come to Edward Gardiner, asking for formal permission to marry Jane, Mary, and Lydia.

Georgiana and Bernard Finch had also come to their own understanding in the days leading up to the ball, but since Bernard was not in a position to marry for another year or so, they decided to enter into an extended courtship instead of a formal engagement. Darcy was glad that his sister was going to be well matched, but also glad not to be losing her quite yet.

It was a night that none of the assembled members of Darcy's families would ever forget.

***Pemberley, Derbyshire***
***21 August 1813***

Over the past five days, Pemberley Manor had been slowly filling to capacity with all of the wedding guests from nearly every county in the whole of England, and a few from Scotland. A welcome surprise guest had been Charlotte Collins. Charlotte rolled up in a fine carriage with the Fitzwilliam Crest on the side on 15 August and alighted with Lady Gwyneth, Colonel Richard Fitzwilliam, Bernard Finch, and her young sister, Maria Lucas.

A fortnight before, Lady Gwyneth, Richard, and Bernard had left Pemberley on some business in London. Elizabeth had never asked the details, but since she was overly busy with preparations for the wedding, she was not concerned with their trip. In truth, Darcy, Bingley, Bristol, and Malcom had sent Richard and Lady Gwyneth to Bernard Finch's law firm in London to renew the male line entailment on Longbourn for the next generation. Lydia's son, Thomas, was legally the closest male issue to Mr. Bennet and, in the event Collins never had a male child, Thomas should be the next in line to inherit. Darcy, Bingley, Bristol, and Malcolm, being the husband and fiancés of Mr. Bennet's daughters, had legal standing to insist that their children be in line to inherit Longbourn.

Upon calling on the Collinses to present them with the entailment renewal, Charlotte decided she wished to see her particular friend and witness the joyous wedding of the three Bennet sisters. Collins refused to go because Darcy's marriage to Elizabeth had upset Lady Catherine very much. She had advised Collins to cut off all communication with the Bennets and the Darcys immediately. She was not temperate in her abuse of all the former ladies of Longbourn, and Elizabeth in particular.

Though Charlotte did not regret her marriage, she was tired of her husband's idiocy. She told him in no uncertain terms that she would be traveling to Pemberley for the wedding and staying for a nice long holiday with her particular friend. She did not anticipate returning to Longbourn for at least two months complete.

The last thing Charlotte left behind were words for her husband to seriously consider over the length of her absence: "I know that you shall always commiserate and console Lady Catherine as well as you can, but I believe we should stand by the nephew. He has infinitely more to give."

On the day Mrs. Bennet gave away three of her daughters to men of quality and money, she was ever the same as she had always been. It would be a good ending, and a happy thing for the sake of her family, if the accomplishment of her earnest desire in the establishment of so many of her children produced so happy an effect as to make her a sensible, amiable, well-informed woman for the rest of her life, but such fundamental changes in one's character are rarely seen. Though Francine Bennet and her sister, Phillips, stood too much in awe of Pemberley and its master to speak with much familiarity, whenever they did speak, it must be vulgar.

Long after all the fairy cakes had been eaten, and the three grand coaches carrying the newlywed couples had strolled down the lane towards wedding trips, which would take the sisters all across the whole of England, Elizabeth and Darcy lay in their bed in a comfortable, loving repose.

"There is a piece of correspondence of which I would speak to you, if you would hear it," Elizabeth murmured.

"If you are speaking of the letter from my Aunt Catherine, I will not! She will not be recognized by me until she renders a full apology for the hurtful things she has said. It was her own fault for arranging a wedding for Anne and myself at the end of July. Stupid, ridiculous woman! If she feels abandoned by our family or humiliated in society, it was of her own making. That is for sure!"

"William, please. I know you are terribly upset by Lady Catherine's hurtful words and unfair expectations, but this missive is one you should perhaps read for yourself." Elizabeth took a folded letter out of a book on her nightstand and handed it to her husband.

After several minutes of perusing the contents, Darcy sighed heavily, rolled to his side and pulled the servant's cord for his valet. A few moments later brought Connor's knock upon the bedchamber door, and the Darcys bid him entrance.

"My man, we've had news today that my cousin, Miss Anne de Bourgh, is set to marry Captain Thurston Finch, the second son of Lord Nottingham, at the Church of Sts. Peter and Paul in Kent County in less than two weeks' time. We shall need to be ready to depart for London as soon as the last of our own wedding guests leave in two days. Please start the preparations for our departure in the morning, and find something for me to wear that is not so heavy around the collar. The temperature will undoubtedly be unbearable in Kent this time of year, and the coat I wore today will not do at all. Thank you."

A giggle escaped his wife as soon as the door was shut. Darcy arched one eyebrow at her in an attempted imitation of his favourite expression of hers, which only increased Elizabeth's giggles to gales of laughter. "Perhaps," she said through large gulps of air, "we should purchase you a few more formal morning suits in a variety of fabrics and colours. With all the marital felicity going around, it would not do to have you appear at each function wearing the same coat. Just think of the gossip such a travesty would inspire! Our reputation would surely never survive."

The End

# Acknowledgements

This novel has been a long time coming. I started writing the original version in the summer of 2015. Creating something from nothing was daunting at first, but I slowly became addicted to the rush of completing each new scene. It was a passion I genuinely did not know was inside of me. So, above all else, I want to say thank you to my husband, Don, for always giving me the space and support to try new, crazy things. It's you and me against the world and we always seem to come out on top, together. Next, to my dear friend Katie, without your guidance and example, this would not have happened. I have watched you write your stories with confidence and excitement for nearly ten years. In every way, you gave me the roadmap to publish my own. Finally, to all my friends and family who supported me on this journey, especially my mom—Mary Ann, my sister—Allison, and my cheerleader—Bernadette. I love you all!

# About the Author

E.M. Storm-Smith is a mother, wife, attorney, former engineer, and literature lover. A lifelong obsession for books drove her to create stories of her own. Several years into the journey of writing about characters she loved, E.M. decided to take her passions to the world and see what happened. When she's not writing, E.M. is spending her time reading others' books—preferably somewhere with lots of sunshine, traveling (*2020 notwithstanding*), and cooking things with chocolate as a primary ingredient.

## Please Leave an Honest Review

The best way to support independent authors is by leaving a review on your preferred platform. On most, you don't even have to have a verified purchase! If you liked this book (*or not*) please consider leaving it a review. You can find links to various distribution review pages on the Storm Haus Publishing website. Also, if you want to get the latest from E.M. and Storm Haus, you can follow us on social media or sign up for our newsletter. Just follow the link below to check out all the great information and other titles available in the Reputation Verse.

https://www.stormhauspublishing.com/reputation

Manufactured by Amazon.ca
Bolton, ON